THE GHOST

DANIELLE STEEL

THE GHOST

Delacorte Press

Published by
Delacorte Press
Bantam Doubleday Dell Publishing Group, Inc.
1540 Broadway
New York, New York 10036

Library of Congress Cataloging in Publication Data
Steel, Danielle.
    The ghost / Danielle Steel.
        p.   cm.
    ISBN 0-385-31695-X
    ISBN 0-385-31982-7 (Large Print Edition)
    ISBN 0-385-32353-0 (Limited Edition)
    I. Title.
    PS3569.T33828G48   1997
    813'.54—dc21   97-26125
                                          CIP

Manufactured in the United States of America
Published simultaneously in Canada

December 1997

10 9 8 7 6 5 4 3 2 1

BVG

To Tom,
beloved and
very special friend,
for the ghosts
you have laid to rest,
and the happiness
we've shared.

with all my love,
d.s.

Chapter 1

IN THE DRIVING rain of a November day, the cab from London to Heathrow took forever. It was so dark it looked like late afternoon, and Charlie Waterston could barely see out the windows as familiar landmarks slid past him. It was only ten o'clock in the morning. And as he leaned his head back against the seat and closed his eyes, he felt as bleak as the weather all around him.

It was hard to believe it had all come to an end. Ten years in London gone, finished, closed, and suddenly behind him. Even now, it was difficult to believe any of it had happened. It had all been so perfect when it began. It had been the start of a life, a career, a decade of excitement and happiness for him in London. And now suddenly, at forty-two, he felt as though all the good times were over. He had begun the long, slow trip down the other side of the mountain. For the past year, he had felt as though his life was slowly and steadily unraveling. The reality of it still amazed him.

And as the cab stopped at the airport finally, the driver turned and looked at him with a raised eyebrow. "Goin' back to the States, are you, sir?" Charlie hesitated for a fraction of a second and then nodded. Yes, he was. Going back to the States. After ten years in London. Nine of them with Carole. Gone now. All of it. In a matter of moments.

"Yes, I am," he said, not sounding like himself, but the driver couldn't know that. All he could see was a well-dressed man in a well-cut English suit and a Burberry raincoat. He had an expensive umbrella with him, a well-worn briefcase that he carried contracts and documents in. But even with all his well-chosen accessories, he didn't look English. He looked like what he was, a handsome American who'd lived in Europe for years. He was completely at home here. And it terrified him more than a little that he was leaving. He couldn't even imagine living in New York again. But he'd been forced into it, and the timing had been perfect. There was no point staying here now anyway, without Carole.

He felt a rock crush his heart, as he thought of her, as he stepped out of the cab and tipped the porter to take his luggage. He was only carrying two small bags. The rest was being held for him in storage.

He checked in at the desk, and then went to sit in the first-class lounge, but he was relieved to see that there was no one he knew there. It was a long wait to board the plane, but he had brought plenty of work with him, and he kept busy until they called the flight. He waited as he always did, and he was the last passenger to board the aircraft. And as the flight attendants showed him to his seat and took his coat for him, his dark brown hair and warm brown eyes did not go unnoticed. He was tall, had long, athletic limbs, and he was undeniably attractive. Besides which, he wore no wedding band, and the woman across the aisle and the flight attendant taking his coat couldn't help but notice. But he was oblivious to all of them, as he slipped into the seat next to the window, and sat staring out at the rain on the runway. It was impossible not to think of what had happened, impossible not to run his mind over it again and again, as though looking for the seam from where the leak began, the place where the lifeblood of their relationship had begun to seep away without their even knowing.

It still seemed incredible to him. How could he have been so blind? How could he have not known? How could he have believed they were so perfectly happy, while she was slipping away from him? Had it changed suddenly, or had it never been the very thing he'd been so sure of? He had been absolutely convinced that they were completely happy, and he still thought they had been . . . until the end . . . until the last year . . . until she told him . . . until Simon. It made Charlie feel so stupid. He'd been such a fool, flying from Tokyo to Milan, designing office buildings, while Carole represented clients for her law firm all over Europe. They were busy, that was all. They had lives of their own. They were planets in separate orbits. But there had been no doubt in anyone's mind how perfect it all was, how it was exactly what they wanted, whenever they were together. Even Carole seemed surprised by what she'd done, but the worst thing about it was that she wasn't willing to undo it. She had tried, but in the end she knew she couldn't.

One of the flight attendants offered him a drink before they took off, and he declined. She handed him the menu then, a set of headphones, and the list of movies. None of it appealed to him. All he wanted to do was think, to try and sort it all out again, as though it would come out differently if he thought about it long enough, and this time, came up with the right answers. It made him want to shout sometimes, to pound his fist into a wall, to shake someone. Why was she doing this to him? Why had that asshole come along and destroyed everything he and Carole had wanted? And yet, even Charlie knew that it wasn't Simon's fault, which left no one to blame except himself and Carole. It made him wonder at times why it was so important to assign the blame. It had to be someone's fault, and lately he had taken to blaming himself. He must have done something to make her turn to someone else. She said that it had happened more than a year before, while they were working on a case together in Paris.

Simon St. James was the senior partner of her law firm. She liked working with him, she laughed about him sometimes, talked about how smart he was, and how outrageous he was with women. He had already had three wives, and he had several children. He was debonair, dashing, good-looking, and extremely charming. He was also sixty-one, and Carole was thirty-nine. She was only three years younger than Charlie, twenty-two years younger than Simon. There was no point reminding her that he was old enough to be her father. She knew all that, she was a smart girl, she knew what a crazy thing it was, and what it had done to Charlie. That was the worst part. She hadn't wanted to hurt anyone. It had just happened.

Carole had been twenty-nine, beautiful, extremely bright, and had a great job with a law firm on Wall Street. They'd been dating for a year before Charlie got transferred, to run the London office of his architectural firm, Whittaker and Jones, but it was never serious between them. He was transferred from New York, where he'd worked for them for two years, and he was delighted.

She came to London on a lark, to see him, and she had no intention of staying. But she fell in love with London, and then with him. It was different here, everything was more romantic. She started flying over whenever she could, to see him on weekends. It was the perfect life for them. They skied in Davos and Gstaad and St. Moritz. She had gone to school in Switzerland when her father worked in France, and she had friends all over Europe. She was completely at home here. She spoke German and French with ease, she fit right into the London social scene, and Charlie adored her. After six months of commuting, she found a job in the London office of an American law firm. They bought an old carriage house in Chelsea and she moved in with him, and they were like two crazy, wild, happy people. They spent almost every night dancing at Annabel's at first, and discovering all the wonderful little out-of-the-way places, restaurants and antiques shops and nightclubs in London. It was heaven.

The carriage house they had bought was in total disrepair when they acquired it, and it took them nearly a year to restore it. And when it was finished, it was spectacular, it was a labor of love for both of them, and they filled it with beautiful things, and all the treasures they collected. They drove through the countryside finding old doors, and remarkable antiques, and when they got tired of traveling around England, they began spending weekends in Paris. They led a charmed life, and between their various business trips they managed to get married, and spend a honeymoon in Morocco, in a palace Charlie had rented for them. Everything they had done had been stylish and fun and exciting. They were the kind of people everyone wanted to know, or be with. They gave great parties, did fun things, and knew all the most interesting people. Everywhere they went, people loved being around them. And Charlie loved being with her more than anything. He was crazy about her. She was long, and lean, and blond, with perfect limbs and a body that looked as though it had been sculpted from white marble. She had a laugh that sounded like bells, a voice that still made him tingle whenever he heard it. She had a deep, sexy voice, and just hearing her say his name made his insides shiver ten years later.

It was the golden life of two careers, two powerful, intelligent, interesting, successful people. The only thing they didn't have, or want, or need, were children. They'd talked about it repeatedly, but it never seemed the right time to them. Carole had too many important, and extremely demanding, clients. To Carole, they were her children. And Charlie didn't really mind. He loved the idea of having a little girl who looked like her, but in truth, he was too crazy about her to want to share her. They had never actually decided *not* to have kids, they just hadn't done it. And in the last five years, they had talked about it less and less often. The only thing that did bother him was now that his parents were gone, other than Carole, Charlie had no other family. No cousins, no grandparents, no aunts and uncles, no siblings. All he had was Carole, and the life they shared. She was everything to him, and now he realized, too much so. There was nothing about his life with her that he would have changed during those years. As far as he was concerned, the life they'd built together was perfection. He was never bored with her, never tired of her, they rarely argued. Neither of them seemed to mind the fact that the other traveled extensively. If anything, it made it more exciting to come back to London. He loved coming back from a trip, and finding her, lying on the couch in their living room, reading a book, or better yet, lying in front of the fire, dozing. More often than not, she was still at work when he returned from Brussels or Milan or Tokyo, or wherever he'd been. But when she was home, she was entirely his. She was good at that. She never made him feel that he came after her work. If he did occasionally, when she had an important case or a difficult client, she was careful not to let him know it. She made him feel as though the world revolved around him . . . and it did . . . for nine exquisite years, and then suddenly . . . it didn't, and he felt as though his life were over.

As Charlie flew inexorably toward New York, he couldn't help counting backward again. The affair had begun exactly fifteen months before, in August. She had told him that, when she told him everything, finally. She had always been honest with him. Honest, truthful, loyal. Other than the fact that she seemed to have fallen out of love with him, he had had nothing to reproach her. She and Simon had been working in Paris together for six weeks. It was an important case, it had been fraught with tension, and Charlie had been at a delicate stage of a major negotiation with huge new clients in Hong Kong. He had been there almost weekly for nearly three months, and the aggravations associated with it had almost driven him insane. He had hardly had a minute to spend with her, which was rare for him, and certainly no excuse for what she'd done, she agreed. But it wasn't his absence that had done them in, she explained . . . it was just time . . . and fate . . . and Simon. He was remarkable, and she was in love with him. He had swept her off her feet, and she knew it was wrong, but she insisted she couldn't help it. She had tried to resist everything she felt for him at first, but eventually she found she just couldn't. She had admired him for too long, liked him far too much, and somehow they found they just had too much in common. It was the way it had been with Charlie a long time since, when everything was still exciting and fun, way back in the beginning. But when did it change? Charlie had asked plaintively while they talked about it on a rainy afternoon as they walked through Soho. It was still fun, he insisted to her helplessly. It was still exactly the way it had once been. He tried to convince her, but Carole only looked at him and shook her head imperceptibly as she listened. It wasn't fun anymore, she said through tears, it was different. They had separate lives, separate needs, they spent too much time with other people. And in some ways, she thought they had never grown up, but Charlie didn't understand that. But unlike being away from Charlie constantly, as they had been for years, because of their travels, she loved being with Simon day after day, and she said he took care of her in ways that Charlie didn't. How, he had begged her to explain, and she tried to, but she found she couldn't. It was more than just what Simon did, it was the complicated world of dreams, and needs and feelings. It was all the small, inexplicable, tiny little subtleties that make you love someone, even when you wish you didn't. She and Charlie had both cried when she said it.

She told herself that the affair with Simon was just a fling when she finally gave in to him. It would be nothing more than a temporary indiscretion, she promised herself, and she meant that. It was the first and only time she'd had an affair, and she didn't want to do anything that would permanently disrupt their marriage. She tried to break it off with Simon when they went home, he said he understood perfectly. He had had affairs before, and he had admitted to her that during his own marriages he had frequently been unfaithful. He regretted it, he explained, but he knew well the landscape of betrayal and indiscretion. He was single at the time, but he was entirely sympathetic to Carole's feelings of guilt and obligation to her husband. But what neither of them had counted on was how much they would miss each other once they were back home, living far from each other in London. Neither of them could bear being apart now. They began to leave the office together in the afternoons, to go to his flat, just to talk sometimes, so she could air her feelings, and she found that what she loved most about him was how well he understood everything, how solicitous he was of her, how much he loved her. He was willing to do anything just to be near her, even if it meant just being friends and no longer lovers. She tried to stay away from him, but she found she just couldn't. Charlie was out of town most of the time, she was alone, and Simon was there, pining for her, as she was for him. She had never realized before how alone she felt, how much Charlie was gone, and how much it meant to her to be with Simon. The physical aspect of the affair with Simon began again two months after they'd tried to end it. And her life was one long deception after that, of meeting him after work almost every night, and pretending to work together on weekends. He actually stayed in town much of the time, to be with her, and when Charlie was gone, they went down to his place in Berkshire for the weekend. She knew what she was doing was wrong, but it was like being possessed. She found she couldn't stop it.

By Christmas that year things were noticeably strained between Carole and Charlie. Charlie was having a crisis with a building site in Milan, at the same time that a deal in Tokyo had gone sour, and he was simply never there. And when he was, he was either jet lagged, exhausted, or in rotten spirits. And although he didn't mean to, more often than not, he took it out on Carole when he saw her, which wasn't often. He was constantly flying somewhere to solve a problem. They were the kind of months that always made them both glad they didn't have children. And it made Carole realize yet again how separate their worlds were. They never had time to talk anymore, or be together, or share their feelings. He had his work, and she had hers, and all they had in between were a few nights a month together in the same bed, and a series of parties and dinners they went to. She suddenly wondered what they'd built, what they'd done, what if anything they really shared. Or was it all just an empty illusion? She could no longer easily answer the question as to whether or not she loved him. And through it all, Charlie was so involved in his own work and woes that he had not the least inkling that anything unusual had happened. He had no idea Carole had been slipping steadily away from him since the previous summer. He spent New Year's Eve alone in Hong Kong, and Carole spent it at Annabel's with Simon. And Charlie was so involved in his business deals, he forgot to call her.

It all came to a head in February, when Charlie came home from Rome unexpectedly, and found her away for the weekend. She hadn't said anything to him this time, hadn't even claimed to be with friends, and something about the way she looked when she got home on Sunday night gave him a shiver of discomfort. She looked radiant and beautiful and relaxed, and the way she used to look when they stayed in bed and made love all weekend. But who had time for that anymore? They were both busy people. In fact, he said something casual about it to her that night, but he wasn't actually worried. Something deep within him had come alert, but the rest of his mind was still sleeping.

It was Carole who made a clean breast of it, and told him everything eventually. She knew that, at a subconscious level, something had struck a nerve with him and she didn't want to wait for something awful to happen, so she came home from work late one night and told him. He just sat and stared at her, with tears in his eyes, as he listened. She told him all of it, when it began, how long it had gone on, it had been five months by then, with a brief interruption after they got home from Paris, when she had tried to stop seeing Simon, and found she couldn't.

"I don't know what else to say, Charlie, except that I think you should know. We can't go on like this forever," she said softly, the huskiness of her voice making her sound sexier than ever.

"What are you planning to do about it?" he asked, trying to remind himself to be civilized, that things like this happened sometimes, but all he knew at that point in time was how hurt he was and how much he still loved her. He couldn't believe how acute the pain of having just been told she was sleeping with another man was. The real question was, did she love Simon or was she just having fun? Charlie knew he had to ask her. "Are you in love with him?" he asked, feeling worlds collide in his head and heart and stomach. What in God's name would he ever do, he asked himself, if she left him? He couldn't even imagine it, and knowing that, he could forgive her anything, and planned to. The one thing he knew was that he didn't want to lose her. But she hesitated for a long, long time before she answered.

"I think so," she said. She was always so goddam honest with him. She always had been. That was why she had told him. Even now, she didn't want to lose that. "I don't know. When I'm with him, I'm sure of it . . . but I love you too . . . I always will." There had never been anyone else in her life like Charlie . . . nor like Simon. She loved them both in her own way. But she knew she'd have to choose now. They could have gone on like this for a long time, people did, she knew, but she was also well aware that she couldn't. It had happened, now she had to deal with it. And so did Charlie. Simon had already said he wanted to marry her, but she knew she couldn't even think about that until she resolved things with her husband. And Simon said he understood that too, and claimed he was willing to wait forever.

"You make it sound like you're leaving me." Charlie had cried just looking at her, and then he'd put his arms around her and they both cried. "How could this happen to us?" he asked her again and again. It seemed impossible, unthinkable, how could she do that? And yet she had, and something about the way she looked at him told him that she was not ready to let go of Simon. He tried to be reasonable about it, but he had to ask her to stop seeing him. He wanted to go to a marriage counselor with her. He wanted to do anything they had to do to fix it.

Carole tried everything she could to make it work with him. She agreed to go to counseling and even stopped seeing Simon. For all of two weeks. But at the end of it, she was crazed, and she knew she couldn't give him up completely. Whatever had been wrong between Charlie and Carole seemed much worse suddenly, and they were both constantly angry at each other. The fights they'd never had before blossomed like trees in spring, and they fought every time they were together. Charlie was furious at what she'd done, he wanted to kill someone, preferably Simon. And she admitted to how unhappy she was to have been left alone so much, she felt as though they were nothing more than good friends and compatible roommates. Charlie didn't take care of her the way Simon did. She said he was immature, and accused him of being selfish. She complained that when he came home from a trip, he was too tired to even think about her, or talk sometimes, until they went to bed and he wanted to make love to her. But that was his way of establishing contact, he explained, it said more about his feelings than words ever could. But it actually said more about the difference between men and women. Their complaints were suddenly deep and ingrained, and Carole stunned him by telling their marriage counselor that she thought their whole marriage was centered on Charlie, and

Simon was the first man she'd ever known who cared about *her* feelings. Charlie couldn't believe what he was hearing.

She was sleeping with Simon again by then, but she was lying to Charlie about it, and within weeks it all became an impossible tangle of deceit and fights and recriminations. In March, when Charlie flew to Berlin for three days, she packed her things and moved in with Simon. She told Charlie on the phone, and he sat in his hotel room and cried. But she told him she wasn't willing to go on living this way. It was agony for all of them, and just too stressful.

"I don't want us to turn into this," she said when she called, crying at her end. "I hate what I've become with you. I hate everything I am and do and say. And I'm starting to hate you . . . Charlie . . . we have to give it up. I just can't do it." Not to mention the fact that she couldn't practice law coherently while trying to juggle this insane situation.

"Why not?" he had blazed back at her. Honest rage was beginning to take hold of him, and even she knew he had a right to be as angry as he was now. "Other marriages survive when one partner has an affair, why can't we?" It was a plea for mercy.

There was a long, long silence at her end. "Charlie, I don't want to do this anymore," she said finally, and he could hear that she meant it. And that was the end of them. For whatever reason, it was over for her. She had fallen in love with another man, and out of love with him. Maybe there was no reason after all, maybe there was no blame. They were only human after all, with unpredictable, erratic emotions. There was no saying why it had happened. It just had, and whether Charlie liked it or not, Carole had left him for Simon.

In the ensuing months, he ricocheted between despair and rage. He could hardly keep his mind on his work. He stopped seeing his friends. He sat alone in his house sometimes, just thinking of her. He sat in the dark, hungry, tired, still unable to believe what had happened. He kept hoping that the affair with

Simon would end, that she would tire of him, that she would decide he was too old for her, too smooth, or maybe even that he was a pompous windbag. He prayed for all of it, but none of it ever happened. She and Simon seemed very happy. He saw photographs of them in newspapers and magazines from time to time, and he hated seeing them. At times he thought the agony of missing her would crush him. The loneliness he felt now was overwhelming. And when he couldn't stand it anymore, he called her. The worst of it was that she always sounded the same. She always sounded so warm and so sensual and so sexy. Sometimes he pretended to himself that she was coming home to him, that she was on a trip, or away for a weekend. But she wasn't. She was gone. Possibly forever.

The house looked uncared for now, and unloved. She had taken all her things. And nothing looked quite the same. Nothing was the same. He felt as though everything he'd ever wanted or been or dreamed had been broken. There was nothing left but shards at his feet, and he had nothing left to care about or believe in.

People in his office noticed it, he looked gray and tired and thin. He was irritable, and argued about everything. He no longer even called their friends, and he declined every invitation they sent him. He was sure that by now everyone was completely swept off their feet by Simon. And besides, he didn't want to hear about them, didn't want to know every little detail about what they did, or have to answer well-meaning questions. And yet, he could never stop himself from reading about them in the papers. The parties they attended and the weekends they spent in the country. Simon St. James was extremely social. Carole had always liked going to parties, but never as much as they did now. It was an important part of her life with Simon. Charlie tried not to think about it all the time, but it seemed impossible to think about much else.

The summer was torture for him. He knew Simon had a villa

in the south of France, because they'd visited him there, between Beaulieu and St.-Jean-Cap-Ferrat. He kept a good-size
yacht in the harbor, and Charlie kept thinking of her on it. He
had nightmares about it sometimes, terrified that she would
drown, and then feeling guilty because he wondered if the nightmares meant that he wished she would drown. He went back to
the marriage counselor to talk about it. But there was nothing
left to say. By September, Charlie Waterston looked sadly battered, and felt even worse.

Carole had called to say she was filing for divorce by then, and
Charlie hated himself when he asked if she was still living with
Simon. Before he even asked the question, he knew the answer,
and could too easily envision her face and the tilt of her head as
she answered.

"You know I am, Charlie," she said sadly. She hated hurting
him. She had never wanted to do this to him. It had just happened. That was all. She couldn't help it. But she was happier
with Simon than she had ever been. It was a life she had never
aspired to, but that she found she loved. They had spent the
month of August at his villa in France, and she was surprised to
find that she liked all his friends. And Simon himself was doing
absolutely everything he could to please her. He called her the
love of his life, and the woman of his dreams, and there was
suddenly a vulnerable quality about him, and a gentleness she
had never seen. She was deeply in love with him, but she didn't
say any of that to Charlie. It only made her realize again how
empty their relationship had been. They had been two self-
centered people moving along side by side, barely touching, and
never meeting. And neither of them had ever realized it. She did
now, but she knew that Charlie still didn't see it. All she wanted
for him was a happy life, she hoped he would find someone, but
it didn't sound as though he was even trying.

"Are you going to marry him?" He always felt as though all the
air had been squeezed out of him when he asked her these kinds

of questions, and yet, much as he hated himself for doing it, he found he had to.

"I don't know, Charlie. We don't talk about it." It was a lie, Simon was desperate to marry her, but that was none of Charlie's business for the moment. "It's not important now. We need to sort things out between us first." She had finally forced him to hire a lawyer, but he almost never called him. "We need to divide up our things, when you have time." He actually felt nauseous when she said it.

"Why don't you just give it another try?" he asked, hating himself for the weakness he heard in his own voice, but he loved her so much, the thought of losing her forever nearly killed him. And why did they have to "divide up their things"? What did he care about the china and the couch and the linens? He wanted her. He wanted everything they'd shared. He wanted their life back, just as it had been. He still hadn't understood any of the things she was saying. "What if we had a baby?" Somehow he assumed that Simon was too old to even think of it. At sixty-one, having had three wives, and a number of children, he couldn't possibly want to have a baby with her. It was the one thing Charlie could offer her that Simon couldn't.

There was a long silence from her end again, and she closed her eyes as she tried to get up the courage to answer. She didn't want a baby with him. She didn't want a baby with anyone. She never really had. She had her career. And now she had Simon. A baby was the last thing on her mind. She just wanted a divorce so they could get on with their respective lives, and stop hurting each other. It didn't seem like too much to ask of him.

"Charlie, it's too late. Don't talk about that now. Neither of us ever wanted a baby."

"Maybe we were wrong. Maybe things would have been different now if we had. Maybe that was the cement between us we were lacking."

15

"It would only complicate things. Kids don't keep people together, they just make it harder."

"Are you going to have a baby with him?" He sounded desperate again. Even he hated the way he sounded when he talked to her. He always wound up as the supplicant, the poor slob begging the beautiful princess to come back to him, and he loathed himself for it. But he didn't know what else to say to her, and he would have done anything if she would just agree to give up Simon and come back.

But she sounded exasperated when she answered. "No, I am not having a baby with him. I'm trying to have a life, of my own, and with him. And I don't want to screw up your life any more than I have to. Charlie, why don't you just let go of it? Something happened to us. I'm not even sure I understand what. Things just work out that way sometimes. It's like if someone dies. You can't argue with it. You can't change it. You can't turn the clock back or bring them back to life. We died. Or at least I did. Now you have to go on living without me."

"I can't." He nearly choked on the words and she knew just how much he meant it. She had run into him the week before, and he looked terrible. He looked tired and pale and exhausted, but oddly enough, she realized that she still thought he was incredibly attractive. He was a very handsome man, and even in misery, he was very appealing. "I can't live without you, Carole." The worst thing was that she knew he believed that.

"Yes, you can, Charlie, you have to."

"Why?" He couldn't think of a single reason these days to go on living. The woman he loved was gone. He was bored with his job. He wanted to be alone all the time. Even the house he had once loved seemed to have lost its spirit. But in spite of that, he didn't want to sell it. He had too many memories with her there. There was too much Carole woven into every fiber of his life. He couldn't imagine ever being free of her, or wanting to be. All he wanted was what he couldn't have, what he had once had with her, all of which now belonged to Simon. The bastard.

"Charlie, you're too young to act like this. You're forty-two years old. You have a whole life ahead of you. You have a great career, an enormous talent. You'll meet someone else, maybe you'll have kids." It was a strange conversation and she knew it, but she didn't know how to let go of him, although she knew that her talking to Charlie like this seriously annoyed Simon. He thought they ought to divide up the spoils, get divorced, and get on with it, as he put it. They were both young enough to have jolly good lives with other people. He thought Charlie was being an incredibly bad sport and putting a lot of unnecessary pressure on Carole, and he was very outspoken about the fact that he didn't like it.

"These things happen to all of us at some point in time, or most of us anyway. My first two wives left me. I didn't lie on the floor having tantrums for a year, I can tell you that. He's quite spoilt, if you ask me," he said irritably. She tried not to talk to Simon at all about Charlie. She had her own guilt and conflicts to contend with. She didn't want to go back to him, but she didn't want to leave him bleeding by the side of the road either. She knew she had run over him. But she had no idea how to fix it for him, how to make it better than it was, or release him gently. She had tried, and she wanted to make it easier for him, but Charlie absolutely refused to let go of her, and every time she talked to him, she had the feeling he was drowning, and if she let him, in his desperate thrashing he would drown her. She needed to get away from him somehow, just for the sake of her own survival.

At the end of September, they finally divided up their things. Simon had family business to attend to in the north of England, and Carole spent an agonizing weekend going through their old house with Charlie. He wanted to discuss each and every item, not because he was trying to keep anything from her, but because he used every moment with her as an opportunity to try and talk her into leaving Simon. It was a nightmare for both of them, and Carole hated hearing it as much as Charlie hated himself for what he was saying. He almost couldn't believe it. But he just refused to let her slip away from him without making piteous screams and hideous noises in the hope that she would change her mind. But she was far from that.

On Sunday night he apologized to her before she left. He smiled ruefully at her, as he stood in the doorway. He looked just awful. And Carole looked almost as bad as he did.

"I'm sorry I've been such a horse's ass all weekend. I don't know what happens to me. Every time I see you, or talk to you, I go crazy." It was the most normal he'd seemed since they'd started inventorying everything on Saturday morning.

"It's okay, Charlie. . . . I know this isn't easy for you." But it wasn't easy for her either. She wasn't sure if he understood that. And he didn't. As far as he was concerned, she had left him. It had been her choice. And she had Simon. She had walked into another man's arms, and she was never alone for a moment, never without company and comfort. Charlie had nothing. He had lost everything he had ever wanted.

"It's a rotten deal," he said, looking into her eyes again. "For everyone. I just hope you don't regret what you're doing."

"So do I," she said, and then she kissed him on the cheek and told him to take care, and a moment later she drove off in Simon's Jaguar. Charlie stood staring after her, trying to make himself believe that it was all over, that she was never coming back again. And as he walked back into the house and saw the piles of her things everywhere, and their china stacked high on the dining room table, there was no escaping what had happened. He closed the door and just stood there and stared, and then he sat down in a chair and cried. He couldn't believe how much he missed her. Even spending the weekend with her, dividing up their things, seemed better than nothing at all.

And when he stopped crying finally, it was dark outside, and in an odd way, he felt better. There was no denying it anymore. No running away from it. She was gone. And he was letting her take almost everything with her. It was all he had left to give her.

But by the first of October, for Charlie, everything was worse instead of better. The man in charge of the New York office of his architectural firm had a heart attack, the partner who could have taken his place announced that he was leaving to open a new firm of his own in Los Angeles, and the two senior partners of the firm, Bill Jones and Arthur Whittaker, flew to London to ask Charlie to come back to New York and take over. It was everything Charlie had never wanted. From the moment he had moved to London ten years before, he had known he never wanted to work in New York again, and he had spent a decade thrilled to be working in Europe. Charlie thought design was far more exciting abroad, particularly in Italy and France, he enjoyed his Asian forays as well, and he had every intention of remaining in Europe.

"I can't," he said with an intractable look when they proposed the idea to him. But both of his senior partners were prepared to be tenacious. They needed him in New York to run the office.

"Why not?" they asked with candor. He didn't want to tell them he just didn't want to, but he didn't. "Even if you want to come back here eventually, there's no reason why you can't come to New York for a year or two. There are a lot of interesting developments in the States right now. You might find that you actually prefer it." He didn't want to explain to them that there was no chance of it, nor did they want to point out to him that, now that his wife had left, he had no reason not to take the job. Unlike the other men they'd thought of, he wasn't tied to anyone, and was free to go anywhere. He had no wife and no children, no family ties anywhere. There was no reason whatsoever why he couldn't rent his house for a year or two, and go to the New York office to keep it on an even keel, or at least until they could find someone else to run it for them. But Charlie was in no way intrigued by the idea, or inclined to do what they asked him.

"It's very, very important to us. Charlie, there's no one else to turn to." He knew that that was true. They were in an awkward spot. The man in the Chicago office couldn't move, his wife had been very sick for the past year. She had breast cancer and was undergoing chemo, and this was no time to ask them to relocate. And no one else in the hierarchy of the New York office was really capable of taking over. Charlie was the obvious choice, and he knew that it would probably alter his professional situation permanently if he categorically refused to go. "We'd really like you to think it over," they insisted, and Charlie was appalled at the realities it entailed. He felt as though an express train were heading for him and were about to hit him. He couldn't believe what was happening, and he just didn't know what to say. He wished he could call Carole to discuss it with her, but he knew that was out of the question.

It was incredible to him that in a matter of months, he had lost his wife, and now he was being forced to give up the life he loved in Europe. Everything around him seemed to be changing, and it was an agonizing two weeks while he mulled over the decision. The senior partners went back to New York after two days, and he told them he'd give them an answer as soon as he'd thought it over. But no matter how much he thought, he couldn't figure out a way to avoid giving them what they wanted.

He couldn't even tell them his wife didn't want him to go. As they knew very well, the decision was all on his own shoulders. And halfway through the month, he knew he had no choice. He had to go. They would never forgive him if he didn't. He tried to negotiate for six months, and they told him they'd try to find someone else to run the New York office by then, but they pointed out that it could easily take them a year, or even more. Important architects following exactly the right path in their design careers were certainly not easy to come by. They were going to replace Charlie in London with his second in command. Dick Barnes was a good man, and Charlie was sure he would do the job. In fact, that was even a matter of concern to Charlie, because Dick Barnes had been lusting after his job for a long time, and this might well prove to be an unexpected opportunity for him to get it. He was equally talented and almost as experienced, and Charlie was afraid that after Barnes had run the London office successfully for a year they might not be willing to let Charlie come back and take over. And the one thing he didn't want was to get stuck in New York. In the end, they signed a contract with him to go to New York for a year. And before he knew it, Charlie felt as though his life had come to an end and he was preparing to move to New York. They had insisted he be there well before Thanksgiving. Carole called him eventually when she heard the news from a mutual friend whose husband worked for Charlie. She congratulated him on the new appointment, although she was surprised to hear that he'd been willing to leave London.

"I don't exactly consider it a step up in the world," he said, still sounding gloomy, but glad that she had called him. It had been a bad year for him, and he could hardly remember the carefree days of happiness and good humor. Ever since she'd left, something terrible seemed to happen every day. "The last thing I wanted to do was go back to work in New York," he said with a sigh. He really hated to leave London, and she knew it. She knew full well how much his life there meant to him, and how happy he had been in London, which was why she had called him. In spite of everything, she wanted to cheer him up, although she knew that Simon would have disapproved of her calling. He spoke to at least two of his ex-wives fairly regularly, but they had been married several times since leaving him, and they weren't clinging to him as Charlie was to Carole.

"Maybe the change will do you good for a while," she said gently. "A year isn't forever, Charlie."

"It sure feels like it," he said, staring out his office window, seeing her far too clearly in his mind's eye. She was so damn beautiful, and still so desirable to him, although he was beginning to wish she weren't. It was going to be so odd being so far away from her. He wouldn't be able to think about running into her anymore. Now there was always the chance he might run into her in a restaurant or a shop, or coming out of Harrods. But not when he left London. "I don't know how I got myself into this mess," he said, thinking about New York.

"It doesn't sound like you had much choice," she said practically.

"I didn't." He had no choice about anything anymore, not about her, or moving to New York. None of it was what he wanted.

And then she asked him what he was going to do about the house. Legally, she still owned half of it, but she didn't mind his living there. She didn't need the cash, and she certainly didn't plan to live in it with Simon. There was no reason why they couldn't just hold on to it for the moment.

"I thought I'd rent it," he said, and she agreed with him. But then she called him back two days later. She had thought about it, and discussed it with Simon at some length, although she didn't say that to Charlie. And it was one thing, as far as she was concerned, if Charlie was living in the house, but she didn't want tenants destroying it, or devaluating the property by causing damage to it. Under the circumstances, she preferred to sell it, and she asked Charlie to put it on the market before he left London.

He felt as though he had lost yet another dear friend when she said that to him. He had loved their house, they both had. But he didn't have the energy to argue with her this time, and he was beginning to understand that there was no point hanging on to any of it. The past was gone, and he might as well let their house go too. He thought about it for a few days, and then put it on the market. And much to their joint surprise, it sold within ten days for a good price, but that was small consolation to him.

By the time he got on the plane, the deal was closed, the house was gone, and everything he owned had been put in storage. Carole had come around the week before to see it for the last time, and to say good-bye to him, and, predictably, it was a painful reunion, filled with grief from his end, guilt from hers, and silent recriminations that seemed to fill the room like people.

It was hard to know what to say to him, as she walked from room to room, remembering little things and funny moments, and finally she just stood in their bedroom, with tears rolling down her cheeks, staring out the window. The garden was bare, the trees were bereft of leaves, and she didn't even hear him walk into the room behind her. He just stood there, looking at her, lost in his own memories, and when she turned to leave, she was surprised to see him.

"I'm going to miss this place," she said, wiping away tears, and he nodded. For once, he wasn't crying. He had been through too much pain, he had lost too much now. He felt almost numb, as she walked slowly toward him.

"I'm going to miss you," he whispered. It was the understatement of a lifetime.

"Me too," she said softly, and then put her arms around him. For a long time, he just stood there and held her, wishing that none of it had happened. As far as Charlie was concerned, if it weren't for Simon, they could still be living there, busy, and distracted, and going their own ways much of the time, but still happy to come home to each other. And if they'd still been together, he could have refused to go to New York for the firm. Her job in Europe was far too important to ask for a transfer. "I'm sorry, Charlie," was all she said, as he stood there wondering how ten years of his life had vanished into thin air. He had lost it all, his wife, his house, and even his residency in Europe.

23

It was as though the clock had been turned back, and he had to start over at the beginning. The real-life game of "Chutes and Ladders." He had climbed the ladder nearly to the top, and with one false step he had slid all the way to the bottom. There was something agonizingly surrealistic about it.

They walked out of the house hand in hand, and a few minutes later, she drove off. It was Saturday, and she had promised Simon she'd drive to Berkshire to meet him. Charlie hadn't even bothered to ask her this time if she was happy. It was obvious that her life was completely intertwined with Simon's. It had only taken him nine months to understand that. And every moment of it had been torture for both of them.

The rest of Charlie's things had gone into storage shortly after that, and he moved into Claridge's for the last few days of his stay in London, at the expense of the firm. There was a very nice dinner for him at the Savoy to celebrate his departure. Everyone from the office came, and a number of important clients. Other friends tried to invite him for dinner before he left, but he said he was too busy tying up loose ends at the office. He had hardly seen any of them since Carole left him. The required explanations were far too painful. It was easier for him not to go out, and leave London in silence.

And when he left the office for the last time, Dick Barnes made a polite little speech about looking forward to seeing him again, but Charlie knew he wasn't. It was obvious and natural that he was hoping Charlie would stay in New York, and leave Barnes running the London office. And Charlie didn't blame him. He didn't blame anyone, not even Carole. He called her to say good-bye the night before he left, but she was out, and he decided it was just as well. There was nothing left to say now except how sorry they both were, and all he ever wanted from her was an explanation of how it had happened. He still didn't understand it. She was far more philosophical than he was. But then again, she had Simon. Charlie had no one in his life to console him.

It was pouring rain when he woke up on the day he left, and he lay in bed at the hotel for a long time, thinking of what was happening, where he was going, and why he was leaving. He felt as though he had a boulder on his chest, and for a minute, he thought about canceling everything, quitting the firm, trying to buy his house back, and refusing to leave London. It was a crazy idea, even to him, and he knew he'd never do it. But for an instant the idea was very appealing, as he lay there, listening to the sound of the rain, trying to make himself get up and get into the shower. He had to be at the airport at eleven o'clock, for a one o'clock flight. The morning ahead of him seemed endless. And as he lay in bed, thinking about it, he had to force himself not to call Carole. He took a long, hot shower, put on a dark suit, a white shirt, and an Hermès tie, and promptly at ten o'clock Charlie was outside the hotel, waiting for a cab, sniffing the London air for the last time, listening to the sounds of traffic moving by, looking up at the familiar buildings. It almost felt like leaving home for the first time. He still couldn't believe he was going, and he kept hoping that someone would stop him before it was too late. He kept wanting her to come running down the street and throw her arms around him, and tell him it had all been a bad dream, and it was over.

But the cab came finally, and the doorman looked at him expectantly, waiting for Charlie to get in. There was nothing left to do but get in the cab and go to the airport. She wasn't coming. She never would again. She wouldn't be coming back to him, he knew that now. She was Simon's.

He had a heavy heart as they drove through town, watching people come and go, to perform their daily tasks or do errands, and as they drove, it poured. It was a freezing November rain. It was typical English winter weather. And in less than an hour, they were at Heathrow. There was no turning back now.

❋   ❋   ❋

"Would you like something to drink now, Mr. Waterston? Some champagne? A glass of wine?" the flight attendant asked pleasantly as he turned from his reverie at the window. They had been in the air for an hour, and it had finally stopped raining.

"No, thanks, I'm fine," he said, looking a little less grim than when he boarded. They had all noticed that he looked desperately unhappy. He declined cocktails, and left his headset unused on the seat beside him. He turned his face toward the window again, and when they came by with dinner, he was asleep.

"I wonder what happened to him," one of the flight attendants whispered to a co-worker in the kitchen. "He looks beat."

"Maybe he's been out every night cheating on his wife," one of the women offered with a grin.

"What makes you think he's married?" The flight attendant who had offered him champagne looked disappointed.

"He's got a mark on his third finger, left hand, and he's not wearing a ring. It's a sure sign he's been cheating."

"Maybe he's a widower," one of them said cheerfully, and her two cohorts groaned at the idea.

"Just another tired businessman fooling around on his wife. Trust me." The oldest flight attendant grinned, and headed down the aisle into first class with fruit and cheese and ice cream sundaes. She stopped to look at Charlie again, he was sound asleep and never stirred, and she rolled slowly past him.

Her colleague wasn't entirely wrong. Charlie had finally taken his wedding ring off the night before he left London. He had taken it off and held it in his hand for a long time, just staring at it, and remembering the day she'd put it on him. It had been a long time . . . ten years in London, nine of them with Carole. And now, as they flew toward New York, even Charlie knew it was over. But he still had his wedding ring in his pocket. And as he slept on the flight, he dreamed that he was with her. She was

26

laughing and talking to him, but when he tried to kiss her, she turned away from him. He couldn't understand it, but he kept reaching out to her. And in the distance he saw a man watching them . . . she was turning toward him . . . and when Charlie looked up, he saw the man beckoning to her, and she went to him. She slipped right through Charlie's hands, as he watched her go to him . . . it was Simon, and he was laughing.

Chapter 2

*T*HEY LANDED ON the runway at Kennedy with a hard thump, which woke Charlie with a start. He had been sleeping for hours, exhausted by the activities and emotions of the past few days, or weeks . . . or months. . . . It had been undeniably hellish. It was just after three o'clock in the afternoon local time, and as the prettiest of the flight attendants handed him his Burberry, he smiled, and she was disappointed all over again that he hadn't woken up sooner, or talked to her during the flight.

"Will you be going back to London with us, Mr. Waterston?" Somehow, just looking at him, she had gotten the impression that he lived in Europe. She was based in London like the others.

"Unfortunately not." He smiled at her, wishing that he was going back to London. "I'm moving to New York," he said, as though she cared. But no one else did either. She nodded and moved on as he put on his raincoat and picked up his briefcase.

The line of people disembarking from the plane moved with the speed of cement, and eventually he made it off the plane and picked up his two bags at the baggage claim, and then found a cab waiting outside for a fare into the city. As Charlie got into the cab, he was surprised by how cold it was. It was only November, but it was freezing. It was four o'clock by then, and he was going to the studio that had been rented by his firm until he found his own apartment. It was in the East Fifties, between Lexington and Third, and if not large, at least it was convenient.

"Where do ya come from?" the driver asked, gnawing a cigar and playing tag with a limousine and two other cabbies. He narrowly missed hitting a truck, and then launched headlong into the Friday afternoon traffic. If nothing else, it was familiar to Charlie.

"London," he answered, looking out the window as Queens sped by. There was no pretty way into the city.

"How long ya been there?" The driver chatted amiably, continuing to dart in and out of traffic. But as they approached the city, and rush hour traffic clogged the road, the sport became less exciting.

"Ten years," Charlie said without thinking, and the driver glanced at him in the rearview mirror.

"Long time. Ya here to visit?"

"I'm moving back," Charlie explained, feeling suddenly exhausted. It was nine-thirty at night for him, and the neighborhoods they drove through were so dreary, it depressed him. The route into London was no lovelier, but at least it was home now. This wasn't. He had lived in New York for seven years after graduating from architectural school at Yale, but he had grown up in Boston.

"There's no place like it," the cabdriver proclaimed with a grin, waving the cigar at the view beyond his windshield. They were just crossing the bridge, and the skyline looked impressive in the twilight, but even seeing the Empire State Building didn't cheer Charlie. He rode the rest of the way into town in silence.

When they arrived at Fifty-fourth and Third, he paid the cab driver and got out, and identified himself to the doorman. He was expected. The office had left his keys for him, and he was grateful to have a place to stay, but when he saw the place they'd rented for him, he was startled. Everything in the single, compact room seemed to be either Formica or plastic. There was a long white counter with gold sparkles in it, and two bar stools covered in fake white leather, a sofa that converted into a bed, cheap furniture with plastic seats in a grim shade of green, and there were even plastic plants that caught his eye as soon as he turned the light on. Looking around at the sheer ugliness of it left him breathless. This was what it had come to. No wife, no home, nothing of his own. The place looked like a cheap hotel room, and all he could think of was what he had lost in the past year. It was impossible to remember anything positive that had come from the upheaval he'd been through. All he could think of were the losses.

He put down his bags, and looked around with a sigh. And then he took off his coat and dropped it on the room's only table. It was certainly going to give him plenty of incentive to find his own place very quickly. He helped himself to a beer from the fridge, and sat down on the couch, thinking about Claridge's, and his house in London. And for a crazy moment, he wanted to call her . . . "You wouldn't believe how ugly this place is. . . ." Why did he always think of telling her the things that were funny or sad or shocking? He wasn't sure which one this was, probably all three, but he didn't even bother to reach for the phone. He just sat there, feeling drained, trying not to see the emptiness of the apartment. There were posters on the wall of sunsets and a panda bear, and when he checked the bathroom, it was the size of a closet. But he was too tired even to take his clothes off and take a shower. He just sat on the couch, staring into space, and finally he lay back, and closed his eyes, trying not to think of anything, or remember where he had come from. He lay there for a long time, and eventually he opened the convertible bed, and he was asleep by nine o'clock. He didn't even bother with dinner.

And when he woke up the next day, the sun was streaming in the windows. It was ten o'clock, but his watch said three. It was still set for London. He yawned and got out of bed. The room looked a mess with the unmade bed in the center of it. It was like living in a shoe box. And when he went to the refrigerator, there were sodas and coffee and beer, but nothing to eat, so he showered and put on jeans and a heavy sweater, and at noon he ventured out into the street. It was a gorgeous, sunny day, and absolutely freezing. He ate a sandwich in a deli on Third Avenue, and then walked slowly uptown, glancing into shops, noticing how different people looked than they did in London. There was no mistaking New York for any other city in the world, and he remembered easily that there was a time when he once loved it. This was where he and Carole had met, where he had started his career, where he had enjoyed his first success in architecture, and yet he had no desire to come back here. He liked visiting it, but he couldn't imagine living here again. But he was, for better or worse, and late that afternoon he bought the *New York Times* and went to look at two apartments. They were both ugly and expensive, and smaller than he wanted. But where he was living was worse. And he was immediately reminded of it when he went back to the studio at six o'clock. Sitting in one tiny room was unbearably depressing. He hated being there, but he was still jet-lagged and tired, and he didn't even bother to go out for dinner. He spent the night working instead, on some papers they'd sent him about current projects in New York. And the next day he walked to the office, even though it was Sunday.

The ugly little studio was only four and a half blocks from the office, which was probably why they got it. They had offered him a hotel, but he had said he preferred an apartment.

The office was a beautiful space on the fiftieth floor at Fifty-first and Park, and when he walked into the reception area, he stood looking at the view for a while, and then walked slowly around the models. It was going to be interesting working here

31

again. Suddenly after all these years, it all seemed so different. But nothing prepared him for how different it really was on Monday morning.

He had woken up at four, and had been waiting for hours, working on a variety of papers. He was still on London time, and he was also anxious to get started. But when he got to the office, it didn't take long to sense that there was a palpable aura of tension. He couldn't put his finger on it, but the associates seemed to be constantly jockeying for position. They told him little secrets about each other's work when he called them in one by one, and one thing was obvious, there was no sense of a team here. They were a group of talented individuals, doing everything they could to get ahead and crawl over each other. But what surprised him most was the kind of work they did. They were supposedly talented, and he got the impression they worked hard, but the designs they were all working on seemed far less advanced than the ones produced by the same firm in Europe. He realized that it was something he had never noticed on his quick trips through town in the past, but he had always been concentrating on the work that he was responsible for in London. This seemed very different, and far less exciting.

Both senior partners, Bill Jones and Arthur Whittaker, were on hand and introduced him to everyone. The staff seemed cautious but pleased, they had all been told about him, and he had been expected. He had even worked with two of the more senior architects ten years before, when he'd been in New York, but what surprised him about them was that they didn't seem to have moved ahead much. They were happy covering the same ground, and doing the same kind of work he remembered. It was a real shock to him now, as he went from desk to desk, from one architect to another, and the young interns and apprentices seemed even more restrained than the people they worked for.

"What goes on here?" Charlie asked casually, as he shared lunch with two of the associates. They had ordered out, and he had invited them into his office, which was a large corner room with wood-paneled walls and a spectacular view all the way to the East River. "I get the feeling that everyone's a little bit afraid here. The designs look surprisingly conservative. How do you explain that?" The two associates shared a long, slow glance, and then failed to answer. "Come on, guys, let's be straight here. I saw more exciting design work here fifteen years ago. This office looks like it's been going backward." One of them laughed in answer, while the other looked seriously worried. But at least one of them, Ben Chow, was brave enough to answer honestly. It was what Charlie wanted. If he was going to run the place effectively, he needed information.

"They pretty much keep a lid on us here," Chow explained. "This isn't Europe. The big guys are here, and they're breathing down our necks all the time. They're ultraconservative, as you know, and they hate taking chances. They think the old ways are the best ways. And I don't think they really care what anyone does in Europe. They want the same kind of work they always did. They claim that's what we're known for. They think of Europe as a kind of eccentric outpost, a necessary evil in the business." But it was that belief that had allowed Charlie all the freedom he'd enjoyed during his ten years in London. This was going to be very different.

"Are you serious?" Charlie looked startled while Chow nodded at him and his colleague looked extremely nervous. If anyone had heard what had just been said, there were going to be serious repercussions.

"That's why none of the interns stick around for long," Ben went on. "They play the game for a while, and then they go off to I. M. Pei, or KPF or Richard Meyer, or one of the other offices that let them show their stuff. You just can't break through in design here," Ben Chow complained, and Charlie listened with interest. "You'll see, unless they let you change things radically. They'll probably sit on you too, if they think they can do it." But at that, Charlie grinned at them. He hadn't come this far, and worked this long and hard, in order to start making cookie-cutter buildings or endorse them. No one was going to make him do that.

But Charlie learned in short order that that was indeed what they expected of him. They made it clear to him right from the beginning. They had brought him to New York to be an administrator, not to change the world, and they had absolutely no interest in the kind of projects he'd done in Europe. They were well aware of them, and they claimed that that was an entirely different market. The people in the New York office did what was expected of them, and what they were known for. Charlie was in shock when he heard what they said to him, and within two weeks of his arrival, he was going crazy. He felt completely violated, totally misled, and completely wasted. This was not what he had come to New York for. He was paraded around everywhere, to all their most important clients, but he was only a front man. They wanted his expertise in selling design, but the designs were never anything he could be proud of, and none of the projects were ideas he could feel comfortable representing. He tried to effect a change, but everytime he did, or altered a design, even superficially, one or both senior partners would be in his office, explaining to him the "climate of the New York market."

"I have to be honest with you," he said finally, over lunch at the University Club with Arthur Whittaker, "the 'climate' you keep talking about is beginning to make me hot under the collar."

"I understand," Arthur said, looking completely sympathetic to Charlie. They had no desire to upset him. They needed him in New York, they had no one else now. "But, Charles, you have to be patient. This is our most important market." It was not, and they all knew it. But it was where the business had started. It was where they lived, and it was obvious that they wanted to run it their way.

"I'm not sure I agree with you," Charlie said as politely as he could. "Europe has been netting the lion's share of the firm's income for you for years. Along with Japan. It's just that the projects aren't quite as large or as well known as what you do here. But in many ways, they're not only more profitable, but more exciting. I'd like to see if we can bring some of that flavor here from Europe." Charlie could see just looking at him that the senior partner was looking for a tactful answer, because he didn't like what Charlie was saying. The only mystery to him was why they were so intent on keeping the New York office so boring. They were completely behind the times now.

"That's really worth thinking about, Charles," Whittaker began, and then wound up with a long speech about Charlie having lost touch with the American market, but they were going to see that he was brought up to date as soon as feasible. In fact, they had already planned a brief tour of some of their major projects in progress. There were half a dozen huge undertakings in cities around the country, and the following week Charlie was flown around in the company jet to see them. But all he saw when he visited them were the same tired designs, the ideas that had been so fresh fifteen years before, and had been done to death now. He just couldn't believe it. While he had been busy in Taipei and Milan and Hong Kong, and doing truly amazing things for them, they had gone to sleep at the wheel in New York, and they were resisting all his efforts to wake them up and change things. In fact, they made it very obvious to him when he returned, and they had heard what he had to say, that change was the last thing they wanted. And after he spoke to them, he felt utterly confused about how to do the job that he had come for. The only thing they seemed to want from him was to shut up and run the office. He felt like a monitor on a playground, and all the employees did was fight because they were so bored, and frustrated with their projects. It seemed like a hopeless situation, and as Thanksgiving approached, Charlie's spirits plummeted. He hated his work and he had been so involved in what he was doing there that he had made no plans for the holiday, and had no one to be with. Both senior partners actually invited him to join them the day before, but he felt so uncomfortable being with either of them that he lied and said he had made plans with some cousins in Boston. And in the end, he sat in his studio apartment watching football on TV, and he ordered in a pizza and ate it at the Formica counter. It was so awful that in a way it was funny. He and Carole had always made a turkey and invited friends, but it was more of an oddity to their English friends, and it had just been an excuse for a dinner party. But Charlie still couldn't help wondering if Carole had celebrated Thanksgiving this year with Simon. He tried not to think about it, and went into the office for the rest of the weekend. He was still looking through photographs, files, and blueprints, and reading the histories of a number of their projects. But the look was always the same. In fact, at times he almost wondered if they'd used the same blueprints. And by the end of the weekend he was certain of what he'd only feared before, he hated everything they were doing. And he had no idea what to tell them.

On Monday, when he went back to work again, he realized he'd forgotten to look at apartments over the weekend. Looking around at the co-workers who still seemed so ill at ease with him, he almost wondered if it was an omen. Half of them still treated him with suspicion, the others seemed to view him as eccentric. And the senior partners spent most of their time trying to either discredit him or control him.

"So what do you think?" Ben Chow asked later that week when he stopped in Charlie's office. He was a smart, talented thirty-year-old guy. He had gone to Harvard, and Charlie liked not only his work, but his candor.

"Honestly?" Charlie looked him straight in the eye, and knew that Ben would never betray him. It was a relief being honest with him after all the sidestepping that seemed to go on in the office. "I'm not sure I've figured this place out yet. I'm confused by the uniformity of design. It's like everyone is terrified to come up with an original design or even think for themselves here. There's something frighteningly mindless about it. Even their attitudes make me uncomfortable. Particularly the way they constantly squeal on each other. Most of the time I have no idea what to say. This is definitely not a constructive, happy office." Ben Chow laughed at his description, and leaned back in the chair across from Charlie.

"I think you've got it, friend. We're just recycling old designs, probably from the days when you were first here." It was truer than either of them knew. They hadn't done anything original in a decade, pretty much since Charlie had left for London. The amazing thing was that no one in Europe had ever noticed.

"But why? What are they all so afraid of?"

"Progress, I guess. Change. They're using formulas that have worked for them for years. They want to play it safe. They won a lot of awards fifteen years ago, and at some time, when no one was looking, the guts went out of the enterprise. No one has any balls now. All the exciting work we do is being done in Europe." He saluted Charlie then and the two men smiled. It was a relief for both of them to talk to each other. Ben Chow hated what he was doing there as much as Charlie disliked being responsible for it.

"But why won't they let you do it here?" Charlie asked, still puzzled.

"Because this is their turf," Ben said clearly, and listening to him, Charlie knew he was right. The two men who owned the firm weren't going to let anything out of their hands that wasn't exactly what they wanted. And as far as they were concerned, what Charlie did was an aberration that only worked in the Far East or Europe.

"Why do you stay?" Charlie asked him, looking curious. "It can't be very exciting for you, and it won't do squat for your portfolio at this rate."

"I know that. But they still have a name that catches people's attention. Most people haven't figured out yet what we know. It'll probably take another five years and then it'll all be over. I want to go back to Hong Kong next year, but I want to put in another year here first." It sounded sensible to Charlie, and he nodded.

"What about you?" Ben had already said to several friends that he didn't think Charlie would last six months there. He was far too advanced, and too creative to waste his time recycling garbage.

"They agreed to send me back to London in a year." But he was already concerned about Dick Barnes, who might not be willing to give up running the London office, and that could turn out to be a serious problem.

"I wouldn't bet on it," Ben said knowingly. "If they like your style, they're going to try and keep you here forever."

"I don't think I could stand it," Charlie said, nearly in a whisper. It was a far, far cry from what he had done in Europe. But he could give them a year. He had promised them that, and he was ready to fulfill his obligation to them. But on Monday morning he got in an enormous argument with Bill and Arthur over a complicated construction they had going in Chicago. It turned into a week-long fight, an ideological debate, and eventually challenged everyone's integrity and ethics. And Charlie absolutely would not relent about it. But everyone was drawn into the debate, and it divided the entire office into factions. By the end of the week, everyone had finally settled down again, tempers had calmed, and most of the participants retreated to compromise positions, though the main issues were not entirely resolved to Charlie's satisfaction. And within days, a similar argument broke out over a project in Phoenix. It was all about design and having the courage to move forward, and not selling the same old tired concepts to unwitting clients. But they were doing the same thing in Phoenix they'd done before, and the building was almost identical to one they'd done in Houston, but the client didn't know it.

"What is going on here?" Charlie ranted at both partners in a closed meeting in his office a week before Christmas. It had been snowing all week, and three of their architectural associates had been unable to come in from the suburbs, which made the pressure on all of them somewhat greater. But the battle about Phoenix had been raging since early morning. "What exactly are we doing? We're not selling anything original. We're not even selling design. We're becoming contractors, that's all we are. Don't you understand that?" Both men sitting in the room with him bristled at the accusations, and reminded him that they were one of the most respected architectural firms in the country. "Then why don't we act like it, and start selling design again, not this crap that could be done by morons. I really can't let you do this," he said, and the two partners looked at each other, but Charlie had his back to them and was looking at the snow out the window. He was completely frustrated by what they were doing, and humiliated by what they were selling. It really had been a disastrous year for him, and as he turned to face them again, he was surprised to hear them remind him of it. They had already discussed it several hours before, and they were trying to salvage a very delicate situation.

"We know you've had a hard time . . . we heard about your wife," they said cautiously, "that must have been stressful for you, Charles. And moving back from Europe after ten years can't be easy either. Maybe we were wrong to ask you to just step right into the job in a matter of days, without even pausing for breath between New York and London. Maybe you need some time to adjust. . . . What about a little vacation? We've got a project in Palm Beach you could go down and supervise for us. In fact, there's no reason for you not to stay there for a while. You could easily spend a month there." As they said it, alternating sentences, they both looked somewhat sheepish.

"A month? In Florida? Is that a polite way of getting rid of me? Why don't you just fire me?" In fact, they had discussed that too, but given his immense success abroad, and the contract he'd signed, they both found it more than a little embarrassing to fire him, and potentially very expensive. His not working out in New York would be a reflection on them as well, and they were both anxious to avoid any possibility of lawsuits or scandal. He was highly respected in their field, and firing him, and all that entailed, would cause comment and controversy, which might eventually hurt them. They wondered if leaving him in Florida for a while would cool him off, and give them a chance to rethink their options. They needed time to discuss it with their lawyers.

"Fire you?" They guffawed at the thought. "Charles! Of course not!" But just looking at them, Charlie knew better. He knew that sending him to Florida was just a ploy to get him out of their hair. And he also knew that not only was he unhappy in New York, but he was making them very nervous. Professionally at least, in his years abroad, he had come to represent everything they hated. He was far too avant-garde now for the New York office, and in their haste to fill the job, they had somehow managed to overlook that.

"Why not just send me back to London?" he asked hopefully. But the truth was, they couldn't. They had just signed a deal with Dick Barnes, guaranteeing him Charlie's old job for at least five years. He had come at them with an incredibly shrewd lawyer. But the contract had been drawn up in the utmost secrecy, and Charlie knew nothing about it. "I'd be a lot happier if I were there, and so would you, I suspect." He smiled at the two men who were his bosses. They weren't bad men, they just had no sense of artistic excitement, and lately they seemed to be lacking courage. They were tired, and so was everything they were doing. And they were running a police state in order to keep everything the way they wanted.

"We need you here, Charles," they explained, looking more than ever like Siamese twins to him. "We're going to have to make the best of a difficult situation." But they didn't sound any happier than he did, and they were desperately groping for a solution.

"Why? Why do anything we don't want to do?" Charlie said suddenly, feeling a strange rush of freedom. He had already lost everything he cared about when Carole left. He had no wife, no ties, no family, no home anywhere, and all his belongings were in storage. All he had now was his job, and he hated it more than he had ever hated anything he'd ever done. Why stay? He suddenly couldn't think of a single reason to be there, other than his contract. But maybe a good attorney could dissolve it. A thought had just come to him while they were speaking, and he was overwhelmed by a sudden sense of liberation. He didn't *have* to be there. In fact, if he took a sabbatical, they might be relieved not to have to pay him. "Maybe I should just leave," he said practically, looking completely unemotional about it. But the senior partners were far more concerned about losing him than he was about leaving. Besides, they had no one else to run the office, and neither of them wanted to do it.

"Maybe a leave of absence," they said cautiously, watching to see his reaction. But he looked happier than he had in the entire seven weeks he'd been there. It was precisely what he'd been thinking. He had realized everything he needed to know now. They didn't own him. He could leave anytime he wanted. And he suddenly didn't care what happened. Eventually, he could always go back to London, even if he left them.

"I think a leave of absence is a great idea," he said, smiling at them, feeling almost dizzy with excitement. It was like skydiving, like floating free in the air, completely unfettered and unchained. "I don't mind if you want to fire me," he said almost

41

nonchalantly, and both men shuddered in answer. Given the contract they had signed, if they fired him, they would have to pay him anyway for two years, or he could turn around and sue them.

"Why don't you just take a few months off . . . with pay, of course." They were willing to pay almost anything just then to avoid their constant battles with him. He was driving them both crazy. "Give yourself time to decide where you want to go from here. You might even decide that we're not so wrong after all, after you give it a little careful consideration." If only he would agree to play by their rules, they could live with him. But for the moment, to Charlie anyway, that seemed out of the question. "You can take up to six months, Charles, if you need it. We'll discuss everything again when you're ready." He was a good architect, after all, and they needed him, but not if he was going to swim upstream and challenge every decision they made about every building. But he nonetheless had a feeling that they had something up their sleeves and weren't being totally honest with him, and he couldn't help wondering if they had ever really planned to send him back to London. He could always go back on his own, of course. But now that he was here, he thought he might spend a month or so traveling to other cities, maybe Philadelphia and Boston. And after that, he wanted to go back to England.

"I'd like to go back to London," Charlie said honestly. "I don't think the New York office will work for me, even in six months, or after a long vacation." He didn't want to mislead them. "The atmosphere here is very different. I can do this for a while, if you need me to, for a short time at least. But I think having me here is counterproductive."

"We've thought of that too, right now anyway," they said, looking relieved. As far as they were concerned, in his years abroad he had become a renegade and a misfit. He had worked independently for too long, and gotten too many European ideas to allow him to readjust his thinking even now that he had left there.

Even Charlie realized that there was always the possibility that he would eventually be able to compromise with them, for a while anyway. And maybe after six months off, he would feel ready to face New York again, but he doubted it. It was too uncomfortable for him, and he couldn't do any of the work here that he was known for. But six months would give them all time to think, and figure out where to put him.

He couldn't help wondering, too, if they were right in another sense. They had implied that he was overwrought and exhausted after his problems with Carole. And maybe he did need some time to recover. Leaving his job, and taking time off, was the wildest thing he had ever done. He had never done anything like it before. He barely used up his annual vacation, and hadn't taken any significant time off since college, nor had he ever wanted to do that. But in the situation he found himself in, it was suddenly very appealing. He had a contract with the firm, and yet he knew he had to get away from the New York office before it drove him completely crazy.

"Where will you go from here?" they asked with concern. As disappointing as his return had been for them, they had always liked him.

"I have absolutely no idea," he said honestly, trying to relish the uncertainty of his situation, rather than be frightened by it. There was nothing for him here. But there was nothing for him in London at the moment either. And he didn't want to risk running into Simon and Carole. It was easier to stay in the States for a while longer. "Maybe I'll go to Boston," he said vaguely. He had grown up there, but had no relatives in the area anymore. His parents were long gone, and most of the people he knew were from his childhood, and he hadn't looked any of them up in ages, and didn't really want to. Particularly now, precariously half out of a job, and with a sad tale to tell them about Carole.

He thought about skiing in Vermont for a week or two, traveling for a while, and then flying back to London, before he made any permanent decisions. He had no plans for the holidays, and he was completely free. He still had quite a bit of money in the bank, after the divorce, and with his salary he could afford to be easy on himself for the time being. He could even go skiing in Switzerland or France, after he went back to London. But he also realized that he no longer had a home there. He had no home anywhere, and his belongings were on a boat on the Atlantic somewhere on their way to storage. But whatever he decided to do in the end, he knew it was a lot more appealing than being squeezed to death in their New York office.

"You'll stay in touch," they said as he came around the desk to shake hands with them. They were enormously relieved by the tone and the outcome of the meeting. For a brief time, they had been afraid that he was going to give them a great deal of trouble, and he could have. According to his contract, he could have insisted on staying there, and they realized now that the battles with him would have been endless.

"I'll be in contact with you about what we do when the leave is over." They had agreed on six months, and although he didn't yet know what to do with it, he was determined to use it and enjoy it. But he seriously wondered if he would ever be able to work for them again. Not in New York, in any case, and he sensed that, despite their agreement with him to send him back after a year, there was some kind of stumbling block about London. He felt as though they were just humoring him, and he wasn't far off the mark, although he didn't know it. Dick Barnes had his old job now, with a slightly different title, and the senior partners of the firm genuinely liked him. He was far more tractable and easy to get along with than Charlie.

He couldn't help wondering, as he packed the few things in his desk, if he would ever return to Whittaker and Jones, in any capacity, in any city. He was seriously beginning to wonder.

He said good-bye to everyone late that afternoon. Everything he had with him was in his briefcase. He had already given them all their files back. He had nothing to work on, to take with him, to read, no deadlines, no projects, no blueprints. He was free now. And the only one he was sorry to leave was Ben Chow, who looked at him with a broad smile just before he left the office.

"How did you get so lucky?" he asked under his breath, and they both laughed. Charlie felt almost euphoric as he thanked the two partners and walked out, not entirely sure if he would eventually quit, be fired, or was really just on a long vacation. But whatever it turned out to be, for the first time in his life, he wasn't even worried. He knew they would have destroyed him artistically if he'd stayed there.

"What now?" he asked himself as he walked back to his apartment. He had told them he'd vacate it in the morning. The cold air and the snow in his eyes sobered him. What was he going to do? Where would he go? Did he really want to go skiing, as he had said, or should he just fly back to London? And if he did, then what? It was going to be Christmas in a week, and he knew that being in London over the holidays would only make him miserable thinking of Carole. He'd want to reach out to her, or at the very least call her. He'd want to buy her a gift and then see her to give it to her. He could feel the whole carousel of agony begin to turn again just pondering the question. In some ways, it would be easier not to be there.

It was hard not to remember that it was going to be their first Christmas apart in ten years. She had even flown to London to be with him for his first year there before they were married. But not this year. This year she would be with Simon.

The skiing idea sounded good to him, and he called and rented a car for the following day as soon as he got to his apartment. He was surprised to find one still available, everyone wanted cars for the holidays, to visit relatives and carry presents. He rented it for a week, and asked for maps of Vermont, New

Hampshire, and Massachusetts, and he figured he could rent ski equipment once he was there. He felt like a kid running away from home as he sat on his couch, thinking of what he'd done. A noble career had just gone right out the window, and he wasn't even sure it mattered. It was utterly and completely crazy. He wondered if he was finally losing his mind after the stress of the past year, and he thought of calling friends in London just to bounce it off them, but he had lost touch with almost everyone. He hadn't wanted to share his grief with anyone, and he had been exhausted by the questions, the probing, and the gossip. Even their sympathy had been exhausting. In the end, it was easier to be on his own, and he had also figured out that most of them were seeing a fair amount of Carole and Simon, and he didn't want to hear about that either. So he just sat there alone, wondering what Carole would say if she knew he had just left the firm, for several months, if not forever. She would probably be stunned, he thought, but on the other hand, the beauty of his situation now was that he didn't owe anyone any explanations.

He packed his bags that night, tidied everything, threw a few things out of the refrigerator, and was ready to roll at eight o'clock the next morning. He took a cab downtown to pick up the car, and as he passed the department stores, he could see the brightly lit Christmas windows. He was glad now that he was getting out of town. It was going to be hard watching everyone else in the office celebrate, listening to their plans, hearing them talk about their wives, and families and children. He had none of that now. He had no one. He didn't even have a job. A year before, he had been a man with a wife, a house, a job, and all the trappings that went with a ten-year marriage. But suddenly, he had none of that. He had a rented car, and two bags, and a handful of maps of New England.

"The car's got snow tires," the man at the car rental explained, "but you'd better put on chains if you go too far North. I'd say anything north of Connecticut," he advised, and Charlie thanked him. "Spending Christmas in New England?" The man smiled, and Charlie nodded.

"I think I'll be going skiing."

"There's lots of snow this year. Don't break anything!" he warned, and then wished Charlie a merry Christmas as he left. Charlie had already asked him if he could return the car in Boston. He thought he might ski for a while, and then leave the car there, and fly from Boston to London. He had no reason to go to New York, not for now at least. Maybe in six months. Or maybe never.

He loaded the white station wagon quickly and drove across town. It was a decent car, and there would be plenty of room for skis if he decided to rent them. For the moment, there were only his two bags in the back, and the chains they had provided. He was wearing blue jeans, a heavy sweater, and a ski parka he had brought with him. And he was smiling to himself as he turned the heat on. He flipped on the radio then and started singing.

He stopped and bought a cup of coffee and a danish before he headed to the FDR Drive. He glanced at the map as he took a sip, and then he started the car again. He had no idea where he was going. North, just as he had said to the man. To Connecticut . . . then Massachusetts . . . maybe Vermont. Vermont might be the right kind of place to spend Christmas. He could ski right through the holidays. People would be in good spirits. And in the meantime all he had to do was drive, keep his eye on the road, watch the snow, and try not to look back over his shoulder. He knew now, more than he ever had before, that there was nothing there, nothing to reach back for, or even take with him.

He was singing softly to himself as he headed out of the city, and he smiled, looking straight ahead. All he had now was the future.

Chapter 3

IT WAS STARTING to snow as Charlie crossed the Triborough Bridge and carefully made his way to the Hutchinson River Parkway, but he didn't mind. It felt more like Christmas somehow, and he felt surprisingly festive as he drove north and began to hum Christmas carols. He was in remarkably good spirits for a man without a job, and he still couldn't believe what had happened. He played it over in his mind again several times, and wondered inevitably if his days with Whittaker and Jones were over. It was hard to guess what would happen in the next six months, but he had already thought about traveling, and maybe even doing some painting. He hadn't had time to even think of doing something like that in ages. But the prospect appealed to him now. He might even teach architecture for a while, if the opportunity presented itself, and he had an idea in the back of his mind about traveling around Europe, and visiting medieval castles. They had fascinated him since college. But first he was going to ski in Vermont, and after that he was going to go back to London and find himself an apartment. It felt like a turning point to him. For the first time in a year, he wasn't reacting to what had been thrown at him. He had made a choice and he was going to do whatever he wanted.

The snow began to collect in drifts, and after three hours on the road, he stopped in Simsbury. There was a small cozy-looking inn that advertised itself as a bed and breakfast. It was the perfect place to spend the night, and the couple who owned it seemed delighted to see him. They showed him to their prettiest room, and he felt relieved again to have abandoned the depressing studio apartment. In fact, his entire stay in New York had been relentlessly unpleasant, and he was delighted that it had ended.

"Going to see your family for the holidays?" the woman who showed him to his room asked pleasantly. She was heavyset and had dyed blond hair, and there was something very warm and friendly about her.

"Actually, no, I'm on my way to go skiing." She nodded, looking pleased, and told him about the town's two best restaurants, both within half a mile, and asked if he'd like her to make reservations for dinner. He hesitated, and then shook his head as he knelt to light a fire with the kindling they had provided.

"I'll just grab a sandwich somewhere, but thanks anyway." He hated going to nice restaurants by himself. He had never understood people who did that. It seemed so lonely somehow to be sitting there drinking half a bottle of wine, and eating a thick steak with no one to talk to. The very thought of it depressed him.

"You're welcome to eat with us, if you'd like." She eyed him with interest. He was good-looking and young, and she wondered what he was doing on his own. It seemed odd to her that he wasn't married. She guessed that he was probably divorced, and was sorry her daughter hadn't come up from New York yet. But Charlie had no idea what she had in mind for him, as he thanked her again, and closed the door behind her. Women were always more interested in him than he realized, but he was usually unaware of it. And he hadn't thought of anything like that in years. He hadn't had a date since Carole left him. He had been far too busy mourning. But now, having divested himself of all the responsibilities in his life so unexpectedly, he was suddenly feeling better.

He went out for a hamburger later that night, and was amazed to see how high the snow was. There were several feet on either side of the carefully shoveled driveway, and he smiled to himself as he drove away from the little bed and breakfast. It was so beautiful here, he would have loved to share it with someone. It was odd to be alone all the time, to have no one to make comments to, or share things with, or talk to. He still hadn't gotten used to the silence. But he sat alone as he ate his hamburger, and took a bag of sweet rolls with him for the morning, and the hotel had promised to provide him with a thermos of coffee. They had offered to make breakfast for him too, but he wanted to get an early start, provided the snow would let him.

It was a clear, quiet night when he went back to the little inn, and he stood outside for a minute, looking at the sky. It was incredibly beautiful and his face tingled in the cold air, and then suddenly he laughed out loud, feeling better than he had in years, and he wished that he could have thrown a snowball at someone. He made one round, firm ball of the crisp white snow, just for the hell of it, and tossed it at a tree. It made him feel like a kid again, and he was still smiling when he went upstairs to his bedroom. It was warm, and the fire was still burning brightly. And it suddenly began to feel like Christmas.

It was only when he got between the clean sheets on the big canopied bed, under the down comforter, that his heart began to ache again, and he wished Carole was there with him. He would have given anything to spend a night with her again, and it made his soul ache just thinking that he would never again do that. She would never spend another night with him, he would never be able to make love to her again. Just letting his mind run over it made him long for her, but he knew as he lay staring into the fire that it was pointless. He couldn't keep doing this to himself, and he couldn't go on pining for her forever. But it was so damn hard not to. It had been so good for such a long time, and he still wondered at the flaw in him that had allowed him not to see what was happening when he had begun to lose her. Maybe if he had seen it then, he could have stopped it. It was like torturing yourself for a life you had been unable to save. The life he had lost was his own, the victim was their marriage. And he wondered if he would ever feel the same about anyone again. He wondered how she could be so sure of herself in going off with Simon. He couldn't imagine ever trusting anyone that much again. In fact, he was sure he wouldn't.

It was a long time before he fell asleep, and when he did, the fire was finally dying. The embers were a soft glow in the room, and the snow had stopped falling beyond the windows. And when he woke up in the morning, the woman who owned the inn was knocking on his door with warm blueberry muffins and a pot of steaming coffee.

"I thought you might like this, Mr. Waterston." She smiled at him, as he opened the door to her with a towel wrapped tightly around his waist. He had sent all his pajamas to storage, and kept forgetting to buy new ones. But she had no objection at all to seeing his long, lean, muscular body. It only made her wish she were twenty years younger.

"Thanks so much," he said, smiling at her, still looking sleepy and a little bit tousled. And when he drew back the curtains, he stood staring at how beautiful it looked. The snow lay in graceful drifts and her husband was outside shoveling the driveway.

"You'll want to be careful driving today," she warned.

"Is it icy?" he asked conversationally, but he didn't look worried.

"Not yet. But it will be later on. They say it's going to snow again this afternoon. There's a storm front coming down from the Canadian border." But he didn't mind at all. He had all the time in the world, and he could drive through New England in twenty-mile increments if he had to. He was in no rush to do anything, not even go skiing, although he was looking forward to it. He hadn't skied in the States since he'd lived there. He and Carole had gone to Sugarbush in the old days, while he'd lived in New York. But he had already decided to go someplace different. He didn't need any more pilgrimages to places where he had memories of her. Especially not over Christmas.

Charlie left the inn an hour later, showered and dressed in ski pants and a parka, carrying the thermos of coffee he'd bought from them. And he got on Interstate 91 without difficulty, and headed toward Massachusetts. He drove steadily for a long time, and he was surprised by how clear the road was. The snow scarcely slowed him at all, and he never even needed to put on the chains the rental company had provided. It was easy driving until he reached Whately, and then it began to snow lightly, and he watched the snowflakes collect on his windshield.

He was tired by then, and he was surprised to see how far he'd come. He had been driving for hours, and he was just on the outskirts of Deerfield. He had no particular destination in mind, but he decided to try and press on for a while, just so he wouldn't have as far to drive to Vermont the next morning. But by the time he passed Deerfield, it was really snowing.

Historic Deerfield was remarkably picturesque, and he was tempted to stop and look around. He had gone there with his parents as a child, and remembered his fascination with seeing the three-hundred-year-old houses that had been preserved there. Even as a child, he had been fascinated with all things architectural, and his visit had made a big impression. But he decided it was too late to stop now, and he wanted to press on. With luck, he might even make the Vermont border. He had no particular route or plan in mind, he just wanted to keep going, and he was constantly in awe of how beautiful it was, how sweet the towns were. He drove through covered bridges and past historical towns, and he knew that there were waterfalls nearby. If it had been summer, he would have stopped and walked, and maybe even gone swimming. New England was where he had grown up. This was his home, and he suddenly realized that it wasn't an accident that he had come here. He had come here to heal, and to touch familiar ground. Maybe at last, it was time for his mourning to end, and for him to recover. Six months before, he couldn't even imagine it, but now he felt as though the healing process had begun because he had come here.

He passed the Deerfield Fort and remembered his boyhood fascination with that landmark, but he only smiled as he drove on, remembering his father. He had told Charlie wonderful tales about the Indians along the Mohawk Trail, which Deerfield was on, and the Iroquois and the Algonquin. Charlie had loved hearing about them as a child, and his father had always had a remarkable store of knowledge. He had been an American history professor at Harvard, and trips like these had always been a special gift from father to son, as had been the tales that he told him. It made Charlie suddenly think about him again now, and wish that he could have told him about Carole. Thinking about both of them brought tears to his eyes, but he had to stop dreaming and concentrate on the road again as the snow began to fall harder. He had only come ten miles in half an hour since Deerfield. But it was getting too difficult to see now.

He passed a sign on the way into a small town, and saw that he was in Shelburne Falls. As closely as he could figure it, he had gone about ten miles northwest of Deerfield, and the frozen river running nearby was the Deerfield River. It was a small, quaint-looking little town, nestled on the hillside, looking out over the valley. And as the snow swirled around him ever more furiously, Charlie abandoned all thought of driving on to Vermont. It didn't seem wise to go any farther, and he wondered if he could find an inn or a small hotel. All he could see around him were small, neatly tended homes as he kept driving. And it was nearly impossible to drive now.

He stopped the car for a minute, unsure which way to go, and then rolled down the window. He could see a street leading off to the left somewhere, and turned the car slowly, deciding to try it. He was afraid to put the car into a skid on the fresh snow, but the snow tires held, and he headed slowly down the street that paralleled the Deerfield River, and just as he was beginning to feel lost and think he had best turn back again, he saw a neat, shingled house with a widow's walk and a white picket fence around it. And the sign hanging outside the fence said simply PALMER: BED AND BREAKFAST. It was just what he wanted. And he pulled carefully into the driveway.

There was a mailbox that looked like a birdhouse outside, and a big Irish setter came bounding through the snow wagging her tail as she saw him. He stopped and patted her, keeping his chin down as the snow swirled around him, and he made his way to the front door and made use of the well-polished brass knocker. But for a long time no one answered, and Charlie began to wonder if anyone was at home. There were lights on inside, but there was no sound, and the Irish setter sat down next to him and looked up at him expectantly as they waited.

He had just given up, and started down the front steps again, when the door opened cautiously and a small white-haired woman looked at him, as though wondering why he had come there. She was neatly dressed in a gray skirt and pale blue sweater, she had a string of pearls around her neck, and she had snow-white hair pulled back into a bun, and brilliant blue eyes that seemed to examine every inch of him as he stood there. She looked like some of the older women he'd known in Boston as a child, and she seemed an unlikely candidate to be running a bed and breakfast. But she also made no move to open the door any farther.

"Yes?" She opened the door only slightly wider to let the dog inside, and she looked up at Charlie with curiosity, but there was no sign of welcome. "May I help you?"

"I saw the sign . . . I thought . . . are you closed for the winter?" Maybe she only ran it in the summer, he thought to himself, some of the bed and breakfasts did that.

"I didn't expect anyone over the holidays," she said cautiously. "There's a motel on the highway to Boston. It's just past Deerfield."

"Thank you . . . I'm sorry . . . I . . ." He felt embarrassed to have intruded on her. She seemed so ladylike and so polite that he felt like some kind of hooligan barging in on her without warning or invitation. But as he apologized, she smiled at him, and he was startled at how alive her eyes were. They were almost electric, they were so full of energy and life, and yet he could tell from looking at her that she had to be in her late sixties, and he suspected that not long since she had once been very pretty. She was delicate and genteel, and she surprised him as she took a step back and opened the door wide enough for him to enter.

"Don't apologize," she smiled. "I was just surprised. I wasn't expecting anyone. I'm afraid I forgot my manners. Would you like to come in for something warm to drink? I'm not really set up for visitors right now. I usually only get paying guests in the warmer weather." He hesitated on the doorstep as he looked at her, wondering if he should drive on while he still could, and find the motel she had recommended. But it was very tempting to come in and visit with her. He could see from the doorway how handsome the living room was. It was a beautifully built old house, possibly even from Revolutionary days, there were heavy beams overhead, carefully laid floors, and he could see that the room was filled with lovely antiques and English and Early American paintings. "Come in . . . Glynnis and I will behave, I promise." She indicated the dog as she said her name, and the big setter wagged her tail furiously as though endorsing the promise. "I didn't mean to be so inhospitable. I was just startled." And as she spoke to him, Charlie found himself unable to resist the invitation, and walked into the warm, welcoming living room that seemed to engulf him like magic. It was even lovelier than he had suspected from the doorway. There was a fire burning in the grate, and there was a remarkably beautiful antique piano in the corner.

"I'm sorry to intrude. I was driving north to Vermont, and the snow got too heavy to drive any farther." He looked at her admiringly, thinking about how pretty she still was, and how graceful, as she walked into her kitchen and he followed. She put a big copper kettle on, and he couldn't help noticing that everything was spotless.

"What a beautiful home you have . . . is it Mrs. Palmer?" He remembered the name on the sign, and she smiled in answer.

"It is. Thank you. And you are?" She looked at him like a schoolteacher expecting an answer, and this time he smiled. He didn't know who she was, or why he had come here, but he instantly knew that he loved her.

"Charles Waterston," he said, extending a hand to her politely, and she shook it. Her hands were very smooth and young for her age, her nails were neatly manicured, and she wore a plain gold wedding band. That and the pearls she wore were her only jewelry. All the spare money she'd ever had she'd put into the antiques and paintings that he saw all around him. But their quality wasn't lost on Charles, who had seen too many fine things in his childhood, and in London, to ignore them.

"And where are you from, Mr. Waterston?" Mrs. Palmer asked as she prepared their tea tray. He had no idea if he was being invited to tea, or would be allowed to spend the night in her establishment, and he didn't dare ask her. If she wasn't going to let him stay, he knew he should press on before the snowstorm got worse, and the roads too icy. But he didn't say a word about it, as he watched her put a silver teapot on an embroidered linen cloth that was much older than she was.

"That's an interesting question," he said with a smile, as she waved him to a comfortable leather chair in front of the fire in her kitchen. There was a George III butler's table in front of it, which she liked to serve tea on. "I've been living in London for the last ten years, and I'll be going back after the holidays. But I've just come from New York, yesterday in fact. I've been there for the past two months, and I was planning to spend a year there, but now it would appear that I can go back to London." It was as simply as he could explain it, without going into all the details. And she smiled gently as she looked at him, as though she understood far more than he had told her.

"A change of plans?"

"You could say that," he said, as he patted the dog, and then looked up at his hostess again. It was as though she had been expecting him, as she put a plate of cinnamon cookies on the table.

"Don't let Glynnis eat them," she warned, and he laughed, and then he thought he should ask her if he was intruding. It was nearly dinnertime, and there was no reason for her to be serving tea to him, particularly if she didn't take in guests during the winter. But she seemed to be enjoying the visit. "Glynnis particularly likes cinnamon, although she's also quite partial to oatmeal." Mrs. Palmer explained about the dog, as Charlie smiled at the owner of the erstwhile Cookie Monster, wondering if she had lived there all her life. It was difficult to look at Mrs. Palmer, and not wonder about her story. She seemed surprisingly elegant, and very fragile. "Will you be going back to New York again, Mr. Waterston, before you return to London?"

"I don't think so. I'm on my way to ski in Vermont, and I thought I'd fly back via Boston. I'm afraid New York isn't my favorite town, although I lived there for a long time. I've been spoiled by living in Europe."

She smiled very gently at him then, as she sat down across from him, at the small, distinguished table. "My husband was English. We used to visit there once in a while, to see his relatives, but he was happy here, and once they died, we never went back. He said he had everything he wanted here in Shelburne Falls." She smiled at her guest, and there was something unsaid in her eyes. Charlie couldn't help wondering what it was, if it was grief, or merely memory, or love for a man with whom she had shared a lifetime. He wondered if, at her age, he would still look like that when he spoke of Carole.

"And where are you from?" he asked, sipping the delicious tea she had brewed for him. It was Earl Grey, and he was a tea drinker, but he had never tasted anything like it. There was something truly magical about her.

"I'm from right here," she said with a smile, setting her cup down. The china was Wedgwood, and as delicate as she was. The entire scene reminded Charlie of the many places and people he'd met on his travels around England. "I've lived in Shelburne Falls all my life. In this house, actually, it belonged to my parents. And my son went to school in Deerfield." He found it hard to believe as he looked at her, she seemed so much more worldly than one would have expected from a woman who had lived in New England all her life, and he sensed that there had to be more than she was saying. "When I was very young, I went to Boston for a year, and lived with my aunt. I thought it was a very exciting place, and that was where I met my husband. He was a visiting scholar at Harvard. And when we were married, we moved here, that was fifty years ago, this year in fact. I'll be seventy this summer." She smiled at him, and Charlie wanted to lean over and kiss her. He told her about his father's teaching career, and that he had taught American history at Harvard. He wondered if he and Mr. Palmer had ever met, and then he told her about his trips to Deerfield as a child, and his passion for the buildings there, and his fascination with the glacial potholes in the huge boulders in the Deerfield River.

"I still remember them," he explained, as she poured another cup of tea for him, and began bustling around her kitchen, and then she turned to him with a warm smile. She felt completely safe with him. He looked entirely wholesome, and was obviously well behaved and very well mannered. She wondered why he was traveling alone during the holidays, and was surprised he had no family to be with, but she said nothing about that as she looked at him with a question.

"Would you like to stay here, Mr. Waterston? It's no trouble for me. I can easily open one of my guest rooms." As she said it, she glanced outside again. The snow was falling furiously, and she would have felt unkind putting him on the road again, besides, she liked him and enjoyed his company. She hoped that he would accept her invitation.

"Are you sure it wouldn't be too much trouble for you?" He had seen the storm outside too, and he wasn't anxious to move on. He also particularly enjoyed her. She was like a glimpse into the past, and at the same time she seemed to have a firm grip on the present, and he was basking in the warmth of her company, as he nodded. "I don't want to be a nuisance. If you had other plans, you don't need to pay any attention to me. But I'd very much like to stay, if you don't mind." It was a sweet minuet between them, and a few minutes later, she took him upstairs and showed him around. The house was beautifully built throughout, and he was more intrigued by how it was built than in seeing his accommodations, but when he saw the room she planned for him, he stood in the doorway and smiled for a long moment. It was like coming home as a child. The bed was huge, the fabrics worn, but all of it was beautifully made. The room was done in blue and white chintz, and there was lovely old china displayed on the mantelpiece, a ship model on the wall, and there were several old, very fine Moran paintings of ships on smooth seas and in storms. It was a room he would have loved to spend a year in. And like the other rooms he'd seen so far, it had a large fireplace, and there were logs standing by, ready to be used. Everything in the house seemed precise and well kept, as though she were expecting her favorite relatives or a house full of guests at any moment.

"This is just lovely," he said gratefully, looking at her warmly. It had been kind of her to take him in, and he appreciated both her hospitality and her effort. And she seemed pleased to see how much he liked it. She loved sharing her home with people who appreciated fine things, and understood what she was sharing with them. Most of the people who stayed with her came by recommendation. She didn't advertise, and it was only in the past year that she'd put out a shingle.

For seven years, taking in paying guests had assisted with her funds, and the people who stayed with her kept her company, and kept her from being too lonely. She had been dreading the holidays, and having Charlie appear at her door had been a godsend.

"I'm glad you like the house, Mr. Waterston." He was examining the paintings in his room as she spoke to him, and he turned to her with a look of pleasure.

"I can't imagine anyone not loving it," he said reverently, and she laughed, thinking of her son. There was a wistful look in her eyes when she spoke of him, but also an unmistakable spark of humor.

"I can. My son hated everything about this town, and all my old things. He loved all things modern. He was a pilot. He flew in Viet Nam, and when he came home, he stayed in the Navy. He was a test pilot for all their most high-tech fighters. He loved flying." There was something about the way she said it that made him afraid to ask, and a look in her eyes that said the subject was very painful. But nonetheless, she continued. There was something about the way she moved, and looked at him, that told him the one thing Gladys Palmer didn't lack was courage. "He and his wife both flew. They bought a small plane after their little girl was born." There were tears in her bright blue eyes as she looked at Charlie, but she didn't waver. "I didn't think it was a good idea, but you have to let your children do as they wish. They wouldn't have listened if I had tried to stop them. They crashed near Deerfield fourteen years ago, when they were coming home for a visit. All three of them were in the plane, and they died on impact." Charlie felt a lump grow in his throat as he listened, and instinctively he reached a hand out to her and touched her arm, wanting to stop the words and the pain. He couldn't imagine anything worse, not even what he had experienced with Carole. This woman had been through so much more, and he couldn't help wondering if she had more children.

"I'm so sorry," he whispered. His hand was still on her arm, and neither of them noticed it, as their eyes met and held. He felt as though he had known her forever.

"So am I. He was a wonderful man. He was thirty-six when he died, and his little girl was only five . . . it was a terrible loss." She sighed and wiped her eyes, as he wished that he could put his arms around her. And then she looked up at him, and what he saw in her eyes made his breath catch. There was such openness, such bravery, such willingness to reach out to him despite the pain she'd suffered. "I suppose we learn something from sorrow. I'm not sure what it is, and it took me a long time. It was ten years before I could talk about it. My husband never could. He was never really well after that. He had a bad heart, even when he was young. He died three years later." She had suffered far greater losses than he had, and he could still see the scars, they were clearly visible, yet she was still there, standing sure and firm, unwilling to be beaten by the hard blows life had dealt her. And he couldn't help wondering if their paths had crossed for a reason. It was so odd that he had come here.

"Do you have other . . . other relatives?" He was embarrassed suddenly to ask if she had other children, as though her lost son could be replaced easily by his siblings, although they both knew he couldn't.

"None," she smiled at him, and what struck him again was how alive she was. There was nothing bitter or sad or depressed about this woman. "I'm all alone now. I have been for eleven years. That's why I started taking in guests during the summer. Otherwise, I think I might have been very lonely." But it was hard to imagine that. She seemed far too lively to wither away, or lock herself up and pine for those she had lost. There was an aura of energy and life all around her. "I would have hated to waste this house too. It's so wonderful, it seemed a terrible shame not to share it. My son James . . . Jimmy and Kathleen would never have wanted it. I suppose eventually, even if he'd lived, I'd have had to sell it." It seemed a terrible shame just hearing about it, and she had no one to leave her treasures to now. It was the same boat he was going to find himself in one day if he didn't do something about his life, marry again, and have children. But none of it appealed to him, even for a minute. He had no desire to marry again, or live with another woman. "And you?" She looked at him before leaving the room. "Do you have a family, Mr. Waterston?" He was the right age to be married and have several children. She guessed him to be slightly younger than he was. She thought he was about Jimmy's age. But at forty-two, he should certainly have been well settled.

"No, I don't," Charlie said softly. "Like you, I have no one. My parents died a long time ago. And I've never had children."

She seemed surprised, and she wondered if there was something about his sexuality that had eluded her, but she didn't think she had missed that. "Have you never been married?" That actually amazed her. He seemed far too attractive and too warm to have avoided a permanent relationship, but when she saw his eyes, she realized there was more to the story.

62

"I have. I'm getting divorced. We were married for ten years, but we never had children."

"I'm sorry to hear that," she said gently, sounding almost like a mother to him, and he felt tears fill his eyes as she said it. "Divorce must be a terrible thing, the tearing asunder of two people who loved each other once, and have lost their way. It must be unbearably painful."

"It is," he said, nodding his head thoughtfully. "It's been very difficult. I've never lost anyone I loved, other than my parents, of course. But the two experiences must be very similar. I feel like I've been in a trance for the last year. She left nine months ago. The incredibly stupid thing is that I always thought we were blissfully happy before that. I seem to be unusually ignorant about other people's feelings. It's not much of a recommendation," he said with a sad smile, and she looked warmly at him. They felt like old friends, although they had only known each other for a few hours. He could have sat and talked to her forever.

"I think you're being hard on yourself. You're not the first man to think everything was fine, and then discover it wasn't. But still, it must be an awful blow not only to the heart . . . but to the ego." She had touched on the crux of it. He was not only feeling the loss and the pain, but his dignity and pride were also mortally wounded. "It sounds cruel to say, but you'll get over it. At your age, you have no choice. You can nurse a broken heart for the rest of your life. It wouldn't be right. You'll need time, I'm sure, but eventually you'll have to come out of your shell. Even I had to do that. I could have closed my doors and sat in this house for the rest of my life, waiting to die, when Jimmy and Kathleen and Peggy died . . . and then again after Roland. But what good would that have done? There's no point wasting the years I have left. I remember them, of course. I still cry sometimes. There isn't a day or an hour or a moment that I don't think of one of them, and sometimes I miss them so much I think I can't bear it

. . . but I'm still here. I have to go on. I have to give something back, to make my time here worth something. If not, the time I've been given here would have been totally wasted. And I don't think we have a right to do that. I think we only have a right to so much time for mourning." She was right, of course, and listening to her say it hit him hard. It was exactly what he needed to hear at that precise moment. And as he thought about it, she looked up at him and smiled again. "Would you like to join me for dinner, Mr. Waterston? I was going to make lamb chops and a salad. I don't eat very much, and it's not as hearty as you'd like, I suspect, but it's a bit of a distance to the nearest restaurant and it's snowing awfully hard. . . ." Her voice trailed off as she looked at him, keenly aware of how handsome he was, and in an odd, subtle way he reminded her of Jimmy.

"I'd like that very much. Could I help you cook? I'm not bad with lamb chops."

"That would be very nice." She smiled at him, and Glynnis wagged her tail, as though she understood what they were saying. "I usually dine at seven. Come downstairs whenever you like," she said formally, and their eyes met and held for a long moment. They had exchanged valuable gifts that afternoon, and they were both distinctly aware of it. In a way that neither of them fully understood, they both knew they needed each other.

Charlie lit the fire in his room, and sat on his bed looking at it for a long time, thinking about her, and what she'd said, about what she'd experienced when her son died, and he was touched to his very soul, and filled with admiration for her. What a remarkable woman she was, and what a gift it had been to meet her. He felt lost in the beauty of her small world, enveloped by the warmth and kindness he had found there.

He took a quick bath and shaved, and changed his clothes before he went back downstairs. He was tempted to put on a suit for her, but that seemed too extreme, and he settled for gray flannel slacks, a dark blue turtleneck sweater, and a blazer. But just as he always did, he looked impeccable in perfectly tailored clothes and hair that had been recently barbered. He was a handsome man, and Gladys Palmer smiled the moment she saw him. It was rare for her to make a mistake about the people she took in, and she already knew that she had not made an error with this one. She hadn't met anyone she liked as much in a long, long time, and like him, she sensed a deeper purpose to their meeting. It seemed as though she had a lot to offer him, the warmth of her home at a difficult time of year, if nothing else, and he brought back the memory of her son for her, and the family she had loved so much and lost years before. The hardest time of year for her was always Christmas.

He cooked the lamb chops for her, and she made salad and mashed potatoes that were delicious, and for dessert they shared bread pudding. It was the kind of meal his own mother would have made for him, and not unlike some of the meals he and Carole had eaten in England. He wished, as he listened to Mrs. Palmer tell her tales, that Carole could have been there and he had to remind himself that it was a waste of time to think that. At some point, he had to stop wishing he could include her in everything. She was no longer a part of his life anymore. She belonged only to Simon. But still it was always painful to remember, and he had begun to suspect it always would be. Looking at Mrs. Palmer he wondered how she had survived, losing her son, her daughter-in-law, and her only grandchild. The agony of it must have been brutal. And yet, she had gone on. He could sense easily that she still felt the pain, like a limb long lost but still remembered. And he knew clearly now that he just had to go on, whatever it cost him.

Mrs. Palmer made him tea again, and they talked for hours, talking about local history, stories of the Deerfield Fort, and some of the people who had lived there. Like his father years before, she was incredibly knowledgeable about the legends and the historical figures of the region. She talked about the Indians who had lived there too, and listening to her revived some of the stories he had long since forgotten, told to him by his father. It was nearly midnight when they both realized how late it was. But both of them had been starving for some warmth and human contact. He had told her about the fiasco in New York too, and she was amazingly sensible in her analysis of the situation. She suggested he go on about his life, use the time well, and see if he even wanted to go back to them at the end of the six months. She thought it might be a great opportunity to explore new avenues to express his talent, perhaps maybe even open his own office. They talked about his love of Gothic and medieval castles and the remarkable work they'd achieved, in his view, and his passion for old houses, like this one.

"There are so many things you can do with your architectural talent, Charles. You don't need to confine it to office buildings or superstructures." He had also confided in her that he had always wanted to build an airport, but for that he was going to have to stay associated with a major firm. For the other things he loved, he could easily have done them through a small one-man office. "It sounds as though you have some serious thinking to do in the next six months . . . and some fun to have as well. It doesn't sound as though you've had much fun lately, have you?" she asked, with a twinkle in her eye. Everything he described about New York, and even the months before, sounded dreadful. "I think skiing in Vermont sounds like a fine idea. Perhaps you'll even have time to get into some mischief." He actually blushed at the way she said it, and they both laughed.

"I can't imagine it, after all these years. I haven't looked at another woman since the day I met Carole."

"Then perhaps it's time now," she said firmly.

He did the dishes for her, and she put away her silver and her china once he was finished. And Glynnis slept by the fire as they talked. It was a cozy scene, and when he said good night to Mrs. Palmer finally and went upstairs, he barely had time to brush his teeth and get undressed before he fell asleep in the huge, cozy bed. And for the first time in months, he slept like a baby.

It was after ten o'clock when he awoke the next day, slightly embarrassed by how long he'd slept. But he had nowhere to go, no duties, no obligations. There was no reason for him to leap out of bed at dawn now to dash to the office. And as he got dressed, he looked out the window. There were several more feet of snow on the ground than there had been the night before, and he was amazed to see that it was still snowing. The idea of driving to Vermont didn't appeal to him much, but he also didn't want to overstay his welcome. He thought maybe he'd best move on, even if it meant staying at another inn or bed and breakfast in Deerfield. But when he got downstairs, he found Mrs. Palmer bustling around. The kitchen was immaculate, Glynnis was once again asleep by the fire, and he could smell cookies in the oven.

"Oatmeal?" he asked, sniffing the extravagantly delicious fumes emanating from her oven.

"Exactly." She smiled at him, and poured him a cup of coffee.

"That's quite a storm outside," he said, looking at the snow swirling up against the window, and she nodded. The skiing ought to be terrific, if he ever got there.

"Are you in a hurry to get to Vermont?" she asked, looking worried. She didn't think he was meeting anyone, from what he'd said, or perhaps he hadn't told her. There could have been a young woman he was too discreet to mention, but she hoped that there wasn't. She was hoping he would stay a little longer.

"I'm not really in a hurry," he explained, "but I'm sure you've got other things to do. I was thinking I could move on to Deerfield." But as he said it, she could barely conceal her disappointment. "I'm sure you have things to attend to before Christmas," he said politely, and she shook her head, trying to hide how bereft she felt. It was foolish really, she reminded herself, she scarcely knew him, and he would have to leave eventually. She couldn't keep him prisoner in Shelburne Falls forever, though she might have liked to.

"I don't want to interrupt your plans," she said, trying not to sound desperate, because she wasn't. But she had been so lonely for so long, and she was so grateful for his company. Talking to him had been like a gift from heaven. "But I'd be more than happy to have you stay here," she said politely, "it's no trouble. In fact . . ." she looked very vulnerable and oddly young. He could easily imagine what she'd looked like as a young woman, and he could see clearly she'd been very lovely, "It's good company for me, Charles. I really enjoyed our dinner, though I imagine you'd have a better time with younger friends . . . but you're more than welcome to stay . . . I have no plans at all . . ." Just surviving Christmas, her heart whispered.

"Are you sure? I wasn't looking forward to driving on, but I don't want to be a nuisance." It was the twenty-first of December, four days before Christmas, a day they were both dreading, though neither of them said it.

"You shouldn't go anywhere in this storm," she said firmly, seeing that he was already convinced, and enormously relieved not to lose him. She wished that he could stay forever, but even a few days were a welcome interruption. She hadn't been this happy in years, and there were things in the area she would have loved to show him, houses she knew he'd be interested in, an old bridge, a remote fort, less well known than the one at Deerfield. There were Indian monuments she would have liked to show him too, because she knew he'd be interested in them, from what he'd said the night before, but it was impossible to show them to him now, with the bad weather. Perhaps, with luck, he might come back to visit again in the summer. But in the meantime, there was lots to do, and she beamed at him as she served him breakfast, and he was embarrassed letting her serve him. She seemed more than an innkeeper. Being with her seemed far more like visiting a friend's mother, and it was almost as though he had known Jimmy, and had come back to see her.

She was talking about houses in the area, and he was asking questions after stoking the fire in the kitchen for her, and then she turned to him with a look that intrigued him. There was a light in her eyes he hadn't seen there before, something happy and young, as though she were keeping a secret.

"You look extremely mischievous," he said with a smile. He was about to put his jacket on to go out and get more wood for her. Usually, she waited until one of the neighbors' sons offered to do it. But as long as Charlie was there, he wanted to do everything he could to help her. She deserved it. And as he looked at her, she was still smiling at him, and he wondered what she was thinking. "You look like the cat that swallowed the canary."

"I just thought of something . . . something I want to show you. . . . I haven't been there in a long time, but it's very dear to me. It's a house my grandmother left me, her grandfather bought it in 1850. Roland and I lived there for a year or two, but he never loved it as I did. He thought it was too remote, and a little too impractical. He preferred living in town, so we bought this house nearly fifty years ago, but I could never bring myself to sell the other. I've just kept it, like a jewel I keep hidden away, with no chance to wear it. I just bring it out occasionally, polish it off, and look at it. There's something very special about it. . . ." She looked almost shy as she said it. "I'd love you to see it." She spoke of it as though it were an object, or a work of art, possibly even a painting, or a piece of jewelry. And he could hardly wait to see it. She said it was in the hills, and she wondered if, with the snow, they'd be able to get there, but she wanted to try it. She seemed to feel sure he would love it, and he was more than willing to go there with her. He had nothing else to do that day, and if it meant so much to her, he wanted to see it. Old houses always intrigued him.

She said that this one had been built around 1790, by a well-known Frenchman in the area. He was a count, and a cousin of Lafayette's, and he had come to the new world in 1777 with Lafayette, but she said very little else about him, except that he had built the house for a lady.

It was after lunch when they set out finally, and they took his car because it was bigger than hers, and she was happy to have him drive her. She pointed out various landmarks on the way, which fascinated him, and she told him still more tales of local legends, but she said very little about the house where they were going. It was five miles from where she lived, in the hills, as she had said, and looked down on the Deerfield River, and as they approached she told him stories about going there as a little girl and loving it. None of her family had ever actually lived in the house before she inherited it, but they had owned it for nearly a hundred and fifty years now.

"It must be quite remarkable. Why is it that none of you ever lived there?" He wondered if it was just impractical, or if there was something more, and the way she talked about it intrigued him.

"It is remarkable. It has a soul of its own, an incredible feeling. It's as though you can still sense the woman it was built for. I tried to get Jimmy and Kathleen to use it as a summerhouse years ago, they used it once, and Kathleen hated it. Jimmy told her a lot of nonsense about ghosts and terrified her, and she would never stay there again. It's a shame, it's the most romantic place I've ever been." He smiled at her as she said it, but he spent most of the time battling the snow as they drove there. The storm had really picked up, and the wind was blowing the snow into high drifts all around them.

They went as far as they could on the road, and Mrs. Palmer told him where to leave the car. He could see nothing but trees all around, and he was worried they'd get lost, but she only smiled at him, as she tightened her coat around her and beckoned. She knew exactly where she was going.

"I feel like Hansel and Gretel in the forest," he said, and they both laughed. "You should have told me to bring breadcrumbs," he said, with his head bowed, holding on to her so she wouldn't fall. He had a firm hand beneath her elbow, but she was strong and spry, and she was used to coming here in all kinds of weather, although she seldom came now. But just being here made her smile, and she looked at him as though she were about to give him a present. "Who was the woman it was built for?" he asked, as they walked along, with their heads bowed against the wind. He remembered that she had said a Frenchman had built it for a woman.

"Her name was Sarah Ferguson," she said, holding on to him then so she didn't stumble, and he walked close to her. They were like mother and son, and he was faintly worried about her. The storm had gotten worse just in the last few minutes, and he was serious about being concerned about being lost in the forest. And if they were on a traveled path, he had no sense of it, but she did. She never hesitated for a moment. And then she began telling him Sarah's story. "She was a remarkable woman. She came from England all alone. The stories about her are quite mysterious and very romantic. She fled a husband who was terrible to her . . . the Earl of Balfour . . ." Just hearing the words sounded exotic to Charlie. "She was the Countess of Balfour when she came here in 1789."

"How did she meet up with the Frenchman?" Charlie asked, intrigued now. There was something about the way she told the story, with little hints, and only the merest glimpses of what lay beyond, that inevitably hooked him.

"That's a long, long story. I've always been fascinated by her," Gladys Palmer said, looking at him, but squinting in the storm, "she was a woman of immeasurable strength and courage." But before she could say more, the trees parted suddenly and they stood in a little clearing. Even in the snow, she had known exactly the road she was on, and Charlie found himself staring at a beautifully built, perfectly proportioned small château, just beyond them. It sat next to a small lake, which Gladys Palmer said had once been filled with swans, but they were long gone now, and even at a distance, in the blinding snow, Charlie was well aware of the extraordinary beauty of the location. He had never seen anything like it. It looked like an exquisite little jewel, sitting there, and as they approached it almost reverently, he could hardly wait to get inside it.

Gladys was smiling as they walked up the front steps, and he was startled to see that they were marble. And as she took out the old brass key and fit it in the lock, she looked over her shoulder at Charlie.

"One of the most remarkable things about the place is that François de Pellerin had it entirely built by the Indians and local craftsmen. He showed them everything, and taught them how to do the work. It all looks as though it was done by master craftsmen brought over from Europe."

And as they stepped inside, they were instantly in another world. The ceilings were high, the floors were inlaid and beautiful, there were long, graceful French windows leading out of every room, marble fireplaces, and the proportion of each room was perfect. It was so beautiful that Charlie could easily imagine it filled with graceful, elegant people, brilliant sunshine, extravagant flowers, and exquisite music. It was like a trip back into history, and yet the warmth and beauty of the place made one want to sit down quietly and just be there. Charlie had never felt this way anywhere, and all he could do was look around and stare. Even the color of the walls was perfect, there were warm creams, and butter-yellows, and pale grays, a blue the color of summer sky in the dining room, and a pale peach in what had apparently been Sarah's boudoir. It was the most beautiful house he'd ever seen, and he could only picture it filled with laughter and love and happy people.

"Who was she?" he whispered reverently as they walked from room to room, and then he looked up in surprise as he noticed murals and gold leaf edging the ceilings. Everything was in exquisite taste, every detail had been seen to, and executed with utter perfection. Charlie wanted to imagine her as they stood in what had been her bedroom. Was she beautiful, was she young, was she old? What had caused the French count to build this tiny perfect palace for her? What had she been that had made him so extravagantly love her? Charlie knew only that he had been a count, and she a Countess, but there was so much more here. Something about the beauty and the spirit of the place told him without actually saying it that they had been real people. And suddenly, he was starving for information about them, but Gladys was very sparing in what she told him.

"Sarah Ferguson was very beautiful, I've been told. I've only seen one drawing of her, and a miniature they have at the museum in Deerfield. She was quite well known around here. She bought a farm when she came, and she lived alone, which apparently created quite a stir. . . . and when he built this house for her, they lived together before being married, which, for the locals of their day, was considered utterly shocking." He smiled at what she was saying, wishing that he could have seen her. He wanted to go directly to the local historical society and read everything he could about her. But the count who had built the house for her fascinated him as much as she did.

"What happened to them eventually? Did they go back to Europe, or stay?"

"He died, and she lived in this house for long years after that. She never left. In fact, she died here." She was buried not far from the house, in a little clearing. "There's a waterfall near here, which the Indians say is sacred and where they were seen to go walking almost every day. He was very involved with the

Indians, and very respected by all the local tribes. He was married to an Iroquois woman long before he married Sarah." Just listening to her filled Charlie's mind with more questions.

"What brought them together then, if they were both married to other people?" He was fascinated and confused and he wanted to know all of it, but even Gladys didn't know all the details.

"Passion brought them together, I suppose. I don't think they were together for many years, but it was clearly a deep love they shared. They must have both been very remarkable people. Jimmy swears he saw her here the summer they stayed in the house, but I don't really think he did. I think I had probably just told him too many stories. Sometimes that can create an illusion." It was an illusion Charlie would have loved to experience. There was something about the house and the place and the feelings that nearly overwhelmed him, and that made him want to know everything about Sarah Ferguson. It was almost as though she were a woman in a dream, and he was suddenly desperate to find her.

"It's the prettiest house I've ever seen," Charlie said as he walked from room to room again. He was unable to tear himself away, and as they went downstairs again, he sat on the stairs, just taking it all in, and thinking.

"I'm glad you like it, Charles." Gladys Palmer looked so pleased. The house meant so much to her, it always had. Even her husband had never quite understood it, and her son had always made fun of her. But she felt something there that was impossible to explain, or to share, unless the other person also felt it. And it was obvious that Charles did. He was so moved, he could barely speak as Gladys watched him. It was as though he was communing with his own soul there. He felt a kind of peace that had eluded him for years, and for the first time in months, he felt as though he had come home to a place he had been seeking. Just sitting there, looking out at the snow, and the valley far below, made him feel something he'd never experienced before, and all he knew was that he didn't want to leave here. His eyes were filled with something very deep as he looked at her, and she knew exactly what he was feeling.

"I know," she said softly, and took his hand in her own. "This is why I never sold it." She loved this house more than any other she had ever lived in. Her house in town was beautiful, and comfortable in its own way, but it had none of the charm or grace or soul that emanated from this one. This house had a spirit of its own, and it was still filled with the warmth and loveliness of the remarkable woman who had lived there, and Gladys knew it always would be. She had left an indelible mark on everything she had touched there, and François's love for her had bathed everything in light and magic. It was an extraordinary place, and Gladys was startled by Charlie's next words, but not entirely. She wondered if that was why she had been compelled to come here with him.

"Will you rent it to me?" he asked with a pleading look in his eyes. He had never wanted anything as badly as he wanted to live here. He believed that houses had souls and destinies, and hearts of their own, and he could feel this one reaching out to him as no house had ever done before, not even the house he had loved so much in London. This was very different. It was an immediate bond he had felt, for reasons he didn't understand, almost as though he had known the people who lived here. "I've never felt anything as strongly," he tried to explain to her, and she looked pensive as she watched him. She had never wanted to rent it to anyone. She had lived there herself for barely more than a year, nearly fifty years before, and Jimmy and his family had stayed there for a few months, but other than that it had literally been uninhabited since Sarah Ferguson herself had lived there. None of Gladys's family had actually lived in the little château. They had simply owned it, as an oddity, and an investment. They had even talked of making a museum of it, but no one had ever done it. And all things considered, it was quite remarkable that it was still in such good condition, but that was to Gladys's credit. She had always made a considerable effort to maintain it, and visited it often.

"I know it sounds crazy," Charlie explained, hoping to convince her of what he so desperately longed for. "But I feel as though this is why I came, why we met . . . as though it was meant to be. I feel as though I've come home," he said, sounding awestruck, and as he looked at her, he knew that she understood him, and she nodded. There was a reason why their paths had crossed, a reason why he had been led here. Their lives were so separate, they were years apart, and yet they had so much to give each other. She had lost so many and so much, and he had lost Carole, they were both alone, but their lives had converged to bring each other something precious and rare. It was a force of destiny neither of them completely understood, and yet they felt the power of it as they stood there. He had come from London, and then New York, and it was as though she had been waiting for him. He was her Christmas gift, and now she wanted to give something to him, and she knew that if she did, he would stay near her. For a while at least, long enough for her to enjoy his company for a few months . . . a year . . . maybe more. It was all she wanted. He wasn't the son she had lost, but he was a special gift. He had come to her so unexpectedly, and now she couldn't deny him. She knew he would take care of it. It was obvious, looking at him, that he already loved it. No one in her family had ever felt remotely as he did about it. Only she had.

"All right," she said quietly, feeling her heart tremble a little bit. It was an act of faith renting it to him, but she knew he realized the enormity of the gift, and he already loved it. And without saying another word to her, he strode toward her then, put his arms around her in a tight hug, and kissed her just as he would have his mother. Her eyes were filled with tears when she pulled away from him, but she was smiling, and he was beaming.

"Thank you," he said, looking down at her with a look of unabashed excitement. "Thank you . . . I promise you, I'll take good care of it. . . ." He was almost speechless with delight, as they stood together in the lovely salon, looking out the windows at the snow falling silently in the valley.

Chapter 4

CHARLES WENT TO all the local stores in Shelburne Falls the next day, and he went to Greenfield's shops for whatever he couldn't find there. Mrs. Palmer had an antique bed for him in the storage room over her garage, and a few modest pieces of furniture, a chest, a desk, a few chairs, and an old, weathered dining room table. He insisted that it was all he needed. He had rented the house from her for a year, and whether he went back to London or to New York eventually, there was no reason why he couldn't stay in Shelburne Falls for the next several months. He was fascinated by everything about it. And if he went back to Whittaker and Jones again, he could come up from New York on weekends. And whatever he did, he knew that if his plans changed, Mrs. Palmer wouldn't hold him to the agreement. But he also knew that if he wanted to, he was welcome to be there for a year at least. She seemed as happy with the arrangement they'd made as he was.

They both looked like happy children when they went back to her house, and he was talking animatedly about everything he needed. He took her out to dinner to celebrate, and it was three days before Christmas when he went to Deerfield to complete his shopping. He stopped at a little jewelry store too, and bought a pretty little pair of pearl earrings for Mrs. Palmer.

He moved into the house on December twenty-third, and as he stood there and admired the view, he couldn't believe his good fortune. He had never been anywhere that was so overwhelmingly beautiful, and so peaceful. And he spent the night exploring every little nook and cranny. He was up half the night unpacking his things, and settling in, although he still had very little with him. He didn't even have a phone yet, and he was glad that he didn't. He knew that if he did, he would have been tempted to call Carole, especially over Christmas.

On the morning of Christmas Eve, he stood at his bedroom window, looking at the view, and he felt melancholy as he remembered back to other Christmases. Only a year before, he reminded himself, he'd been with her. And he sighed as he turned away from the window.

But his first night in his new home had gone very smoothly. There had been no problems, no odd sounds, and he smiled at the ghost stories Mrs. Palmer had told him her son had teased them all with, and his claim that he'd actually seen Sarah. Charlie was still fascinated with her, and wanted to know everything he could about her. He had already promised himself to go to the local library, and the historical society, right after Christmas. He wanted to read everything he could about Sarah and François, he was anxious to learn everything there was to know about them.

And although Shelburne Falls was obviously a quiet little place, for Charlie, there was a lot to do here. He had bought a sketch pad and some pens and pastels and he was itching to get out and do some drawing. He had already sketched the house several times, just playing with some ideas, and he had made quick drawings of it from several angles. It was amazing even to him how much he loved it. And Gladys Palmer was thrilled to hear it when he drove by to visit.

When he came to have dinner with her on Christmas Eve, he found three of her friends visiting her, and when they left, all he could do was talk about the house. He had already discovered several hidden cabinets, and what he thought was a secret cupboard, and he was dying to get into the attic. He sounded like a boy to her, and she laughed as he rattled on, and she listened.

"And what do you think you're going to find there?" she teased. "A ghost? Her jewels? A letter from her to François? Or perhaps a letter to you? Now, that would be something!" She couldn't resist playing with him. It made her happy to be able to share her love of the house with someone. All her life she had gone there to look and think and dream. It had always been the place where she had gone to find comfort. And when Jimmy died, she had spent a lot of quiet afternoons there. And she had done the same again after she lost Roland. Going there had always helped her. It was as though Sarah's benevolent presence eased her anguished spirit.

"I wish I could find a drawing of her somewhere. I would love to know what she looked like. You said you saw a sketch of her once," he reminded his new friend. She had bestowed the greatest gift of all on him, her trust along with the gem of a château that had been built by François for Sarah. "Where was it?"

She thought about it for a long time, as she handed the cranberry sauce to him. She had made a proper turkey dinner to eat with him on Christmas, and he had brought her a bottle of wine. He was sleeping at the château that night again, but he was planning to come back the next day to give Gladys the pearl earrings. But as she looked at him, she finally remembered. "I'm almost positive the historical society has a book about her. I think that's where I saw the drawing. I'm not certain, but I'm fairly sure of it."

"I'll go in and check after Christmas."

"I'll look through the books I have as well," she promised Charlie. "I might have a book or two about him. François de

Pellerin was quite an important person in this part of the world in the latter half of the eighteenth century. The Indians all considered him one of theirs, and he was the only Frenchman around here whom both the settlers and the Indians were genuinely fond of. I think he was even quite respected by the British, which was a real feat for a Frenchman."

"Why did he come here?" Charlie asked her again, he loved hearing everything she knew about it. "I suppose the Revolutionary War brought him here initially. But there must have been another reason why he stayed."

"Maybe just because of his Iroquois wife . . . or perhaps for Sarah. I don't remember all the details. I was always more intrigued by her, although I loved hearing about both of them when I first heard the stories. My grandmother loved to talk about it. Sometimes I used to think she was almost in love with what she knew of François. Her grandfather had actually met him. He died a long, long time before Sarah."

"How sad for her," Charlie said quietly. They were so real to him, but he had also been thinking of Mrs. Palmer, of how lonely she must have been ever since her husband died.

But at least she had Charlie now, to distract her. She had friends in Shelburne Falls, lots of them. But Charlie was someone new, and very special.

"Tell me, are you still going skiing, Charles?" she asked, as they ate apple pie with homemade vanilla ice cream. This time, he hadn't cooked for her, he had been too busy settling into his house all afternoon, and everything had been ready when he arrived wearing a dark suit, and a tie. Mrs. Palmer was wearing a black silk dress her husband had bought her twenty years before in Boston, and the pearls he had given to her at their wedding. And Charlie thought she looked lovely. He was grateful to be with her. This Christmas together provided him with the family he no longer had, and he did the same for her. They were well met and well matched, and happy to be together. And in the excitement of moving in, he realized that he'd forgotten all about going skiing.

"Maybe over the New Year," he said vaguely, and she smiled at him. He looked so much happier and more at ease than he had when he'd arrived. He seemed younger now, and a little more carefree. He had lost some of that anguished, tortured expression that he had worn for the past year, although she couldn't have known that. "It seems such a pity to leave now," he said, looking distracted. Vermont was a long way from Shelburne Falls, and going there seemed a lot less appealing. He didn't want to leave his new friend or his house yet.

"Why don't you go to Charlemont? It's only twenty minutes from here. I'm not sure if the skiing is quite as good, but you could try it. And you can always go to Vermont a little later." When the thrill of the house wore off, and he felt less compelled to be there. She understood completely.

"That's a great idea," he agreed. "Maybe I'll go in a few days." It was so convenient. He even had ski terrain twenty minutes from his doorstep. He had truly found the perfect location.

They talked again for a long time that night. It was a difficult time for both of them, and neither of them wanted to let go, and be left alone with their private sorrows and demons. There had been too much grief in both their lives, particularly hers, to make either of them want to spend Christmas Eve alone. And Charlie didn't leave her until he was sure she was ready to go to bed. He kissed her gently on the cheek, and thanked her for dinner, and then he let himself out, while Glynnis wagged her tail and watched him.

He crunched briefly through the fresh snow. It was knee-high even on the road, and over his head in some of the drifts along the road to Deerfield. It was even higher in places near his château. And he loved seeing it. The world looked so pure and so idyllic with everything blanketed in smooth white cotton. And as he drove home he saw hares darting through the snow, and a deer watching him from the side of the road. It was as though all the people had disappeared, and all that was left were the animals, and the stars, and the angels.

He reached the road to his château easily, and left the car where he knew he could still get it out the next day, and walked the rest of the way in, just as he had with all of his supplies, and the men he'd hired had done with the few pieces of furniture he had borrowed from her. But he didn't mind the inconvenience. It made the house seem even more remote, and the place where he was even more special.

He was humming to himself as he walked in that night, and he felt more at peace than he had in a long time. It was amazing how fate or life or God had provided for him, and found a place where he could heal and think and be. Charles knew without a moment's doubt that this house was just what he needed. And as he turned the brass key in the lock and walked in, he felt the same happiness and ease that he had felt here right from the beginning. It was as though there had once been so much joy there that it had lasted for two centuries, and he could still feel it. There was nothing eerie, or odd, or even remotely spooky about it. Even late at night, it seemed filled with light and love and sunshine. And he knew with total certainty that it wasn't just the colors of the walls, or the size of the rooms, or the view, it was the aura he felt there. If there were spirits there, they were obviously extremely happy ones, he thought to himself as he walked slowly upstairs, thinking about Mrs. Palmer. He was already incredibly fond of her, and wished he could do something special for her. He was thinking about doing a painting, perhaps of the valley from the vantage point of his bedroom. And as he thought about it, he walked into his room, and turned the light on. And as he did, he gave an enormous start. There was a woman standing there, looking at him. She was wearing a white gown, she held a hand out to him, and she was smiling. She looked as though she were about to say something to him, and then she walked away and disappeared behind the curtains. She had long, jet-black hair, and skin so fair it looked like ivory, and he had noticed that her eyes were distinctly blue. He had noticed every detail about her, and there was no question in his mind about who she was or how she'd gotten there. This was no ghost. This was a woman who had gotten into his house, probably to play a trick on him, and he wanted to know where she'd gone, and where she came from.

"Hello!" He spoke clearly into the room, waiting for her to come out from behind the curtain where he had just seen her. But when she didn't, he realized she was embarrassed to do so. And she should have been. It was a foolish trick to play, particularly on Christmas. "Hello!" he said louder this time. "Who are you?" And with that, he strode across the room, and pulled the curtain back with one long, swift motion. But there was no one there. There was not a sound. And the window was open. He was sure he'd left it closed, in case it snowed again while he was out, but he also realized that he could have been mistaken, and he might have forgotten to close it.

He moved along to the next curtain then. There was something very odd about what was happening. He knew she had to be somewhere in the room, and he was vaguely aware of how beautiful she had been. But that was not the point now. He didn't want the locals playing with him, or letting themselves into his house through the French windows. He could only imagine that that was how she had entered. The windows were very old, and despite the two-hundred-year-old locks, if you pushed them hard enough, they opened. Everything in the house was original, all the fixtures, all the hardware, even the glass in the windows had been handblown and you could see the irregularities and the fluid marks in them. The only things that had been changed in the past two centuries were the electricity and the plumbing, and even that was not very recent. Gladys had last had it seen to in the early fifties. And Charlie had already promised her he would check it for her. The last thing they wanted was an electrical fire, which could destroy the house after she and all her ancestors had been so careful to preserve it. But that was not on his mind now. The only thing he was interested in was the woman he had seen in his bedroom. He checked all the curtains then, and the bathroom, and the closets, but she was nowhere, and yet when he walked around the room, he could feel that he was not alone. It was almost as though she were watching him. He knew she was there, but he just couldn't find where she was hiding.

"What are you doing here?" he asked, sounding annoyed, and he heard a rustle of silk just behind him. He turned swiftly then, ready to confront her, but he saw nothing, and then he felt an odd sense of peace come over him, as though she had introduced herself to him, or he had recognized her. Suddenly, he knew exactly who he had seen in his room, and he no longer believed she had come in through the French windows.

"Sarah?" he said, in a whisper, feeling suddenly very foolish. What if it wasn't her? If there was truly a live human being watching him, waiting to report to her friends what a fool he'd been, and yet he no longer believed that. He could feel her. And he stood silently, his eyes sweeping the room, but he saw nothing. He stood there for a long time, immobile, and yet he never had the sense that she had left him. He could still feel her standing near him. But there was no sound, no movement, and the woman in the white gown was gone. And yet he had seen her so clearly. She had looked right into his eyes, and smiled at him, as though she were welcoming him to her bedroom. And he already knew from Gladys that he had instinctively chosen the room she had shared with François, it was the room in which she had lain with him, and where Gladys said she had borne their children.

He wanted to say her name again, but he didn't dare, and it almost felt as though she knew what he was thinking. He felt no hostile presence there, and he wasn't afraid of her. All he wanted was for her to appear again, so he could see her more clearly. But what he had seen was already etched in his memory, and he knew he would never forget her.

He went to the bathroom finally, and undressed. He had bought new pajamas for himself because it was cold in the house at night, and he came out wearing them. The heating system worked well and there were fireplaces everywhere, but he didn't always want to use them. And he was hoping that when he came back into the room, he would see her again, but he didn't. And after a few minutes of glancing around the room, he carefully turned the light off, and got into bed. He hadn't bothered to pull down the shades because the morning light never bothered him, and as he lay in his bed, the room was filled with moonlight.

And as mad as it seemed, and he would have hated to have to explain it to anyone, he could still feel her near him. He was aware of no other presence in the room, only her, but he was absolutely certain it was Sarah. Sarah Ferguson de Pellerin. The name sounded so elegant and so noble, just as she had looked when he saw her. She was a rare beauty. And then, as he lay there, thinking of her, he laughed at himself, and the sound filled the room as he chuckled. His life had certainly changed in the past year. He had spent Christmas Eve with a woman about to turn seventy, and the rest of the night with the ghost of a woman who had been dead for a hundred and sixty years, and had been in her prime two centuries before. It was certainly a change from spending Christmas with his wife in London. And he knew that if he told anyone, they would be absolutely certain he had lost his marbles. But he was just as sure he hadn't.

And as he lay there, thinking of her, remembering what he'd just seen, and those eyes that had looked at him so clearly, he whispered her name again in the darkness, but there was no answer as he listened. He wasn't sure what he expected of her, some sound, some sign. He had never heard of spirits talking to anyone, and yet she had looked as though she were about to say something. She seemed to be welcoming him, and she had been smiling. And this time, he spoke clearly in the darkness.

"Merry Christmas," he said in the silent room that had once been hers and François's . . . but there was no answer, only the gentle feeling of her presence. And in a little while, Charlie was sound asleep in the moonlight.

Chapter 5

WHEN CHARLIE AWOKE on Christmas Day, the vision of Sarah he'd seen the night before seemed more than ever like a dream to him, and he decided instantly that he wasn't going to tell anyone about it. At the very least, he would have been accused of drinking. And yet he knew how real it seemed, how certain he had been that she'd been in the room with him. He'd been absolutely sure of her presence, and he had seen her so clearly. So much so that he'd been convinced it was one of his neighbors, but it surely wasn't. He even went out to check the snow around the house, and there were no tracks there other than his own, going in and out. Unless she'd flown in by helicopter, and come down through the chimney like Santa Claus, he had had no visitors the night before. Whoever and whatever he'd seen in his bedroom on Christmas Eve had definitely not been human. And yet, in his entire life, he had never believed in spirits. For him, it was a serious dilemma. He didn't know what to think, and in the clear light of day, it seemed more than a little crazy. He didn't even think he wanted to tell Gladys. In fact, by the time he was dressed and ready to visit her, he was certain he wasn't going to say anything about it. And as he walked across the fresh snow, he kept his eye out for tracks again, but there were none other than his own, and as he got into his car, he felt the box with the pearl earrings safely stashed in his pocket.

And when he got to her house, Gladys Palmer was delighted to see him. She had just come home from church, and Charlie had even thought of going with her, but in the end he had decided not to. He had told her the night before not to wait for him, and after she gave him a warm hug, she scolded him for not coming.

"I'm such a heathen, I'd probably scare all the angels away."

"I doubt that. I think God must be used to heathens. If we were all angels, it would be very boring." He smiled at her, and a few minutes later, he handed her the present, and she opened it very carefully, smoothing the ribbon with her hands, and then opening the paper as delicately as possible so as not to destroy it. He always wondered why people did that. What were they planning to do with all the saved ribbon and paper? They never seemed to use it. But she put it aside as his grandmother had done when he was young, and opened the box with great caution, as though a lion might be in it, or a mouse, and she gave a little shout when she saw them. She loved the pearl earrings he'd bought her, and her eyes filled with tears as she thanked him. She said that Roland had bought a pair for her much like them long since, and she had been heartbroken five years before when she lost them. These were almost identical, only they were slightly nicer, and she said so.

"What a dear boy you are, Charles," she said with deep feeling. "I don't deserve you. You really are my Christmas gift, aren't you?" She didn't even want to think now about how much lonelier she'd be next year, without him. She couldn't imagine him staying in Shelburne Falls forever. But she was grateful for his presence in her life now, his sudden appearance and unexpected arrival. He was like an answer to her prayers. "I shall wear them every day, forever. I promise." They were hardly worth the fuss she made, but he was pleased that she liked them. And then she startled him, by giving him a book of poetry that had been her husband's. She gave him that and a warm muffler she'd bought for him in Deerfield. She had noticed that he didn't have one, and he was touched by both her gifts, particularly by the poetry. And there was still an inscription in it from her to Roland, dated Christmas, 1957. It seemed a long time ago, as he thought of it, but not nearly as long as the time when Sarah had lived, and then he thought about telling her what he had seen the night before, but he was almost afraid to. And as Gladys looked at him, over the tea she'd made for him, she sensed something.

"Is everything all right? At the house, I mean?" It was as though she knew, or expected him to see her. Her eyes were looking deep into his, and he was trying to look casual as he set his cup down, but his hands were shaking.

"Everything's fine. It's cozy and warm, everything works, even the heating and the plumbing. I had lots of hot water this morning," he said, still thinking about the night before, but not saying anything as she eyed him sharply. And then she floored him with her next question.

"You've seen her, haven't you?" Her eyes were deep and sharp as she watched him, and he felt a gentle tremor.

"Seen who?" He looked vague, and helped himself to an oatmeal cookie while Glynnis watched him with envy, and he slipped her a little morsel. "I haven't seen anyone," he said innocently, but Gladys knew instinctively he was lying, and she smiled and shook her finger at him.

"Oh, yes, you have. I knew you would. But I didn't want to scare you. She's beautiful, isn't she?" He was about to deny it again, but he couldn't as he looked at her. He valued their friendship too much, and he wanted to know so much more about Sarah.

"You've seen her then?" He looked awestruck, and it was actually a relief to be able to talk to her about it. It was like a dark secret between them, except that there had been nothing dark about Sarah. She was all air and light and springtime.

"I've only seen her once," Gladys admitted to him, as she sat back in her chair with a wistful look. "I was fourteen, and I've never forgotten it. She was the most beautiful woman I'd ever seen, and she stood looking at me for the longest time, in the salon, and then she smiled and disappeared into the garden. I ran outside to look for her, and I never found her. I never told anyone either, except Jimmy, and I don't think he ever believed me. He just thought it was a ghost story, until Kathleen saw her in their bedroom. But it terrified her, and she wouldn't stay in the house again. It's odd how she appears to people there, as though she wants to welcome us to her home. The odd thing was that as young as I was when it happened to me, I was never frightened. All I wanted was to see her again, and I was devastated when I didn't." He knew exactly how she had felt, as he nodded. After the initial shock of seeing her, all he wanted was for her to return and appear to him again. He had waited for her until he fell asleep in his bedroom.

"I thought it was a neighbor playing a prank on me. I was sure of it, and I went around the room rustling all the curtains. That's where she was when I last saw her. I even went out into the snow this morning and looked for someone's footprints, but there was nothing. And then I realized what had happened. I wasn't even going to tell you about it, and I probably wouldn't have if you hadn't pressed me. I don't believe in those things," he said soberly, but there was no other way to explain it.

"I had a feeling she'd come to you, because you're so receptive to her, and so interested in her story. And to tell you the truth, I don't really believe in those things either. There are lots of stories around here about goblins and ghosts and people who practiced witchcraft. I've always been absolutely sure it was all nonsense . . . but not Sarah . . . somehow, I have the strongest feeling that she's different. She seemed so real to me when I saw her . . . I still remember it as though it had been yesterday." She looked pensive as she said it.

"She seemed real to me too," he said with a thoughtful look. "I was so sure it was a real woman. I wasn't even frightened to see someone in my house, just annoyed that they would do a thing like that. I really thought it was a joke of some kind. I wish I'd understood who she was right from the beginning." And then he looked reproachfully at Gladys Palmer. "You should have warned me." But she only laughed at him and shook her head, wearing the new pearl earrings she was so proud of.

"Don't be silly. You'd have had me locked up, and been convinced that I was senile. Would you have warned me if the tables were turned? I don't think so." He smiled at what she said, and he knew it was true. If she had warned him, he would never have believed her.

"I suppose you're right. What happens now?" He asked with interest. "Do you suppose she'll come back again?" It wasn't likely if Gladys had only seen her once in seventy years, and he was sad to think that he would never have another chance to see her.

"I have no idea. I don't know much about these things. I told you, I don't believe in them."

"Neither do I." But he was aching to see her, and he didn't want to admit it even to Gladys. It made him wonder about himself that he was suddenly fascinated by the ghost of a woman who'd lived in the eighteenth century. It didn't say much about his love life. And for the rest of the afternoon, they talked about Sarah and François, and Gladys tried to remember everything she'd ever heard about them. And finally at four o'clock, Charlie left her and drove slowly back to the château, thinking of Sarah. And as he drove through town he thought about calling Carole, so he stopped at a pay phone. It seemed so odd to have spent an entire Christmas without her, and he had been thinking about calling her ever since that morning. He wasn't even sure where she was, but he thought it was worth a try calling Simon's number. He was almost certain she'd be there, unless they'd gone to the country for the weekend. It was nine o'clock at night for them, and even if they'd been out with friends, he was sure that they'd be home by then, as long as they had stayed in London over Christmas.

He stood next to the phone and thought about it for a long time, and then finally, he dialed the number. He was just about to decide that she wasn't there, when she answered on the fifth ring, and she sounded a little breathless, as though she'd run upstairs, or in from another room. It was Carole, but he stood in the snow on Christmas afternoon, freezing at the outside pay phone, and for just an instant he couldn't even answer.

"Hello?" she said again, wondering who it was. She could hear the far-off tinny sound of long-distance. Maybe because of the phone he'd used, they didn't seem to have a great connection.

"Hi . . . it's me. . . . I just wanted to wish you merry Christmas," and ask you to come back, and if you're still in love with me. . . . He had to force himself not to tell her how much he missed her, and he suddenly knew that calling her had not been a great idea. Just hearing her again made him feel as though he'd been punched in the stomach. He hadn't spoken to her since he left London. "How are you?" He tried to sound nonchalant and failed abysmally, and even worse, he knew she could hear it.

"I'm fine. How are you? How's New York?" She sounded happy and alive and busy. And here he was chasing ghosts around New England. Just hearing her made him want his old life back.

"New York is fine, I guess." There was a long pause, and then he decided to tell her. "I left last week."

"To ski?" She sounded relieved, at least that sounded normal. At first she thought he sounded depressed and nervous.

"Eventually. Actually, I took a six-month leave of absence."

"You *what?*" It was so unlike him, she couldn't believe it. "What happened?" Even though she had left him for someone else, she still worried about him.

"It's a long story, but the office was a nightmare. They're cranking out designs from twenty years ago, and selling zillion-dollar clients tired, reworked old blueprints. I don't know how they've stayed in business this long. And their office is a snake pit. It's all about politics and turning your best friend in. I don't know how Europe got to be so different, or how we never noticed what they'd turned into. I just couldn't do it. And I was driving them crazy. I kept asking too many questions. I don't even know if I'll go back again. They told me to take six months off, and I figure that sometime in April I'll try and sort out what I'm doing. I just can't see myself putting up with that kind of bullshit."

"Are you coming back to London?" She sounded shocked at what he had said, and sad for him. She knew how much he loved the firm, and how loyal he had been. It must have been a real blow to him to leave them, even for a leave of absence.

"I'm not sure yet. I have to figure out some things, like what to do with the rest of my life, for instance. I just rented a house in New England for a year. It's kind of a special deal. I might stay here for a while and then come back to London and look for an apartment."

"Where are you?" She sounded confused. She didn't understand what he was doing, but the trouble was, neither did Charlie.

"I'm in Massachusetts, in a little town called Shelburne Falls, near Deerfield." She had only a vague notion of where that was. She had grown up on the West Coast, in San Francisco. "It's really beautiful, and I met the most amazing woman here." He was talking about Gladys, not Sarah, and at her end, Carole looked enormously relieved. She had been waiting for this to happen. It would take a lot of the heat off of her, and change his attitude about both her and Simon. She was suddenly delighted he had called her.

"Oh, Charlie, I'm so glad. I'm happy for you. You need that. We all do."

But he was smiling wistfully as he heard her. "Yeah, I know. But don't get too worked up. She's seventy years old, she's my landlady. She owns the most beautiful little château. It was built in 1790 by a French count, for his mistress."

"It sounds very exotic," she said, a little confused by what he was saying to her. She wondered if he was having a nervous breakdown. What was he doing renting a château in New England, and walking out on his job for six months? What in hell *was* he doing? "Are you all right, Charlie? I mean . . . really . . ."

"I think so. I'm not sure some of the time. And then at other times, I think I'm going to make it. I'll let you know what happens." And then he couldn't help himself. He had to know. There was always the slim chance that she had dumped Simon since Charlie had left London.

"How are things with you? How's Simon?" Tired of him yet? Hate him? Has he gone off with someone else? Are either of you cheating? He didn't give a damn what Simon did. Charlie wanted his wife back.

"He's fine," Carole said quietly, "and we're fine too." She knew exactly what Charlie was asking.

"I'm sorry to hear that," he said, looking like a kid, and she laughed. She knew exactly the expression he was wearing, and in her own way, she still loved him, but not enough to want to be married to him anymore. She was very much in love with Simon. And she still wasn't sure what had happened to them, but she knew that somewhere along the road, she had fallen out of love with her husband. And in spite of everything different he wanted to believe, Charlie knew that. It was just a question of learning to live with it for the next forty or fifty years. But at least now, he told himself with a rueful smile, he had Gladys . . . and Sarah. But he would have traded them both for Carole in a minute. He tried not to think of her, of how she looked, of those long graceful legs, and the tiny waist that had always dazzled him, as they went on talking. She had just told him they were going to St. Moritz over New Year's.

"I was on my way to Vermont, when I stopped here," he explained to her. "That was five days ago, and then I met the woman who owns the château, and . . . I'll tell you about it sometime." It was too long a saga to go into, standing at an open phone in Shelburne Falls, Massachusetts. And as he listened to her at the other end, it started snowing.

"Let me know where you are," she said to him, and he frowned as soon as she said it.

"Why? What difference does it make?"

"I just want to know you're all right, that's all." She was instantly sorry she'd said it.

"I'm getting a phone and a fax next week. I'll call you when I have the numbers." At least it was an excuse to call her, but she was already starting to feel uncomfortable about the conversation, and Simon had just come into the room to see where she was. They had dinner guests, and she had taken forever.

"Just fax it to my office," she said, "I'll get it." But he could tell immediately that she was no longer alone, and it seemed ironic to him. A year before, she had been cheating on him with Simon, and now she was afraid to live with him and talk to her husband. It wasn't that she was afraid of him, it was that she just didn't want to, and Charlie knew that.

"I'll call you sometime . . . take care of yourself . . ." he said, feeling as though she were fading away. And she was. He could hear other people in the room now. Their guests had all come into the room where she'd been speaking. It was an informal gathering, and they had come into Simon's den after dinner to have coffee.

"You too," she sounded sad as he said good-bye, and then as an afterthought, she shouted after him, "Merry Christmas . . ." I love you, she wanted to add, but knew she couldn't. And even if Simon hadn't been there, she knew that she could no longer say that to Charlie, he wouldn't have understood it, how she could love both men, but only want to live with Simon. Charlie was like her dearest, oldest friend now. But she knew it would have been unkind to confuse him.

And after he'd hung up the phone, he stood staring at it for a long time, with tiny snowflakes swirling slowly around him. He wanted to hit something, or cry, or ask her again why it had happened. What was she doing there, at Simon's house, with his friends, pretending to be married to Simon? She was still his wife, for God's sake, the divorce hadn't gone through yet. But it would eventually, and he supposed he knew what would happen. He just couldn't bear to think about it. And he got back in the station wagon with a sigh, and drove slowly up into the hills, thinking of Carole.

He was still thinking about her when he got to the clearing where he usually left the car, and he walked through the snow back to the house he had fallen in love with. It was dark, and there was no sign of life, and he wondered if the same woman he had seen was waiting for him there. He needed something, someone, someone he could love and talk to. But all he wanted as he unlocked the door was Carole. And there was no one in the house this time. Nothing stirred, there was no sound, no apparition, no feeling. The house was empty, and he sat down in one of the few chairs he had, in the dark, looking out the window into the darkness. He hadn't even bothered to put the light on. He just wanted to sit there and think about her for a while . . . the woman he had loved and lost . . . and then the woman he had caught a glimpse of the night before, and could only dream of.

Chapter 6

CHARLIE WAS UP early, and feeling energetic, the day after Christmas. He was going to town with a list of things he needed to polish the floors and to clean the marble steps and the fire-places. And before he went out to shop, he got a ladder, and let himself into the attic. It was a large, well-lit space, with four large, round windows, and he had no problem finding his way around there. There were some boxes of old clothes and things that Gladys told him she'd stored, and then, sadly, he found some of Jimmy's things, his Navy uniforms, some toys from when he was a child, and some things of Peggy's. It tore at Charlie's heart to see them. And he suspected that Gladys kept them there so she wouldn't have to come across them.

It took him an hour to go through everything, there were about a dozen small trunks and cardboard boxes. But he didn't find anything particularly interesting, and none of it appeared to have been Sarah's, and when he came back downstairs, he was more than a little disappointed. He wasn't sure what he had expected to find, but he had somehow hoped that over the years some of her things had gotten left there. But Gladys was far too neat and organized to overlook something as important as a box of Sarah's belongings. He wasn't even sure what he would have done with them, but he felt as though it might have brought him a little closer to her just to see them. He reminded himself that the woman had been gone for nearly two centuries, and if he wasn't careful, she might become an obsession with him. He had enough real problems in his life without believing in a ghost, let alone falling in love with her. How would he ever have explained *that* to Carole? But as it turned out, he didn't have to. He found none of her things, and he was sure from what Gladys had said that Sarah wasn't likely to appear to him again. In fact, in the clear light of day, two days afterward, he almost wondered if what he'd seen had been a figment of his imagination, a sign of the incredible pressure he'd been under, first with the divorce, and everything that led up to it, and then with his office when he left them. Maybe there had never been a woman there at all. Maybe he'd fallen asleep, and only dreamed it.

But when he stopped at the hardware store that afternoon in Shelburne Falls, he couldn't resist going to the historical society right next to it. It was a narrow shingled house that had been donated to the town years before, and housed an extensive library about local history, and a small museum. Charlie wanted to see if there were any books available about François or Sarah. But as he stepped inside, he was in no way prepared for the reception he got there. The woman at the desk had her back to him, and when she turned and looked at him, in spite of a face that looked like a cameo, she had eyes full of sorrow and hatred. And her response to his "Good afternoon" was curt almost to the point of rudeness. She looked as though she was furious at him for coming in at all, and it was obvious that she didn't want him to disturb her.

"I'm sorry," he apologized with a warm smile, but nothing in her eyes or face responded. He wondered if maybe she'd had a rotten Christmas, or a rotten life, but actually, he decided as he looked at her, maybe she was just a rotten person. She was a very pretty girl. She had big green eyes, and dark auburn hair, and creamy skin that went with it. She was tall and thin and her features were very delicate, and he saw, as she put her hands on the desk in front of her, that she had long, graceful fingers. But everything about her told him not to come near her. "I was looking for some books on Sarah Ferguson and François de Pellerin, if you have anything. I'm not quite sure of the dates, but I think they lived here at the end of the eighteenth century, and she must have been around for a bit longer. I think whatever I'd want is somewhere around 1790. Are you familiar with them?" he asked innocently, and she stunned him again by almost snarling at him, as she jotted down the names of two books on a piece of paper and handed it to him.

"You'll find them over there." She pointed coldly at a rack of books across the room, just behind him. "I'm busy right now. If you can't find them, let me know." He was really annoyed at her attitude, and it was surprisingly unlike everyone else he'd met in either Shelburne Falls or Deerfield. Everyone else seemed anxious to make him feel at home, and they'd been excited to hear he'd rented the château. But not this woman. She was like the kind of people he'd encountered on the subway in New York, on the rare times he'd taken it, but even they had been more pleasant.

"Is something wrong?" he couldn't resist asking her. It seemed impossible that she would be that disagreeable without a reason.

"Why?" She looked at him with eyes like green ice. In fact they were just a shade more yellow than emeralds, and he wondered what she would look like if she were smiling.

"You seem upset," he said gently, his own warm, brown eyes like melted chocolate looked into her cold ones.

"I'm not. I'm just busy." She turned away from him again then, and he found the two books, and leafed through them. He was planning to take them home with him, and he was curious to see if there were any drawings of either of them, but his breath caught as he flipped through the pages of the second book, and found one. There was no question of who he had seen. The likeness was extraordinary, even the look in her eyes, the shape of her lips, the way she had seemed about to smile, or speak, or laugh at him. It was the same girl with the long black hair and huge blue eyes. It was the very same woman as the one he'd seen . . . it was Sarah.

And as she turned to look at him again, the young woman at the historical society saw his look of amazement. "Is she a relative?" she asked, intrigued by his obvious fascination. And she felt only slightly guilty for being so short with him. But it was unusual for anyone to come in, except now and then in tourist season. Most of the time the historical society was just used as a reference library, and Francesca Vironnet had taken the job of curator and librarian because she knew she would have very little contact with people, and would have plenty of time to herself, to work on her thesis. She had earned an art history degree in France years before, and another in Italy, and she could have taught, but in recent times, she had far preferred books to people. She was proud of the historical society, kept good track of the books they kept there, repaired them when necessary, and zealously guarded the antiques that were on the second floor in the rooms designated as a museum. It was really only in summer that people came to see them.

She looked annoyed when she glanced up, and saw that Charlie was watching her with interest. She was uncomfortable under his scrutiny, and he was surprised she had even bothered to ask him a question. She seemed anything but friendly.

"No, I've heard about Sarah and François from friends," he explained. "They must have been interesting people." He pretended not to notice her standoffish expression.

"There are a lot of myths and legends about them," she said cautiously, trying not to appear intrigued by him. He looked intelligent and sophisticated, more like the Europeans she knew, but she resisted any impulse to get to know him. "I suspect most of them aren't true. They seem to have grown larger than life in the last two centuries. They were probably very ordinary, although there's no way to prove it." It seemed a depressing outlook to him, and he hated the idea of reducing them to the size of mere mortals again. He much preferred the great passion to which Gladys had referred, the touching love story, and the courage to flaunt the mores of the times out of love for each other. He wondered what had happened to this girl to make her so angry and unpleasant. But paradoxically, in spite of her sour face and angry eyes, she was almost a beauty. "Was there anything else?" she asked Charlie then, as though he were a nuisance. It was obvious that she was anxious for him to leave and end their conversation. And then she told him that she was closing early.

"Do you have anything else about them? Even some old books where they're mentioned?" he asked stubbornly, he wasn't going to be rushed out the door just because she hated people. He had read her correctly. She loved the books and furniture and artifacts she was responsible for, and their history. But books and furniture would never hurt her.

"I'll have to look into it," she said coolly. "Do you have a number where I can reach you?" But he shook his head in answer to her question.

"Not yet. I won't have a phone till next week. I'll call you and see what you've come up with." And then, as though wanting to warm her up, though he didn't know why, except that somehow her coolness challenged him, he told her that he had just rented the house that François and Sarah had once lived in.

"You mean the château on the hill?" she asked, intrigued this time, and her eyes warmed slightly, but only for an instant.

"Yes, that one," he said, still watching her. It was as though a door somewhere had opened just a fraction of a crack, but just as quickly she had slammed it.

"Have you seen a ghost yet?" she asked sarcastically, amused that he was so interested in Sarah Ferguson and François de Pellerin. It was a sweet story, but she had never paid much attention to it.

"Is there a ghost?" he asked casually. "No one's told me about it."

"I don't know. I just assumed there was. I don't think there's a house in this part of the world that doesn't claim at least one. Maybe you'll see the lovers kissing one night at midnight." She laughed at the thought, relaxing for just a fraction of an instant, and he smiled, but she looked away from him when he did. She looked frightened to see him smiling.

"I'll call and let you know if I see anything." But she seemed to have lost interest. The door was not only closed, but locked and bolted very firmly. "Do I need to sign the books out?" he asked in a businesslike tone. She nodded and slipped a piece of paper across the desk to him, and reminded him that he had a week to return them.

"Thanks," he said, barely saying good-bye to her, which was unlike him, but she was so cold, so closed, that he almost felt sorry for her. It was hard to say, but he wondered if something really awful had happened to her. It was difficult to imagine being as hard and cold as that at her age. He figured her for about twenty-nine or thirty. He couldn't help remembering Carole at the same age, she had been all warmth and laughter, and very sexy. This woman was like a long thin shard of winter sunlight. He couldn't imagine her warming anything, least of all a man's heart. Not his at any rate. She was a pretty girl, but she was made of ice. And as he got back in his car again and drove back to the château, he forgot about her.

He could hardly wait to read the books he'd borrowed from

the historical society. He wanted to know everything he could about Sarah and François.

And when Gladys came to visit the next day, he showed the books to her and told her all about them. He had already finished one, and had started the second one early that morning.

"Have you seen her again?" she asked, looking at him conspiratorially, and he couldn't help laughing.

"Of course not," he said quietly. He had already begun to doubt he had seen her the first time.

"I wonder if you will," she mused, noticing the few things he had done since he'd been there. Everything was neat and clean, and orderly, and even the little he'd added had a great deal of style. It did her heart good to know that he was living in the little château she had always loved. It always seemed so sad to her when it stood empty. It had made her unhappy when her daughter-in-law had refused to stay there.

"You never saw her again," Charlie reminded her, and she laughed at his remembering what she'd told him.

"Perhaps I wasn't pure enough, or wise enough, or didn't have a strong enough spirit," she said, playing with him a little bit, and he smiled at her as he answered.

"If those were the criteria, rest assured I would never have seen her either." And then he told her that he had spoken to his ex-wife two days before, and had told Carole all about her. "She thought you were going to be my next wife. I think she was quite pleased at first, but I told her I didn't think I could ever be that lucky." He loved teasing her, and she loved playing with him. Gladys Palmer thanked her lucky stars every day for the afternoon he'd walked into her life, fresh off the highway. They both thought it had been kismet.

"How was it when you talked to her?" Gladys Palmer asked him kindly. He had already admitted to her how much pain he'd been in for the last year, and although she didn't know him well, she worried about him.

"Difficult. He was there. They had guests. It's so odd thinking about her having a life with someone else. I wonder if I'll ever get used to it, and stop being angry every time I see him."

"You will. One day. It may take a while. I suppose we can get used to anything if we have to." Although she was very grateful that nothing of the sort had ever happened to her, she felt certain it would have killed her if Roland had ever left her. It was bad enough losing him to illness and age, but losing him to someone else early in their marriage would have been an agony and humiliation she couldn't bear to think of. And she had a great deal of respect for Charlie for surviving all he'd been through. What's more, he didn't seem bitter to her. He seemed decent, and kind, and whole, and he still had a healthy sense of humor. She could sense the scars here and there, and there was something sad about his eyes at times, but there was nothing even the least unpleasant or unkind about him.

"I thought I should call her to wish her merry Christmas. I guess it was a mistake . . . I suppose next year I'll know better," he explained to Gladys.

"Maybe next year you'll be with someone else," she said hopefully, although he couldn't imagine it. He couldn't even dream of living with anyone but Carole.

"I doubt it," he said with a rueful smile, "unless I manage to entice Sarah."

"Now, there's a thought!" Gladys Palmer laughed with him, and before she left, Charlie told her that the next day he was going skiing. He was going to Charlemont as she had suggested to him, and he had rented a room for four days, so he could ski over New Year's. He asked her if she'd be all right on New Year's Eve, or if she'd like him to come home to be with her, and she was deeply touched by his offer. It seemed typical of the little she knew of him. He was always offering to do things for her, to chop firewood, or do errands, or buy groceries, or cook a meal for her. He was like the son she hadn't seen in fourteen years,

105

and missed so much. He was a blessing life had bestowed on her, and she smiled warmly as she answered his question. "You're a dear to ask," she applauded his kindness, "but I haven't celebrated New Year's Eve in years. Roland and I never went out. We stayed home and went to bed at ten o'clock, while everyone else stayed out and got drunk, cracked up their cars, made fools of themselves. It was never a night that appealed to me much. No, you're kind to ask, but I won't miss it. You stay in Charlemont and go skiing." He promised to leave the name of his hotel with her, in case she needed him, and she kissed him fondly when she left, and wished him a good time skiing.

"Don't break anything!" she warned, as he settled her in her car. "Sarah wouldn't like it!" she teased, and he laughed at her. He loved the look in her eyes when she spoke of Sarah and François.

"I wouldn't like it either, believe me! The last thing I need is a broken arm or leg," he said with feeling. A broken heart had been enough in the past year, broken limbs would have been a massive inconvenience.

He waved as she drove off to visit a friend in town, and he walked back to the house, and finished reading the second book on Sarah and François. He found it fascinating, and this one spoke mostly about François's work with the Army, trying to negotiate treaties with the Indians. He had been the main spokesman for the Indians in this part of the world, and had been very involved with all six Iroquois nations.

Sarah didn't come to him again that night. In fact, he felt nothing at all, as he wandered around the house. He just felt comfortable and at ease there. And before he went to bed he packed his things to go skiing. He set his alarm for seven the next morning. And just as he fell asleep, he thought he heard the curtains move, but he was too tired to open his eyes again, and as he drifted off to sleep, he was sure he felt her near him.

Chapter 7

*T*HE SKIING AT Charlemont was surprisingly pleasant for him, although Charlie had been spoiled by the many ski vacations he and Carole had taken in Europe. They were particularly fond of Val d'Isère and Courchevel, although Charlie liked St. Moritz and had a great time in Cortina. Charlemont was fairly tame compared to all that, but the trails were good, the expert runs challenging, and it felt great to be on the slopes again, out in the air, doing something he was good at. It was just what he had needed.

He hadn't been skiing in a year, and by noon he felt like a new man as he went up the lift for a last run before going in for lunch, and a steaming cup of coffee. The weather was crisp and it had been cold when he left the house, but he felt warm in the sun, and he smiled as he got on the chairlift with a little girl who was half his size. He was impressed that she was skiing alone, and going all the way up the mountain. There were expert trails, and he was surprised her parents weren't worried. But as the bar came down, she turned to him with a broad smile, and he asked if she came there often.

"Not too much. Whenever my mom has time. She's writing a

story," she said informatively as she looked carefully at Charlie. She had big blue eyes and strawberry-blond curls, and he wasn't sure how old she was. He thought somewhere between seven and ten, which was a broad range, but he didn't know much about children. She was a pretty little girl and she looked completely at ease with herself as they rode up the mountain. She hummed a little song and then she looked at him again with her impish smile, and eyes full of questions.

"Do you have children?" she asked, and he smiled as he answered.

"No, I don't." He almost felt as though he should apologize, or at the very least explain it, but she nodded as though she understood. She was just trying to establish who and what he was for the brief ride, and she looked interested in him as she continued to look him over. He was wearing black pants and a dark green parka. She was wearing a bright blue one-piece suit almost the same color as her eyes, and a red hat that looked just right with her outfit. She reminded him of the children he'd seen whenever he and Carole skied in France. There was something very European about her, the little cherub face, the bright eyes, the curls, she looked happy and innocent and healthy. And although she seemed perfectly at ease with him, she wasn't rude or precocious. There was nothing overly sophisticated about the child, she just seemed very wise and very happy, and he liked sitting next to her, and couldn't resist her infectious smile.

"Are you married?" she asked him then and he laughed at her. Maybe she was more sophisticated than he'd thought at first glance. Her mother had warned her not to say too much to people she met on the lift, but she loved talking to them, and had made a lot of friends there.

"Yes, I am," he said almost by reflex, and then thought better of it. There was no reason to lie to a child. "Actually, it's kind of complicated to explain, but no, I'm not. I am . . . but I won't be for much longer." He was exhausted after chasing his own tail, but this time she looked serious as she nodded.

"You're divorced," she said solemnly, "so am I." The way she said it made him smile again. She was an irresistible little pixie.

"I'm sorry to hear that," he said, trying to look serious for her benefit, as they slowly reached the top, "how long were you married?"

"All my life." There was a look of tragedy as she said it to him, and then he realized what she meant. She wasn't teasing him. She was talking about her parents. They had obviously gotten divorced, and she felt that she had been divorced as well.

"I'm really sorry," he said, and meant it this time. "How old were you when you got divorced?"

"Nearly seven. Now I'm eight. We used to live in France."

"Oh," he said, with fresh interest. "I used to live in London myself. When I was married. Do you live here now, or are you just here for a visit?"

"We live pretty nearby," she said matter-of-factly, and then turned to him again, happy to supply more information, whether or not he asked for it. "My father's French. We used to ski in Courchevelles."

"So did I," he said, as though they were old pals now. "You must be pretty good if your parents let you come all the way up to the top of the mountain by yourself."

"I learned to ski with my dad," she said proudly. "My mom skis too slow for me, so she lets me ski alone. She just says not to get into trouble, not to go anywhere with anyone, and not to talk too much." He was glad that she hadn't learned her lessons too well. He was actually enjoying her company. She was an enchanting little person.

"Where did you live in France?" They were old buddies as they reached the top and had to hop off. And as they did, he gave her a hand. But he could see by the way she got off the chairlift that she was a good skier and she was completely comfortable as they moved off toward an expert trail that would have daunted most grown-ups.

"We lived in Paris," she answered him, adjusting her goggles. "On the rue du Bac . . . in the Septième . . . my daddy lives in our old house." He wanted to ask her why she had come here, and if her mother was American. Charlie assumed she was, as the child spoke English like a native. He wanted to ask her a lot of things, but he didn't think he should, and as he watched her, she started down. She moved with the speed of a little snow bunny, heading almost straight down the mountain, and making smooth perfect turns. He followed her easily, and was only a few feet behind her. She looked up then, and saw him skiing near her, and her broad grin told him she was happy about it. "You ski just like my dad," she said with a tone of admiration, but it was Charlie who was in awe of her. She was a remarkable little skier, an adorable little girl, he felt as though he had made a new friend on the mountain. And he had to laugh at himself as he skied swiftly behind her. His life was certainly different these days. He was spending all his time with a seventy-year-old woman, ghosts, and children. It was a far cry from his busy, settled, predictable life in London, running an architectural firm. Now he had no job, no friends, no wife, no plans. All he had was the brilliant white of the snow beneath his skis, and the sunlight on the mountains as he followed the little skier most of the way down.

She stopped finally, and he came to a flashy stop beside her, as she commented on his style. "You ski great. Just like my daddy. He used to be a racer. He was in the Olympics for France. That was a long time ago. Now he thinks he's old. He's thirty-five."

"I'm even older than that. And I was never in the Olympics, but thank you." And then he thought of something and turned to ask her a question, as she looked up at him and brushed her curls back. "What's your name?"

"Monique Vironnet," she said simply, with a perfect French

accent, and he realized that she probably spoke French flaw-lessly. "My daddy's name is Pierre. Did you ever see him race?"

"Probably. But I don't remember the name."

"He won a bronze medal," she said, as he watched her eyes grow sad.

"You must miss him a lot," Charlie said gently, as they looked at the bunny slopes far below. Neither of them seemed to want to finish their run and go down. He liked chatting with her, and she seemed to be enjoying his company a lot. He assumed she missed her father, she talked about him a great deal.

"I visit him on holidays," she explained. "But my mother doesn't like me to go there. She says being in Paris isn't good for me. When we lived there, she cried all the time." He nodded. He knew the feeling. He had cried a lot in London in the past year. The end of any marriage hurt a lot. He wondered then what her mother was like, if she was as pretty and as lively as her little girl. She had to be, everything about the child was sunny and warm. That didn't happen by itself. In the case of children, it usually came from reflected light from their parents.

"Shall we go down?" he asked her finally. They had been on the mountain for a long time, and it was later than they thought. It was well after one. And he was starving. And as he followed her down the side of the mountain, they skied in perfect unison, and they were both glowing at the end of their run. "That was terrific, Monique. Thank you!" He had told her his name was Charlie by then, and she looked at him with her most brilliant smile.

"You ski great! Like Daddy." From her, it was the highest praise, and Charlie sensed that.

"Thank you for that. You're not bad yourself." And then he didn't know what to do with her. He didn't want to just take off his skis and walk away from her, and he didn't think he should take her with him. "Are you supposed to meet your mom some-where?" He was only mildly concerned. The resort at Charlemont seemed wholesome and safe. But still, she was only a child, and he didn't want to leave her to her own devices now that they were off the mountain.

Monique nodded at him. "Mom said she'd see me at lunch."

"I'll walk you inside," he said, feeling very proprietary about her, and protective of her. It was rare for him to encounter children, and he was surprised at how comfortable he was with her, and how much he liked her.

"Thanks," she said, as they walked onto the deck, and wove their way through the crowd, but she told Charlie she didn't see her mom anywhere. "Maybe she went back up. She doesn't eat very much." He had visions of a tiny, delicate, modern-day Edith Piaf, although Monique had never said her mom was French, just her father.

He asked her what she'd like to eat, and she asked for a hot dog, a chocolate shake, and french fries. "Daddy makes me eat good stuff in France. Yuk." She made an awful face and he laughed as he paid for her lunch and ordered a hamburger and a Coke for himself. After skiing with her at full speed, he wasn't even cold. And he had had a great time.

They took over a small table together, and they were halfway through their lunch when Monique gave a little shout, jumped up, and started to wave at someone in the distance. And Charlie turned around to see who she had seen in the crowd. There were flocks of people everywhere, people waving, talking, shouting, clumping by in their heavy boots, excited about their morning runs, and anxious to get back on the mountain. He couldn't tell who she'd seen, and then suddenly, she was there, beside them. A tall thin woman in an elegant beige parka trimmed in fur. She was wearing beige stretch pants and a beige sweater and she took her dark glasses off as she frowned at the little girl. Charlie had the feeling he'd seen her somewhere before, but he couldn't remember where. Maybe she was a model, or their paths had crossed in Europe somewhere. There was something very stylish about her, and she was wearing a good-looking fur hat. But she looked anything but pleased as she glanced from him to her daughter.

"Where were you? I looked everywhere for you. I told you to meet me at the restaurant at twelve o'clock." Monique looked mollified as she looked up at her mother, but what surprised Charlie was that the woman was as cold as ice with her, and the child was so warm. But the elegant young woman was also angry because she had been worried, and he couldn't entirely blame her.

"I'm very sorry," he apologized. "It's probably my fault. We rode up on the lift together, and then we skied down and took our time. We started to talk." She looked even angrier at that.

"She's an eight-year-old child." She glared at him ferociously and something rang a bell in his mind, but he had no idea what it was. She looked so familiar to him, and he still had no idea why. But as he looked down at her, he could see that Monique was about to cry. "Monique," her mother glared down at her relentlessly, "who paid for your lunch?"

"I did," Charlie explained, sorry for the little girl in the face of her mother's tirade.

"What happened to the money I gave you this morning?" The young woman looked frustrated and angry as she took off her hat, and revealed a long mane of dark auburn hair. And Charlie had already noticed that she had deep green eyes. She didn't look anything like her daughter.

"I lost it," Monique told her as two tears finally escaped from her brimming eyes. "I'm sorry, Mommy. . . ." She hid her face in her hands so Charlie wouldn't see her cry.

"Really, it's nothing," Charlie tried to soothe them both. He felt terrible about the stir he'd caused, first making her late, and then paying for her hot dog. It wasn't as though he was trying to pick her up. He was well aware that she was a child. But the look in her mother's eyes was still ferocious, and after thanking him angrily, she took Monique by the arm, and led her away without even letting her finish her lunch. Just watching them together made Charlie angry. There had been no reason to make a scene and embarrass the child. She was right not to let her hang around with strangers, but he certainly looked harmless enough. She could have been good humored and a lot more pleasant about it, and she wasn't. And as he finished his hamburger, he thought about them, the little girl he'd enjoyed talking to so much, and the mother who was so angry and afraid . . . and then suddenly he remembered. He knew exactly where he'd seen her before, and who she was. She was the disagreeable woman from the historical society in Shelburne. And he had disliked her almost as much there as he did this time. She seemed so bitter and so frightened. And then he remembered what Monique had said, that in Paris her mother had cried all the time. It made him wonder even more about them. What was she running away from? What was she hiding? Or was she as unpleasant as she looked? Perhaps, in fact, there was no one inside.

He was still thinking about them when he took the chairlift alone this time, and ran into Monique at the top. She still seemed embarrassed, and she was more hesitant about talking to him this time. But she had hoped she'd see him. She hated it when her mother acted like that. Nowadays, she did it a lot. And that was more or less what she told Charlie, as she looked up at him with her great big eyes.

"I'm sorry my mom got mad at you. She gets mad a lot now. I think it's because she gets tired. She works really hard. She stays up really late at night, writing." It was still no excuse for the way she behaved, even the child knew that, and she was really sorry her mother had been so mean to Charlie. There seemed to be no way to make it up now. "Do you want to ski with me again?" she asked sadly. She seemed so lonely, and he suspected from the way she looked at him, that she missed her father. With a mother like that it was no wonder. And he hoped for the child's sake that her father was warmer than the woman with the sharp tongue and broken look in her eyes.

"Are you sure your mother won't mind?" He didn't want her to think he was a pervert, some crazy pedophile chasing her little girl. But they were out in the open, on the mountain, there wasn't much that could be misconstrued from that. And he didn't have the heart to reject the child. She seemed so hungry for a companion.

"My mommy doesn't care who I ski with. I just can't go inside with anyone, or to their house, or in their car," she explained sensibly, "and she was really mad because I let you pay for my lunch. She said we can take care of ourselves." She looked up at him with huge eyes then, apologizing for her extravagance. "Did it cost a lot?" she asked, looking worried, and he laughed at the innocence of the question.

"Of course not. I think she was just worried about you, and that's why she got angry. Moms do that sometimes," he said sensibly, trying to allay her worries, "and so do Dads. Sometimes parents are afraid something bad has happened when they can't find you, so when they do find you, they get all wound up. I'm sure she'll be fine by tonight." But Monique was not as certain, she knew her mother better than Charlie. Her mother had been moody and unhappy for so long, Monique could no longer remember a different person, although she thought her mother had been happier when she was little. But their life had been different then, her illusions had not yet been shattered, there had still been hope then, and faith, and love. Now there was only bitterness and anger, and unhappy silence in their lives.

"In Paris, Mommy used to cry all the time. Here, she gets angry." She sounded like a barrel of laughs, and Charlie couldn't help feeling sorry for the child. It was so unfair of her mother to take her unhappiness out on her daughter. "I don't think she's very happy. Maybe she doesn't like her job."

115

He nodded, suspecting easily that it was more than that, but he wasn't about to explain it to an eight-year-old. "Maybe she misses your daddy."

"No," Monique said firmly, as they made a sharp turn side by side. "She says she hates him." That was nice. What a great atmosphere for a kid to grow up in, Charlie thought, growing still more annoyed at the mother. "I don't really think she does," Monique said, looking hopeful, but her eyes were sad. "Maybe we'll go back one day," she said wistfully. "But Daddy is with Marie-Lise now." It sounded like a complicated situation, and it appeared to have taken a heavy toll on the child. It reminded him a little bit of his plight with Carole, but at least there were no children to get damaged by it. And Monique seemed to be surviving, in spite of her mother.

"Is that what your mommy says?" he asked with idle interest, not because of any interest in the mother, but only because he had grown fond of the child. "That you'll go back?"

"Not really . . . not yet anyway. She says we have to stay here now." He could think of worse fates. He wondered if they lived in Shelburne Falls, and on the way down he asked her, and she nodded. He knew her mother worked there, but he didn't know if they lived somewhere outside town or in Deerfield. "How did you know?" she asked him with interest.

"Because I've seen your mom. I live there too. I just moved there from New York, at Christmas."

"I went to New York once, when we came back from Paris. My grandma took me to F.A.O. Schwarz."

"It's a great toy store," he said, and she agreed heartily with him, and they got to the bottom of the run and rode up on the chairlift together this time. He decided it was even worth risking her mother's ire, just so he could enjoy talking to Monique again. He really liked her, and he could sense an unstoppable enthusiasm and warmth and energy in the little girl, despite her problems with her parents. She was so bright and alive and so loving, and she had obviously been through a lot of pain, and yet there was nothing dreary about her. Unlike her mother, who had obviously been beaten down and never came out the other end. Or if she had, whatever there had once been in her of life and hope and happiness had altered. It was almost as though she had died, and a bitter, tired, battered soul had taken her place. In a way, Charlie felt sorry for her. Monique would survive. Her mother obviously had not.

They talked about Europe this time on the way down, and Charlie loved talking to her. She saw everything through the fresh, funny, always slightly humorous eyes of a child. And she told him about all the things she loved about France. There were a lot of them. She thought she would go back one day, when she got big enough to live where she chose, and she was going to stay with her daddy. She spent two months in the summer with him now, and she liked it very much. They spent a month in the south of France. She said her dad was a sportscaster on TV, and he was very famous.

"Do you look like him?" Charlie asked casually, admiring the soft gold curls and the big blue eyes, as he had since they met that morning.

"My mom says I do." But he suspected that that also made her mother unhappy. If he was an Olympic ski champion and a sportscaster, and had a girlfriend named Marie-Lise, there was always the possibility that Monique's mother had gotten a bum deal, or maybe not. But if she used to cry all the time it didn't exactly speak well for her husband. And he found himself thinking on the way down, as Monique chattered on, what messes most people made of their lives. Cheating on each other, telling lies, marrying the wrong woman or man, losing respect, losing hope, losing heart. It seemed miraculous to him now that anyone managed to make it work and stayed married. He certainly hadn't. He had thought he was the happiest man in the world, until he found out his wife was madly in love with another man.

It was so classic it was embarrassing, and he found himself wondering again what had happened between Monique's parents. Maybe there was a reason for the grim look her mother wore, the heart-shaped lips set in a firm, hard line. Maybe she'd been someone else before Pierre Vironnet had turned her bitter. Then again there was the possibility that she was a shrew, and he'd been thrilled to get rid of her. Who knew? And in the end, who cared? Charlie didn't. He only cared about the child.

Monique went to find her mother on time this time. Charlie had asked her about any rendezvous they had, and at three o'clock sharp he sent her off, and went up alone for a last run. But he found that even without the child, he skied no better, no faster, no wilder than he had with his young friend. She could keep up easily with him, and Charlie could see that her father had taught her well. And as he came down the mountain alone this time, he couldn't help thinking about the little girl who'd lived in Paris. Meeting her almost made him wish that he and Carole had had children. It would have complicated things, and they'd be in the same mess now probably, but at least there would be something to show for their ten years together. Now all they had were some antiques, a few nice paintings, and half the linen and china. It seemed precious little to have left to mark ten years together. After ten years, they should have had more.

Charlie was still mulling over it when he went back to the hotel. But the next day, when he skied again, he didn't see Monique, or her mother, and he wondered if they'd gone home. He hadn't asked her if they were planning to stay, and he guessed that they hadn't. He skied alone for the next couple of days, and although he saw some pretty women here and there, none of them seemed worth the trouble. These days, he felt as though he had nothing to say, nothing to offer anyone, no succor, no support, no amusing anecdotes. His well had run dry. The only person who had drawn him out successfully was an eight-year-old. It was a sad statement on his psyche, and his perspective on life.

And he was startled when, on the day of New Year's Eve, he ran into Monique again. "Where've you been?" he asked with delight, as they met putting on their skis at the base of the mountain. He noticed that her mother was nowhere in sight. Again he wondered about someone who was so concerned about who bought the kid a hot dog and fries but let her ski alone. She certainly didn't hang around with Monique much. But she knew that at Charlemont, Monique was safe. They had come here almost every weekend for the past year, ever since they'd moved here. And despite the bitter taste that Pierre had cast on almost everything they'd done in France, skiing was still important to them, although her mother skied milder slopes than she did.

"We went back because Mom had to work," she explained to Charlie as she beamed at him. It was like the meeting of old friends. "But we're going to stay here tonight, and go home tomorrow."

"So am I." He had already been there for three days, and wasn't going back until New Year's night. "Are you going to stay up tonight for New Year's Eve?"

"Probably," she said hopefully. "My dad lets me drink champagne. My mom says it'll rot my mind."

"That's possible," he said, looking amused, thinking of all the champagne he'd drunk in the past twenty-five or thirty years, although it was debatable as to the effect it had had. "I think you'll be all right with a few sips."

"My mom won't even let me have that." And then on a happier note, "We went to the movies yesterday. It was very nice." She seemed pleased and then moved ahead of him for a little while. And this time, at exactly noon, he sent her down to her mother. But they met again that afternoon, and Monique brought a friend with her. He was a boy she knew from school. He was a little hot dogger on the slopes, Charlie observed, but

Monique whispered to him with a serious look that Tommy was a rotten skier. And Charlie smiled as the children flew ahead of him. Charlie was a little more cautious than they were on the way down, and by the end of the day he was tired. Monique had left the slopes by then, and he was surprised to run into them in his hotel that night after dinner. They were sitting in the lodge's large living room, and Francesca had stretched her long legs out in front of the fire. And as she said something to Monique, Charlie actually saw her smile. And he hated to admit it, but she looked gorgeous. She was a beautiful woman despite the icy, sorrowful look in her eyes.

He hesitated at first, but finally decided to walk over and say hello to them. He had spent so much time with Monique by then, that he felt rude not acknowledging her mother. She wore her hair down her back in a long ponytail, and as he approached, he couldn't help noticing the enormous almond-shaped eyes and the deep red color of her hair in the firelight. There was something mysterious and exotic about her when she smiled. But the moment she recognized him, everything closed again, like shutters on windows. Charlie had never seen anything like it. She was obviously determined to hide.

"Hello again," he said, trying to look more comfortable than he felt. He wasn't good at this anymore. And he didn't want to be. He felt like a fool, standing there with Francesca glaring at him. "Great snow today, wasn't it?" he said casually, and saw her nod. The eyes fluttered up at him once and then looked back into the fire without interest.

But she forced herself to glance up at him finally, and answer his question. "It was great snow," she conceded, but he noticed that it seemed to cause her considerable pain to speak to him at all. "Monique told me she saw you again," she added, seeming almost expansive, but he didn't want this woman to think there was anything clandestine about his dealings with her child. They were just ski partners, and she was obviously hungry for male companionship because she missed her father. "You've been very kind to her," Francesca Vironnet said quietly as Monique went to talk to another child, but she didn't invite him to sit down with her. "Do you have children of your own?" She assumed he had. Monique hadn't told her much about their conversations. She particularly didn't tell her that she had told Charlie about her father.

"No, I don't have children," Charlie explained. "I like her," Charlie said, and then complimented Monique profusely. But he couldn't help noticing again how withdrawn the woman was. She was like a wounded animal deep in a cave. All you could see were her eyes glistening in the dark from the light of the fire. He wasn't sure why, but even if only out of curiosity, he would have liked to draw her out. These were the kind of challenges he had loved years before, but had learned not to tackle even before he was married. More often than not, challenges such as these were not worth the agony, or the time. And yet . . . something in her eyes whispered volumes about her sorrow.

"You're very lucky to have Monique," he said quietly, and this time she looked up into his eyes, and at last he saw the merest flicker of something warm from behind the glacier where she was hiding.

"Yes, I am lucky . . ." she conceded, but didn't sound as though she meant it.

"She's a great skier too," he smiled, "she outran me a number of times."

"She outruns me too." Francesca almost laughed, but caught herself. She didn't want to know this man. "That's why I let her ski by herself. She's too fast for me. I can't keep up with her." She smiled at him, and looked almost beautiful, but not quite. It would have taken a lot more fire to make the difference.

"She tells me she learned to ski in France," he said casually, and with those words he saw everything in Francesca's face slam shut. It was like watching the door to a vault close electrically.

121

Locked and sealed and barred, and nothing short of dynamite would have opened it before the appointed hour. He had obviously reminded her of something she could not bear to think about. And she had locked the door, and run far, far away from him. She was still wearing a look of startled agony when Monique wandered back, and Francesca stood up and told her it was bedtime.

Monique looked devastated. She had been having such a good time. And she wanted to stay up till midnight. And Charlie knew that, in part, her removal was his fault. Francesca had to run away from him now, to stay safe, and she had to take her daughter with her. He wanted to tell her that he wished her no harm, that he had wounds of his own. He was no threat to anyone. They were like two wounded animals, drinking at the same brook, there was no need to injure each other again, nor to run and hide. But there was no way to tell her what he felt. He wanted nothing at all from her, no friendship, no intimacy, he wanted to wrest nothing whatsoever from her. He was just standing quietly along her path. But even that faint threat, that hint of a human presence in her life, even for a moment or two, was too much for her. He wondered what she was writing about, but he wouldn't have dared to ask her about that.

He tried to make a last plea for his young friend. "It's awfully early to go up on New Year's Eve, isn't it? How about some ginger ale for Monique, and a glass of wine for us?" But that was even more threatening, and Francesca shook her head, thanked him, and within two minutes, they both were gone, and he was sorry when they left. But he had never met a woman as badly injured as she, and couldn't imagine what the sportscaster had done to leave her so damaged. Whatever it was, Charlie suspected it must have been pretty awful. Or at least she thought it was, which was enough. But despite the suit of armor she wore so effectively, he sensed now that somewhere deep within, she was probably a decent person.

He went to the bar and stayed until ten-thirty, and then finally he went up to his own room. There was no point standing around downstairs, watching everyone else laugh and shout and get drunk. Like Gladys Palmer, New Year's Eve was a night he had never loved. And at midnight when the horns blew and the bells rang and couples kissed, promising that this year would be different, Charlie was sound asleep in bed in his room.

He woke up bright and early the next morning, and saw that it was snowing and the visibility was poor. A strong wind had come up and it was cold, and he decided to go back. Charlemont was so close to where he lived, he could come back anytime he wanted, he didn't have to ski in bad weather, or force himself to stay, when he'd rather be at home doing things in his house. Three days of good skiing there had been enough for him.

He checked out at ten-thirty, and in twenty minutes was back at his house. The snowdrifts were building again, and there was an exquisite silence blanketing everything. He loved watching it, and sat for hours in his den, which had been Sarah's boudoir, reading and glancing up from time to time to see the snow still falling outside.

He thought of the little girl he had met in Charlemont, and her life with the mother who was at the same time so angry and so sad. He would have liked to see the child again, but it was obvious that he and her mother were not destined to be bosom companions. And as he thought of her, he remembered the two books he had to take back to the historical society. He had lent one of them to Gladys Palmer and he wanted to see her anyway, so he made a mental note to himself to stop by the next day and pick it up. He could drop both books off at the historical society after he left her.

But as he thought about them, there was a strange shuffling noise in the attic over his head, and in spite of himself, he jumped, and then he laughed. He felt so foolish, in a house with a history like this, everything was attributed to the supernatural.

It never occurred to anyone that there might be a chipmunk in the attic somewhere, or even a squirrel, or a rat.

He decided not to pay any attention to it, but as he read some new architectural journals he'd bought, he heard the same sound again. It sounded like an animal dragging something, and at times it sounded almost like a man. And then, there was a gnawing sound, which told him exactly what he'd thought before. It was a rodent. For once, he didn't even begin to suspect it was Sarah's ghost. He had already resigned himself, after what Gladys said about only having seen her once in her life, he was sure the vision was not returning for a second time. He still couldn't quite explain it to himself, but whatever it was, it was gone, and the house was empty. Except for the rat in the attic over his head.

It annoyed him all afternoon, and at twilight, as the snow still fell, he got out the ladder, and decided to go up and check it out. If it was a rat, he didn't want the wiring destroyed. The house was old enough without having rodents devour what was left, and cause a fire. He had promised Gladys repeatedly that he would be careful about that.

But when he opened the trapdoor that led to the attic, and lifted himself into it, he found everything quiet there, and no telltale signs of anything amiss. He knew he hadn't imagined it, and hoped they hadn't found a way to slip between the walls. But he was certain that the sounds he'd heard were directly above him. He had brought a flashlight with him, and he looked everywhere. There were all the same boxes he had seen before, the uniforms, the toys, an old mirror leaning against a wall, and then at the far end, he spotted something he hadn't seen on his first foray up here. It was an old hand-carved cradle, and he gently ran a hand over it, wondering if it had belonged to Gladys or Sarah, but in either case, there was a sadness to it now, an emptiness that touched him. The babies in both their lives were gone, and worse than that, they were all dead now. He turned

away from it, and the bittersweet feeling it gave him, and cast a
light into the far corners, just to make sure no little furry crea-
ture had built a nest there. He knew chipmunks did that sometimes. It might even have lived there for a long time, and as he
walked slowly back toward the ladder, he noticed a little alcove
beneath one of the big round windows, and tucked away in it was
an old battered trunk. He didn't think he had seen it there
before, although from the look of it, and the cloud of dust that
rose when he touched it, it was obvious that it had been there
forever. It would have been easy to overlook it, its battered
leather cover seemed to blend into the wall. And when Charlie
tried to open it, he found it was locked. The fact that he couldn't
get into it intrigued him.

There were no identifying marks on the trunk, no initials, no
name, no crest. As both people who had lived in the house
before had been both European and titled, he wouldn't have
been surprised to see a crest somewhere on it, but he didn't. And
as he played with the lock a little bit, some of the very old leather
flaked off. The covering on it looked extremely fragile, but the
trunk itself was not. And when Charlie tried to lift it, it felt like it
was filled with rocks. But it was small enough to carry with some
effort, and Charlie carried it as far as the ladder, and then slowly
let himself down, balancing it on his shoulder, and careful not to
drop it.

It fell with a thud to the floor of the hall when he got down
again. And after he closed the trapdoor, satisfied that there were
no visible rodents upstairs, he took the trunk to the kitchen, and
got out some tools to pry open the lock. He felt a little awkward,
wondering if Gladys Palmer had some small treasures hidden
there, or some papers she didn't want anyone to see. He almost
called her before he started trying to force it. It seemed something of a violation, and yet at the same time, the trunk seemed
so old, and something about it mesmerized him. He couldn't
stop what he was doing. He couldn't let go, and as he wrestled

with it, the lock suddenly gave way and fell off. The leather was dry and frail, and there were brass nail heads in it, and it was easy to believe that the trunk had been there as long as the house. And as Charlie touched the lid, he felt strangely breathless. He had no idea what he expected to find, money, jewels, treasure, papers, maps, a small dried skull, some ghastly, wonderful trophy or trinket from another century, but his heart was pounding as he lifted the lid, and he almost believed he heard a rustle by his side as he did it. He laughed in the silence of the old kitchen, knowing that he had imagined it. This was only a thing, an object, an old box, and as it opened, he felt a small wave of disappointment wash over him. It was filled with small leather-bound books, they looked almost like prayer books or hymnals. They were carefully bound, and had long silk markers in them. There were over a dozen of them, and they were all the same. He suspected the leather might have once been red, but it was a dull, faded brown now. He picked one up, and opened it, wondering if the books had come from a church somewhere, or to whom they had belonged. There were no markings on them, no titles, but they had the look of something reverent, and then as he glanced inside, at the very first page, he felt a shiver as he saw her name in her own hand. The writing was small and elegant and clear. The ink had been dry on the page for more than two hundred years, and in the corner she had written "Sarah Ferguson, 1789." Just seeing what she had written and reading her name filled him with longing . . . how long ago it had been . . . what had she been like? If he closed his eyes, he could imagine her, sitting in this room, writing.

And with the utmost gentleness and caution, afraid it would disintegrate at his touch, he turned the next page, and then he realized what he had in his hand. This was no hymnal. These were diaries, Sarah's journals. His eyes grew wide as he began to read. It was like a letter from her to all of them. She was telling them what had happened to her, where she had been, whom she

had seen, what had been dear to her, how she had met François
. . . how she had come there, and from where. And as Charlie
began reading the words that had survived two centuries, a tear
rolled down his cheek and fell on his hand. He could scarcely
believe his good fortune, and he felt a shiver of excitement run
through him as he began to read.

Chapter 8

SARAH FERGUSON STOOD at the window, looking out over the moors, as she had for the last two days. Although it was August, the mists had hung low since morning, the sky was dark, and it was easy to discern that there would be a storm before much longer. There was a dark, ominous look to everything around them, but it suited the way she felt, as she stood and waited. Her husband, Edward, Earl of Balfour, had been gone for four days.

He had said he was going hunting four days before, and he had taken five of his servants with him. He had told Sarah he was meeting friends. And she never asked questions. She knew better. She had told the men who were searching for him to look for him at the inn, or in the next town, or even among the serving girls at their farms or on their property. She knew Edward well, had known him for a long time. She knew his cruelty, his infidelity, and his unkindness, the mercilessness of his tongue, and the viciousness of the back of his hand. She had failed him bitterly and often. The sixth child she'd borne him, dead at birth this time, had been buried only three months before. The only thing Edward had ever wanted from her was an heir, and after years with her, he still didn't have one. All the children she had borne him had miscarried or been stillborn, or died within hours of their birth.

Her own mother had died in childbed with her second child, and Sarah had lived alone with her father since she was a little girl. He was already old when Sarah was born, and when Sarah's mother died, he never remarried. Sarah had been so beautiful, so whimsical, and such a joy to him, and he had cherished her. And as he grew older, and became increasingly frail, Sarah nursed him devotedly, and kept him alive for years longer than he might have without her. And when she was fifteen, it was obvious even to him that he couldn't last much longer. He knew he had no choice anymore, he could not delay, a decision had to be made. He had to find her a husband before he died.

There were numerous possibilities within the county, an earl, a duke, a viscount, some of them important men. But it was Balfour who was the most anxious, who wanted her so desperately, and whose lands were adjacent to her father's. It would make a remarkable estate, he'd pointed out to Sarah's father, one of the largest and most important in England. Sarah's father had added enormous blocks of land to his own over the years, and she had a dowry fit for a monarch.

It was Balfour who won her in the end. He was too astute, his interest too keen, his arguments too convincing to be ignored. There had been another, younger man, whom she far preferred to him, but Edward had assured her father that, having lived with an old man for so long, she would never be happy with a boy close to her own age. She needed someone more like her father. And Sarah knew so little of Edward, she didn't know enough to beg for mercy, to plead to be spared.

She was traded for land, and became the Countess of Balfour at sixteen. The wedding was small, the estate huge, and the penalties endless. Her father died within five weeks of her wedding.

Edward beat her regularly after that, until she got pregnant.

Then he only threatened and berated her, slapping her as often as he dared, and telling her he would kill her if she failed to produce an heir. Most of the time, he was far from home, traveling over his estates, lying drunk in pubs, ravaging servant girls, or staying with friends all over England. It was always a bleak day when he returned. But the bleakest of all was when their first child died within hours of its birth. It had been the only ray of hope in her life. Edward was less distraught than she, as it was only a girl. The next three had been sons, two stillborn, one born far too early, and the last two had been girls again. She had held the last one for hours, lifeless, wrapped in swaddling clothes, just as she had prepared all of them. She had been half out of her mind with grief and pain, and they had had to take the baby from her and lay it to rest. Edward had barely spoken to her since then.

Although Edward was careful to hide his cruelty to her, like everyone in the county, she knew he had countless bastards, seven of them sons, but that was not the same. He had already warned her that if she did not produce an heir, he would recognize one of them in the end, anything rather than pass the title and his estates to his brother, Haversham, whom he hated.

"I will leave you nothing," he had spat at her. "I will kill you before I let you live on the face of this earth without me, if you do not give me an heir." At twenty-four, she had been married to him for eight years, and a part of her had been killed by him long since. There was a dead look in her eyes that she herself saw in the mirror sometimes. And particularly since the last infant died, she didn't care anymore if she lived or died. Her father would have been beside himself if he had known the fate to which he had condemned her. She had no life, no hope, no dreams. She was beaten, abused, detested, scorned, by a man she loathed, and with whom she had been forced to sleep for the past eight years, and constantly try to give him children, above all an heir.

At fifty-four, he was still a handsome man, he had aristocratic good looks, and young girls on farms and in pubs, who didn't know his ways, still thought him handsome and charming, but within a short time, they would be used and cast aside and savaged by him, and if a child came later of it, Edward had no interest in the girl or the baby. He cared for nothing, he was fueled by jealousy and hatred of his younger brother, and by the greed that caused him to devour every piece of land upon which he could lay his hands, including her father's lands that became his when the old man died. Edward had long since used all her money, sold most of her mother's jewels, and taken even that which her father had left her. Edward had used her in every way he possibly could, and whatever was left of her was of no interest to him. Still, even now, after so many disappointments, so much tragedy in her young life, all he wanted from her was an heir, and she knew that in the end, child or not, he would see her dead trying. She didn't even care anymore. She only hoped that the end would come soon. Some accident, some treachery, some merciless beating, a baby in her womb never to be born with whom she could slip into another world. She wanted nothing from him, only death and the freedom she would derive from it. And as she waited for him to return now, she was sure that he would come riding in on the spiteful horse he rode, fresh from some vile adventure. She couldn't imagine anything happening to him. She was certain that he was lying drunk somewhere, with a harlot in her arms. And eventually he would come home in order to abuse her. She was grateful for his absence, though this time everyone was worried, except Sarah, who knew he was too mean to die, too wily to disappear for long.

She turned from the window at last and looked at the clock on the mantel again. It was just after four. She wondered if she should send for Haversham, if she should ask him to come to search for Edward. He was Edward's half brother and would have come if she asked him. But it seemed foolish to worry him, and if Edward found him there when he came home, he would be livid, and he would take it out on her. She decided to wait yet another day before she called Haversham to her.

She walked slowly into the room again, and sat down, her wide green satin gown shimmering like a jewel, with a dark green velvet bodice, which molded her lithe figure so tightly, she looked like a young girl again. And the creamy gauze of her blouse beneath the gown seemed almost the same color as her skin. There was something very delicate, and deceptively frail about her, but she was sturdier than she looked, or she wouldn't have survived the beatings.

The ivory of her skin was in sharp contrast with her shining black hair. She wore it in a long braid looped around several times to form a large bun at the back of her head. Sarah had always been elegant without being stylish. There was a classic dignity to the way she carried herself that belied the despair in her eyes. She always had a kind word for the servants, always went out to the farms to help with the sick children, and bring them nourishment. She was always there to help them.

She had a deep passion for literature and art, and had traveled to Italy and France with her father as a young girl, but she had been nowhere since. Edward kept her locked up, and treated her like a piece of furniture. Her exceptional beauty was something he didn't even notice anymore, it was of absolutely no consequence to him. He treated his horses better than he treated Sarah.

It was Haversham who had always noticed her, and cared about her, who saw the sorrow in her eyes, and was distressed whenever he heard that she was ailing. He had been appalled for years at the way his brother treated her, but there was very little he could do to make Sarah's life less of a hell than it was at the hands of his brother. He had been twenty-one when Edward married her, and by the time she bore her husband their first child, Haversham had been deeply in love with her. It had taken him another two years to tell her, but when he did, she had been terrified of what would happen if she reciprocated his feelings. Edward would kill them both. She forced Haversham to swear he would never speak of it again. Yet, there was no denying what they felt. For long years now, she had also been in love with him. But she kept it a secret. She would never, ever have told him, for to do so would have been to risk his life, which seemed far more important to her now than her own.

They both knew there was never any hope of getting together. And four years earlier, he had finally married one of his cousins, a foolish but well-intentioned seventeen-year-old girl named Alice. She had grown up in Cornwall, and was in many ways far too simple for her husband, but it was a good match economically, their families had been pleased, and in the past four years, she had given him four adorable little girls. But other than Haversham himself, there was still no heir, and Haversham's daughters did not solve the problem, since women could not inherit land or titles.

As the light began to fade, and Sarah quietly lit the candles, she heard a stirring in the courtyard, and closed her eyes as she trembled, praying he had not returned yet. As wicked as she knew it was of her to think so, her life would be forever blessed if indeed something had befallen him, and he never came back at all. She could not bear to think of spending the rest of her life beside him, however short it was, it would be far, far too long to be beside Edward.

Setting the candle down, she walked swiftly to the window, and then she saw it, his horse, riderless, being led by half a dozen of their men. And then behind them, she saw his body laid out on his cloak, on a farmer's cart. He looked as though he were dead. Her heart pounded like a bird in her chest as she waited. If he was dead, they would remain solemn, and someone would come to tell her. But they began running and shouting for help almost as soon as they entered the courtyard. Someone was sent to fetch the doctor, and four of the men set him on a board, and began carrying him into the house. She had no idea yet what had happened to him, but her heart sank as she realized he was alive, and they were still hoping to save him.

"God, forgive me . . ." she whispered as a door exploded at the far end of the huge drawing room where she had been sitting, and his men carried him in. He looked dead to her, but she knew he wasn't.

"It's his lordship, he's fallen," they said urgently, but Edward never stirred. She motioned them to follow her upstairs to his bedroom, and she watched quietly as they set him down on his bed. He was still wearing the clothes he'd worn when he left, and she saw that his shirt was torn and dusty. His face was gray and his beard was full of brambles.

He had started his journey with a woman at a farm nearby, and he had sent his men on to an inn to await him. And they had waited for him patiently there for the better part of three days. It wasn't unusual for him to take that long to dally, and they only laughed and joked as they waited for him, and drank gallons of ale and whiskey. And then finally they went to find him again, only to discover, when he did not surface, that he'd left the woman on the farm three days before. They called the sheriff out and began a search for him, and it was only that morning that they had found him. Edward had fallen from his horse and had lain delirious for days. At first they thought his neck was broken, but it wasn't. He had come to his senses once for a moment on the way home, and then fallen unconscious again, and now he looked as though he were dead as he lay there. To Sarah they said only that he'd had a bad fall and, they suspected, hit his head very sharply.

"When did it happen?" she asked quietly, and she did not believe them when they said that morning. He had blood and vomit caked on him that looked several days old. She knew almost nothing to tell the doctor, when he came, and the men took him aside and told him quietly what had happened. He was familiar with these things. His lordship's wife did not need to know where he'd been or what he'd been doing. What he needed was to be bled now, and some leeches, and they'd have to wait for the outcome. He was a healthy, vital man, with a strong constitution, and even at his age the doctor thought it was possible, though not certain, that he might survive his mishap.

Sarah stood next to him dutifully while they bled him, and he never stirred. It was the leeches she hated most of all, and when the doctor left finally, she looked almost as ill as Edward as she left the room. She went to her desk and wrote to Haversham then. He needed to know what had happened, and if there was any danger that Edward might die during the night, he should be there.

She sealed the letter and sent it with one of their runners. It was an hour's ride to where Haversham lived, and she knew he would come at once that night. She went back then, to sit with Edward. She sat silently in the chair, looking at him, trying to understand what she felt. It was not anger or hatred, it was indifference, and fear and disdain. She could not even remember a time now when she had loved him. It had been so brief, so based on lies, and so long ago as to have faded almost entirely from her mind. She felt nothing at all for him. And there was a part of her that sat there that night, silent, strong, unbroken, unbridled, praying he would die before morning. There were times when she thought she could not live with him another moment. She could not bear the thought of surviving his touch, or letting him paw her. She would rather die than bear him more children, and yet she knew that if he lived, it was only a matter of time before he took her again, and forced her.

Margaret, her serving girl, came to her just before midnight, to ask if there was anything she could bring her. She was a sweet girl, the same age that Sarah had been when she came to Balfour, a mere sixteen. And Sarah was surprised to find she was still up, and sent her to bed. Margaret was passionately devoted to

135

her, she had been at her side when the last baby died, and she thought Sarah was the most remarkable woman she had ever known. She would have done anything she asked her.

Haversham didn't arrive until two o'clock that morning. His wife was ill, two of the girls had given her measles, and she was miserable, as were they, all broken out with spots and itching unbearably and coughing. He had hated to leave them, but when he got Sarah's note, he knew he had to come.

"How is he?" He was as tall and dark and handsome as Edward had been in his youth. Haversham was only twenty-nine, and Sarah could feel her heart stir, as it always did, as he crossed the room and took her hands in his own and held them.

"They bled him hours ago, and leeched him, but he hasn't stirred, or made a sound. I don't know . . . Haversham . . . I think . . . the doctor thought he had bleeding somewhere inside him. There's no sign of it, nothing's broken . . . but he looks as though he might not survive it." As she said it, he could read nothing in her eyes. "I thought you should be here."

"I wanted to be with you." She looked up at him gratefully, and they walked slowly to Edward's room. There had been no change. It was only when they emerged again, and the butler brought Haversham a glass of brandy in the drawing room that he looked at his sister-in-law, and admitted that Edward already looked dead. He couldn't imagine him surviving. "When did this happen?" he asked, looking troubled. If Edward died, a great deal of responsibility was about to fall on him. He had never really thought that would happen. He had always assumed that, at some point, she and Edward would have a son, although he himself certainly hadn't managed it, despite four children. But since she'd had three sons who died, he couldn't imagine her not having another, and hoped that the next one would survive past childbirth.

"They tell me it happened this morning," she said quietly, and as he looked at her, he realized, as he always did, how strong she

136

was. She was far stronger, and more courageous, than most men, and surely more so than he was. "They're lying," she said calmly. Haversham wondered how she knew that. He crossed one leg over the other as he watched her, trying desperately to resist the urge to take her in his arms. "Something rather more complicated must have happened," she went on, "but perhaps it's not important. Whatever happened, wherever they found him, it doesn't change the condition he's in now." He appeared to both of them to be mortally injured.

"Was the doctor hopeful?" Haversham asked, still looking anxious, and then as she looked noncommittal, he set down his glass and took her hand in his own again. "Sarah, if something happens to Edward, what will you do then?" She would be free of him at last, only Haversham and a handful of the servants knew how brutal he had been.

"I don't know. Live again, I suppose," she sat back in her chair with a sigh and smiled, "breathe . . . just be. Finish my life quietly somewhere." Perhaps, if he left her anything, she'd rent a small house of her own, or even a farm and live peacefully. She wanted nothing more than that. He had killed all her dreams. All she wanted was to flee him.

"Would you go away with me?" She looked shocked at the question. They hadn't spoken of such things in years, and she had forbidden him to speak to her of love ever since his marriage to Alice.

"Don't be ridiculous," she said quietly, trying to sound as though she meant it. "You have a wife and four daughters here. You can't just abandon them and run off with me." But it was exactly what he wanted to do with her, and always had. His wife meant nothing to him. He had only married her because he knew he could never have Sarah. But now . . . if Edward died . . . he couldn't bear losing her again. "Don't even think of it," she said firmly. She was, above all, a woman of honor. And there were times when, much as she had loved him for a third of her life, Haversham acted like a schoolboy. Never having the burden of the title, he had never been forced to grow up and take the responsibilities that went with it. But without the title, he also didn't have a penny, except his wife's dowry.

"And if he lives?" he whispered in the light of the flickering candles.

"Then I will die here," she said sadly, hoping it would be sooner rather than later.

"I can't let you do that. I can't bear it any longer, Sarah. I can't watch him murdering you day after day, year after year. Oh God, if you knew how I hate him." He had even less reason to do so than she did, although Edward had done whatever he could to complicate Haversham's life ever since he'd been born. Haversham had been born of their father's second wife, and the two men shared a common father, but had different mothers. Haversham was twenty-five years Edward's junior. "Come away with me," he said then, the brandy had gone to his head, but only slightly. He had tried to concoct a plan to flee with her for years, but he had never before gotten up the courage to ask her. He knew how sensitive she was to his marriage, far more so than he was. Alice was a sweet girl, and he was fond of her, but he had never loved her. "We'll go to America," he went on, clasping her hands now. "We'll be free of all this. Sarah, you must do it." He spoke to her urgently in the dark, chilly room, and if she had been honest with him, she would have told him that she would have liked nothing better. But she knew she couldn't do it. Not to him, or to his wife. And if Edward was still alive, she knew with utter certainty that he would find them and kill them.

"You mustn't talk such nonsense," she said firmly. "You would risk your life for nothing." She wanted more than anything to calm him.

"Being with you for the rest of our lives is not 'nothing,'" Haversham said heatedly. "It would be worth dying for . . . truly . . . I mean it . . ." He moved ever closer to her, and she felt breathless being so near him, but she couldn't let him see that.

"I know you do, dear man." She sat, holding his hands and smiling at him, wishing their lives had been different, but she would do nothing now to risk him. She loved him far too dearly. But as he looked at her, he sensed the love she felt for him, and he couldn't restrain himself any longer. He reached out and pulled her into his arms, and kissed her. "Don't . . ." she whispered when he stopped, wanting to be angry at him, wanting to send him away from her, if only to save him, but she had been starved for too long and found she couldn't do it. He kissed her again, and she didn't resist him, and then finally she pulled away and shook her head sadly. "We must not do this, Haversham. It's impossible." And very, very dangerous, if anyone saw them.

"Nothing is impossible, and you know that. We'll find a ship in Falmouth and set sail for the new world, and have a life together. No one can stop us." She smiled at how naive he was, how innocent, and how little he knew his brother. Not to mention the fact that neither of them had any money.

"You make it all sound so simple. And we'd live a life of infamy and shame. Think of what your daughters will learn of you when they're old enough to be told . . . and poor Alice . . ."

"She's a child, she'll find someone else. She does not love me either."

"She will in time. You'll grow used to each other eventually."

She wanted him to be happy where he was, no matter how much she loved him. In an odd way, he was more boy than man. He really didn't understand the dangers with which he was flirting, but he was angry that she wouldn't agree to go with him, and he sat looking sullen for a while, and then they walked upstairs hand in hand to check on Edward. It was nearly dawn by then, and there was no one up in the house, except the manservant sitting with her husband.

"How is he?" she asked quietly.

"There's been no change, your ladyship. I believe the doctor will return to bleed him again in the morning." She nodded, it was what she had been told as well. But Edward didn't look as though he'd live long enough to see it. And when they left the room again, Haversham looked hopeful.

"Bastard, when I think of what he's done to you for all these years." It made his blood boil.

"Don't think of it," she said quietly, and then she suggested that he go to sleep in one of their guest rooms. He was planning to stay until Edward either woke or died, and he had brought his own servants with him. They had been sent to bed downstairs when he arrived, but Haversham was grateful for a bed when she suggested it, and surprised that she didn't intend to go to bed herself. She seemed to go on forever, as tireless as always.

When Haversham had left her, she went back to her husband's bedroom, and offered to sit with him for a while to relieve the others. She could doze in the chair, next to him, and as she did, she found herself dreaming of his brother. What he had said to her was extraordinary. The idea of going to America was amazing. And however appealing it might sound, she knew that there was absolutely not the remotest possibility they could do it. If nothing else, no matter how irresponsible Haversham was, she would never have done that to Alice or her daughters, though she would gladly have fled Edward, even if it killed her.

Her head bobbed down on her chest for a while, and she was sound asleep when the sun came up and the roosters crowed. There was no one in the room with them, and suddenly as she slept, she felt a vise seize her arm and shake her. It seemed like part of her dream, and eventually she thought an animal of some kind had taken her arm, and had gripped it in its teeth until she thought her arm would be torn off her body. She woke with a start and a small murmur of pain and fear, and then was even more startled to realize it was Edward, clutching her arm and squeezing it until she had to fight not to cry out in anguish.

"Edward! . . ." He was awake, and as evil as ever. "Are you all right? You've been very ill for days, I believe. They brought you home on a farmer's cart, and the doctor had to bleed you."

"You must be sorry that I lived," he said coldly, his eyes taking her in with obvious hatred. He still had a grip on her arm, and it amused him that even in his weakened state, he was still able to hurt her. "Did you call my fool of a brother?" His eyes blazed as he let go of her arm just as suddenly as he had grabbed it.

"I had to, Edward . . . they thought you might be dying," she said, looking at him with the caution you would use with a poisonous snake, because indeed he was one.

"How disappointed you both must be . . . the grieving widow, and the new Earl of Balfour. Not so soon, my dear. You will not be so lucky quite so quickly," he said, squeezing her face hard in his fingers. It was amazing that he had so much strength after having been so deeply unconscious. She imagined that his wickedness must fuel it.

"No one wishes you any ill, Edward," she said, lowering her eyes as he released her, and then she moved slowly to the door, on the pretext of getting him some gruel for breakfast.

"I won't get my strength back on that slop," he complained, but from what she could see, and had just felt, he had regained quite enough strength already to suit her.

"I'll see if we can make you something better," she said calmly.

"Do that." He looked at her evilly, and then she saw his eyes glitter at her in anger. It was a look she knew well, and that had terrorized her when she was younger. Now she simply forced herself not to think of it, and to rise above it. It was the only way she had survived him. "I know the way my brother thinks," he said thoughtfully, "and how weak he is. He will not rescue you from me, my dear, if that's what you think. And if he should try, whatever his plan, wherever he goes, wherever you go, rest assured, I will find you, and kill him, or kill you both. Remember that, Sarah. . . . I mean it. . . ."

"I'm sure you do, Edward," she said smoothly. "You have nothing to fear from either of us. We were very worried about you," she said, and swiftly left the room, feeling her knees tremble beneath her. It was as though he knew, as though he had heard them the night before when Haversham tried to convince her to leave for America with him. How foolish Haversham was to think he could escape him. And she did believe that Edward would happily kill him. She could never put Haversham in that position, even if she had wanted to. She could never let him touch her, no matter how much they loved each other. In fact, she wondered now if she should flee, alone, for his sake. Then there would be no more accusations.

Her head was full of wild ideas as she went to the kitchen and prepared a tray for him herself, and when she brought it back to him, with Margaret carrying it for her, one of his manservants had shaved him. He looked remarkably civilized and he seemed almost himself by the time he finished breakfast. She had brought him fish and eggs and scones that had been made just that morning. But he thanked her for none of it. He was giving orders to everyone and although he was very pale, and she suspected he still felt quite unwell, the doctor couldn't believe his lordship's remarkable recovery when he returned to bleed him. He still wanted to, in fact, but Edward wouldn't have it, and threatened to throw him out bodily if he tried. The poor old man was quaking as he left the room, and Sarah apologized, as she always did, for her husband.

"He must not get up too quickly," the doctor warned, "and he must not each such hearty meals yet." He had seen the remains of the breakfast she had prepared for him, and the cook had just sent him a roast chicken. "He will fall into unconsciousness again if he is unwise now," the doctor said nervously. He was the same physician who had attended her deliveries, and seen her babies die as she held them, or come into the world blue and still and dead from before she bore them. He knew her well, and admired her. And he was terrified of Edward. He had actually refused to deliver the news of the last three stillbirths. The first time, Edward had hit him, as the bearer of outrageous tidings. He had even accused him of lying.

"We'll take care of him, Doctor," Sarah said as she saw him into the courtyard. And she stood there for a long moment after he left, feeling the sun on her face, wondering what she would do now. There had been a small ray of hope the night before, but there was none now.

And when she went back to see Edward again, Haversham was with him. He was quite stunned, as they all were, to see the recovery Edward had made, and he was less philosophical than Sarah.

When he met her in the hall that afternoon, bringing soup to him, after he had thrown the first bowl at her and burned her arm, Haversham looked at her in anguish. "You must listen to me, Sarah . . . you have no choice now . . . you cannot stay here. He's worse than ever. I think he's quite mad," he said angrily. Edward had warned Haversham that morning to stay away from her, or promised he would kill him if he did not. He had said he was not through with her yet. He was going to squeeze an heir from her loins yet, if it killed her, which was of no import to him, as long as she left him a son.

"He's not mad, just vicious," she said calmly. None of it was new to her, although he seemed less anxious to conceal it now. He was willing to let everyone watch him abuse her. In fact, he seemed to like it.

"I will find a ship," he said urgently, but she looked furiously at him this time, and winced when he touched her arm where Edward had burned it.

"You'll do no such thing. He'll kill you. He means it," Sarah warned. "Stay away from me, Haversham. I will not go anywhere with you. Stay where you are and forget me."

"I will never, ever do that," he said heatedly, and he looked desperate.

"You must." She spat the words at him, looked at him as ferociously as she could, and went back to Edward's bedroom. And that evening she was told that Haversham had left to go home to his wife and children. With Edward on the road to recovery, there was no further reason for him to be there. But she was worried about what he'd do about the ship. He was just foolish and romantic enough to try and follow through on his plan, but she would not let him risk his life for her, or abandon his family because he thought he loved her. They both had to accept the fact that they had no future together.

She went back to her own bedroom that night and slept fitfully, and she woke at dawn when the rooster crowed and she found herself thinking. There was no reason why Haversham's plan couldn't work for her, no reason she had to go with him. It was the maddest idea she'd ever had, but as she thought about it, she knew it was possible, if she made her plans carefully, and told no one. She still had a few of her mother's jewels left after Edward had taken most of them. She suspected that he had given them to harlots and friends, and she had heard from someone that he had sold them. But there was still enough left for her to make a life on. She would never live in grandeur again, but she had no desire to. All she wanted was to escape and to live in safety and freedom. And even if she drowned on the way to the new world, at least she would not be dying in terror and bondage, abused by a man she hated, and who hated her. She was willing to take her chances. And as she got up and dressed, she thought about it all morning. There was suddenly new purpose to her life.

Edward was full of venom and complaints, and he slapped two of his men while they tried to get him up and dress him. She could tell he still did not feel well, but he wouldn't admit it. By noon he was dressed and in the drawing room, looking deathly pale and somewhat grim, but in his usual unpleasant humor. He drank some wine with lunch, and after that he seemed to feel better. But he was no kinder to her. The kindest thing he ever did for her was ignore her.

And as he dozed in his chair after lunch, she slipped quietly from the room and went back to her bedroom. She had a great deal to think about, a lot to plan, and she opened the locked box where she kept what was left of her mother's jewelry. She wanted to make sure it was still there, and that Edward had not taken it and sold it. But there were still a few fine old pieces left, and just looking at them reminded her of her father.

She wrapped them in cloth and put them in the pocket of her cloak, and hung it carefully in her wardrobe and then locked the box again. There were a number of things she had to do now, and that night, she spoke to Margaret in a whisper. She asked her if what she had always said to her was true, that she would do anything for her, if she had to.

"Oh yes, ma'am," she said, dropping a curtsy.

"Would you go somewhere with me, if I asked you to?"

"Of course." She smiled easily as they whispered. She was imagining a secret journey to London, perhaps to meet Haversham, she thought. It was easy to see how much he loved her.

"What if it were far away?" Margaret wondered if that meant France. She knew there was trouble there, but for Sarah, she would brave it.

"I would go anywhere with you," Margaret said bravely, and Sarah thanked her, and urged her not to say anything to anyone about their conversation. And the young girl promised dutifully.

But the next night was more difficult. Sarah put on a heavy dress, and her wool cloak, and she stole silently down to the stables at midnight, and she was certain no one saw her.

She saddled her own horse, and prayed that they wouldn't

make too much noise, then she led Nellie out as quietly as she could. She didn't even mount her until she was far, far down the road, and then she quickly hopped onto her back, and rode her sidesaddle as hard as she could all the way to Falmouth. It took her just over two hours, and she was there at two-thirty in the morning. She had no idea if anyone would be awake, but she hoped to see someone, and find out what she could. But she was lucky, there was a group of sailors working on a small ship, preparing to set sail with the tide at four o'clock that morning.

They told her of a ship that was returning from France in the next few days. They implied it had been used as a gunrunner, and it was sailing for the New World in September. They knew most of the men on it, and said it was a good ship, and she would be safe on board, though they warned her there would be few comforts. And she assured them it didn't matter. They were curious about who she was, as well, but they didn't ask, and they told her who to talk to in the port, to book her passage. And after she left, they all agreed that there was something very mysterious about her. She was very beautiful, even with her face half concealed by the cloak, and she actually went and woke the man they had told her to talk to. He was quite shocked to be woken up by an unknown woman. And even more so, when she said she had no money to pay him with, and instead she offered him a ruby bracelet to pay for her passage to Boston.

"What am I to do with that?" he said, dangling it from one hand with a look of amazement.

"Sell it." It was probably worth more than the ship for which he was the agent. But there was no turning back now. She was going to do everything she had to, to be on it when it sailed.

"It's dangerous sailing to America," he said to her, still in his nightshirt and cap. "People die on shipboard." But she still did not look frightened.

"I will die if I stay here," she said, and the way she looked when she said it, he believed her.

"You're not in trouble with the law, are you?" It suddenly occurred to him that the bracelet might be stolen, although he was sure they had transported felons to the New World before. This would not be the first time. But she shook her head in answer. And even to him, she looked honest. "Where shall we bring your ticket?"

"Keep it here. I will get it when I come. When do you sail?"

"On the fifth of September, with the full moon. If you miss it we leave without you."

"I'll be here."

"We'll sail with the tide, early in the morning. And we make no stops between here and Boston." She was pleased to hear that too. There was nothing he had told her that had warned her off, and she wasn't even frightened. She had an idea of how hard it would be, or she thought she did. But she didn't care now. She left the bracelet with him, and signed her name on a piece of paper. She wrote only Sarah Ferguson, and hoped that they wouldn't know who she was, or connect her to the Earl of Balfour.

The ship was sailing in three weeks, and it was four o'clock in the morning when she left Falmouth. It was a hard ride back, and her horse stumbled once and almost threw her, but she got back just as the cock crowed in the courtyard. And as she looked up at the window of the room where Edward slept, she smiled for the first time in years. In three weeks, it would be over, and her tortures at Edward's hands would be at an end at last.

Chapter 9

THE LAST THREE weeks Sarah spent with him seemed interminable. And the minutes seemed to tick by like days. She had taken no one into her confidence, except Margaret knew they were going on a trip, and she promised not to tell even her parents.

Sarah had sewn the rest of her jewels into the lining of her cloak by then, and the only thing suspicious about it was that it had grown remarkably heavy. But Sarah spent all her time doing needlework, and trying to avoid Edward. He had recovered from his mishap in less than a week, and gone hunting again, and at the end of August, he came home with a group of friends who spent all their time with him eating and drinking in the main hall. They were a rowdy, demanding, badly behaved lot, and it was a relief when they left. When Edward had his cohorts around, Sarah always feared for the female servants, and other than keep the young pretty ones completely out of sight, which she did sometimes, there was precious little she could do to protect them.

She hadn't seen Haversham again since his visit while Edward was so ill. She had heard that the rest of the children had come down with measles as well, and Alice was still ill, and they were beginning to fear pneumonia. It was easy to imagine that he had his hands full, but she was sorry he didn't come to visit. She would have liked to see him one last time, just to lay eyes on him again, to say something, and then in the end, she decided it was just as well she couldn't. He might divine something, or sense something different about her. He knew her far better than Edward.

There were no telltale signs of her plan. She followed the same daily routine she always did. She only seemed a little happier these days, and she sang to herself sometimes as she went about her work at the far end of the castle. She had been darning tapestries for months, trying to preserve them. In fact, it was there that Edward found her. She was alone, and she didn't hear him come into the long, drafty hall where she was working. She was planning to go back to her own room as the light was fading. And she gave a little start when she saw him.

"Where have you been all afternoon? I couldn't find you." She couldn't imagine why he wanted to, he never bothered to look for her, and she was suddenly terrified, wondering if someone from the port had located her about her ticket. But it wasn't possible, she reminded herself. They had no idea where she lived, and they had no reason to come and get her.

"Is something wrong?" Her face was calm, but her eyes were still worried.

"I wanted to talk to you."

"What about?" She looked him squarely in the eye as she set her work down, and then she realized that he'd been drinking. He had been drunk incessantly all summer, not that it made much difference to her. It made him more violent sometimes, but she tried to be careful not to provoke him. And he had made no move to sleep with her since the death of the last baby. It was nearly three months now.

"Why are you hiding here?"

"I'm repairing some of your father's tapestries. I think the mice have been gnawing at them. I was hoping to preserve them," she said calmly.

"Is this where you meet my brother?" he asked her with a vicious look and she was startled by the question.

"I don't meet your brother anywhere," she said sharply.

"Of course you do. He's in love with you. Don't tell me that he doesn't ask you to meet him in secret. I know him. He's a sly, stupid boy, and that's just the kind of thing he would do."

"Haversham would never do that, Edward. Nor would I."

"That's sensible of you, because you know what I would have to do to you if you did, don't you?" She lowered her eyes as he advanced on her with a cruel look in his eyes, and she didn't want to show him she was frightened. He was standing right in front of her by then, and he grabbed her hair hard and yanked it backward, so her face was looking straight up at his, and her eyes rose slowly toward him. "Shall I show you what I would do, my dear?" She didn't answer. She knew that anything she said would only worsen the situation. There was nothing to do but wait for him to tire of torturing her. She prayed it would end quickly. "Why aren't you answering me? Are you protecting him? You thought I was going to die a few weeks ago, didn't you? What were you going to do with him then? Tell me . . . what did you do while I was ill?" He snarled his words right into her face, and then pulled back his arm and hit her in the face with the full force of it. She would have reeled backward against the wall, but he was still holding her hair in a firm grasp, and he rent her lip with his ring as he hit her.

"Edward . . . please . . . we didn't do anything . . ." she said, trying not to whimper as her blood dripped on her dress. She was wearing white cotton, and the blood looked bright and shocking, like his actions.

"You're a liar and a whore," he screamed, and hit her with his fist this time. He hit her cheekbone, and she thought she felt it splinter. She was dizzy when she looked at him and he hit her again, and then much to her surprise he yanked her into his arms and kissed her. Her blood mixed with his saliva, and she had an overwhelming urge to bite him, but she knew that if she defended herself in any way, he would hurt her more. She had learned that lesson the hard way. Instead, she felt herself falling backward and hit her head hard on the floor as he fell on her, and with one hand tore her skirt as he yanked it up, and then pulled her pantaloons down.

"Edward, you don't have to do this . . ." she whispered, choking on her own blood . . . they were married. He didn't have to humiliate and beat her. He didn't have to rape her on the stone floor of the old castle, but this was where he wanted her, and how he wanted to do it. And whatever his lordship wanted was what she was expected to deliver. She had lived in hell with him for the past eight years, but she would soon be free. "Edward . . . don't . . . please . . ." She was still whispering as he forced himself inside her, and battered her against the floor, while she was too afraid someone would hear them to make a sound. It was too humiliating to have everyone know what he did to her, and she knew that if she made a noise, he would only hurt her more. So she just let him. She thought she could feel sand loose in her head, as he banged her head against the floor again and again and ripped at her buttocks. And then finally he'd had what he wanted, and released her. He fell on top of her for a long moment, crushing the air out of her as he lay there, and then he got up and looked down at her like so much garbage at his feet.

"You'll give me a son now, won't you . . . or die trying . . ." he said, and then turned and walked away as she lay there. He was long gone before she caught her breath, pulled up her pantaloons, smoothed down her skirt, and began sobbing. She couldn't even imagine the horror of having another of his babies. All she wanted now was to go quietly and die somewhere . . .

even if it was on the *Concord*, on her way to Boston. And if there was a child this time, and they both lived, she vowed never to tell Edward about it. She would truly die before she would let him take a baby from her, or ever do anything to her again. It was over.

And as she walked slowly back to her room, covered with blood everywhere, her hair disheveled, her lip split and swollen, her cheek bruised, her head pounding, she knew she truly hated him as she had hated no one before him. He was the lowest of animals, the cruelest of beasts, and when he saw her in the hall afterward, having made an attempt to clean up his damage, he smiled at her evilly and bowed solicitously, with a look of cruel amusement.

"Have you had an accident, my dear? How unfortunate. You must be more careful about falling," he said, and swept by her. But she wore no expression as he passed her by. She had nothing to say to him, or to anyone, and she knew at that moment that there would never be a man in her life again. No lover, no husband, and now she hoped no son, no children. She wanted nothing more from life, except her freedom from him.

Edward left her alone after that. He had gotten what he'd come for, or so he thought. In the past, a single act, however brutal it might have been, had always been enough to get her pregnant, and he assumed it would do so this time. And all she wanted now was to find out it hadn't. But she wouldn't know that until she was on the Atlantic.

The last days finally crawled by without event, or further disaster, and the night of her flight came at last with the full moon high in the sky, and the stars shining brightly. She wanted to feel something, some relief, some sorrow as she left, perhaps even some nostalgia, but as she stole to the stables, with Margaret and their two small bags, she felt nothing. She would have liked to leave a note for Haversham, but knew she couldn't. She would write to him from the new world. And she left no note for

Edward, lest he find it before she reached Falmouth safely. And as it turned out, he had gone hunting the day before, and hadn't returned yet. It made their flight at midnight somewhat less frantic. And as they rode toward Falmouth, both women were in high spirits. Margaret especially, she thought it was going to be an excellent adventure.

And just as it had before, it took two hours to get there. It was an easy ride this time, and no one bothered them on the way. Sarah had been slightly afraid of that, but she had said nothing to Margaret about being concerned about highwaymen or robbers. The girl would never have come with her. Bandits would have gotten nothing from them anyway, Sarah had her jewels and the little money she had sewn into all her linings.

As they rode through Falmouth, Sarah let their horses slow to a walk, and they made their way to the dock in silence. And then, as soon as they got there, Sarah saw it. The *Concord* was much smaller than she had expected. She was two-masted and square-rigged, and the small ship barely looked sturdy enough to cross the channel, but there was no turning back now, and Sarah didn't care if she drowned. She was going. But Margaret looked puzzled when she saw the ship, Sarah had still not told her where they were going, though she had warned her that she would not see her parents for a long, long time, but the girl insisted she didn't mind. She assumed now that her guess had been correct, and they were going to Italy, or perhaps even France, despite the unrest there. In either case, she was aching to see a foreign country. And she only listened casually as Sarah conversed quietly with the captain, he seemed to be handing her quite a bit of money. He was an honest man, and he was returning the difference between their passage and what he'd gotten for her ruby bracelet. He had actually been able to sell it to a well-known jeweler in London, and they'd paid him a king's ransom for it.

Sarah was thanking him as Margaret joined them. "How long

will the journey take?" the young girl asked cheerfully, as Sarah and the captain exchanged a look, and he answered her.

"Six weeks if we're lucky, two months if we hit storms. Either way, we should be in Boston in October." He nodded, and Sarah silently hoped the crossing would go well, although she was going in any case. She had nothing to lose now. But Margaret was looking horrified at what she'd just heard from Captain Mac-Cormack.

"Boston? I thought we were going to Paris!" she said, with a look of terror. "Oh, I can't go to Boston, your ladyship . . . I can't do it . . . I can't . . . I'd die . . . I'd die, I know it, on a little boat like that. Oh no, please," she began to sob and clutch at Sarah's hands, "don't make me do it . . . please send me back." Sarah put her arms around her as she sighed. She had been afraid something like this would happen, and it would be awkward for her to travel alone, but she didn't have the heart to force the girl to come with her. She was far too frightened, and after a few minutes, Sarah told her to calm down and held both her hands.

"I won't make you go anywhere you don't want to go," she said quietly, trying to will the girl out of her hysterics, but it was no small task. "I want you to swear to me that you won't tell anyone where I've gone . . . no matter what his lordship does, or anyone says . . . or even Mr. Haversham . . . you must promise me you won't tell anyone where I am. Otherwise, if you think you might tell, you must come with me," she said sternly, and Margaret nodded frantically as she cried. Sarah had no intention of taking her anywhere now, but she'd rather frighten her a little bit, so the girl didn't go back to Edward and expose her. "You must swear now." She lifted her chin with one finger, and the girl clung to her like a child.

"I swear . . . but your ladyship . . . please don't go on that boat, I beg of you . . . you'll drown . . ."

"I would far rather drown than live as I do now," she said

calmly. She could still feel the bruise on her cheek, and it had taken days for her swollen lip to go down. And after his most recent rape, she still did not know if she was with child. But rather than tolerate his brutality, she would rather sail ten times around the world in the smallest boat they had. "I'm going, Margaret." And since the girl was going back, Sarah told her to take the horses back with her. She had originally planned to abandon them in Falmouth, and had told the man at the stables to sell them for whatever he could get, but there was no reason now to do that. "You must be very strong when they ask you about me. Tell them only that I left you, and I took the London road on foot. That will keep them busy for a while." Poor Haversham. Sarah was sure that Edward would accuse his brother without mercy, but in the end, his very real innocence would be his best defense. And once she was in the new world, there was nothing Edward could do to bring her back. She wasn't chattel after all, she wasn't a slave he had bought and owned, although he thought so. She was only his wife. All he could do was disown her, and refuse to pay her debts. But she wanted nothing more from the Earl of Balfour. She was going to sell the jewels she had, and do the best she could after that. At worst, she could become a governess, or a companion to a proper lady, if she had to. She had never tried it, but she was not afraid of work. She was only afraid of dying at Edward's hands. Or worse, not dying soon enough, and living long enough to be tortured by him until he died. And even at fifty-four, he could still live for a long time. Far too long for Sarah.

Sarah and Margaret shared a tearful farewell on the dock, and the young girl clung to her, crying piteously, terrified her mistress was about to die. But as Sarah boarded the tiny brig alone, she looked unafraid. There were half a dozen other passengers on the deck, and they wanted to be off before first light.

She was still standing there, waving, as the ship set sail and Margaret could see her through her tears, as they left the dock.

"Good luck!" she shouted in the morning breeze, but by then Sarah couldn't hear her. She was smiling broadly, and feeling happy and free and alive for the first time. And as the ship turned slowly around and left the English coast, Sarah closed her eyes and thanked God for giving her a new life.

Charlie sat in total silence for a long time, as he closed the book. It was four o'clock in the morning, and he had been reading for hours. What an extraordinary human being she had been. What an incredible thing to do, to dare to leave her husband, at that time, and set sail for Boston, on a tiny ship, with neither companion nor friend to go with her. And from what he could gather from what she'd written, she knew no one at all in the new world. He couldn't even imagine the courage she had, or the life from which she'd fled. The stories she'd told of Edward made him shiver, and he wished that he could have reached out to her, or been there to help. He would have loved to know her, and to be her friend, even to be on the brig with her that left Falmouth for the new world.

He closed the journal carefully, looking at it as the precious thing that it was. He felt as though he were sharing a remarkable secret, and as he went upstairs to her room, he longed to see her. He knew so much more about her now, knew who she was, where she had been. He could only imagine what the trip over on the ship had been like. He was tempted to stay up all night and read about it, but he knew he had to get some sleep before morning.

He lay in bed that night, thinking about her, wishing he could hear her, and thinking of the incredible good luck that had brought him to the trunk. Or was it? Perhaps there had never been a chipmunk or a rat, perhaps she had wanted him to find her journals. Perhaps she had led him to them, but then as he thought about it, he smiled again, knowing that was impossible.

Even for him, the idea that she had brought her journals to him was just too far-fetched for him to believe. But however he had come to them, he was infinitely glad he had. And all he wanted to do now was pick them up again.

Chapter 10

WHEN CHARLIE AWOKE the next morning, he wondered if it had all been a dream. It was cold outside, and it was still snowing. He wanted to fax some notes to his lawyer in London, and he should have made a couple of calls to New York. But all he wanted to do once he was up, and had taken a shower, and dressed, was grab a cup of coffee and read Sarah's journals for the rest of the morning. They were almost hypnotic in the rhythm with which she wrote, and he wanted to sit in one spot until he finished all of them, or at least the one he'd been reading.

But finally, after he'd done a little bit of work, he let himself sit down in a comfortable chair he had bought, and start reading about her crossing on the ship. He felt like a kid with an enormous secret. He was going to share the journals with Gladys eventually, but not just yet. He wanted them to himself first. There was not a single sound in the house as he picked up the journal he had put down the night before, and started reading again.

✿   ✿   ✿

The *Concord* was a small brig that had been built five years before, it had two masts, and a square stern. There was a small section underneath them, between decks, and four cabins for a total of twelve people traveling to the new world. And as they set sail slowly from Falmouth, Sarah finally went downstairs to take a look at the cabin which she and Margaret had been meant to share. But nothing had prepared her for what she saw there. The cabin itself was about six feet long, and four across, and two excruciatingly narrow mattresses rested on two terrifyingly narrow wooden shelves, which were meant to be their beds. It didn't even bear thinking what they would have done, if either of them had been fat. The shelves would have collapsed. And just above the beds were two ropes that would be used to lash them into their beds in the event of storms on the Atlantic.

The others had all been told that they had to share their cabins, but as one of only two women on the ship, Sarah of course did not. The other woman was traveling with her husband, and their five-year-old little girl. The child's name was Hannah, and Sarah had already seen her on the deck. They were American, from the Northwest Territory in the Ohio region, she'd been told, and their name was Jordan. They'd been visiting Mrs. Jordan's family for the past several months, and were now on their way back home. Even to Sarah, it seemed brave of them to have come.

The rest of the people on the ship were all men, there were four merchants, a pharmacist who might prove useful, a minister going to work with the heathens in the West, and a French journalist who talked a lot about the American diplomat and inventor Ben Franklin, whom he said he had met five years before, in Paris. By the time they hit the first swells, almost all the passengers were feeling ill, and they could already barely see the coast of England. But Sarah was amazed at how alive she felt. She stood on deck as the sun came up, breathing in the air, enjoying her first taste of freedom. She felt as though she could have flown, she was so excited. And when she finally went below-decks again, she ran into Martha Jordan just coming out of their cabin with Hannah. She wondered how three of them could sleep there.

"Good afternoon, Miss," Martha Jordan said primly, lowering her eyes. She and her husband had both commented on how odd it was that Sarah was traveling without chaperone or escort. And just the way she looked at her made Sarah realize that she had to come up with an explanation for it. Not having Margaret with her was going to make things very awkward, particularly in Boston. She knew that even there a woman traveling alone would be considered most unseemly.

"Hello, Hannah," Sarah said gently, smiling at the little girl. She was plain but very sweet, she looked just like her mother, and they were both looking a little pale. Sarah wondered if they were seasick. "Are you well?"

"Not very," the little five-year-old said, and her mother looked up in spite of herself and both women curtsied.

"I'd be happy to have her stay with me anytime you and your husband want a little time together," Sarah said kindly. "I have another bed in my cabin. I have no children of my own, unfortunately, but my late husband and I always hoped that we'd have them." She didn't mention the six that had died at birth and been stillborn. But what she had said had immediately caught the attention of Martha Jordan, which was what she had intended.

"You're a widow then?" Martha Jordan said with visible approval. Then that explained it. She still should have had a maid or a female relative with her, but if she were a widow, it was much less shocking and could be explained.

"I am. Only recently." Sarah lowered her eyes demurely, and wished that it were true, but sadly, it wasn't. "My niece was to have made the journey with me," she said, assuming Martha might have seen Margaret sobbing on the dock when she left

her, "but she was much too frightened. She'd have been hysterical all the way to Boston. I just couldn't bring myself to force
her, although I promised my parents that I would take her with
me. But it seemed too unkind to hold her to her agreement,
though it's put me in a dreadful position," Sarah said, looking
mortified, and Martha Jordan became instantly sympathetic.

"Oh, my dear, how terrible for you, particularly being a recent
widow." And the poor thing hadn't even any children. She didn't
know how old she was, but she thought her very beautiful, and
guessed her correctly to be in her mid-twenties. "If there's anything we can do for you, please let us know at once. Perhaps
you'd like to visit us in Ohio." But Sarah didn't think so. She was
determined to get to Boston.

"You're very kind," Sarah said as she thanked her, and then
went into her cabin. She had worn a large black silk hat that tied
under her chin, and a black wool gown, which corroborated her
story. Though she didn't look like she had been grieving. Her
eyes literally danced as they reached the high seas and England
disappeared on the horizon.

And for the first few days, the trip was quite peaceful. They
had brought some pigs and some sheep with them, to slaughter
and eat during the trip, and the cook seemed to be making an
effort with their meals. But Sarah noticed that the crew were
quite noisy at night, and Seth Jordan told her that they drank
rum and got utterly drunk every evening. He had been very firm
about suggesting that she and his wife should keep to their cabins after supper.

Most of the merchants stood along the deck and chatted every
day, and despite a little seasickness here and there, everyone
appeared to be in good humor. Captain MacCormack chatted
regularly with each of them, and he had told Sarah he was from
Wales, and he didn't say anything to her, but he was overwhelmed by her beauty. He had a wife and ten children on the
Isle of Wight, but he admitted to her wistfully that he rarely saw

them. He hadn't been home in two years. And at times he found it hard to concentrate, whenever Sarah stood on the deck, looking far out to sea, or even when she sat quietly somewhere writing in her journal. She had the kind of rare looks that made men catch fire as they looked at her, and with each passing hour, they smoldered more. The captain was sure that she was unaware of her effect on all of them. There was a quiet strength and humility about her that only made her more attractive.

They'd been at sea for nearly a week when they hit the first storm, and it was a beauty. Sarah had been asleep in her bunk when it hit, and one of the sailors walked into her room, and told her he had to lash her to the wall with the ropes that hung there for that purpose. And as she looked at him, she was very frightened. He had woken her from a sound sleep, and he reeked of rum, but his hands were gentle and sure as he tied the knots, and then hurried back on deck to the others. And as she listened, she could hear every inch of the small ship groan and strain beneath them.

It was a long night for all of them, and all of the passengers were extremely ill from the constant rising and sinking of the ship, and she closed her eyes and prayed each time it shuddered and fell. None of them came out of their cabins for two days, some of them for considerably longer, and a week after the storm, Martha Jordan still hadn't emerged, and Sarah asked her husband how she was faring.

"She's never been very strong," he explained, "she had the influenza last year, and it nearly killed her. She's been very seasick ever since the storm," he explained, looking vague and a little worried. He had his hands full with Hannah. And that afternoon, Sarah knocked on the cabin door and went in to see his wife. She was lying on her bunk, deathly pale, and there was a slop bucket just beneath her. It wasn't a pretty sight, and as soon as Sarah walked in the door, the poor woman began retching.

"Oh my dear, let me help you," Sarah said, genuinely concerned, it was obvious that the poor thing felt as though she were dying. Sarah held her head for her, and when Martha Jordan could speak again, Sarah learned that she was not just seasick, she was pregnant. But the happiest news for Sarah was that she had discovered only the day before that she wasn't. She was enormously relieved to realize that she would never again have any link to Edward. She was truly free now. And if he wanted an heir, he was going to have to find another female. But as she looked at the poor woman retching in her arms, Sarah knew that hers was an entirely difficult situation.

"We could have stayed in England with my family until the baby was born," Martha said unhappily, as she leaned against Sarah with her eyes closed. "But Seth thought we should get back to Ohio," and then she started crying. "It'll take weeks to get back there after we reach Boston." And even that was two months away, two months of rising and falling and swaying on the ship. Sarah couldn't imagine anything worse at this stage of her confinement, and she was more grateful than ever not to have to deal with it herself. Just knowing she had Edward's child in her would have driven her to distraction.

But as she looked down at Martha in her distress, she turned her thoughts to what she could do to help her. First, she went to her cabin to get some lavender water she'd brought with her, and a clean cloth, and she bathed her forehead in the cool, scented water. But even that faint smell made her nauseous. Then she attempted to wash the woman's face and pull her hair back. She switched the slop bucket to an empty pail, and she promised to bring her back a cup of tea, if she could get someone in the galley to make one.

"Thank you," the poor woman whispered hoarsely, "you can't imagine what this is like . . . I was sick the entire time with Hannah . . ." But Sarah knew it all too well, and had done it far too often, which made her even more sympathetic to this woman. And mercifully, after a cup of tea, and some biscuits the cook provided for her, by late afternoon, she actually felt a little better and had stopped retching. Seth Jordan said Sarah was an angel of mercy, and thanked her profusely, and then she took Hannah with her, and played games with her for a little while. She was a sweet child, and all she wanted was to be with her mother. Sarah took her back to her mother after a little bit, but Martha was too ill to care for the child, she was vomiting again, and Hannah had to go back on deck with her father. He was talking to some of the men and they were smoking cigars one of them had bought in the West Indies. They were very fine ones, and the smell was so pungent even in the sea air that Sarah was tempted to try one, but she knew what a harlot the men would think her. She told Seth Jordan as delicately as possible how ill his wife was again, and he thanked her for doing what she could to help her.

They enjoyed a few more calm days after that, and then hit another storm, and after that they didn't see good weather for two weeks, nor did they see many of the passengers out of their cabins. They had been on board for three and a half weeks by then, and the captain estimated they had done half the journey. Providing they didn't hit any really awful storms, it was going to take them a total of seven weeks to reach Boston. Despite the bad weather, Sarah walked around the deck at times, looking up at the sails and watching the crewmen. And she couldn't help wondering what Edward had thought of her disappearance. She wondered if he had figured it out by then, or if Margaret had told him where she'd gone, or if she'd kept her promise. But there was nothing he could do now. He couldn't force her to come back. He couldn't do anything. All he could do was hate her, and he had before anyway, so she saw virtually no difference.

One morning, she was joined by another brave passenger, Abraham Levitt, one of the merchants. "Have you relatives in Boston?" he asked her. He was a prosperous man, and had done extremely well in commerce. He was precisely the sort of man she never would have met before, and it fascinated her to be able to talk to him, and hear about all his trips and trades, and travels through the Orient and the West Indies. And he was impressed by the questions she asked him. She was most unusual for a woman. And she kept trying to ask everyone everything she could about Boston and the settlements to the north and west of it. She wanted to know all about the Indians and the forts and the people in Connecticut and Massachusetts. She had read about a picturesque place called Deerfield, where there were waterfalls and quite an elaborate stockade, as well as Indians, which intrigued her. "Will you be visiting people there?" the man asked once he learned she had no connections whatsoever in Boston.

"I think I might like to buy a farm there one day," she said pensively, as she looked out to sea, as though she were trying to make her mind up, and he looked at her in consternation.

"You can't do that. You can't just buy a farm. Why, a woman alone would have nothing but trouble. How would you run the farm? And the Indians would just carry you off the first time they saw you." It was what he would have liked to have done, but Captain MacCormack ran an extremely proper ship, unlike some, and he was keeping a fatherly eye on Sarah. All of them had been disappointed. She was so beautiful that sometimes all they wanted was to be able to look at her, and stand near her. They bumped into her sometimes, just so they could reach out and touch her. All the men were aware of it, and Sarah had no suspicion of it whatsoever.

"I don't think the Indians will carry me off," she said, laughing at him. He was a pleasant man, she knew he had a wife in Connecticut, and he was in his early thirties. And it was obvious from the enterprise he ran that he was going to make a lot of money, and although she knew she shouldn't have, she admired him for it. She knew that things were different in America, and she hoped that one day, in a place like that, he would be respected for all that he'd accomplished, and she said as much to him as they stood by the rail, chatting until dinner.

"You're a remarkable woman, Mrs. Ferguson. I really like you," he said bluntly. And then the first lieutenant announced that dinner was served, and Abraham Levitt walked her in to dinner.

Seth and Hannah Jordan were already there, Martha hadn't come to dinner in weeks. She never left her cabin anymore, and she was looking very ill and very frail each time Sarah saw her. It was frightening to see her, but even the pharmacist seemed to have no clue as to what to do for her. He had exhausted all his remedies, and so had Sarah.

Sarah shared a lively dinner with all of them, as she always did, as they all exchanged stories and legends and tales, and even ghost stories. They all agreed that Sarah told the best ones. And she told the best children's stories too. She told one to Hannah that night and helped her get to bed, so her father could stay up on deck with the other men. And in her cabin, Martha was sleeping. She had been vomiting for weeks, and she seemed to be wasting away before their eyes, but no one could help her. But Sarah imagined that other women had been through it before, at least that was what the captain said. No one had ever died of seasickness. But the storm they encountered that night made her doubt that.

Captain MacCormack said afterward that it was one of the worst ones he'd ever been in. It lasted for three days, and all the sailors on deck had to be lashed to the masts, the passengers tied to their bunks in the cabins, and two men were washed overboard as they attempted to save the sails. One of them had torn in half, and equipment was floating everywhere around them. And this time when the ship came down after a swell, it felt as though it were crashing into rocks. The *Concord* shuddered so hard as she hit the water that it seemed as though every piece of wood on her would splinter. Even Sarah was terrified this time, and she cried in her bunk wondering if she would be taken at her word, and drown at sea rather than stay with Edward. But even if she did, she didn't regret it.

On the fourth day, the sun came out, and the sea calmed a little bit, though not completely. And as the passengers came out of their cabins after that, they all looked more than a little ragged. All except Abraham Levitt. He said he had been in far worse storms on his way to the Orient, and he told tales that left everyone horrified. They were all looking a little weak and pale, but when Seth and Hannah came up, he looked terribly worried and he came to find Sarah.

"It's Martha," he said, with a distracted air, "she's not well. I think she's delirious . . . she hasn't taken even a sip of water in days, and I just can't seem to make her do it."

"You must try," Sarah said with a worried look. She knew that women had died of dehydration.

But the pharmacist shook his head. "She should be bled. It's a shame we don't have a doctor on board to do it."

"We'll do without," Sarah said firmly, and went downstairs to check on the ship's only other woman. But Sarah was even more shocked when she saw her. The woman looked gray, her eyes had sunken back in her head, and she was whispering softly. "Martha . . ." Sarah spoke gently to her, but the other woman gave no sign that she had heard her. "Martha . . . you must get better now . . . come . . . we're going to try to drink a little water. . . ." She held a spoon of it to Martha's lips and tried to force it in, but it only ran down her cheeks and her chin, she would not take it.

Sarah sat with her for hours that night, trying to urge a little water into her, but the woman never recognized her, never spoke coherently, and never took a single sip despite all of Sarah's efforts.

It was late when her husband finally came back downstairs, and Hannah was nearly asleep in his arms. He laid her on the bunk he shared with her, and she fell asleep instantly, as Sarah and Seth worked frantically on her mother. But by morning, it was obvious that the inevitable was going to happen. They had done everything they could, but there was no way to turn the tides back. Martha was four months pregnant by then, and so piteously frail that Sarah felt sure that if her body had still had the energy to fend for itself, she would have surely lost the baby. Perhaps it was even dead already. There was no way of knowing. And just as the sun came up, she opened her eyes, and smiled peacefully at her husband.

"Thank you, Seth," she said sweetly, and took her last breath, and then she was gone as he held her. It was the saddest thing Sarah had ever seen, except when her babies died. But this had an ache of sadness to it that touched her deeply, and when Hannah woke up shortly after that, she turned and looked at her mother. Sarah had combed her hair by then, and tied a gauze scarf of her own around the woman's neck, and she actually looked almost pretty.

"Is she better?" the little girl asked hopefully. Martha looked as though she were sleeping.

"No, dear," Sarah said with tears in her eyes. She hadn't wanted to intrude on them, but Seth hadn't wanted her to leave him. "She's not. . . ." She waited for Seth to say something, but he didn't. He looked at her imploringly through his tears, and his eyes begged Sarah to tell her. "She's up in heaven now. See how she's smiling . . . she's with the angels. . . ." Just like her own little babies. "I'm so sorry," she said with tears in her own eyes for this woman she had scarcely known, but felt so sad for. She would never see her daughter grow to be a woman. She would never get back to Ohio. She had left them.

"Is she dead?" Hannah asked, with wide eyes, looking from Sarah to her father, and they both nodded. And then she started to cry for her mother. They took her up on deck finally, after

Sarah got her dressed, and Seth had to talk to the captain about what they were going to do with Martha.

He suggested they put her in the captain's cabin until noon, and then they would have a burial at sea. It was the only thing they could do, and Seth hated the thought of it. He knew how much she had always wanted to be buried on their farm or with her family in England.

"There's no choice here," the captain explained to him bluntly. "We can't keep her until we reach Boston. We have no way to do that. You'll have to bury her here." It was rare for them to have a trip without a burial, either of a passenger or a crew member. Someone always fell ill, or had an accident, or slipped overboard. It was to be expected when you traveled a great distance, and they all knew it, but still it was a shock when it happened.

Two of the sailors carried Martha's body up to the captain's cabin, and wrapped her in a cloth they carried for the purpose. They put weights in what became her shroud, and at noon they took her out and lay her on a plank amidships, while the captain said a prayer for her, and the preacher took over. He read from Psalms, and talked about what a decent woman she had been, although none of them really knew her. And then the men tipped the plank slowly on one end, and her body slipped into the sea as they moved swiftly past where they had dropped her. And weighted as the body was, she disappeared before they'd even left the spot, as poor little Hannah screamed for her mother. She sobbed in Sarah's arms for hours, and Seth looked as though he had done the same when he came to Sarah's cabin to thank her. It had been a difficult day for all of them, and she was lying on her bunk with a headache. But she got up again to talk to Seth Jordan. She felt so sorry for him, and for his sake and Hannah's, she hoped they reached Boston quickly. It was time now. They had been on the boat for five and a half weeks, and she hoped that in the next week or ten days, they would see Boston on the horizon.

"You can come to Ohio with us, if you'd like," he said awkwardly, and she was touched by the invitation. She had grown fond of them in the past few weeks, particularly Hannah. "I'm going to have a real hard time taking care of her now," he said tentatively, and Sarah wondered if he'd go back to England, to Martha's family, so they could help him. But she was sure that they were hardly anxious to undertake another journey across the Atlantic.

"I think I'll be staying in Massachusetts," she said, smiling at him. "You can visit me on my farm, when I find one." She didn't say she had to sell some more jewelry first and hoped that someone in Boston would want it for good money.

"There's more land at better prices in Ohio." But Sarah knew it was a harder life, and the Indians were less peaceful. "Maybe you'll come west and see us," he said hopefully, and she nodded, and offered to take care of Hannah for him that night, but he said they wanted to be together.

But for the next week, the little girl clung to her, and Sarah felt as though her heart would break as she held her. She was keening for her mother, and Seth looked distraught as each day wore on. And finally, he talked to Sarah one night. They had been on the ship for seven weeks then. He had knocked on her door, after he left a sleeping Hannah in his cabin. She had been inconsolable ever since her mother died, and the only person she wanted with her now was Sarah.

"I don't know how you'll feel about this," he said, looking anxious, as he glanced around the small cabin. She was wearing a blue silk dressing gown over her nightgown. "Maybe it'll sound strange to you, but I've been thinking a lot about this since Martha died." He was starting to strangle on his words, and Sarah was beginning to get worried. She could sense what was coming next. She would have liked to stop him, but she didn't know how to. "We're both kind of in the same situation . . . I mean . . . with Martha and your husband and all . . . I mean . . . you know what it's like . . . except you don't, because I have Hannah . . . I just can't do this alone," he said, as tears filled his eyes. "I don't know what I'm going to do without her. . . . I know this isn't the way to say it . . . and I'm sure there are better ways to ask . . . but Sarah, would you marry me and come to Ohio with us?" Martha had been dead for ten days, and Sarah was momentarily speechless as she listened. She felt desperately sorry for him, but not enough to want to marry him, even if she could have. What he needed was a girl to work for him, or a woman who did want to marry him, maybe one of their friends when he got home, or a widow like the one she was pretending to be. But for Sarah, it was out of the question and she gently shook her head as she looked at him with consternation.

"Seth, I can't," she said firmly.

"Yes, you can. Hannah loves you, even more than she loves me. And we'll get used to each other in time. I wouldn't expect too much, not at first. . . . I know this is fast, but . . . we'll be in Boston soon, and I just had to ask you." His hands were trembling as he touched her, but she was very sure. She didn't want to mislead him. There was no chance of her marrying Seth Jordan.

"It's impossible. For many reasons. I'm very flattered, but I can't." Something in her eyes told him that she meant it. This was the last thing she wanted, even if he was a kind man, and Hannah was a sweet child. She wanted her own life now. That was what she had come for, and nothing was going to make her lose that. Besides, she still had a husband, and he was very much alive, unfortunately, in England.

"I'm sorry . . . I probably shouldn't have asked . . . I just thought you being a widow and all . . ." He was blushing furiously and trying to back out of her cabin as she reassured him.

"It's all right, Seth. I understand." She smiled at him, and closed the door, and sat on her bunk with a sigh. It was time to get to Boston. They had been on the ship for long enough. In fact, too long.

Chapter 11

*I*N THE END, the crossing took exactly seven weeks and four days. The captain said he could have done it in less, but they had run into several storms, and he had wanted to proceed with caution. But all the discomforts of the trip were quickly forgotten as they sighted shore, and everyone began to shout, and run around on deck. It was nearly two months since they'd left England. It was the twenty-eighth of October, 1789, and the weather in Boston was crisp and sunny.

The passengers disembarked onto the long wharf, looking a little unsteady as they reached firm ground, and all of them talked excitedly and laughed. The port was a veritable maelstrom of excitement. There were settlers and men in uniform, and soldiers from the garrison. There were hundreds of people selling things, and animals being herded on and off ships. There were carts being loaded, and carriages bringing passengers to and from the boats all around them. And Captain MacCormack was very solicitous of her, as he helped her organize her belongings and hire a carriage to take her to the boardinghouse he had recommended.

Others were moving on to find stagecoaches, or hire horses, to go home or to boardinghouses nearby. Abraham Levitt made a point of saying good-bye to her, and the pharmacist, and the preacher heading west, and several of the sailors came to shake her hand. And then poor little Hannah threw her arms around Sarah's legs and begged her not to leave her. But Sarah explained that she had to, and promised to write to her, although a letter might take a long time to reach her, but she would try.

She kissed her and held her for a long moment, and then she stood and shook hands with Seth. He was still faintly embarrassed around her, and wished she'd agreed to marry him, and come to Ohio to live on his farm with them. She was a glorious-looking woman, and he was going to dream about her for a long time, and she had been so kind to his little daughter.

"Take care of yourself," Sarah said gently, with the voice he'd become so fond of.

"You too, Sarah. Don't do anything foolish . . . be careful if you buy a farm. Don't get anything too far out of town."

"I won't," she said, and knew she was lying. That was exactly what she wanted, to taste the exhilaration and independence of this new land. What good was it if she bought a house in town somewhere, or sat in the stockade, or right next to the garrison? She wanted a place where she could move around and enjoy her freedom.

She got into the carriage Captain MacCormack had found for her, and he directed her to the Widow Ingersoll's at Court and Tremont. She had no reservation, knew no one, had no plans. But she wasn't even frightened as she waved at all of them, and drove slowly away from the port up State Street into Boston. Something told her that everything was going to be all right here.

And as he read the last line of that particular entry, Charlie sat and thought about how brave she was and almost cried. There was nothing she had been afraid of. She had lived through so much pain, and she had still been willing to brave more. She was never afraid to try. The very thought of her trip over on the *Concord* terrified him. He was sure he would never have survived it. She was absolutely amazing, and he wondered where she was going to buy her farm. It was like reading the best novel he'd ever read before, but the best part was that the people were all real, and it had all happened.

He stood up and stretched and put the journal down. He knew her handwriting so well by now, he read it as easily as his own. And when he glanced at his watch, he was amazed by how the day had flown. He still wanted to drop by Gladys Palmer's, and he had to go to the historical society and return the books he'd borrowed the week before. He wondered if Francesca would be there.

He had a cup of tea with Gladys when he picked up the book, and he was dying to tell her what he'd found in the attic. But he wanted to read them all first, and think about them, before he shared them with anyone, even Gladys. It was as though Sarah belonged to him for the moment. It was more than a little odd to realize that he was entranced with a woman who was so long gone. But reading her words, her adventures, and her feelings, brought her more alive to him than any living woman.

They chatted about some of the news from town, Gladys always had lots of things to tell him. One of her friends had had a heart attack the previous afternoon, and an old acquaintance from years past had written to her from Paris. And hearing her speak of France reminded him to ask her about Francesca. She said she had seen her once or twice, and everyone in town had commented on how pretty she was when she first came. But she had a reputation for keeping to herself, and no one seemed to really know her. Gladys had no idea why she'd come to town. "She's a pretty woman though," she said with cautious admiration. He agreed with that, but would have liked to know more about her. She intrigued him, and he was enchanted by her child.

He left Gladys just after four-thirty, but when he got to the historical society, it was closed, and he was left standing outside with the books in his hand and nowhere to leave them. He thought of leaving them on the front step, but he was afraid they might get stolen or ruined if it snowed. So he put them back in his car, and stopped at the grocery store at the shopping center on the way home, promising himself to come back the next day, or the day after.

He was just buying cereal for himself, when he looked up and saw Francesca. It reminded him of his conversation about her with Gladys. She seemed to hesitate before she smiled, and then, looking cautious and somewhat afraid, she said hello to Charlie with a careful little nod.

"I just missed you," he said casually, putting the cereal he wanted in his basket, as he noticed that she was alone. There was no sign of her daughter. "I tried to return the books. I'll come back again in a couple of days."

She nodded, looking serious again, and yet there was something in her eyes that was warmer than the last time they'd met. He wasn't sure what it was, but there wasn't the terror he'd seen in her eyes when he invited her for a drink on New Year's Eve, and he wondered what, if anything, had changed. What had happened was that she'd thought a lot about it and realized that she had really been rude to him. She didn't want to establish a friendship with him, but she had to admit, he'd been incredibly nice to Monique and there was no reason to shun him completely. And since he didn't appear to be in any way unsavory, he was obviously nice to the child because he was good-hearted. She had worked that much out after their last meeting.

"How was New Year's Eve?" she asked, trying not to sound nervous.

"Fine," he said with the grin that most women loved and she pretended not to notice. "I went to sleep. And I came home the next day. I've been pretty busy for the last couple of days . . .

getting settled in the house." And reading all about Sarah . . . but he said nothing to her about it. It was still his secret.

"Have you found any other material on Sarah and François?" It was just a casual question, but she was surprised to see him jump when she said it.

"I . . . uh . . . actually . . . no." It was as though he had a guilty secret, and he immediately grabbed at a straw to deflect the interest back to her. "Monique says you write." He knew that his just asking her that would probably make her uncomfortable, and keep her at bay at least for a while, but this time he was surprised. There was a warm look in her eyes in answer to his question.

"It's just some material on the local Indian tribes. I'm doing my thesis. But I've thought about turning it into a book afterward, if I get enough. It's pretty dry." Unlike Sarah's journals, which had turned him upside down. He couldn't help wondering what Francesca would think if she knew about them.

"How's Monique?" he asked, running out of conversation. He could sense that she was constantly watching him and trying to decide if he was foe or friend. It seemed sad to be so afraid of everything that came through your life. It was so unlike what he had read of Sarah in her journals. Nothing had frightened her or stopped her, not even Edward with all his brutal cruelty, although Charlie had to admit, it had even taken her a while to escape him. She hadn't run out the door the first time he hit her. It had taken her eight years to walk out on him, but thank God she had. Charlie was aching to read about her meeting François.

"Monique is fine," Francesca answered. "She wants to go skiing again." His first instinct was to offer to take her, but he knew he couldn't do that. Francesca would have run away right on the spot. He had to move around her with extreme caution, and seem not to care at all how she'd react. He wasn't even sure why he was working so hard at not scaring her off, he told himself it was because he liked her daughter. But even he knew, it was more than that. He wondered if he was attracted by the challenge, but that was so obvious, he hated to admit it.

"She's such a great little skier," he said admiringly. She was a wonderful little girl, and this time when Francesca smiled at him, her eyes were warmer. She started to say something as they walked to the checkout together, and then she thought better of it, and stopped. "What were you going to say just then?" He decided to take the bull by the horns, and see if he could pull her back, and force her to be more open.

"I . . . I was just going to say I was sorry I was so disagreeable when we met at Charlemont that day . . . about lunch . . . I just don't want her going off with strangers, or letting people pay for things that might make her feel obligated in ways she doesn't understand yet."

"I know," he said quietly, meeting her eyes squarely, and he could see her start to pull away, but this time she held her ground. It was as though he had lured her from her hiding place in the forest, and she was a lovely young doe, standing very still, listening to each sound with caution. "I understand." He smiled, and when she looked away from him, he saw pain in her eyes. What had happened to her that was so awful? How much worse could it have been than what Sarah had survived? Was it worse than what Carole had done to him with Simon? What was so special about her heart? Why was it that much more fragile? "It's a lot of responsibility having a child," he said as they waited on line. It was a way of telling her he respected what she was doing. There were other things he would have liked to say as well, but he doubted that he'd get the chance. But she was the only woman even close to his age that he knew here. The others were either seventy years old like Gladys, eight like Monique, or Sarah, who was gone. Francesca was the only real, live, eligible woman, and he figured if he didn't at least try to talk to her now and then, he'd lose the knack completely. It was a funny reason for establishing a friendship with her, but as they moved closer to the register at the end of the counter, Charlie told himself it made sense. Better yet would have been if two damaged, wounded people could become friends here. But that was a lot to ask of Francesca. Neither of them had any idea what had happened in the other's life. All he knew was what he had gleaned from Monique about when they lived in Paris.

Without saying anything further, he helped her put her groceries on the counter. She had hamburger and steak and chicken, frozen pizza, ice cream, marshmallows, three kinds of cookies, lots of fruit and vegetables, and a huge container of milk. He suspected they were all the things Monique liked.

All he had were club sodas and frozen food and ice cream, and the cereal he'd been buying when they first met. It was obviously bachelor food, and she smiled as she glanced into his basket.

"Not exactly health food, Mr. Waterston." He was startled to realize she had remembered his last name. He didn't think she had paid that much attention.

"I eat out a lot." Or at least he had in London and New York, but maybe here she was right to look surprised when he said it.

"I'd love to know where," she said with a small laugh, although they both knew there were plenty of nice restaurants in Deerfield, but many were closed, especially in the winter months, and most of the locals stayed home except for special occasions. It was too cold to go out a lot of the time and Francesca looked at him with amusement.

"I guess I'm going to have to start cooking again," he said pensively. "I'll come back tomorrow and buy more stuff." He looked boyish when he smiled at her, and he waited around to help her carry her bags to her car. She had three bags and they would have been heavy for her, it seemed natural, but she looked uncomfortable anyway at his assistance.

He helped her put the groceries in the backseat, and then closed the door, and looked down at Francesca. "Say hi to Monique for me," he said, but he didn't tell her he'd see her again, or promise to drop by, or even offer to call her. She got into her car with a cautious smile, but without looking quite as terrified this time.

And he couldn't help wondering to himself, as he walked back to his car, what it would take to thaw her.

Chapter 12

*I*T WAS ANOTHER snowy day again, as Charlie looked out the window. There wasn't even a pretense today of having work to do. What he wanted was to go back to Sarah's journals, and find out what had happened to her when she left the ship in Boston.

But he stood at the window for a moment, with the small leather-bound volume in his hand, thinking about Francesca. He couldn't help wondering what kind of woman she was, or exactly what had brought her back from France, and why she was in Shelburne. It seemed an odd place for a woman who had obviously once had a sophisticated lifestyle. He also wondered if he'd ever know her well enough to ask her. And then, putting her out of his mind again, he sat down in his only comfortable chair and pored over Sarah's neat, lacy hand again. In less than a minute, he had forgotten everything but Sarah.

Sarah stayed at Ingersoll's Boardinghouse, at the corner of Court and Tremont Streets, when she got to Boston. It was big enough, four stories tall, comfortable, and Captain MacCormack had suggested she stay there. In fact, George Washington had stayed there only a week before, and found it very pleasant.

But Mrs. Ingersoll and her housekeeper had been surprised when Sarah checked in with only two bags, and no female to escort her. Sarah explained that she was a widow and had just arrived from England, and at the last moment, her niece had become too ill to make the trip. The woman who ran the hotel was immediately sympathetic to her story, and the housekeeper was asked to take her to her rooms.

She had a large, handsome suite of rooms, with a drawing room done in heavy red brocades, and a bedroom adjacent to it done in pale gray satin. It was a sunny room with a view of Scollay Square, and in the distance she could see the harbour. It was a bustling city then, and she loved walking everywhere and looking at the shops, and listening to the people. She heard a lot of Irish accents, and English like her own. Most of them were soldiers and merchants and hardworking people who had come from Europe. There were very few people like her around the streets, and even in simple clothes, it was more than obvious that she was aristocratic and well-born.

She was still wearing the plain dresses she had brought to wear on the ship, the bonnet that was battered now, and after the first few days, looking around, she asked Mrs. Ingersoll to direct her to some shops. She needed to have some warm clothes made, it was chilly there, and other than the cloak where she had concealed her jewels, she had nothing appropriate to wear in Boston.

She found a small dressmaker on Union Street, and looked through some sketches that one of the clients had brought from France the year before. She was a very grande dame, and she bought most of her clothes in Europe, but she had five daughters as well, and the dressmaker had copied designs for them, and Sarah was well pleased with the imitations. She ordered half a dozen dresses, and the dressmaker suggested a milliner who could make the hats to go with them.

The dresses Sarah saw in Boston were, for the most part,

simpler than what she had worn in England. And they were much, much plainer than what women wore in France. The French women she knew had always had lovely gowns. But now that the revolution had begun there four months before, no one was concerned with clothes anymore, the issues at hand were more important. But what Sarah needed now was not high fashion for the life she led here. She needed serious, serviceable clothes that were practical and looked dignified and suited her new station in life as a widow. In fact, in order to convince everyone of it, most of what she ordered from the dressmaker was black and a little dreary. But she couldn't resist one really lovely velvet gown, they were going to make it in a deep blue, almost exactly the color of her eyes. She couldn't imagine where she would wear it. She knew no one there for the moment, but eventually she thought she might meet some people, and attend a ball or some assemblies, and she didn't want to look like a total dowdy, so she indulged herself with the blue velvet gown.

The dressmaker promised to have most of it ready in a week or two, only the more complicated blue velvet gown wouldn't be ready until the end of the month. But she'd have the rest very quickly, and after the dressmaker, she went to the bank. She explained her situation there too, her widowhood, her recent arrival from England, her lack of connections in town, and she quietly admitted that eventually she'd like to buy a farm outside Boston.

"How would you run it, Mrs. Ferguson?" Angus Blake, the bank manager asked, with a look of concern. "Managing a farm is no small task, especially for a woman alone."

"I'm well aware of that, sir," she said discreetly. "I would have to hire people to help me, but I'm sure I can find the people I need once I find the land." But he looked at her over his spectacles with strong disapproval, and told her she'd be far better off in town. There were lovely houses there, in handsome neighborhoods, and he was very sure that in a short time, she'd have many friends there. She was a very pretty young woman, and he didn't say it to her, but he was certain that in a very short time she'd be remarried. It was pointless for her to buy a farm. And it seemed foolish of her to want it at all.

"I wouldn't do anything hasty, Mrs. Ferguson. You need to acquaint yourself with Boston first, before you make up your mind." And he made it a personal crusade to make her feel at home in Boston, and introduce her to several customers of the bank. She was obviously genteel and distinguished, in fact, his wife was convinced that there was more to Sarah Ferguson than first met the eye.

"There's something very unusual about her," she said when her husband first introduced them. She had children nearly Sarah's age, and she had never met anyone, any woman, as intelligent, and capable and strong. Just thinking about the journey she'd made on the *Concord* made Belinda Blake shudder, and she completely agreed with her husband, that it was an absurd idea for her to even contemplate buying a farm. "You must stay here in town." She added her voice to her husband's, but when she said it, Sarah only smiled.

The Blakes took it upon themselves to introduce her to their many friends, and within a short time, Sarah received a number of invitations to dinner and tea. She was cautious about where she went, and hesitant about making friends. She was always afraid that someone from England might recognize her. She and Edward had not gone to London a great deal, nor gone out very much, but it was possible that the story of her flight had become well known or even published. She had no way of discovering that, now that she was here. She thought of writing to Haversham to inquire, but she dared not risk it. So she went out to dinner once or twice, and slowly began making friends.

Angus had also been good enough to introduce her to a discreet jeweler, and he was more than a little shocked at the pieces she unwrapped and spread out on his desk so he could view them. There were half a dozen truly important pieces, and some smaller ones she hadn't yet decided to sell. But she was anxious to sell the larger ones, particularly a handsome diamond necklace that Edward had somehow overlooked when he sold her mother's jewelry. With that alone, she could have bought several farms, or a truly splendid house in Boston. She had already seen several handsome brick mansions and Belinda Blake kept urging her to look at them, in the hope that she'd buy one. But she still had her heart set on a farm on the outskirts of town.

The jeweler bought the necklace from her very quickly. He had a client for it, and knew that if he didn't sell it in Boston at once, he could sell it in New York. And the money he paid her for it went directly into her account at the bank. By the end of November, she had a handsome sum there, and was surprised herself by how many people she knew in town now. Everyone had been wonderful to her, inviting her to luncheons, and in spite of her caution not to do so, she had caused quite a stir among the more distinguished people in town the few times she ventured out. It was impossible not to see how aristocratic she was, nor to realize how unusual, and her beauty was rapidly becoming a topic of constant conversation among all the prosperous, eligible men in Boston, many of whom gathered at the Royal Exchange Tavern, where more than a few mentioned Sarah. Almost overnight, Sarah Ferguson had become the object of everyone's attention, and more than ever, it made her anxious to go away and live quietly, before reports of her whereabouts crossed the Atlantic and reached Edward. Even at such a great distance, she feared the long reach of his arm.

She shared the Thanksgiving celebration with the Blakes, and two days later was invited by the illustrious Bowdoins for a dinner party, which was a sign of her acceptance into the first circles of Boston. She wasn't even going to accept the invitation at first, she had no real interest in entering the elite social circles, and making herself conspicuous to all concerned. But Belinda was so upset when she said she wasn't going to go, that in the end, after considerable badgering from the Blakes, she agreed to go.

"How will you ever get married again?" Belinda scolded afterward, she treated Sarah like one of her daughters. And Sarah only shook her head with a wistful smile. There was so much she would never be able to tell her.

"I don't intend to marry again," she said firmly, and there was something in her eyes that told Belinda how irreversibly she meant it.

"I know you feel that way now," Belinda comforted her with a gentle hand on her arm, "and I'm sure Mr. Ferguson was a lovely, kind man." Sarah's stomach almost turned over as she thought of Edward. There had never been anything lovely or kind about him, not even in the beginning. He had been a wise match, at best, and nothing more than that. And in time he had become a monster. "But I'm sure that one day you'll find someone quite as fine as he was. You must marry again, Sarah, dear. You're far too young. You can't stay alone forever, and perhaps you'll be fortunate enough this time to have several children." But at that, something died in Sarah's eyes and Belinda saw it.

"I'm not able to bear children," she said stiffly, and Belinda would never have dared to ask her how she knew that to be the case.

"That may well not be true," Belinda said gently, taking Sarah's hand in her own, "I had a cousin who was barren for many years, and at forty-one, she discovered that she was expecting. She had twins," Belinda beamed at her, "and *both* lived. She was the happiest woman on earth, and you're far younger than she was. You must not despair. You will have a whole new life here." It was what she had come to America for, a whole new life, but certainly not marriage, or babies. Much to her chagrin, she'd already had one terrifying union. And she would never have misled anyone into responding to her supposedly being single. She was careful not to flirt with the men, or lead anyone on. At the dinner parties where she went, she conversed mainly with the other women. But the men spoke of her constantly anyway, and even Sarah had to admit, she often found them more intelligent to speak to. But her interest in them was only in learning a little more about business, discussing their land with them, or trying to learn more about farming. It only made her more fascinating to them. The other women only spoke of each other's clothes and their own children. And her refusal to lure the men closer to her only made her that much more appealing. She was a constant challenge to them. In fact, several men had come to call on her at Ingersoll's. They had left flowers and cards, enormous baskets of fruit when it could be found, and even a slim book of poetry reached her hand. It was the gift of a young lieutenant she had met at the Arbucks'. But she refused to see all of them, no matter how generous their gifts, or how lavish the flowers they left her. She had no interest whatsoever in pursuing, or being pursued by them, although Lieutenant Parker was particularly persistent, and she accidentally ran into him several times waiting around for her in the parlor. He was hoping to lend her his protection in any way he could, carry her packages for her if she was going in or out, or escort her to whatever public place she planned to visit. He was twenty-five years old, had come to Boston from Virginia the year before, and he was head-over-heels in love with Sarah. And in spite of his endless kindnesses to her, she found him exasperating each time she saw him. She was always falling over him like a large, panting dog, aching to play, and only succeeding in making himself an intolerable nuisance. She only wished he would fix his affections on someone else, and find a more eligible young woman to play with. She had already told him that she was in mourning for her late husband, and had no intention of ever remarrying, but it was evident he didn't believe her, or care how old she was.

"You have no idea how you will feel about it six months or a year from now," he said firmly, but she always shook her head and tried to make herself clear to him as she rebuffed him.

"Yes, I do know how I'll feel a year from now . . . or two . . . or ten. . . ." Unless Edward died, she would be feeling very married. And even if he did, she had no desire to marry again. Her years with Edward had soured her on the experience forever. She knew without a doubt that she would never again expose herself to being the object of a man's violence, or a possession to be used and battered. She couldn't even imagine how other people stood it. And she knew that many husbands were kind men, but she had no desire to take another gamble. She would be very content to stay alone forever, although young Lieutenant Parker remained to be convinced, as did the other men she had met in Boston.

"You should be grateful you have so many suitors, instead of complaining about them!" Belinda Blake always scolded when Sarah grew annoyed about them.

"I don't want suitors. I'm a married woman!" she said one day without thinking, and then realized what she'd said almost as quickly as she'd said it. "Or I was . . . it's just that I know better than all this nonsense," she said demurely.

"I'm sure you do. Marriage is such a blessing, it makes mere courtship seem like crumbs at a feast. Still . . . you can't have one without the other." It was hopeless to explain it to her, and Sarah gave up eventually. It was useless.

It was in early December that she met Amelia Stockbridge, and subsequently her husband. Colonel Stockbridge was the commander of the Deerfield garrison, and the string of forts all along the Connecticut River, and Sarah found him fascinating to talk to. She questioned him extensively about the area, and he enjoyed sharing what he knew of it with her. She was particularly intrigued by the Indian tribes, and surprised when he told her that most of them were very peaceful.

"We only have a few of the Nonotucks and Wampanoags there

now, and they haven't caused any trouble in a long time. There's the occasional problem of course, too much firewater, or an argument over some land, but most of them don't cause any problems." In fact, he sounded as though he liked them, and Sarah commented that everyone had warned her that the outlying areas were too dangerous, because of the Indians, and other problems.

"That's true of course," he said, smiling at her, surprised that she had any interest in the subject at all. "We see some Iroquois in the spring when the salmon run. And there's always the danger of a band of renegades or a Mohawk war party coming down from the north. They've been known to make trouble for the settlers." They'd had an entire family murdered the year before, husband and wife, and seven children, just north of Deerfield, but he didn't tell her that, and generally it was quite rare now. "But on the whole, the really dangerous ones are in the West. The worry of course is that the problems with the Shawnees and the Miamis will spread east, but I can't imagine they'll come as far east as Massachusetts. They could though. They've certainly been causing enough trouble out there. The president is very upset about it, he thinks we've spent enough money on Indian wars, and he's very sympathetic about the land they've lost. But they can't just continue to go around killing settlers constantly because they're angry. They're giving our people a devil of a time at the moment." She had heard about it, but it was far more exciting hearing about it firsthand, and her eyes shone as she listened.

The colonel was in Boston for the Christmas holidays. The Stockbridges had a house in town, where the colonel's wife stayed most of the time. She hated living at the garrison in Deerfield, and the colonel visited her whenever he could get away. But it wasn't very often, as Deerfield was a four-day journey.

A few days later they invited her to a small Christmas party they were giving for their friends and a few of the colonel's men who were on leave in Boston, and she happily accepted. It was a congenial group, and everyone sang while Amelia Stockbridge played the pianoforte.

Sarah enjoyed the evening thoroughly, and the only difficulty for her was that they had also invited Lieutenant Parker. He hung around her like a puppy much of the time, and Sarah did everything she possibly could to avoid him. She was far more interested in talking to the colonel, and she was fortunate enough to have a few minutes alone with him toward the end of the evening, and he was somewhat shocked by what she asked him.

"I suppose it's possible," he said, frowning as he looked at her. "It's quite a trip, particularly in the snow at this time of year. You couldn't come alone, you'd have to hire a guide or two, it's a good four- or five-day journey." And then he smiled ruefully. "Even my wife won't do it. Several of the younger men have wives in the area, or at the garrison, and the settlers are all around us. We're quite civilized, but it's not very comfortable. I very seriously doubt that you'd like it, even for a visit." He really felt an obligation to discourage her, but it was obvious to the colonel from the questions Sarah asked that she was determined to go to Deerfield, and see it. "Have you friends out there?" He couldn't think of any other reason for her to leave the comforts of Boston. It was so pleasant here, and she looked far too delicate and too elegant to undertake such a journey. And yet he knew that she had come to America on a small, dismally uncomfortable ship, without so much as a companion to escort her. Sarah Ferguson was obviously a great deal tougher than she looked, and he couldn't help but respect that. "I'd like to pick your guides for you, if you do decide to go. I wouldn't want you in the hands of some ruffians who'd get lost on the road, or get drunk. Let me know when you'd like to go, and I'll find some men for you. You should bring two guides, and a driver. You'll need all of them, and a good sturdy carriage. I doubt if you'll enjoy the trip, but at least you'll get there safely."

"Thank you, Colonel," she said with a light in her eyes he had never seen before, and it was obvious to him then that nothing he could have said would have stopped her. He tried to explain that to his wife, when he told her about the exchange and she scolded him soundly.

"How can you even think of letting a girl like that go to Deerfield? It's far too rough a place, she has no idea what it's like. She could get injured, or lost, or ill from the long journey." She thought his allowing her to go, and even offering to find guides for her, was an outrage.

"She came here, all the way from England, on a very small ship, all alone. I don't think Sarah Ferguson is the little drawing-room flower you think she is, my dear. In fact, after talking to her tonight, I'm quite sure she isn't. I think there's a great deal more to that girl than any of us has guessed, or than she's told us." He was a wise man, and he could see in Sarah's eyes that she had come far over a long, hard road, and as long as she could do anything about it, nothing was going to stop her. She had the kind of determination he'd seen in the people who'd gone west, to eke their living out of the land, and face the unknown, and even fight the Indians. The ones who had survived it had been just like Sarah. "She'll be fine. I'm quite sure of it, or I wouldn't have told her I'd help her."

"You're an old fool," Amelia growled at him, and then a little while later, she went to bed and kissed him, but she still thought he was mistaken about Sarah, and that her plan to go to Deerfield was completely crazy. She only hoped that Sarah would meet someone in town and forget all about it.

But Sarah came to see the colonel again the next day. She had thought about what he'd said all night. In fact, she had been so excited she couldn't sleep. And she wanted to accept his very kind offer, and ask him to help her find guides to bring her to Deerfield. She asked when he was going back, and he said in another week. He was going right after the New Year, and this time he planned to stay until spring. Amelia was going to be busy enough without him, as their oldest daughter was expecting a baby any minute.

"I'd come along with you," Colonel Stockbridge said thoughtfully. "But I'm going with some of my men, we're going to ride hard, and cover the ground a little more quickly. You'll be more comfortable if you come at your own pace." And then he smiled at her, and made a suggestion. "I could leave Lieutenant Parker to go with you, if you like." But Sarah was quick to decline his suggestion.

"I'd much rather you didn't," she said softly. "I'd prefer just hiring guides, as you suggested last night. Would you be able to find some?" she asked cautiously, and he nodded.

"Of course. Would you like to go in the next month?" he asked as he mentally wandered over a list of men he would have trusted to go with her.

"I'd love that," she said, and they exchanged a long, warm smile. None of his daughters had ever offered to go and see him. They went once every few years, with their families, under great duress, and considered it a remarkable adventure. This girl on the other hand acted as though it were the opportunity of a lifetime. And to Sarah, it was. It was all she wanted.

The colonel promised to get in touch with her in the next few days, and they both agreed not to give his wife any of the details. They both knew that she was going to be furious at what Sarah was doing, and the fact that her husband was going to help her do it. But he felt sure that she was going to be quite safe, otherwise he wouldn't have helped her with her plan to get to Deerfield.

Sarah thanked him profusely, and walked back to her hotel,

although it was quite a long distance. But she was so exhilarated she wanted to get some air, and as the wind stung her face, and burned her eyes, Sarah only smiled as she pulled her cloak more tightly around her.

Chapter 13

Sarah set out on the fourth of January, 1790, in a very old, but very solid, rented carriage. The driver she'd hired with it was young, but he'd traveled the area for a long time. In fact, he'd grown up within a day's journey of Deerfield. He knew all the trails for miles around, and his brother lived at the Deerfield garrison, and Colonel Stockbridge had been well pleased with him when he found him. His name was Johnny Drum and he was just a little older than Sarah. The other two men rode on horseback alongside. One was an old trapper, George Henderson, who'd spent years traveling up to Canada to trade furs, and had spent two years in his youth as a prisoner of the Huron. Eventually, he had taken a Huron bride, but that had been long since. He was old now, but people said he was one of the best guides in Massachusetts, and the other guide was a Wampanoag. His name was Tom Singing Wind, and his father was the sachem of his tribe, a holy man and a leader. Tom worked as a guide at the garrison, but he had come to Boston to see some men about trading for farm equipment for his tribe, and Colonel Stockbridge had asked him to do him a favor, by traveling with Sarah. He was a serious-looking young man, with long dark hair, and sharply carved features. He wore buckskin breeches and a buffalo coat, and he spoke only to the men whenever possible, and never to Sarah. It was a form of respect for her, but she couldn't keep her eyes off him as he rode alongside them, when they began their journey. He was the first Indian she had ever seen, and he looked every bit as noble and stern and ominous as she would have expected. Yet he didn't frighten her, and she knew from everything the colonel had explained to her that the Wampanoags were a peaceful tribe of farmers.

It was snowing as they rolled slowly out of town and headed west, and Boston was already stirring in the early morning. They were carrying with them all their supplies, furs, blankets, food, utensils, water. The two guides were expected to cook for them, and the old trapper was reputed to be a fine cook, but Sarah was more than willing to help him.

They rolled out of Boston at first light, and Sarah sat in the carriage, watching the snow fall outside, and she had never felt as excited in her life, not even when they set sail out of Falmouth on the *Concord*. It was as though she knew this was one of the most important journeys of her life. She wasn't sure why, but she knew without a doubt that she had been meant to come here.

They left town from Scollay Square, and traveled for five hours before they stopped to rest the horses. Sarah got out and walked for a little while, and she marveled at the beauty of the countryside. They were already just past Concord, and after half an hour they rolled on again. It had stopped snowing by then, but everything was covered in thick, white snow as they reached the Mohawk Trail and headed west toward their destination. Sarah wished she could be on horseback with them, but the colonel had insisted that she be driven. It would have been hard terrain for her, but she knew she was equal to it, and she was impatient to move ahead quickly and reach their destination.

They ate roasted rabbit on a spit, prepared by Henderson that night. They had packed it in snow, and brought it with them from Boston, and after the long day's ride, it tasted delicious. And as always, Singing Wind said very little to them, but he seemed pleasant and good-humored. He cooked some dried squash he had brought and offered it to all of them, and Sarah thought she'd never tasted anything as delicate or as sweet. It seemed like a feast to her, and after they ate, and attended to their various needs, she curled up in the carriage under the trapper's heavy furs and slept like a baby.

She woke at first light, when she heard the others stir and the horses begin to commune with each other. It had stopped snowing and the dawn lit up the day like a fire in the heavens. And as they began to roll, Johnny Drum and Henderson began singing. And as she bumped along in the coach alongside, Sarah sang softly with them. They were singing songs she had learned long before in England.

And when they stopped to eat that night, Singing Wind once again provided all kinds of dried vegetables and he was a master at cooking them in ways that would please the settlers' palates. While Johnny took care of the horses, Henderson shot three small birds, and they ate them too, and it was yet another meal that Sarah knew she would never forget. Everything was so simple here, so much more real, so honest, and so infinitely precious.

And on the third day, as they rode on, Henderson told them tales of when he had lived with the Huron. They were all in Canada now, but when they had been allied with the French against the English they had been all over this part of the world, and a real menace. In fact, he claimed they had kidnapped him not far from Deerfield. But Sarah knew they were long gone, and she wasn't frightened as she listened. They talked of the trouble Blue Jacket of the Shawnees was causing in the West, and the stories Singing Wind told of him were quite unnerving. Sarah began speaking to him then, and asking him questions about his tribe, and she thought she saw the flicker of a smile in his eyes as she asked him all the things she wanted to know about his customs. He told her that all of his family were farmers, that his father was the sachem, the chief, but his grandfather had been a powwaw, a spiritual leader even more important than the sachem. He explained that his tribe had a special bond with all things in the universe, that everything around them had its own spirit, and in its own way, was sacred. He told her how Kiehtan, which seemed to be his word for God, had control over all things in the universe, all creatures, all beings, and one must always give thanks to him for food, for life, for everything that Kiehtan gave them. He explained the Green Corn Festival to her, which was their celebration of an early harvest, and she listened to him with wide eyes, in rapt attention. He explained that all beings must be fair to each other, and be guided by Kiehtan, and that if a man mistreated his wife, in his tribe, the woman could leave him. And as she looked at Tom, so proud, so strong, as he sat astride his horse, she wondered why he'd said that, if he knew or sensed that she had been mistreated. He seemed unusually wise for a young man, and the values he described to her sounded more than reasonable. In fact, they sounded very civilized and quite modern, and in some ways nearly perfect. It was hard to imagine that these were the people the early travelers to this part of the world had called "savages," and some did even now, particularly in the West. There was obviously nothing savage about him. And it intrigued her too to realize that one day this man would be the sachem, the chief of his tribe, and how wise he would be to our ways, after spending so much of his time with the settlers. His father was a wise man to send him forth among them, as an ambassador of sorts. And as she watched him ride, she knew that in a lifetime she would never forget this moment.

The fourth day seemed the longest one as they reached Millers Falls, and continued their journey. They saw several forts, but only stopped once, and were given some food and fresh water. They knew it was not far now, but at nightfall, they had still not reached the garrison, and the question was whether to continue through the night, or wait till morning. They were all anxious to get to their destination. On their own, they would have pushed on, but with a woman with them, none of them dared to press her. But it was Sarah herself who said she thought they ought to go on, as long as there was no danger.

"There's always some," Johnny, the young driver, said fairly. "We can always run into a war party, or lose a wheel." The road was rutted, and icy at night. He felt responsible for her, and was not inclined to take risks, which had been his reputation.

"That could happen in daylight too," Sarah reminded him, and in the end, they all agreed to press on for a few hours and see if they could make good time. The two guides estimated that if they kept going, they could reach the fort by midnight.

They rode hard that night, and Sarah made no sound as the old carriage bounced along. It was almost as lively as a good swell on the *Concord* at times, but she would never have complained. All she wanted was to get there. And just after eleven o'clock, they saw the lights of the garrison in the distance. The four of them sent up a cheer, and pressed their horses forward, and this time Sarah felt sure they'd lose a wheel in the last stretch, but they arrived alive and in one piece at the main gates as Johnny shouted out to the sentry. But Singing Wind had ridden ahead, and they had recognized him immediately. The gates swung slowly open, and the carriage rolled slowly in and stopped just inside them. And with shaking legs, Sarah stepped down and looked around her. There were about a dozen men walking in the dark, talking quietly, some were smoking, and there were horses tethered to posts, wearing blankets. The garrison housed several long, simple buildings, in which the men were quartered. There were a few cabins for the families that lived there, and stores where they got their supplies. There was a main square, in fact, it looked very much like a village, all self-contained, all safely surrounded and guarded, with settlers living in the outlying areas all around them. They came here for help, and relied on the garrisons and the forts to protect them. Even late at night, with no one around, Sarah had a sense of belonging as she stood here, and there were tears in her eyes as she shook hands with the men and thanked them. As far as she was concerned, it had been an unforgettable, and entirely pleasant, journey from Boston. And looking back at it, the four days had virtually flown by. And when she said it, they all laughed, even Singing Wind, who had found the going slow, because of the woman.

Johnny took the carriage to the main barn to leave it there, and water his horses, and the two guides disappeared to find friends, as Sarah was left with one of the soldiers who had met them. He had been instructed by the colonel, when he'd arrived two days before, after a hard ride, to take her to one of the women. There were several families who lived here, and Sarah was to stay with them. He felt certain she'd be most comfortable with the women and children. And when the young soldier knocked on the door, a woman in a cotton gown and an old flannel wrap and cap came to the door wrapped in a blanket. She looked sleepy and young, and Sarah could see two homespun wooden cradles in the room just behind her. They all lived in one or two rooms, and she had come here two years before as soon as she had married.

The young soldier explained who Sarah was, and the young girl smiled and said her name was Rebecca. She invited Sarah to come inside, out of the wind, and Sarah came in, carrying her only bag. She had brought very little with her, and she looked around in the light of Rebecca's candle. It was a small, rough room, in what appeared to be a log cabin, and when Sarah looked at her again, she saw that Rebecca was pregnant. And for an instant she almost envied her her simple life, in this perfect place, with her babies all around her. How sweet it would have been to live like that, rather than beaten in a castle, living with a man she hated. And all of that was behind her now, the agony, as well as the lost hope of mercy or fulfillment. But she did have what Tom Singing Wind had described as a kind of communion with the universe. She was, as he had said, in the hand of Kiehtan. And Kiehtan, according to Singing Wind, was fair with all beings, as he had been with her, when he let her find her freedom. She wanted nothing more now.

As Sarah thought of it, Rebecca led her to their only bedroom. It was a tiny room, roughly the size of her cabin on the *Concord*, and it boasted a small rough-hewn bed, just barely big enough for two people. It was the bed she shared with her husband, and Sarah could see that she'd been sleeping in it, with her large, round stomach. But she offered it to Sarah now, and said she could sleep on a blanket in the other room near her children, if Sarah preferred that. Her husband was away with a hunting party, and wouldn't be home for several days. And Rebecca didn't mind giving up her bedroom to her guest, if Sarah preferred it.

"Of course not," Sarah said, touched by her willingness to give up even her bed to an unknown woman. "I can sleep on the floor if I have to. I don't mind at all. I've been sleeping in a carriage for four days and I didn't mind that either."

"Oh no!" Rebecca blushed furiously, and then finally the two women agreed to sleep together in the only bed. Sarah undressed quickly in the dark, so as not to disturb her more than she had to, and five minutes later, the two women who had just met lay side by side like sisters. It was a whole new life here. And as she lay thinking about it, Sarah whispered shyly in the dark, as if they were two children trying not to wake their parents.

"Why did you come here?" Rebecca asked her. She could not resist asking her the question. Perhaps there was a man she was in love with. Rebecca had thought she was very beautiful, and didn't think she was very old. Rebecca herself had just turned twenty.

"I wanted to see it," Sarah said honestly. "I came here from

England two months ago to make a new life. . . ." She thought she'd best propagate the same lie here she'd told since the beginning. "I'm a widow."

"How sad," Rebecca said with real feeling. Her own husband, Andrew, was twenty-one, and they had known and loved each other since they were children. She could not even imagine a husband and wife sharing less than that, let alone a life like the one that had forced Sarah to flee England. "I'm sorry."

"It's all right. . . ." And then she decided to be at least somewhat honest with her, it seemed unfair not to be. "I never loved him."

"How terrible," Rebecca said with a look of amazement. They were sharing confidences that they never would have in a drawing room, and yet they were sharing the same bed, in this magical place which seemed so close to God . . . and Kiehtan. Sarah smiled at the legends Singing Wind had told her. "Will you stay at the garrison for long?" Rebecca asked with interest, and then yawned. She could feel the baby move inside her, and she knew that soon her other two would wake her. The days were long for her, particularly with Andrew away hunting. There was no one else to help her. Her family was in North Carolina.

"I don't know how long I'll stay," Sarah said, yawning too, it was contagious. "I'd like to stay forever." Rebecca smiled in answer and drifted off to sleep then, and a little while later, Sarah fell asleep too, unable to believe her good fortune just to be there.

Rebecca was up and out of bed long before the dawn the next day when she heard her youngest stir. She knew from the heaviness in her breasts that it was time to nurse him. It gave her pains when she did that sometimes, and she was afraid that the baby in her womb might come early, but her little one was so young, it seemed wrong not to nurse him. He was only eight months old, and he'd been frail. She didn't know how pregnant she was, but she thought maybe seven months or so. She was much bigger than the time before. Their first baby was a girl, and she was eighteen months old now. And once she woke up, Rebecca had her hands full. She tried to keep them from waking her guest, and she kept them both busy with a bowl of porridge and a crust of bread for each. It was easier for her being in the garrison than on a farm somewhere. She would have had no way to work the land, and they were safer and had more food here. This way Andrew didn't need to worry about her whenever he left her.

And by the time Sarah woke at nine o'clock, Rebecca had washed both children, dressed them and herself, done the laundry, and there was bread baking in the oven. She had had a busy morning. And as she saw her hostess bustling around the tiny cheerful room, with a fire in the grate, Sarah was embarrassed to have slept so late and been so lazy. She must have been more tired than she thought. She had slept like the dead until the sound of horses and carts outside finally woke her. She knew that by the time she woke up that day, her carriage would have gone back to Boston. And both guides had said they were moving on early that morning. Singing Wind had to go back to his father and report on the farming utensils and equipment he'd bought for them, and George, the trapper, was heading north to trade with the settlers on the Canadian border. It was more dangerous there, he knew, but he didn't mind it. He knew most of the tribes, and all but a few of them were friendly.

"Would you like something to eat?" Rebecca asked her kindly, holding the baby in one arm, and trying to steady her little girl and keep her out of the sewing basket with the other.

"I'll take care of myself. You look as though you have your hands full."

"I do," Rebecca said with a broad smile. She was small and wore her hair in braids, and in the bright sunshine she looked more like twelve than twenty. "Andrew helps me with them when he can, but he's away a lot, checking on the settlers, visiting the other forts. He has a lot to do here." But so did she, and her belly looked enormous now to Sarah.

"When will the baby come?" Sarah asked with a look of concern as she helped herself to a cup of coffee. It looked like any minute.

"Not for a month or two, I think . . . probably two . . . I'm not sure." She blushed. Each of her babies had come right on the heels of the other, but she looked healthy and happy. But even Sarah could see that it was not an easy life here. It was simple and rugged, and devoid of all the conveniences that people were accustomed to. It seemed as though it was in another world than Boston, and it was. This was an entirely different life here, and she knew just from being here and sniffing at it, this was exactly what she wanted.

Sarah made the bed, and asked if she could help Rebecca with anything, but she said she was fine and planning to visit a friend on a neighboring farm who had just had a baby. And when Sarah felt sure she wasn't abandoning her, she left to find the colonel.

She found his office easily, but he wasn't there, and she walked around the garrison for a while, watching everything that went on, the blacksmith shoeing horses, the men laughing and exchanging tales, the Indians who came and went, who looked different from Singing Wind, and she suspected they were the Nonotucks she'd heard of. They were an equally gentle tribe as the Wampanoags. There were no fierce Indians left around here, or so she thought, until she saw a group of men ride hard through the gates, and she thought she had never seen anything so ferocious. They were a group of about twelve men, most of them Indians, and looked as though they'd had a long hard ride. They had four supply horses galloping behind them, and the men who led them seemed to stop for nothing. The Indians looked nothing like Singing Wind, or the Nonotucks she'd seen that morning. They had a fierce harshness to them, in the way they looked, and even in the way they handled their horses.

Their hair was long and black, and they wore beads and feathers, and one of them was wearing a spectacular breastplate. But even the way they spoke to each other frightened Sarah a little. But no one else in the garrison seemed to pay any attention to them. And as they pulled their horses up not far from where she stood, Sarah felt herself tremble. And she was annoyed at herself for her reaction. But they were so powerful, so breathtaking, they were like a storm rushing past her. And then she heard one of the men shout something to the others, and they laughed. There was a powerful sense of camaraderie among them, which even seemed to include the white men. And as their horses still pranced nervously, they dismounted. She saw several soldiers eyeing them, but they said nothing, and the Indians spoke quietly amongst themselves. It was obviously not an attack, but it looked like a delegation of some sort, and there was an undeniable sense of strength and unity about them. She stood watching them silently, unobserved, wondering who and what they were, and she found herself staring at their leader. He was the most mesmerizing of all, he had long, shining dark hair that flew out behind him as he walked, and he wore beautiful buckskins and boots. He looked almost European, but not quite, he had the noble carriage, and harshly carved face of the Indians he rode with, and he spoke in Indian dialect to the men around him. It was obvious just from the way he moved and the way they answered him, how much he was respected. He was a natural leader. He seemed almost like a prince of some kind in his warlike dignity, and it was easy to believe that he was the sachem, the chief, or perhaps the son of a chief. He looked to Sarah as though he were in his late thirties.

He turned sharply then, as she watched him, carrying an enormous musket, with a bow slung across his back, and she found herself face-to-face with him unexpectedly, and she jumped as he saw her. She was in no way prepared to face the man, however spectacular she thought him. He was like a painting she wanted to observe, an exquisite unknown sport of some kind, just watching him move and speak and turn was like listening to music. He was the most graceful and powerful man she'd ever seen, and at the same time very silent. But he was also terrifying, and she couldn't move from where she stood as he watched her. He stopped dead, staring at her, looking more ominous than any man she'd seen, and yet she did not feel like he would hurt her. He was like the Prince of the Unknown, he represented a world she could only dream of, and as his eyes searched hers, he turned away then, and walked into an office. And she was horrified to realize she was shaking violently once he'd passed her. Her knees were knocking so hard she almost couldn't stand, and she let herself down on the steps of the building she'd been standing near, as she watched the others disband their supplies, and move across the garrison. She still wondered what tribe they were from, and who they were, and why they had pounded into the garrison as though they had a legion of devils just behind them.

It took her ten minutes to stop shaking after her encounter with the leader of the group, and when she walked back across the garrison to the colonel's office again, out of curiosity she asked a soldier what tribe the Indians were from that she had noticed. It was easy to describe them.

"They're Iroquois," he explained, looking unimpressed. He'd seen them many times before, but Sarah hadn't. And their entrance had been quite remarkable, as far as she was concerned. She knew, like so much else she'd seen here, she would never forget it. "They're Seneca actually, which is part of the Iroquois nation, and one of them is Cayuga. There are six Iroquois nations." He reeled them all off to her as she listened avidly: "Onondaga, Cayuga, Oneida, Seneca, Mohawk, and the last to join the confederacy were the Tuscarora. They've only joined up with the Iroquois for the past seventy years, and they're originally from North Carolina. What you're seeing here, though, is Seneca, and the little short one is Cayuga."

"Their leader is quite an impressive sort," she said, still a little overwhelmed by the impression he'd made on her. She felt as though she had faced all the terrors of the new world, embodied in one man, and failed to be terrorized or defeated. But it had been close for a minute or two. He had been more than a little daunting. But she'd survived it. And here at the garrison, she knew it was unlikely that anyone would try to hurt her. And what had comforted her, as terrifying as he was, was that no one else seemed worried by him.

"Who rode in with them?" the soldier asked, but she could only describe him. "I'm not sure who that was. Probably one of the chief's sons. He might have been Mohawk, they're a little more frightening-looking than the Seneca. Particularly in war paint," which they obviously weren't wearing. That was a relief anyway. Probably if they had, with the best will in the world, she felt sure she might have fainted.

She thanked the man for the information then, and went on to find the colonel. He had returned from his morning's ride by then, and seemed pleased by what he'd seen. His territory was in good order. And he looked particularly happy to see Sarah. It seemed years since he'd seen her in Boston. And he was extremely relieved to hear that the long trip had gone well, and she had arrived safely. It was impossible not to notice how pretty she looked too. Even in a simple brown wool gown, with a plain bonnet to protect her from the cold, she was a rare beauty. The cream of her skin looked almost like snow, her eyes were the color of a summer sky, and the lips which wore no rouge would have begged a younger man to kiss them. Yet she was perfectly demure, proper in every possible way, and the light he saw in her eyes was only excitement to be there. There was a subtle sensuality about her, but she kept it so well hidden, that all one sensed about her, if one didn't look too far, was warmth and friendship.

And she thanked him profusely for letting her come here, which made him chuckle as he listened.

"Amelia has always treated her visits to me as sheer torture, and something I must apologize for from the moment she arrives until the moment she leaves us." In the past five years, she had not come often. At forty-nine, she felt she was too old now for hardship. And it was easier for him to see her in Boston. But Sarah was another story. She had the land in her veins. And he teased her and said she was born to be a settler, but he was sure she knew he didn't really mean it. It was just a compliment he paid her.

He had organized a small dinner for her that night, and hoped that she was comfortable enough where she was staying. They had no rooms for guests, and had to rely on the soldiers' wives to accommodate people when they came. His own wife had to share his billet, which was some of what she hated. Sarah said that she was fine, and had already grown fond of Rebecca. But later at dinner she found that the colonel had invited Lieutenant Parker to dinner. And he was still as besotted with her as he'd been in Boston. She did everything she could to discourage him, until she finally reached the point of being quite rude to him, but he didn't seem to mind it. In fact, she almost feared he liked it. He interpreted her sharp answers as a form of interest. And she was even more distressed to find that some of the other guests thought she had come to Deerfield to see him.

"Not at all," she said quite soberly to the wife of a major. "As you know, I'm a widow," she said sternly, feeling like her own grandmother as she said it, but trying to look extremely daunting. Had she seen herself, she would have giggled. But the woman she said it to was not nearly as impressed as Sarah had hoped for.

"You can't stay alone forever, Mrs. Ferguson," she said sweetly, casting an appreciative eye at the young lieutenant.

"I intend to," Sarah said sharply, and the colonel laughed as he listened. And then he lowered his voice as Sarah prepared to leave. The lieutenant was lingering in the hope of escorting her to Rebecca's.

"Shall I offer you my protection?" the colonel asked kindly, and she nodded. He had understood her situation, and didn't want her to feel awkward. She was his guest after all, and clearly didn't reciprocate the lieutenant's tender feelings.

"I'd appreciate it very much," she whispered, and the colonel smiled at her and informed Lieutenant Parker that he was very kind to wait for Mrs. Ferguson, but that he intended to see her home himself. He thanked him again, and told him he would see him in the morning. Sarah already knew that they had a meeting planned with an important delegation from the West, who had gone to discuss peace with the troublemakers led by Little Turtle. But after the colonel's words the lieutenant looked extremely dejected when he left them.

"I'm sorry, my dear, if he annoyed you. He's young, and very taken with you, I'm afraid. I can't blame him. If I were thirty years younger, I'd be tempted to make a fool of myself as well. You're only very lucky that I have Amelia to keep me behaving." She laughed at the compliment and blushed as she thanked him.

"He refuses to understand that I'm determined not to marry again. I've told him very clearly. And he doesn't think I mean it."

"I should think not," he said firmly, as he helped her put her cloak on. The last of the guests had just left them. "If you do, you're very much mistaken. You're far too young to close a door on life. You have at least half your life left, more if you're lucky. It's too soon to end the party." He smiled again and offered her his arm, and she didn't argue with him, but she knew her mind. And to change the subject she asked him about his meeting the next day, and the unrest caused by the Shawnees and the Miamis, and he was immediately drawn into her questions. And he was almost sorry to leave her at Rebecca's. He wished his own children expressed as much interest in what he did, as she did.

But they were far more involved in their families, and the social life of Boston. Sarah was much more intrigued by the budding world around them, and it was obvious that she was thrilled to have come to Deerfield.

She thanked him again for the dinner party, and the excellent food. They had had venison, delicately prepared by his Nonotuck cook with vegetables all grown on the farms nearby. And she promised to visit him the next day after his meeting, or in the late afternoon. She was planning to take a ride out into the surrounding country, if she could find someone to ride with her, other than Lieutenant Parker. And the colonel said he would fix it up and urged her to be careful.

When she went inside the little log cabin that Rebecca was so generously sharing with her, she found that Rebecca had already gone to bed, the babies were asleep, the fire was out, the room was cool, and she was too wide awake to undress and go to bed beside Rebecca. She stood outside for a little while, thinking about her ride the next day, and the things that had been said that night at the dinner table, and the fierce-looking Indians she'd seen that afternoon. It made her tremble to think of what an actual war party would look like, and she was grateful she'd never seen one. As fascinated as she was with this part of the world, she had no desire to go west and become a pioneer. That was too rugged a life, even for her, and she knew she would be content to stay right here in Deerfield.

As she thought about it, she wandered a little way from the house, and decided to get some air. It was quiet all around her, and she knew that she was safe here. Most of the men had gone to bed. The sentries were at the gate, and most of the people in the garrison were sleeping. It was a lovely feeling being there, walking with the snow beneath her feet, looking up at the stars shining brightly above her. It reminded her of what Singing Wind had said about being part of the universe, every person, being, animal was at one with the universe, he had said, and as she looked back to earth again, she gave a tremendous start. There was a man not three feet from her, watching her, his brows knit, his face tense, his entire being poised either in flight or attack, and she could not keep from gasping. It was the leader of the Iroquois delegation she had seen ride into the garrison that afternoon and he had already terrified her once, and now he had done it for a second time. He stood there watching her in total silence as she felt her heart pound. She was not at all sure whether or not he would attack her, but it seemed a definite possibility as he glared at her with, what seemed to her, a look of fury.

There was a long terrifying moment of silence when neither of them moved, and she considered turning and running back to Rebecca's house as fast as she could, but she knew just looking at him that he would outrun her, and she did not want to bring danger to Rebecca and her children. And if she screamed, he might kill her even before someone heard her. There was nothing for her to do but stand her ground and refuse to be frightened, but it was no small task as she saw the jet-black hair flying in the wind, and one long eagle feather flying out behind him. He had a face almost like a hawk, and yet even in its terrifying starkness, she was aware of his beauty. And then he startled her even further.

"What are you doing here?" he asked softly, in perfectly clear English, although she was aware of some kind of an accent.

She was tense and straight as she answered him, never taking her eyes off his, her whole body taut in terror. "I am visiting the colonel," she said very distinctly, hoping that the mention of the commander's name would cause him to hesitate before he killed her. She was shaking violently, but she hoped that in the dark, he would not see it.

"Why have you come?" he asked, as though he were angry that she had come. She was yet one more intruder. She noticed then that his accent sounded almost French, and wondered if he had learned English from the French soldiers years before. Perhaps he was not Iroquois, but Huron.

"I came from England," she said in a small, strong voice. "I came to find a new life," she said bravely, as though he might understand, though she was sure he wouldn't. But she had not come here to be murdered by one lone Indian under a starry sky in the most beautiful place she'd ever been. She would not let him do this. Just as she had not let Edward kill her.

"You don't belong here," he said quietly, and some of the tension in his face eased, but only slightly. It was the oddest exchange she'd ever had, alone in the darkness speaking to this warrior, who was angry that she had come to Deerfield. "You should go back where you came. There are already too many white men here." He had seen too clearly for too many years the harm they'd done, but so few people understood that. "It is dangerous for you here, you don't understand that," he said, and her knees stopped trembling just a little bit. Why was he saying this to her? Why was he warning her? What business was it of his? And yet the land was his, not theirs, perhaps he did have a right to say it.

"I understand," she said quietly. "But I have nowhere else now. I have no one, nowhere, no place to go. I love this place. I want to be here." She said it sadly, not wanting to anger him more than she had, yet wanting to let him know how much she loved his country. She had not come just to exploit the land, or take it from him. She had come to give herself to it. That was all she wanted. And he looked at her long and hard and said nothing. And then finally, he asked her one more question.

"Who will take care of you? You have no man with you. You cannot live alone here." As though it mattered. It would matter even less if he killed her, but she was almost sure now he wasn't going to. At least she hoped not. What she didn't know was that the whole garrison was talking about her, and this man had heard about her all afternoon and did not approve of her coming, and had said so.

"Perhaps I can live alone," she said softly. "Perhaps I will find a way to do it." But he shook his head again, always amazed by the stupidity and innocence of the settlers. They thought they could just be here, take the land, and never pay the final price for it. The Indians had died for their land. And the settlers did too, more often than they admitted. A woman alone was sheer insanity. He wondered if she was mad, or just very foolish, but looking at her in the moonlight with her pale face and dark hair beneath the hood of her cloak, she looked almost like a spirit. It was that that he had been staring at when she first saw him. She looked like a ghost to him, a rare vision of beauty, and she had startled him, as he had been walking, thinking about his meeting with the colonel in the morning.

"Go back now," he said. "You are a fool to be alone here."

She smiled then, and what he saw in her eyes startled him. He was completely unprepared for the passion he saw there. He had only known one woman like her. She was Iroquois. . . . Oneida. . . . Crying Sparrow. . . . the only name he could think of for this woman was White Dove . . . but he said nothing. He only watched her. And then, saying nothing at all, knowing she would not dare move until he did, he turned on his heel and left her. She let out a long breath when she saw that he was gone, and she ran all the way back to Rebecca's.

Chapter 14

Sarah told no one about her encounter with the warrior the night before, for fear that they wouldn't let her venture around the garrison alone again. And she was thrilled to find the colonel had arranged for a scout to take her out riding in the morning. He was a young private, and his commanding officer thought he could be spared for a day of riding with her. He was extremely shy and fairly new to the area, and he wasn't quite sure what she wanted to see. No one had told him what was expected of him, other than to be polite to her, so he asked her, and she said only that she wanted to see the surrounding areas. She said a woman at dinner the night before had mentioned a place called Shelburne, somewhere nearby, and she said it had a lovely waterfall, although at this time of the year, it would be mostly frozen. But as Will Hutchins rode along with her, he said he didn't know it, so they started out, heading north, in a rambling way, and as they rode, Sarah was impressed with the ever more beautiful country, the rolling hills, the denseness of the trees, the deer they saw everywhere. It was like a fairyland, and she felt euphoric as they rode ever farther from Deerfield.

By lunchtime, Will thought they should go back, the sky

looked faintly threatening, but they hadn't seen any waterfalls yet, and she wanted to go just a little farther, and as the horses were doing well, and didn't seem tired yet, he agreed to let her. They could still get back by nightfall. So they continued riding.

They ate lunch from their saddlebags when they were hungry, and shortly after two o'clock, they saw it, a spectacular waterfall coming from far above, and at the base of it huge boulders filled with gigantic potholes. And the moment she saw it, Sarah exclaimed excitedly that this was precisely the spot the woman spoke of. She was absolutely sure of it. It was Shelburne Falls. The young soldier was pleased for her, although he was far less interested in it than she was. They had been riding for four hours by then, on a rugged trail, and he was anxious to get back to the garrison by nightfall. He knew the colonel and his commanding officer would be furious with him if any harm came to this woman. And being beyond the garrison walls after dark was something they all knew should be avoided. No matter how peaceful the neighboring Indians were, there was still the occasional mishap, besides which it would be easy enough to get lost in the darkness. And Will scarcely knew the area better than she did. He had only been there since November, and with the heavy snows, they hadn't ventured out much. Unlike the colonel, who was wise to her ways, the boy's commanding officer had been naive enough to believe she just wanted a little exercise and a tour around the garrison on horseback. He had had no idea how intense her desire for exploration was, or how far afield it would lead them. They had traveled for nearly twelve miles, and just as she had guessed, they were in Shelburne, it was a small, distant community, north of Deerfield.

As soon as she saw the waterfall, she insisted on dismounting and leading her horse closer to it, and walking for a while. She thought it was the most beautiful spot on earth, and wished that she'd had time to sketch it. And then finally, with the utmost reluctance, she mounted her horse again, and they began the long ride back to Deerfield, but within a mile of the waterfall, she stopped suddenly, as though she'd seen something she'd lost, and could go no farther till she reclaimed it.

"What is it?" Will thought something was wrong, and he looked anxious as she stopped and looked around her. She seemed to be listening and the young private looked as though he were about to cry. He did not want to run into a war party with this woman.

But she had heard no human sound, and it was clear to him that she had seen something, and it had stopped her in her tracks like a bolt of lightning. All he saw as he glanced where she stared was a large clearing, and some old trees, and a view across the valley. "What's wrong?" he asked her miserably. He was cold, and he would have liked to be back in his billet.

But she had seen precisely what she wanted. "Who owns this land?" she asked softly. She was staring around the clearing as though it were haunted, but she knew what she had seen in her head a thousand times since she had decided to come here. It was the perfect location.

"The government, I think. You should ask the colonel." It had all belonged to the Indians once, but it had been taken from them. It was a magical place, and she could easily envision a house here. There was a spring in the back, the waterfall was nearby, and if you listened, she imagined, you could hear it. And there was a family of deer standing in the clearing, looking straight at her. It was like a message from the King of the Universe. Singing Wind had spoken about it to her . . . Kiehtan . . . she knew with utter certainty that she was meant to be here. But as she sat, immobile on her horse, with her escort at her side, it was getting darker.

"We must go, Mrs. Ferguson," he said urgently. "It's getting late." He didn't want to tell her, but he was frightened. He was seventeen years old, and he didn't know why, but she scared him.

"All we have to do is go down these hills to the valley floor and then cross it heading southeast," she said calmly. She had an excellent sense of direction, but it did little to calm him. She hated to leave the spot where they stood, but she knew that she would find it easily again. All she had to do was return to the waterfall, and she could find it from there. It was completely distinctive. And to please the boy, she began moving again. He was right, it was getting dark, but unlike him, she wasn't frightened.

They traveled for the next two hours without incident, or making comment. It was a hard ride, but a pleasant one, and they went faster than usual, as they were racing against nightfall, but the horses were strong, and most of the time, the trail was clear, there were only one or two occasions when they were not quite sure which way to go at a fork in the road, or in a clearing, but her sense of direction was keen, and led them almost all the way back to Deerfield. She knew they were back on the valley floor when they reached a clearing, but when they saw it for the second time she knew they had seen it twenty minutes earlier. It was nearly dark by then, and in the twilight, she questioned her sense of direction, but said nothing. When they returned to the clearing for the third time, she faltered.

"We can't be far from the garrison," she said, looking around, trying to remember the notches she'd seen in the trees before, a little trick she'd been shown by her father as a child, when he taught her to find her way in the forest. She'd always found the things she'd learned from him extremely useful, but this time, her knowledge failed her.

"We're lost, aren't we?" Will asked, beginning to panic.

"Not really. We'll find our way. It's just a question of observation." But the changing light and the snow had fooled her, and this was unfamiliar terrain to her. Unconsciously, she had remembered several key things on their way out earlier that day, but now they looked different in the early darkness. And there were odd, eerie sounds all around them. All the boy could think of were war parties, although there had been none in the three months he'd been there. "I'm sure in a moment, we'll find our way again," she said calmly, and offered him a sip of water from the flask they carried. Even in the darkness, she could see that he was pale and frightened. She didn't like the situation much herself, but she felt more in control than he did. But then again, she was a great deal older.

They tried another path this time, but wound up back in the same place. It was like a magic merry-go-round they could not escape, round and round and round they went, always to end in the same clearing.

"All right," she said finally, they had tried three ways by then, and there was only one more, a fourth one. It seemed entirely wrong to her, and appeared to be heading north instead of south, but she was willing to try it. "We'll go this way, and if that fails, we'll just keep going. Even if we don't reach the garrison, we'll end up at one of the forts on the river eventually, or a homestead. We can always spend the night there." He didn't like the idea at all, but he didn't want to argue with her. She was extremely strong-headed, he could tell, and she had gotten them into this mess in the first place, insisting on finding the waterfall, and then stopping in the clearing as if she were looking for gold or something. He was beginning to think she was more than a little crazy, and he didn't like it. But he had no better suggestions.

She pointed to the way they should go, and he followed her reluctantly. She was clearly in the lead now, and they didn't return to the clearing again, but she could tell by the stars that they weren't going in the right direction either. But at least they were not going around in circles anymore, and if they could find the river, she knew that, eventually, they would find civilization. But they rode for a long time and saw nothing, and this time she knew they were truly lost. It had been more than two hours since

217

nightfall. She wondered if the colonel would send out a search party for them, but she hated to cause him all that trouble. And just as she thought of it, she realized they had run out of water. There was always the snow of course, but they had not taken adequate provisions for an overnight journey, and the air around them was suddenly crisp and freezing. Both of them were shivering. But there was nothing for them to do but keep going.

And as they rode steadily along, their horses beginning to stumble by then, she heard the sound of hooves in the distance. There was no mistaking it, and she turned to the boy beside her. He had heard it too, and he looked at her with wild frightened eyes, ready to bolt and ride hell-for-leather in any direction.

"Stay still," she said harshly to him, grabbing his reins with one hand, and pulling his horse sharply into the deeper brush alongside her own. It was even darker there, and she knew their horses would give them away, but perhaps if the other horses were far enough away, they wouldn't find them. There was nothing she could do but pray, and she was as frightened as Will, but she knew she couldn't show it. She knew full well it was her fault they were lost, and she was sorry to have gotten him into this mess, but there wasn't a great deal she could do now to save them.

The sound of hoofbeats grew stronger very quickly, and their horses danced but made no sound, their eyes almost as frightened as the boy's were, and then in a rush of horses and men, she saw them. There must have been a dozen of them, Indians, riding hard through the forest, as though it were broad daylight. They must have known the trail like their own hands, but as soon as they hurried past, one of the men called out sharply and they stopped within twenty yards, their horses dancing wildly. She was not yet sure if they had seen them, and she wished that she and Will could dismount and flee, but she didn't dare, and she was sure that these men would find them. They were far too at home in the forest. She put a finger to her lips as she looked at the boy in the darkness and he nodded. The Indians they had seen were riding slowly back toward them, in single file, glancing to either side. They were almost upon them, and the urge to scream was overpowering, but with every ounce of will she had, she forced herself not to, instead she dug a hand into the young private's arm, and wished she dared to close her eyes so she would not see them kill her, but she couldn't. Instead, she watched wide-eyed and terrified as the Indians rode toward them, she could see the snowshoes tied to their saddles, now they were so close. They stopped on the trail not ten feet from them, as one of the men spoke, the others halted, and he rode slowly toward them. He rode swift and straight until he was barely more than an arm's length from them, and Sarah could feel the hair on her arms and the back of her neck rise as their eyes met in the darkness. She knew him now. There was no escaping him this time. She knew that this time he would not let her flee him. He was the leader of the Iroquois she had seen at the garrison. She did not know his name, but she did not need to. She kept her hand on the boy's arm, but her eyes never wavered from the warrior's, and there was no expression in his eyes whatsoever. The men behind him sat very still as their horses pawed the ground. They were not sure what was happening, and she did not think he would protect her from them. She was prepared to die at his hands, but not to beg. It no longer mattered to her. But she was prepared to bargain for the boy's life. He still had long years before him, if he was lucky.

The warrior looked as fierce as he had before, and when he spoke to her, she trembled. "I told you, you did not belong here," he said angrily. "You do not know this place. You are not safe here."

"I know that," she said in a voice that was barely more than a croak in her dry throat, but her eyes never wavered, and she sat very straight in her saddle. He saw that the boy next to her was crying, but paid no attention to him. "I apologize for coming here. It is your land, not mine. I only wanted to see it," she said, trying to sound calmer than she felt, but sure that he did not give a damn about her explanations, and then she did what she knew she had to do for the boy's sake. "Let the boy go," she said, "he will do no harm. He is very young," she said in a voice that sounded suddenly stronger as the warrior's eyes looked deep into hers. If she had reached out to him, she could have touched him.

"And you? You will sacrifice yourself for him?" His English was very sophisticated, and it was obvious that he had lived and studied with the white man. But his face, his hair, his dress, his fierce aura proclaimed his proud heritage as he glared at her in open anger. "Why do I not save you, and kill him?" he asked, demanding an explanation from her she could not give him.

"It is my fault we are here." She wished that she knew his name but perhaps it didn't matter to him. The warrior and the woman sat locked together silently, their eyes never leaving each other's, and then he backed his horse slowly away. She wasn't sure what he was going to do, but it was as though she could breathe a little better with him not quite so close to her, and he made no move to pull her or Will off their horses, though she saw both of his muskets very clearly.

"The colonel is very worried about you," he said angrily, still staring at her. "There have been Mohawk here recently. You could start a war with your stupidity," he said, barking at her as his horse danced. "You do not know what you are doing. The Indians need peace, not trouble caused by fools. There are already enough of those here." She nodded silently, moved by what he said, and then he shouted something to the others in the dialect they spoke. And she saw the others glance over at them with interest. His voice was quieter when he spoke to her again, and she waited to hear their verdict. "We will lead you back to the garrison," he said, glancing at both of them, "you are not far." And with that, he turned, and led the others ahead of her, all but one who followed behind them, so they would not get lost again.

"It'll be all right," she said softly, to the boy next to her who finally stopped crying. "I don't think they'll hurt us." He nodded, speechless at what she had tried to do for him, and deeply ashamed at the same time, yet very grateful. She would have traded her life for his. He couldn't imagine ever knowing another woman who would do that for him.

Less than an hour later, the garrison came into sight as they left the woods, and the Indian party paused, watching them, and then after a brief exchange amongst themselves, they decided to ride all the way back with her. They had already lost hours, and it seemed just as easy to stay there for the night now, and leave in the morning. And Sarah felt a wave of exhaustion wash over her as they passed through the gates and the sentry called out, and Will started grinning. But she was still feeling too shaken to even smile. A horn sounded then somewhere, and the colonel came rushing out of his quarters with a frantic look, which turned to relief the moment he saw her.

"We have two search parties out looking for you," he said, glancing from her to Private Hutchins, "we thought you'd had an accident," he said, and then glanced at the group of Indians standing all around them. Some of them had started to dismount, and the warrior in charge got slowly off his horse and walked over to them. She dared not even leave her saddle yet, for fear that her legs would not carry her, but the colonel helped her gently down, and she prayed that the warrior who had brought her back would not see how weak and frightened she was, or that her legs would buckle beneath her. It was far different facing him here than it had been bargaining for her life with him in the forest. "Where did you find her?" the colonel asked him bluntly. There was an obvious respect between the two men, and they seemed well acquainted with each other, but Sarah had not been sure how benevolent the warrior was. He had seemed quite warlike to her from the first moment she saw him, but he was clearly an educated man and she got the odd feeling that the colonel liked him.

"I found them less than an hour from here, lost in the wood," he said with disgust, and then he looked straight at Sarah. "You're a very brave woman," he said with the first mark of respect she'd seen from him in either of their encounters, and then he looked back at the colonel. "She thought we were going to kill her," he said with the same trace of accent she'd heard before. "She tried to trade her life for the boy's." He had never known a woman who would do that, and doubted there were many in the world. But he still thought she didn't belong here.

"Sarah, why did you do that? Private Hutchins was there to protect you." What the colonel had just heard truly shocked him, and at the same time filled him with admiration. But he could see that there were tears in her eyes now. She'd been through an awful lot since that morning. And she was, after all, only a woman.

"He's only a child," she said, her voice sounding hoarse for a moment. "It was my fault we were lost . . . I dallied near the waterfall . . . and I read the signs on the road wrong . . . I thought I remembered the way we'd come, but I didn't." She was full of apologies now, and confusion, and then remembering why they'd been delayed, she looked at the colonel, and told him of the clearing. But she did not say yet that she wanted to buy it. That would have to come later.

The colonel thanked the young Indian again, and then as though remembering his manners, turned to Sarah. "I assume you two have met, though in rather an odd way." He smiled, as though introducing them in a drawing room, rather than on a freezing night after she had thought he was going to kill her. "François de Pellerin . . . or should I say count?" The man she had thought was an Indian glared at him, and Sarah stared at them both in utter confusion.

"But I thought . . . you are . . . what . . . how . . . how *could* you?" she asked, looking suddenly livid. "You knew what I thought . . . you could have said something last night, or at least tonight when you first found us. . . ." She couldn't believe he'd let her think that they were going to kill them, even for a moment. The sheer cruelty of it almost made her want to hit him.

"But I could have been," he said with the same accent she'd heard before, and now she realized he was not Huron, but French. He was a Frenchman, although she did not understand how he had come here. He looked like the fiercest of warriors to her, but if she tried, she could imagine him in knee breeches and all that went with it. Dressed as he was, he appeared to be Iroquois, but in other garb, he could in fact have been a very handsome Frenchman. But the cruelty of his deception was something she knew she would never forgive him. "I could have been Mohawk," he said without apology. She needed to understand the dangers of the land she was visiting. This was no game to them. She could have been marching to Canada by then, tied with ropes, and killed on the trail if she did not walk quickly. "We could have been Mohawk, or worse. . . ." He had recently seen what the Shawnees had done, on his trip west, and none of it was pretty. They were completely out of control, and the government, thus far, had been unable to stop them. "Even last night, I could have stolen over the fence while the sentries weren't looking. You are not safe here. You should not have come. This is not England. You have no right here."

"Then why are you here?" she challenged him, braver now, as the colonel watched the exchange with interest. Will had long since gone back to his barracks, and had already had two stiff whiskeys.

"I came with my cousin, thirteen years ago during the revolution," he said, although he did not feel he owed her an explanation. He also did not tell her his cousin was Lafayette, and they had both been formally forbidden to come by the king, but had come anyway. Lafayette had gone back ten years before. Unlike his cousin, François knew his destiny was in America, and he could not bring himself to leave his friends here. "I have fought for this country, and bled for her. I have lived with the Iroquois, I have every reason to be here."

"The count has been negotiating for us with the tribes in the west for the past two months.

"Red Jacket, the chief of the Iroquois, regards him almost as a son," the colonel explained, with obvious respect, but he did not tell her that François had once been the chief's son-in-law, until Crying Sparrow and their son were killed by the Huron. "He was traveling north tonight, on his way to visit the Mohawk chief in Montreal and he said he would look out for you on the trail. We were very worried when you didn't come back by nightfall."

"I'm very sorry, sir," she said contritely, but the peace had not yet been made between her and the French count masquerading as an Indian brave. She could not imagine the sheer audacity of his not telling her who and what he was either the night before, or when she had met him on the trail. He had terrified her, and he knew it.

"You should go back to Boston," the Frenchman said, looking at her. He did not look happy either, although something in his eyes said he had been impressed with her, and he had said as much to the colonel when he was told she was missing.

"I will go exactly where I want to, sir," she said sharply to him, "and I thank you for escorting me back this evening." She dropped an elegant curtsy to him, as though they had been in an English ballroom. She shook the colonel's hand then and apologized again for the confusion she'd caused, bowed to him, and walked back to the cabin where she was lodged, without saying another word, or looking back at either of them. Her legs held her unsteadily as she made her way across the garrison, and she quietly opened the door, and stepped into the darkened room, closed the door, and slid slowly to the floor sobbing in relief and anguish.

François de Pellerin had looked after her as she went and said not a word, but the colonel was watching his face, curious about what he saw there. He was a hard man to read. There was more than something a little wild in his soul, and at times the colonel wondered if he wasn't part Indian by now. He certainly knew how they thought, and at times he behaved like them. He had disappeared with them for several years, and only resurfaced when his Indian bride had died, and the colonel understood he never talked about her. But everyone else in the area knew the story.

"She's quite remarkable," the colonel said with a sigh, still puzzled by a letter he had received from his wife only that morning. "Says she's a widow . . . but Amelia heard a remarkable story from a woman she met in Boston, just arrived from England. It seems she's a runaway, the husband is alive somewhere . . . not a very pleasant sort apparently. The Earl of Balfour . . . that makes her a Countess, doesn't it? Bit of a coincidence, you a count, and she a Countess, sometimes I think half the nobility of Europe winds up here." All the misfits and the runaways, and the mad, wild boys. But that still didn't explain Sarah's story. But François was smiling at him wistfully, thinking of his cousin years before . . . the men he had fought beside and known . . . and now this girl . . . willing to trade her life for that of a stranger . . . she had been so brave and so bold in the forest that night. He had never seen anything quite like it.

"No," François said, "they don't all come here, Colonel . . . only the best ones."

He said good night to the colonel then, and went back to his men. They were sleeping as the Indians always did, outside, under the shelter of the garrison, and without a sound, or a word to them, François joined them.

Sarah was in bed by then, thinking of the man she had been so sure would kill her. All she could think of were his fierce dark eyes, as he looked at her in the forest, the dancing of his horse, the powerful movement of his arms as he controlled it . . . his guns flashing in the moonlight. . . . She wondered if their paths would ever cross again, and as she closed her eyes and tried to force him from her mind, she hoped not.

Chapter 15

CHARLIE HAD READ Sarah's journal for an entire day from morning till almost midnight that night, and when he put it down, he smiled reading of her meeting with François. How little she knew of what was to come. But just as François had been, Charlie was overwhelmed by her bravery during their meeting in the forest in Deerfield.

Charlie couldn't even imagine knowing a woman like that, and it made him lonelier than ever when he thought about her. He realized then that he hadn't called Carole in a while, not since the Christmas Day fiasco, when he had called her while she was entertaining friends with Simon. It made him feel lonely again thinking of her, and he decided to step outside and get a breath of air. It was a cold, clear night, with a sky full of stars. But everything he did seemed to make him feel more lonely. There was no one to share things with anymore, no one to talk to now about Sarah. He didn't even wish he could see her ghost again, if there was such a thing, he wanted something so much more real than that, and as he went back inside, he could almost feel the air squeezed out of him, thinking about what he had lost in England. There were times when he thought he would mourn his lost life forever. He couldn't imagine loving anyone again, sharing his life with someone else. And it was impossible not to wish she'd tire of Simon. He knew he'd have taken her back in a second.

But all of that was irrelevant as he walked slowly upstairs, thinking first of Carole, and then of Sarah and François. How lucky they had been, how blessed when their paths had crossed. Or maybe they had been special people, and each of them had deserved the blessing. He was still thinking of them that night, as he lay in bed, wishing he could hear some sound, or believe that they were still near him. But there was no sound, no breeze, no sense of spirits in the room. Maybe it was enough to have her words . . . just to have found the journals.

He drifted off to sleep, dreaming of them again, they were all laughing and chasing each other through a forest . . . he kept hearing odd sounds through the night, and thought it was a waterfall . . . he had found it . . . the place she'd been the day she got lost . . . and then when he woke in the morning, he realized it was raining. He thought about getting up, and the things he could have done that day, but he realized he didn't want to. He made himself a cup of coffee instead, and went back to bed with her journals.

He was faintly worried about himself. Reading Sarah's journals was becoming an obsession. But he couldn't stop now. He had to know everything that had happened. He opened her journal to the place he'd marked the night before, and lost himself in it again, without pausing for an instant.

The trip back to Boston, for Sarah, had been uneventful. And as though to punish her for worrying them, Colonel Stockbridge had sent the still-infatuated Lieutenant Parker with her. But he was impeccably behaved, and she was far more tolerant of him than she had been. Before she left the garrison, she had had a long talk with the colonel, and although he disapproved of it, she had gotten from him exactly what she wanted.

She returned to Ingersoll's in high spirits, and it took her several days to learn that someone who had recently arrived had been spreading rumors about her. They ranged from the vague to the absurd, and one rumor had her directly related to King George III of England. But it was clear that someone had come through town who knew that she'd been married to the Earl of Balfour. Some said he was dead, others that he was alive. Some spoke of a terrible tragedy where he'd been murdered by highwaymen, others said he was insane and had tried to kill her so she fled. Most of the stories were quite romantic, and the town seemed to be buzzing with them, but if anything they made her even more desirable than she had been, and she admitted nothing to anyone, she simply went on presenting herself as Mrs. Ferguson, and left the rest to their imaginations. But one thing she knew, if the news of who she'd been married to had come out, it was only a matter of time before Edward learned she was in Boston. And knowing that made her even more intent on her plan. The colonel had introduced her to some good men, and they had promised to start their work by spring. She had ridden out with several men before she left Deerfield and found the clearing very quickly. And this time, the ride back had been much shorter and far less exciting. She still had not forgiven François de Pellerin for his deception.

The men she'd contracted with in Shelburne said she'd have her house by late spring, particularly since what she wanted was so simple. She wanted a long, plain log house, with a main room, a small dining area, a single bedroom, and a kitchen. She needed sheds and outbuildings, but they could come later, and a cabin for the two or three men she'd need to help her. Nothing more. And the men she'd hired said they'd have it put together for her in no time. Possibly June, maybe even before that. Everything was going to be made locally. They'd use whatever hardware they had on hand, only the windows had to be made in Boston and sent to Shelburne by oxcart. There were actually some handsome houses near her too, but they were even more elaborate than what she wanted. Sarah wanted only the simplest of dwellings. She had no need and no desire for anything fancy.

And all she could think about that spring was the house she was building in Shelburne. She had spent the winter peacefully in Boston, reading, keeping her journal, being entertained by friends. She heard that Rebecca gave birth to a little girl and knitted a little cap and sweater for her. And then finally in May she could stand it no longer. She took the long trip back to Deerfield again, and rode to Shelburne as often as she could to watch them build her house, log by log, piece by piece, bit by bit, as they fitted it magically together. And they had been as good as their word. By the first of June, she was ready to move in. And she hated going back to Boston again, to pack up her belongings, but there were still some things she needed. It took her two weeks to find them, and in mid-June she set out again, in a carriage, with a cart piled high with her things, and two guides and a driver. And there were no incidents. She arrived safely first in Deerfield, and then at last in Shelburne. And as she unpacked her things, she was overwhelmed by how beautiful the area was in summer. The clearing she lived in was lush and green, the trees reaching far above her and shading the house that had been built for her, exactly to her specifications. She had half a dozen horses, some sheep, a goat, two cows. And she had hired two boys to help her.

For the moment, they hadn't planted much of anything. She wanted time to study the land, to learn about it, although they had planted corn. That was easy. And one of the boys she'd hired had spoken to some neighboring Iroquois about what to plant, they were so wise about everything that grew in the region.

By July, the colonel had come out to see her once, and she had prepared a wholesome dinner for him, cooked by her own hands.

She cooked for her two hired hands every night, and treated them as her children. The colonel was not only touched by the simple beauty of her home, and the few but lovely things she'd chosen to bring with her, but he found he could not understand why she had given up what must have been a privileged, noble life in England, and it would have been almost impossible to explain it to him. The horror of her life with Edward still gave her nightmares. And she was grateful every moment, every hour, every day for her freedom.

She walked almost daily to Shelburne Falls when she had the time, and as summer wore on, she came to love it more and more. She sat on the rocks for hours sometimes, sketching, writing, thinking, with her feet in the icy water. She loved jumping from one rock to the other, and trying to imagine how the enormous holes in the rocks had come there. She knew the Indians had wonderful legends about it, and she could imagine celestial beings using them as toys, hurtling them across the heavens. Perhaps once long ago, they had been comets. But in her time at the falls, she found a peace she never had before, and she could feel old wounds begin to heal at last. It had taken that long. She looked healthier than she ever had before, and freer. She had finally left all the demons and the sorrows far behind her. Her life in England seemed like a dream now.

She was walking home from the falls one afternoon, singing to herself in the late July sunshine, when she heard a sound nearby, and then she saw him. Had she not known his history by then, he would have frightened her again, so fierce did he look, as he sat watching her, bare-chested and in buckskin pants, riding bareback. It was the Frenchman.

She looked up at him, and neither of them spoke, and she imagined he was on his way to the garrison. In fact, he had already been, and he and the colonel talked about her.

The colonel still considered her remarkable, and his wife was still mourning the fact that she had been unable to convince her to stay in Boston.

"But she seems to want to live out here, in the wilderness, don't ask me why, a girl like that. By all rights, she should be back in England. She doesn't belong here." And François quite agreed with him, though for different reasons. He thought the life she'd chosen for herself was dangerous for her, yet her indomitable courage when they'd met six months before had indelibly impressed him. He had thought of her more than once since that time, and as he rode north alone from Deerfield, on his way to visit the Iroquois, he had decided to stop by and see her, somewhat on the spur of the moment. One of the boys who worked for her had told François where she was, although the boy had been frightened of him at first, and thought he might be a Mohawk. But François had been extremely polite to the boy, and tried to be careful not to scare him. He said that he and Mrs. Ferguson were old friends, although that was not quite the case, and she would have been surprised to hear it. And when she saw him watching her, she looked less than pleased to see him.

"Good afternoon," he said finally, dismounting, aware of his state of undress in the native style, and wondering if she would be bothered by it. But she seemed not to even notice. What she objected to was his spying on her. She had seen him sitting there, watching her, as she walked home on the trail. She couldn't help wondering why he'd come there. "The colonel sends you his greetings," he said, falling into step beside her, as she glanced at him, still surprised to see him.

"Why did you come?" she asked him bluntly, still angry over the terror he had caused her in the forest the previous winter. She had thought they would never meet again, and was surprised to see him.

He looked at her for a long moment, and then bowed his head, as his horse followed behind them. He had thought of this for a long time, and was sorry now he hadn't come sooner. He had heard from some of his Seneca friends that she was living near Shelburne, in a clearing in the forest. There were few secrets in that part of the world, the Indian world was filled with rumors.

"I came to apologize," he said, looking straight ahead, and then finally he looked at her. She seemed surprised, as she moved along beside him. She wore a plain blue cotton gown with a white shirt and an apron, not unlike the clothes the servants had worn on her father's farm when she was a child in England. She led a simple life now, not unlike her father's servants. But François saw her very differently. She seemed like a spirit from another world, the kind of woman he had never met but only dreamed of. "I know I frightened you very badly last winter. I shouldn't have done that, but I thought it was wrong of you to be here. This is not a place for most women. The life is hard, the winters long . . . there are many dangers." She heard his accent again, and in spite of herself found she liked it. It was mostly French, and had just a touch of Indian, from speaking their dialects so much of the time for so many years. He had learned English as a boy and spoke it well, and he no longer had the opportunity to speak French very often. "The cemeteries are filled with people who should never have come here. But," he conceded with a slow smile that lit his face in a way she'd never seen before, it was like watching sunlight on the mountains, "perhaps you, my brave friend, are meant to be here." He had come to think differently about her ever since that night in the forest, and for months, he wished that he had told her. He was glad to have the opportunity to do so now, and happier still that she was willing to listen. She had been so angry at him that night, that he feared she would never let him near her. "There is an Indian legend about a woman who traded her life for her son's . . . she died for his honor . . . and lived forever among the stars, a beacon for all warriors to find their way in the darkness." He looked up at the sky as though there were stars there even though it was still daylight, and then he smiled at her again. "The Indians believe that all our souls go up to the sky and live there when we die. I find that comforting sometimes when I think of the people I have known, and who have left me." She didn't want to ask him who they had been, but what he had just said made her think about her babies.

"I like that too," she said softly, glancing at him with a shy smile. Perhaps he wasn't as wicked as she had once thought him, though she still didn't completely trust him.

"The colonel tells me we have something in common," he said, walking along slowly beside her. "We have both left lives behind us in Europe." That much was obvious from their respective accents, and she wondered suddenly if the colonel had told him something more than that, though she couldn't imagine that he knew anything more than the rumors she herself had heard in Boston. "It must have taken a great deal to bring you here, on your own . . . you're still young. Giving up your life there must have cost you dearly." He was still trying to figure out why she had come. Despite what the colonel had said to him six months before, he sensed that it would have taken more than her husband being "an unpleasant sort" to drive her all the way to Deerfield. And he wondered if she was happy in her retired, simple life, tucked away near Shelburne. But he could tell from looking at her that, if nothing else, she was at peace here.

He walked all the way back to her log cabin with her, and then seemed reluctant to leave and ride on. She hesitated as she looked at him. Despite what he had said, they seemed to have very little in common. He lived among the Indians, and she lived alone here. But in some ways, he could have been an interesting friend. She was intrigued by the legends and the Indian lore she had heard, and she was always anxious to learn more about them.

He stood watching her once they got back, and she smiled at him, remembering how fierce he had once seemed to her. But now, in his buckskins and his moccasins, with his hair loose in the wind, he seemed exotic but harmless.

"Would you like to stay for dinner? It's nothing fancy. Just stew. The boys and I eat very simple fare." She'd had a stew pot on all afternoon, both Patrick and John, her hired hands, were from Irish families, and they came from Boston. All they cared about was that the food was plentiful, and she kept them well housed and well fed, and was grateful for their assistance. Both boys were fifteen, and were good friends. And as François looked down at her, he nodded.

"If this were an Indian family, I would be expected to bring a gift. I have come with empty hands," he said, apologizing again. But he hadn't intended to do more than check on her, give her the colonel's greetings, and then move on. But something about her, her soft voice, her gentle manner, the intelligent things she talked about, made him want to stay there.

He wore a buckskin shirt when he came into the cabin that night. He had fed and watered his horse, and washed his face and hands. His hair was tied back in a leather thong, with a feather and a small knot of bright green beads, and he wore a necklace of bear claws. And they sat at table together, as though they were in Boston, and had known each other forever. The boys had eaten earlier and she had set the table for the two of them with a lace tablecloth, and used the china she had bought from a woman in Deerfield. It was from Gloucester, and had been brought from England years before. And the candles in the pewter candlesticks flickered a warm light on their faces and cast shadows against the wall, as they chatted.

They talked about the Indian Wars years before, and he explained some of the tribes to her, mostly among the Iroquois, but he told her about the Algonquin, and the local tribes as well. He told her how different it had been when he first came there, how many more Indians there had been before the government had forced them to go north, and west. Many of them were in Canada now, many of them had died on the long march north. It made it easier to understand why the Western tribes were fighting so viciously for their land against the Army and the settlers. In some ways, he sympathized with them, although he hated what they were doing to the settlers. He would have liked to see some kind of peace treaty signed, so things could calm down. But so far, they had accomplished nothing.

"No one wins in these wars. It's not an answer to the problem. Everyone is hurt by them . . . and the Indians always lose in the end." It saddened him, he had a great respect for the Indians, and Sarah loved hearing about them. More than that, she loved watching him, as he told his many tales. He was a man of many lives, many interests, many passions. He had given so much of himself to the new world, and she knew he had long since won the respect of settlers and Indians as well. And as they sat and talked, his eyes were filled with questions about her.

"Sarah, why did you really come here?" he asked finally, she had let him call her by her Christian name almost as soon as they sat down to dinner.

"It would have killed me if I'd stayed there," she said sadly. "I was a prisoner in my own house . . . or his house actually . . . my husband's. I was traded at the age of sixteen for a good-size piece of land. Rather like a treaty." She smiled at him, and then her eyes saddened again. "He treated me abominably for the next eight years. He had an accident one day, and it seemed as though he might die. For the first time in all that time, I thought of what it would be like to be free again, not to be beaten . . . not to come to any harm . . . and then he recovered, and everything was just the same as it always had been. I ran away to Falmouth, bought passage on a small brig that was scheduled to set sail, and came to Boston. I had to wait three weeks for the ship to set sail once I booked passage on her, and every day seemed like a year." She smiled as she remembered it, and then she frowned again. "He beat me again . . . terribly . . . and

. . . did terrible things to me, just before I left, and then I knew that even if I died at sea, I had to do it. I couldn't have stayed another hour, and truly, I think if I'd stayed, he would have killed me." If he hadn't beaten her to death, or broken her spirit, she would have died in childbed almost certainly with their next baby. But she said nothing of that to François, and asked him instead why he had never gone back to France. She was curious about him as well, and grateful for the company he provided. She read so much and spent so much time alone that it was a pleasure to have another intelligent human being to talk to. The boys who worked for her were sweet, but they were simple and uneducated and talking to them was like speaking to children. But not so with François. He was sophisticated and wise, and truly brilliant.

"I stayed here because I love it . . . and I'm useful here," he said quietly as she listened. "I would have served no purpose at all if I'd gone back to France. And now the revolution has come, I'd be dead by now if I'd gone back to Paris. My life is here," he said simply. "It has been for a long time." It was clear that he didn't want to talk about himself. But she nodded, it was easy to understand why he stayed. She couldn't imagine being in England again. It was part of another life. "And you, my friend?" he asked. It was easy to forget how they had met now, sitting at her table, eating the dinner she had prepared. "What will you do now? You cannot live alone forever in this outpost of yours. It's an odd life for a young girl." He was fourteen years older than she was, but she laughed at what he'd just said about her.

"I'm twenty-five. You can hardly call that young anymore. And yes, I can live here alone forever, that is precisely what I intend. I want to build onto the house next year. And there are some things we still need to do to it before winter. I'm going to have a good life here," she said firmly, but listening to her, he frowned.

"And when a war party comes? What will you do then? Trade your life for those two boys outside, as you did last year?" He was still impressed by that, and would never forget the look in her eyes when she offered him her life for the young soldier's.

"We are no threat to them. You said yourself the Indians are peaceful here. I wish them no harm. They will know that."

"The Nonotuck and the Wampanoag perhaps, but if Shawnee come from the West, or Huron from the North, or even Mohawk, then what will you do, Sarah?"

"Pray, or join my Maker," she said with a smile. She was not going to worry about it. She felt safe where she was, and the other settlers said there were rarely problems. They had already promised to send her word if any war parties were seen in the environs.

"Can you shoot?" he asked, still looking worried about her, and she smiled at his interest. He no longer looked fierce to her, he was her friend now.

"I went hunting with my father as a young girl, but I have not done so for many years." He nodded, he knew what he had to teach her. And there were things about the Indians he still felt she should learn. He was also going to spread the word among his friends in the neighboring tribes that there was a woman here, unarmed, alone, and that she was under his protection. The word would travel far and wide among them. They would be curious about her, some would come to look, or watch from the distance. They might even visit, or come to trade with her. But once they knew she was connected to him, they would do her no harm. He was White Bear of the Iroquois. He had been in the sweat lodges with them and danced with them after their Wars. He had shared their ceremonies with them. And Red Jacket of the Iroquois had accepted him as his son many years before. And when his wife and infant son had died, murdered by the Huron, they had been buried with her ancestors, and taken by the gods, while François mourned them.

Sarah watched him, as they finished dinner, and after she cleared the table, they walked outside again. The night was warm, and François felt odd standing next to her. It was a long time since he had visited this way with a white woman. There had been no woman of significance in his life since Crying Sparrow, and now as he looked at Sarah, standing next to him, he felt frightened for her. She was so innocent in her brave new world. He would have liked to watch over her, to teach her many things, to glide with her in the long canoes, to take her down the other rivers, to ride with her for many days, but there was no way to explain to her what he felt, or his worries about her. She was an innocent in a potentially complicated world, and he knew that she understood none of the dangers.

He slept outside, near the horses that night, under the stars. And he lay thinking about her for a long time. She had come far from where she started, just as he had so many years before. But it was so much harder for her, and she was so much braver. She seemed to realize none of it, as she came out of her kitchen the next day, and he could smell bacon frying in her kitchen. She had baked corn bread for him, and there was steaming, hot coffee. It was a long time since he'd had a breakfast like that, made by a woman.

"You'll make me lazy," he smiled, and after breakfast he took her out with his musket and his rifles. He was surprised to find that she was a good shot. They both laughed with pleasure when she brought down several birds in rapid succession, and he told her he would leave a musket with her, and ammunition, and he said that she should buy guns for the boys she'd hired, so they could protect her.

"I don't think we'll need them," she said firmly, and asked him if he'd like to walk to the waterfall with her before he left.

They walked side by side in silence for a long time, each of them lost in their own thoughts, and when they got there, they both stood quietly looking at the spectacular cascade of water. She always felt her soul had been restored when she saw it and listened to the sounds, something about the rushing water always

239

touched her deeply. He smiled as he looked down at her again, but he seemed more distant now and she didn't know what he was thinking. As with his Indian friends, it was often difficult to tell what was on his mind. He had picked up many of their habits.

"Send word to the garrison, Sarah, if you ever need me. They'll know where I am, or they can send out an Indian scout to find me." It was an offer he made to none, but in her case he meant it, but she thanked him and shook her head.

"We'll be fine," she said firmly, and believed it.

"And if you're not?"

"Your friends will tell you," she smiled, "between the soldiers and the Indians, there seem to be few secrets in this part of the world." There was more truth to that than she knew, and he laughed at what she was saying. Considering how remote they were, everyone seemed to know what everyone else was doing. It was no different than Boston, in some ways, though it took longer for news to get around.

"I'll come back again this way next month," he said, without waiting for an invitation, "to see how you are, and if you need help with the house."

"Where will you be until then?" His life intrigued her. She could easily imagine him living in the long houses of the Iroquois among his friends, or traveling in their canoes with them, for long distances on the rivers.

"I'll be up North," he said simply. And then he said something very odd to her in response to what she had said the night before. "You won't be alone here forever, Sarah." It was something he believed as well as felt. But she surprised him with her answer, and the quiet look in her eyes, which confirmed it.

"I'm not afraid to be alone, François," she said clearly, and meant it. She had accepted that fact of her life for a long time, better that than to be chained to a man like Edward, or another one like him. Even the Indians gave their women the right to leave a brave who abused them. Her supposedly civilized world didn't even do that. "I have no fear here," she said with an easy smile, balancing on her beloved rocks while he watched her. At times, she looked almost like a child. And old as she thought she was, to him, she was barely more than a girl, and she looked it. There was still something young and trusting in her eyes, as she looked at him.

"What are you afraid of then?" he asked, mesmerized by her as she sat down on a smooth, warm rock that had been warmed by the sun all morning.

"I was afraid of you," she laughed, "terrified in fact . . . that was wretched of you," she scolded him now, comfortable enough to tell him how desperately frightened she had been. "I fully expected you to kill me."

"I was so angry at you, I wanted to shake you," he confessed, ashamed now of the terror he had caused her. "All I could think of was what a Mohawk war party would have done, and I wanted to frighten you all the way back to Boston, to save you. But I see now that you're far too stubborn to be influenced by the sensible arguments of an honest man."

"*Sensible! Honest!*" She jeered at him. "How honest were you, masquerading as an Indian warrior, scaring me to death? That's hardly a 'sensible argument' if you ask me, now, is it?" She was laughing at him by then, and as he sat next to her, splashing his bare feet next to hers, their arms were agonizingly close, but not quite touching. It would have taken nothing to put an arm around her, to pull her close to him and hold her. But even knowing her as little as he did, he sensed the high wall around her, and he wouldn't have dared to approach it. "I'll get you back for it one day," she said calmly, "I'll put on a terrifying mask, and come and frighten you in your lodge."

"I think I'd like that," he said, leaning against the rock, looking at her, as they basked in the warm sun together.

"Well, then I'll have to think of something much worse to do to you." But in truth, she couldn't. Having lost a wife and a child, the worst had been done. It didn't matter to him that his marriage would not have been recognized by the court, his native France, or even the settlers. For him, the Iroquois bond that had tied them together was sacred enough to last a lifetime.

"You had no children in England, did you?" he asked casually, almost sure that she didn't, and thinking that the subject was safe enough. But he was wrong. He saw immediately in her eyes the enormous pain he'd caused, and wished that he could tear out his tongue as he watched her. "I'm sorry, Sarah . . . I didn't mean . . . I thought . . ."

"It's all right," she said gently, looking at him, with worlds of wisdom and sorrow in her eyes. "All my children either died at birth or were stillborn. Perhaps that's why my husband hated me so much. I failed to provide him with an heir. He has many bastards, all over England, I believe, but I never gave him a legitimate son. Of the six that died," she said in an anguished tone, looking out over the water, "three of them were sons."

"I'm so sorry," he said softly, barely able to imagine the grief she must have gone through.

"So was I," she smiled sadly. "He was relentless, he wanted an heir at any price, and I think he would have beaten me senseless until I produced one. He got me with child again and again, and even then he beat me, not enough to injure the child, just enough to remind me that I was dirt beneath his feet. I used to think he was quite mad sometimes, and then I thought I was . . . I used to sit in church and pray that he would die. . . ." François cringed just thinking of it, and then as though to share his grief with her, he told her of Crying Sparrow and their baby, and how much he had loved them. He said he had thought he would die of grief when they were both killed in an Indian raid on their village. He had thought he could never care about anyone else again, but now he was not as sure, although Sarah was very different than anyone he had known. But he was surprised himself how much he cared about Sarah, despite the little he knew of her. He did not say as much to her, but they had each had their private sorrows, they each carried a heavy burden on their heart. It had been a long time for him now, but he could see in Sarah's eyes that her wounds had not yet healed. Her last child had died only a little over a year before, but the pain was not as sharp now as it had once been. She had had such a happy, easy life since she'd come here.

They sat in the sunshine for a while, thinking of the confidences they'd shared and the pain it eased, and she marveled at the fact that the man who had frightened her so much six months before had just become her first real friend since she'd been here. She was almost sorry that he was leaving, and as they walked back to her house in the late afternoon, she asked him if he'd like to stay for another meal, but he said he'd best move on, he still had far to travel. He said he had promised to meet up with his men farther north, but the real reason was he didn't trust himself with her if he stayed close to her for too long. And he knew from talking to her that she was not ready to take anyone into her life yet. If he wanted to be close to her, all he could hope for was her friendship.

She gave him stores of corn bread and ham and bacon to take with him when he left, and he reminded her to buy guns and ammunition. She still had his musket, and he waved as he rode away from her, bare-chested again, his hair flying in the wind, the only thing that set him apart from his adopted brothers was that he would not wear their breechclout, but instead he wore buckskins, and moccasins, and walked on silent feet, just as they did.

She watched him until he left the clearing, and when she went back into the house, something bright caught her eye on the table where they had dined the night before, and when she went to look, it was the bear claw necklace, and the string of bright green beads he'd been wearing the night before at dinner.

243

◊　◊　◊

And as Charlie put the journal down again, the phone was ring-
ing and he could see from the light that it was late afternoon. He
felt disoriented, having just come back from a moment in time
distant by two hundred years. He assumed it was probably
Gladys. When the phone had been put in he told Gladys and the
office in New York his phone number, and of course he faxed
Carole, who really had no reason to call him.

But when he answered, he gave a start. She hadn't called him
since he left London. And he hadn't called her himself in nearly
two weeks. It was Carole, and he couldn't help wondering if
she'd come to her senses. Maybe Simon had done something
terrible to her, or maybe she finally missed him. But whatever
the reason for her call, just listening to her voice seemed delicious to Charlie.

"Hi," he said, still lying in bed, as he had been since that
morning. He had just put the journal down, and could still envision the green beads François had left her on the table. "How
are you?" His voice and his smile were warm as he lay there
thinking of Carole.

"You sound funny. Are you all right?" She worried about him,
more than he ever suspected.

"I'm fine," he explained. "I'm in bed." He had his head on the
pillow, and he sounded relaxed. He couldn't help thinking that
she'd love the house. He wanted to tell her about it. He had
wanted to ever since the first time he'd seen it. But first, he
wanted to know why she'd called him.

"Don't you do any kind of work anymore?" She sounded nervous and she still didn't fully understand what had happened in
New York. She still wondered if he'd had some kind of nervous
breakdown. It wasn't like him to just walk out on a job and take
six months off, and now he was talking about lying around in bed
at four o'clock in the afternoon. To Carole, it sounded awful, and
highly suspicious.

"I was reading," he said, sounding hurt, but he didn't tell her what. "I'm just taking some time for myself, that's all. I haven't done that in years." And after all she'd done to him in the past year, she ought to understand that, but in her busy legal world, it was not the kind of thing that normal, healthy people did. You didn't just walk out on an important job, and spend the next six months in bed, reading.

"I'm not sure I understand what's happening to you, Charlie," she said sadly, and he laughed when he answered her. He was in great spirits, now that she had called him.

"Neither do I. So what's up, why did you call me?" In London, it was nine o'clock at night. It was easy to believe that she had just left the office, or so he thought. Actually, she was still at her desk, but she had told Simon she was going to call him. They were meeting at Annabel's at ten o'clock and she knew he'd ask her about it. "Are you okay?" She hated hearing what a good mood he was in, she didn't want to spoil it, but she wanted him to know before she told anyone else, and before he heard it from any of their old friends. Word always got around London very quickly.

"I'm fine. Charlie, there's no way to tell you this, except straight out. . . . Simon and I are getting married, in June, after the divorce is final." There was an endless silence, and she closed her eyes and bit her lip. For an eternity, Charlie said nothing. He felt as though he had just been hit in the stomach with a boulder. By now, it was a familiar feeling.

"What do you expect me to say?" he said, sounding sick suddenly. "Beg you not to? Is that why you called? You could have just sent me a letter."

"I wouldn't do that to you, and I didn't want you to hear it from someone else." She was crying, telling him was turning out to be much worse than she thought. And although she couldn't hear Charlie, he was crying too, and wishing she hadn't called him.

"What difference does it make who I hear it from? And why the hell are you marrying him? He's old enough to be your father for chrissake, and he's just going to dump you like he did all his other wives," Charlie said, fighting for his life now. He couldn't let her do it. He felt as though he were flying down a hill out of control, and he couldn't stop as he tried to warn her about Simon.

"Two of them left him," Carole corrected him, and Charlie made a bitter little sound at his end. "He only left the third one."

"Great recommendation. What does that make you? Number Four? How charming. Is that what you want? Why don't you just have an affair with him? You already did that," he said, beginning to turn nasty.

"And then what?" She slammed the ball back at him now. He made her feel terrible, and she didn't have to call him. She had just done it to be nice. "What do you expect from me, Charlie? To come back and start all over again where we left off? How would you even know I'm back? Neither of us were ever there, we were just two executives sharing a house and a fax machine. Christ, that wasn't a marriage, do you know how lonely I was?" she said, sounding anguished, and listening to her, he felt sick. He had never noticed.

"Why didn't you tell me? Why didn't you say something instead of just going out and fucking someone else, goddammit! How was I supposed to know what was going on in your head, if you never said anything about it?"

She was sobbing now, and there were tears running down his cheeks. "I'm not sure I knew myself," she said honestly, "until it was over. I think we were so busy running away from each other all the time that I stopped feeling after a while. I was just a robot, a machine, a lawyer . . . and every now and then, when either of us had time, which wasn't often, I was your wife."

"And now?" He wasn't just torturing himself, he wanted to

know. He needed to know, for himself. "Are you happier with him?"

"Yes, I am," she admitted to Charlie. "It's different. We eat dinner together every night, he calls me three or four times a day if we're apart. He wants to know what I'm doing. I don't know what it is, but he makes more time. He makes *me* make more time. If he goes away, he takes me with him, or he comes with me, if he can, even if he just flies over to Paris or Brussels or Rome or wherever I am, for the night." He was infinitely more attentive.

"That's not fair," Charlie said, looking unhappy, "you both work for the same firm. I wasn't even as close as Paris for chrissake, at least not all the time. Half the time I was in Hong Kong or Taipei." It was true, but there was more to it than that, and they both knew it. They had let something between them die, it had just slipped away while they weren't looking.

"It wasn't just the trips, Charlie . . . you know that. It was everything. We stopped talking to each other . . . we never had time to make love . . . I was always working and you were always jet-lagged." It was truer than he was ready to admit, and her reference to their absentee sex life only made it worse. He was not enjoying the conversation.

"And I suppose a sixty-one-year-old man is going to make love to you every night? What does he have, an implant? Give me a break, Carole."

"Charlie, for God's sake . . . please . ''

"No, you please!" He sat up sharply in bed, ready to fight back. "You had an affair with him. You never told me how unhappy you were. You just walked right out there and hired someone else for the job without even telling me I'd been fired. You never even gave me a chance to fix it, and now you're all wrapped up in this romantic bullshit that he's heaping on you because he's oh so suave and debonair, and you're telling me that you're getting *married*. And just how long is that going to last? You're kidding yourself, Carole. You're thirty-nine years old. He's sixty-one. I give it a year, two at most."

"Thanks for the vote of confidence, and the gracious good wishes," she said, sounding really angry. "I knew you couldn't handle it. Simon thought I should call you, he said it was the proper thing to do. And I said you'd act like a complete jerk. Looks like I was right." She was being a bitch now, and she knew it, but she hated the way he sounded, hated knowing he was still so hurt. What if he never recovered and it was all her fault forever? But even thinking that didn't make her want to go back to him. All she wanted was to marry Simon.

"Why didn't you just have Simon call?" he asked meanly. "It would have been so much simpler. None of this messy stuff, just a lot of crap about being a good sport, hail-fellow-well-met, God save the Queen, and all that . . ." He was crying again, she could hear it, and then there was an endless silence. He sniffed, and he sounded terrible when he spoke again. "I can't believe you're getting married in June. The ink on the divorce won't even be dry yet."

"I'm sorry, Charlie," she said softly. "I can't help it. This is what I want." He was quiet again, thinking about her, remembering how much he had loved her, wishing she had given him a chance. But she hadn't. And it was Simon's turn now. She had thrown away everything she'd ever had with Charlie. He still couldn't believe it.

"I'm sorry, baby," he said, and the gentleness of his words tore her heart out. They were far more effective than his anger, but she didn't say that to him. "I guess the only thing left for me is to say good luck."

"Thanks." She sat at her desk, silently crying. She wanted to tell him she still loved him, but she knew that wouldn't be fair. But in a way, she knew she always would. It was all so confusing, and so painful, but at least, by calling him, she felt she'd done the right thing. "I'd better go now." It was after nine-thirty, and she had to meet Simon in half an hour at the club.

"Take care," Charlie said hoarsely, and a moment later they both hung up. He was sitting up in bed and lay his head back against the headboard and closed his eyes. He couldn't believe what she'd said. And for a crazy minute he'd thought she was calling to tell him it was over with Simon. How stupid could he have been? But now he couldn't believe the pain she had inflicted on him.

He got up and wiped his eyes and stared out the window. It was a sunny afternoon, and suddenly even Sarah's journals didn't seem as important. All he wanted was to get out of the house and scream. He didn't know what he was going to do, but he got out of bed and pulled his clothes on. He brushed his hair, and put on a heavy sweater with his jeans. He put on warm socks and boots, and a jacket, locked the house and got into his car. He didn't even know where he was going, he just knew that for a while at least, he had to get out. Maybe she was right, maybe there was something wrong with him just taking time off for a while. But things had been such a mess in New York, he hadn't felt he had any options.

He drove aimlessly toward town and saw in the rearview mirror that he looked ragged. He hadn't shaved since the day before and his eyes suddenly looked sunken in his head. It was as though she had hit him with a brick. But he knew he had to get over it at some point. He couldn't go on crying over her for the rest of his life, or could he? And if this was the way he felt now, what would it be like in June when they got married?

He drove by the historical society as he asked himself a thousand questions, and then without knowing why he did it, he stopped. Francesca was the wrong person to talk to. In her own way, she was even more wounded than he was. But he had to talk to someone. He couldn't just sit there reading the journals anymore, and somehow he didn't think that, in this instance, talking to Gladys Palmer would help him. He thought of just going to a bar and having a drink. He needed to hear noise and see people, he needed to do something to blunt the pain of what he'd just heard from Carole.

He was still sitting in the car, wondering if he should go in, when he saw her. She had just locked the door, and was halfway down the steps, and then as though she sensed someone watching her, Francesca turned and saw him. She hesitated for a moment, wondering if it was coincidence or intentional, and then she turned and began to walk away. And without thinking about why he did it, he got out of the car and ran after her, and all he could think of as he did was Sarah and François. At some point François had had to have the courage to be there. He had come back, even after he'd frightened her, in order to give her the green beads and the bear claws. Charlie hadn't even frightened Francesca, he reminded himself. But all she'd ever done since he'd met her was run away from him. She was perennially frightened, of life, of men, of people.

"Wait!" he shouted as he came up two steps behind her, and she turned then, with a worried look in her eyes. What did he want from her? Why was he running after her? She had nothing to give him, she knew only too well. She had nothing to give anyone anymore, and certainly not Charlie. "I'm sorry," he said, looking suddenly embarrassed, and she noticed instantly that he looked awful.

"You can bring the books back tomorrow," she said, as though he would have come tearing down the block for two books he'd forgotten to return. Not likely.

"Screw the books," he said bluntly. "I need to talk to you . . . I need to talk to someone . . ." He flung his arms around in despair, as though he were thrashing, and she could see suddenly that he was close to crying.

"Is something wrong? Did something happen?" In spite of herself, she felt sorry for him. It was easy to see that he was in a lot of pain. He sat down on the steps leading to a darkened house, and she looked down at him the way she would have at her little girl. "What is it?" she asked gently this time, sitting on the step next to him. "Tell me what happened." She sat very close to him, and he stared into space, wishing he had the courage to take her hand while he told her.

"I shouldn't bother you with this . . . I just had to talk to someone. I just got a call from my ex-wife . . . I know . . . I'm crazy . . . she's been seeing this guy for over a year, seventeen months actually. She had an affair with him, he's the senior partner of her law firm, and he's sixty-one and been married three times . . . so she left me for him, ten months ago to be exact. Last fall we filed for divorce, and it's a long story but I got transferred to New York, and it didn't work out so I took a leave of absence . . . and now she calls me . . . she called and I thought she was going to tell me that she came to her senses." He laughed an empty little laugh and Francesca watched him. She could already guess what was coming.

"Instead, she called to tell you she's getting married," she said sadly, and he looked startled.

"She called you too?" He grinned at her sadly, and they both laughed.

"She didn't have to. I got that call too, quite a while ago," she said with a look of sorrow.

"From your husband?"

She nodded. "His was a little more exotic. He had an affair publicized on national French TV at the Olympics. He's a sportscaster, and he got involved with a young girl, the French ski champion. They became everybody's darlings. No matter that he was married, and had a child. That was completely unimportant. Everyone fell in love with Pierre and Marie-Lise, she's the cutest little thing you've ever seen. She was eighteen, he was thirty-three. They posed for pictures, were on the cover of *Paris-Match*. They even gave interviews together, and he told me it wasn't important. It was good publicity for the ski team. Anything for God and country. I got a little upset about it though, when she got pregnant. They made a big fuss about that on TV too. People kept sending baby clothes they made for her, only they kept sending them to me. He kept telling me he loved me, and of course he's crazy about Monique . . . and he's a good father . . . so I stayed . . ."

"And cried all the time," he filled in for her.

"Who told you?" She looked surprised for a minute, and he smiled gently at her.

"Monique. But she didn't say anything else." He didn't want to get the little girl in trouble, and Francesca smiled wisely and shrugged.

"Anyway, I stayed, and she got bigger and bigger. More interviews, more cover stories, more coverage on TV, national sportscaster and gold medal Olympic ski teenager. It was perfect. More Headlines. News Flash: she's having twins. More little booties arrive at the house. Monique thought I was having a baby, try explaining that to a five-year-old kid. Anyway, Pierre kept telling me I was being neurotic and old-fashioned. According to him, I'm a constipated American and it was all very French and I refused to understand it. Trouble was, it was déjà vu for me, my father is Italian, and did almost the same thing to my mother when I was six. It wasn't much fun then either, but to tell the truth, this was worse." She made it sound almost funny, but it didn't take much to figure out that it had been a nightmare. Having your husband cheat on you in front of TV cameras had to be even worse than what Carole had done to him. Even Charlie thought so. "Anyway, the babies were finally born. And of course they were adorable, naturally, a boy and a girl. Jean-Pierre and Marie-Louise, two little darling replicas of them. I took it for about two weeks after that, and then I got the hell out of Dodge. I packed up Monique, and told him to let me know if he had any more children, but in the meantime, he could find me in New York, at my mother's. Once I got there, I thought about it for a while, and my mother drove me crazy, screaming about him. It was like her own divorce revisited for her. After a while, I didn't want to hear it. I filed for divorce. The French press said I was a very poor sport. I guess they were right. The divorce was final a year ago, just before last Christmas. I got the same call you did just last Christmas Eve. They wanted to share the good news with me. They had just gotten married in Courchevel on the slopes, with the babies on their backs, and they just knew I'd want to share their joy with them. Monique tells me she's pregnant again, she wants to have another one before she starts training for the next Olympics. It's all too cute. But what I keep wondering is why he bothered with me? He could have just waited around for her, and skipped over the whole episode that included me. It never really played all that well for TV anyway. As the French press said, I was very American, and pretty boring."

She still sounded angry and bitter, and listening to what she'd said, it didn't sound like a mystery to him. She was obviously deeply hurt by the loss and the humiliation, and her father having done the same thing when she was a kid couldn't have helped much. He wondered what that meant now for Monique. Was she now a third-generation loser, guaranteed to fail at marriage? It was hard to know how these things affected people. His parents had been happily married, so had Carole's. It had still happened to them. Did that mean everyone failed at marriage? Or just some? What did it all mean?

"How long were you married?" he asked her.

"Six years," she said, leaning gently against him. She wasn't even aware of doing it, but it had felt good to tell him her story. Listening to his, she didn't feel quite as alone now, and neither did Charlie. "What about you?" she asked with interest. They suddenly had a lot in common. They'd been dumped by experts.

"We were married for nine years, nearly ten. Tower of observation that I am, I thought we were blissfully happy. I never even noticed there was a problem till she was already practically living with someone else. I don't know how I missed that. She said we were too busy, traveled too much, didn't pay enough attention to each other. Sometimes I think now we should have had kids."

"Why didn't you?"

"I don't know. I guess she's right," he confessed, it was easier admitting it to Francesca than Carole. "Maybe we were too busy. It just didn't seem like something we needed to do, and now I'm sorry, especially when I meet a kid like yours. I've got nothing to show for nine years of marriage."

Francesca smiled at him, and he liked what he saw there. He was glad he had stopped her on the street. He had needed to talk to someone and maybe better her than someone else. At least she understood him, and what had happened.

"Pierre said it happened to us because I was too wrapped up in Monique. I stopped working when I had her. I was modeling in Paris when we met, and when we got married, I gave up modeling, studied art and history at the Sorbonne, and got my master's. But when I had her, I just fell in love with being a mother. I wanted to be with her all the time. I wanted to take care of her myself, I thought that was what he wanted. I don't know, Charlie . . . maybe you can't win sometimes. Maybe some marriages are doomed from the beginning." She thought so.

"That's what I've been thinking lately." Charlie nodded in agreement. "I thought we had this great marriage, and now it turns out I was crazy, and you thought you were married to the French edition of Prince Charming. How would you say that, 'Prince Charmant'?" She nodded and grinned. "And it turns out we were both crazy. Now Carole is going to be married to some old fart who collects women, and your ex-husband is married to a twelve-year-old with twins . . . go figure . . . how are you ever supposed to know when you've got it right? Maybe you can't know. Maybe you have to take your chances and work it out as you go along. I'll tell you one thing, next time, if there ever is one, I'm going to listen like crazy. I'm going to ask questions all the time . . . how are you? . . . how am I? . . . how are we? . . . are you happy? . . . is this good? . . . are you cheating on me yet?" She laughed at him, but he wasn't entirely kidding, he had learned something from what had happened, but Francesca looked sad as she shook her head.

"You're braver than I am. There's not going to be a next time for me, Charlie. I've already made up my mind." She told him that now because she was willing to be his friend, but nothing more. Romance was not on her menu.

"You can't make your mind up about a thing like that," he said gently.

"Yes, you can," she argued with him. "I have. I don't ever want to have my heart and my guts trampled on again."

"What about without TV coverage next time?" he teased her. "Or maybe just foreign rights and a percentage of the tabloid sales. How about a share of the box office?" he teased, and she smiled halfheartedly. She was very, very wounded, and badly scarred by all that had happened to her.

"You don't know what it was like," she said with feeling. But looking in her eyes, he could see a glimmer of it. All that was left there now was pain, and he remembered the little snippets of what Monique had said, about her crying. It was why she was so closed down to everyone, why she had been so unpleasant to him at first. But all he could think of now was how lonely it must have been for her, and still was, and without thinking, he put an arm around her and pulled her closer. But there was no threat in it, he just wanted to be her friend, and she sensed that and didn't fight him.

"Tell you what, kid," he said gently, "if it ever happens again, and you decide to take a wild leap into marriage, I'll be your agent." But she laughed at that and shook her head.

"Don't wait for that job, Charlie . . . it'll never happen. Not to me. Not again." And he knew how emphatically she meant it.

"Shall we make a pact then? Neither of us will ever make fools of ourselves again, or if one of us does, the other has to, sort of a joint suicide pact . . . kamikaze marriage . . ." He was teasing, but she didn't mind it. It was the first time she had ever laughed about her situation, and she was surprised to find it made her feel better, although she didn't think she'd done much for him, but when she said so, he denied it. "I needed to talk to someone, Francesca . . . and I'm glad it was you." They both stood up then, and she looked at her watch apologetically, and reminded him that she had to pick up her daughter.

"I'm really sorry to leave you. Will you be all right?" she asked, and he saw a person in her he hadn't seen in the short time he'd known her, but he was relieved to see her now. She seemed much kinder, and more open.

"I'll be fine," he lied. He wanted to go home and think about it, to ponder about Carole and Simon, and try and adjust to their marriage in his mind. In his own way, he needed more time to mourn her. But he had an idea as he looked at Francesca. "What about dinner, the three of us, tomorrow night?" He didn't want to frighten her by asking her out on a date. "And I'll bring my books back. I promise," he added as an incentive, as she walked him back to his car. Hers was down the street, just beyond it. "What about it? Just pizza or spaghetti or something? It might do us all good to get out." She hesitated and he had the feeling she was going to decline the offer, but as she looked at him, she knew he wouldn't harm her. She had told him where things stood. And he knew that all she could offer him was to be his friend and if he was willing to accept that, she was willing to have dinner with him.

"All right." She looked determined and he smiled.

"Maybe we'll do the big time. Dinner in Deerfield. You know, maybe even black tie." He was silly and he made her laugh, and then he drove her to her car. "I'll pick you up at six," he said, feeling almost human again, and then he looked at her gently as she got out. "Francesca . . . thanks!"

She waved as he drove away, and he thought about the things she'd told him. It must have been hard for her . . . worse than that . . . heartbreaking . . . and humiliating. . . . People were so rotten to each other sometimes, it was hard to understand it. Carole hadn't been rotten to him, he thought to himself, as he drove home, she had just broken his heart. That was all. Nothing more serious than that, at the moment.

And as he unlocked the door to his house again, he thought of Sarah, the pain she had gone through with Edward, and the joy she must have found with François. He wondered how one bridged the two lives, the two moments . . . how did one go from intolerable pain, and no longer trusting anyone . . . to being whole again, forgiving, and starting life over? He didn't have the answers yet, he knew, as he turned the light on. Even after talking to Francesca, all he could think of now was Carole. And that night, as he lay in bed, he thought of her instead of Sarah and François. And as he mused on the mysteries of life, he decided not to read the journals again for a few days. He needed to work this one out, go back to the real world, and deal with his life now.

Chapter 16

*C*HARLIE PICKED THEM up at six o'clock, and drove them to Di Maio in Deerfield for dinner. Charlie and Francesca were both feeling a little shy, but Monique chatted animatedly all the way to Deerfield. She talked about her friends at school, the dog she wished she had, the hamster her mother had promised her, wanting to go skating the next day, and she complained about her homework.

"I used to get a lot more homework in France," she conceded finally, referring obliquely to their life in Paris, and Charlie glanced at Francesca. She was staring out the window.

"Maybe we should start teaching you German, or Chinese or something, just to keep you busy," he teased her, and Monique made a face, two languages were enough trouble as far as she was concerned, although she was completely fluent in both. And then she looked at him brightly.

"My mom speaks Italian. My grampa was from Venice." And according to her, a bastard just like her husband, Charlie remembered. They were touching on all her favorite subjects. It was going to be a great evening. But she said nothing. "They have a lot of boats there," Monique told him, and he tactfully changed the subject and asked what kind of dog she wanted. "Something little and cute," she answered immediately, she'd obviously given it a lot of thought. "Like a Chihuahua."

"A Chihuahua?" He laughed at the suggestion. "That's so small, you'll get it mixed up with your hamster." She guffawed when he said it.

"No, I wouldn't." He told her about Gladys's dog then, the big friendly Irish setter, and offered to take her to meet her. She liked that, and Francesca almost smiled then. She was so serious, and so sad sometimes, it made his heart ache for her. But at least Monique was happy. It said something about Francesca's mothering skills, and the fact that she must love her, and had protected her fairly successfully from the horrors that had happened to them in Paris.

And a few minutes later, they reached Deerfield.

The restaurant was busy and cheerful, and Monique ordered spaghetti and meatballs almost as soon as she sat down at the table. The adults took a little longer, and finally ordered capellini with basil and tomato. He ordered wine for them, and he noticed that Francesca spoke to the waiter in Italian. He seemed delighted, and Charlie listened with pleasure.

"I love to hear that." He smiled at her. "Did you ever live there?"

"Until I was nine. But I always spoke Italian to my father, when he was alive. I'd like Monique to learn it. It's always useful to know another language." Though now that they were living back in the States, it seemed less important. "She might want to go back to Europe one day to live," Francesca conceded, though in her heart of hearts, she hoped not. And then she turned to him with eyes full of questions. She had learned a lot about him the day before, but only about his marriage. "What about you? What will you do? Go back to London?"

"I don't know. I just stopped here on my way to Vermont to go skiing. And then I met Gladys Palmer, and saw the house and fell in love with it. I rented it for a year, but even if I go back to Europe, I can come here for vacations. But I'm happy here for now, though I feel a little guilty for not working. This is the first time in my life I've ever done this. But eventually, I'll have to be an architect again, hopefully in London."

"Why?" She looked puzzled, after all he had told her. Was it to pursue his wife, or were there other reasons? Her eyes asked a myriad questions.

"I have a life there," he said firmly, and then reconsidered, as Monique dug into her meatballs. "At least I used to. I sold my house just before I left." And now he wasn't even sure he had a job there. "Besides, I love London," he said stubbornly. But he also loved Carole. Maybe he would forever. Even after she married Simon, but he didn't say that to Francesca. The thought of it depressed him.

"I loved Paris too," Francesca said softly. "But I couldn't stay afterward . . . I tried. But it was just too difficult. It would have driven me crazy, expecting to see him every time I turned a corner, waiting to run into him, hating him when I did. I cried every time I turned the news on, and saw him, but I couldn't make myself stop watching. It was sick. So I left. I can't imagine living there now." She sighed, and smiled at him over their capellini.

"Will you stay here?" He liked talking to her. It was such a relief to talk to someone, and air the things that had almost killed him. Talking about it made it all seem so much smaller.

"Maybe," she answered. She hadn't made up her mind. "My mother thinks I should bring Monique back to New York to get a 'decent' education. But we're happy here, the school is fine. She loves to ski. I like our little house at the edge of town. And it's so peaceful. I want to finish my thesis while I'm here, I can decide after that. This would be a good place to do some writing." Or reading. He thought about Sarah's journals and said nothing.

"It would," he agreed. "I want to do some painting." His style had always been a little bit like Wyeth's, and particularly with the snow, the landscape around Shelburne Falls was perfect.

"A man of many talents," she said, with a twinkle in her eye, and he suddenly smiled at her. He liked it when she teased him. And eventually they drew Monique back into the conversation, but she'd been happy for a while, listening to them, and eating her spaghetti. Monique talked about her life in Paris then, the apartment she loved, going to the Bois de Boulogne every day after school, and the trips she'd taken with her parents, mostly skiing, since it was her father's passion. And listening to her made Francesca look nostalgic, which worried Charlie. He didn't want her closing up on him again. This was good for both of them, and she relaxed again when Charlie changed the subject, and then he had an idea, and decided to ask her.

"What about going skiing this Saturday? We could just go to Charlemont for the day." He knew from Gladys that many of the locals did that often. And Monique was instantly enthusiastic.

"Come on, Mommy . . . pleasssseeee . . ." She drew out the word like taffy, and Francesca smiled at the invitation.

"You're probably busy, and I should really get some work done. I don't think . . ."

"Come on," he said gently. "It would do us all good." He was thinking of the jolt he'd had the day before, when Carole called, and the things Francesca had told him. They all needed a little fun in their lives, and a day of skiing sounded perfect. "You can spare a day. We both can." He had nothing else to do, except read Sarah's journals. "Let's do it." He looked so sweet, and sounded so persuasive that she eventually relented, although she was still feeling a little hesitant about being indebted to him. She didn't want to do that. He might come to expect something she couldn't give him.

"All right, just for the day then." Monique's spirits rose dramatically after Francesca said it. She chatted and giggled and laughed and talked about the runs there and compared them to

261

Courchevel and Val d'Isère, and Francesca laughed at that, and so did Charlie. The skiing was not exactly comparable, but it would be fun anyway. And they were all looking forward to it, when he drove them back to Shelburne Falls after dinner.

He stopped outside their house, and got out. It was a small neat wooden house, painted white, with green shutters, and a picket fence around it. And when they got out of the car, Francesca thanked him for dinner.

"I really enjoyed it," she said carefully, and Monique immediately chimed in.

"So did I. Thanks, Charlie."

"You're welcome. I'll see you both on Saturday. What time should I pick you up?" He made no move to go into the house with them. He knew instinctively that it would have scared Francesca. She still wore the look of a young doe, about to dart back into the forest, particularly now that they were on her turf. It was obvious that she didn't want him too near her, no matter how pleasant their conversations.

"How about eight o'clock?" she suggested in answer to his question. "We can be on the slopes by nine then."

"That sounds fine. See you then," he said, and watched them go into the house and close the door. He saw all the lights turn on, and the house looked cozy and warm, as he stood staring at it from the outside. And he was surprised at how lonely he felt on the drive back to his place. He always seemed to be on the outside now, watching Francesca and Monique, hearing about Carole and Simon . . . reading about Sarah and François. He didn't belong to anyone anymore, and he realized again how much he missed it. And as he thought about it, he drove slowly out of the way and decided to stop, on his way home, at Gladys Palmer's. She was in good spirits, looked well, and was delighted with the surprise visit. She made him some chamomile tea, and offered him a fresh plate of gingerbread cookies.

"How are things at the house?" she asked comfortably, and he smiled in answer. He was thinking about Sarah and the journals that he was still keeping secret, even from Mrs. Palmer. He wanted to finish them before he told her about them.

"Fine," he said noncommittally, and then told her about the evening he had just spent with Francesca and her daughter.

"That sounds promising," she said, looking pleased for him.

"We'll see," he said, as he finished a second cup of tea, and then finally left her to get back to the house. And when he did, he felt surprisingly less lonely. Seeing her always seemed to have remarkable restorative powers for him. She was almost like a mother to him.

And as he let himself into his house, he thought he heard a sound upstairs before he turned the light on. He stood very still, listening to it, wanting it to be her, convinced he had heard a footstep. But he stood there for a long time in the silence. It was nothing. And he finally turned the light on.

After he went upstairs, he thought about reading the journals again, but he realized he needed some breathing space from them. He was so involved with her and François now. They were becoming far too real to him, and all he wanted was to be with them. It wasn't healthy.

He picked up a novel that night, and forced himself to read it. But it was so dull, compared to Sarah's words, that by ten o'clock, he was sound asleep, and he stirred when he heard a sound in the room. He opened his eyes and looked around for a minute, but he was half asleep and he didn't see her.

He hadn't touched the journals all week when he left the house to pick up Francesca and Monique on Saturday. He stopped by to see Gladys on the way, and gave her a book he'd been saving for her. They had a quick cup of tea, and then talked about Francesca again, and Gladys was pleased that he was seeing her again. It made her happy to know he had a friend, and she hoped to meet her one day, if Charlie continued to see her.

When he arrived at their house, Monique was wearing a bright red one-piece suit, and Francesca was looking extremely stylish in a black stretch suit. It was easy to believe she'd been a model, she was very striking. And they both looked in good spirits. They put their skis in the car, and fifteen minutes later, they were in Charlemont, and Francesca was threatening to put Monique in ski school. She didn't want her cruising all over the mountain by herself, picking up strangers. Charlie could see her point, but Monique was bitterly disappointed.

"They're all terrible in ski school," she complained, "no one knows how to do anything fun. I don't want to," she pouted, and Charlie felt so sorry for her he volunteered to ski with her. He had really enjoyed her. It was how they had met after all, and what had started their friendship. But Francesca didn't want to impose on him any more than they had already.

"Don't you want to ski on your own?" she asked him honestly, and he couldn't help noticing how green her eyes were, although he was trying not to.

"She skis better than I do," he grinned, "I can hardly keep up with her."

"That's not true," Monique said fairly with a smile, "you're pretty good. You've got good style, even on the moguls," she complimented him, and he laughed at her assessment. She definitely had her father's genes, at least as far as skiing. And Charlie thought it was funny.

"Thank you, miss. So, are you skiing with me?" and then he turned to her mother. "Would you care to join us? Or are you too expert for us?" He had never actually seen Francesca ski, he realized, only her daughter.

"She's okay," Monique conceded, and Francesca laughed at her, as the threesome decided to ski together that morning. But Charlie was duly impressed when he saw Francesca head down the mountain.

He didn't know if her Olympic champion ex-husband had

taught her some tricks, or if she'd skied like that before him, but she was much better than she had told him. She was almost as good a skier as her daughter, though not quite as confident, and she was very humble about it. She skied with such elegance and grace that it caught several people's attention, and he could only admire her when they stopped again at the bottom.

"You're *very* good," he said admiringly.

"I like it," she admitted. "We used to go to Cortina when I was a kid. My father was a great skier, but I've always been a little too cautious," she said, and Monique nodded vehemently. She liked to go a lot faster. Francesca was a woman of many charms, many talents, most of them either unsung, or hidden. She had so much going for her, and she was so unwilling to share it. It seemed a terrible waste to Charlie. But he found as the day wore on that he really enjoyed being with her. The sharpness that had so irritated him before never showed itself once, she just seemed happy and relaxed, and it was easy to see how much she loved skiing. And she enjoyed being with him too. By the time they took their last run, they felt like old friends, and looked like a family, as Monique skied in front of them. Francesca always kept an eye on her, but most of the time she skied with Charlie. And when they took off their skis at the end of the day, they stopped at the restaurant at the base for brownies and hot chocolate. Monique looked tired by then, but Francesca seemed to glow with exhilaration. Her creamy skin was warmed to a rosy color, and her eyes looked brilliant.

"I had a great time," she said as she thanked him. "I used to complain that the skiing isn't as good as Europe here, but I don't care anymore. I enjoy it anyway. Thank you for bringing us," she said, taking a sip of her hot chocolate and looking at him warmly.

"We should try some of the other resorts near here. Or go up to Vermont. Sugarbush is pretty good skiing," he said calmly.

"I'd like that," she said, before retreating into herself again, but she seemed completely at ease with him now, and she sat very close to him at the small table. He could feel her long, graceful legs next to his own, and it sent a small thrill through him. He hadn't felt that way for anyone since Carole left him. He'd been asked on a couple of dates in London, but they'd sounded awful. And he had never tried it. He knew he wasn't ready. But this woman, with her fine mind, intense shyness, and great pain, was beginning to warm him.

In fact, he hated to go back to Shelburne Falls, and he suggested dinner on the way, which Monique accepted on behalf of her mother. They stopped at the Charlemont Inn and had delicious hot turkey sandwiches with mashed potatoes, and they talked animatedly about a variety of subjects, including architecture, and they discovered that, like him, she had a passion for medieval castles. Monique was almost asleep by then, and when they went back to the car, she was yawning, and almost stumbled but Charlie caught her. It had been a long, happy day for all of them. And this time, when they reached their house, Francesca asked him if he'd like to come in and have a drink or a cup of coffee. She felt as though she had to do something to thank him.

"I have to put Monique to bed," she whispered over her head, and then took her into the back of the house, to her small, cozy bedroom while he waited in the living room, and looked at the wall full of books Francesca had brought with her from Europe. There were some wonderful volumes she had collected over the years, mostly about European history, and a number of them about art, and she even had several first editions. "Can you tell I'm a book freak?" she said when she came back into the living room, and noticed that he had lit the fire. It was a small, comfortable room, full of well-worn things that meant something to her, most of which she had brought from Europe. It was an insight into her to see it. She had seemed so cold to him at first, so distant, but this room told a different tale, and so did her eyes when he turned and looked at her. He wasn't sure what to do now, there was something very strange and very powerful happening between them, and he knew that if he acknowledged it, she might never see him again, so he decided to ignore it. And as though to confirm that, she left the room to make coffee and he found her in the kitchen. He was very careful about what he said then. He decided that Sarah Ferguson was probably a safe subject.

"I've been reading about Sarah Ferguson," he explained. "She was a remarkable woman, with incredible courage. She came over on the tiniest ship I've ever read about, it was an eighty-ton brig out of Falmouth, that carried twelve passengers, and it took over seven weeks to get here. I can't even imagine an experience like that. I get sick thinking about it. But she did it, and survived, and started a whole new life here." He stopped before he said any more, because he still didn't want to tell her about the journals, but Francesca looked puzzled.

"Where did you read that? I've never found anything like that about her, and I've searched our library very thoroughly at the historical society. Did you find something about her in Deerfield?"

"I . . . uh . . . yes, I did actually. And Mrs. Palmer gave me some articles." He would have loved to tell her what he'd found, but he didn't dare yet. He was satisfied to simply talk about it with her, and they talked about Sarah's courage for a little while, and the parallels in their own lives. "She had a whole new life here. Apparently, she left a terrible man in England." They exchanged a look as Francesca nodded thoughtfully. She had left a terrible man in Paris. Or maybe he wasn't even terrible after all, just stupid, like Carole. Or perhaps what their mates had found elsewhere was really what they needed to complete their own lives. It made Charlie pensive as he thought about Carole and Simon.

"Do you still miss her terribly?" Francesca asked gently, she could see from the look in his eyes what he was thinking.

"Sometimes," he said honestly, "I think I miss what I thought we had, rather than what we did have." Francesca understood that perfectly. All she could think about with Pierre afterward, was the happiness of the beginning and the horror of the ending, never the ordinary reality of the middle, which had been most of it, but that seemed to have been forgotten.

"I think we all do that," she agreed with him, "we remember the fantasy we create rather than the reality we lived with, whether that fantasy was beautiful or ugly. I'm not sure I even remember who Pierre was anymore, just the man I came to hate in the end, whoever he was."

"I suppose I'll get that way eventually with Carole. Even now, some of it gets a little hazy." Everything seemed either better or worse than it had been, and sometimes he could see that. And then he thought about Sarah again. "You know, the remarkable thing about her," he said to Francesca thoughtfully, "was that she fell in love all over again, with the Frenchman. From everything I've heard, the important part of her life was with him. Even after everything that happened to her, she wasn't afraid to start over. I admire that," he said with a small sigh, "but I'm not sure how to do it."

"I couldn't," Francesca said firmly, it was a confirmation of everything she'd said to him already. "I know myself well enough to know that."

"You're too young to make a decision like that," Charlie said sadly.

"I'm thirty-one," she said firmly. "That's old enough to know you don't want to play again, ever, and I don't. I wouldn't survive the hurt next time." And although he still felt an attraction between them that couldn't be denied, he also knew she was telling him not to try it. And if he did, she was fully prepared to run out of his life forever. He had heard the warning, very clearly.

"I think you have to think about that, Francesca." It made him want to give her the journals to read, but he wasn't ready to tell her about them. And he realized that maybe he never would be.

He still felt very private about them, and he would have had to be very close to her to share them.

"Believe me, I've thought about nothing but for the past two years," she said sternly, and then she asked him a strange question and he wasn't sure how to answer. "Are you sure you've never seen her . . . Sarah, I mean . . . with all the stories you hear about ghosts . . . and spirits living in houses, in this part of the world, it's hard to imagine that you haven't. Have you," she persisted with a smile, "seen her ghost . . . ?" She was looking straight at him as he denied it, and he wondered if she believed him.

"No, I haven't . . . I . . ." He hated lying to her, but he was afraid to tell her what he had seen for fear she'd think he was crazy. "I . . . I've heard some noises a couple of times. But I don't think it's anything. I think that's all local legend." Her eyes searched his, and she smiled a funny little smile, that made him want to lean over and kiss her, but he knew he couldn't.

"I'm not sure I believe you, and I don't know why. You seem amazingly well informed about her . . . why is it that I think there's something you're not telling me?" she asked pointedly in a sexy voice, and he laughed nervously, and wondered how she knew he was lying.

"Whatever it is I'm not telling you has nothing to do with Sarah," he said, sounding husky, and they both laughed. But he reassured her again after that that he had seen nothing. "I'll be sure to let you know if I do though. You know, Ghost-Watch." He was teasing her, and she laughed, and she had never looked prettier as she did it. When she relaxed a little bit, she was so beautiful and so warm and so appealing, but the door always slammed shut just before he could reach her. It drove him crazy.

"I'm serious," she insisted. "You know, I believe in that. I think there are spirits around us sometimes, and we're not aware of them. But we could be, if we paid attention." He was fascinated by the earnestness with which she said it.

"I'll have to go home and concentrate," he said, still teasing. "Any suggestions about how I do it? A Ouija board maybe, or just meditation?"

"You're impossible," she said. "I hope she wakes you up from a sound sleep, and scares you."

"Now, there's an appealing thought. I'll have to sleep in your living room tonight if you make me too nervous." But somehow she didn't believe that he was susceptible to that kind of terror, although he would have loved an invitation. And when he finally did leave, he wasn't sure what to say to her. He could feel the attraction between them again. It was so powerful, but so unspoken.

And then he decided to brave it, and invite her to spend the next day with him, and her daughter. It was Sunday. But she was quick to decline the invitation. They were getting too friendly.

"I can't. I've got some work to do on my thesis," she said, averting her eyes so she didn't have to look at him.

"That doesn't sound like much fun," he said sympathetically, looking disappointed.

"It isn't fun," she acknowledged, and she could have put it off. But she didn't want to. He was becoming a threat now. She was much too comfortable with him. "But I really have to do it."

"You could come to my place and we could go ghost-hunting," he teased, and she laughed at him.

"That's a difficult invitation to resist, but I'd better stick to my books. I haven't done much lately. Maybe some other time, but thank you."

She stood in the doorway and watched him go, and he thought of her all the way home, sorry that he hadn't just grabbed her and kissed her. But he knew full well how dangerous that would have been. He would never have seen her again. And yet, he could feel an incredible tension between them. And when he got home, and walked around his empty house, thinking about her, and not Sarah for once, he was really bothered that she hadn't accepted his invitation for Sunday. They had such a good time together, she had no right to shut him out. Besides, he even liked her kid, and it was obvious how much Monique enjoyed him. He sat there, muttering to himself about it, and then finally, he couldn't help himself. He picked up the phone and called her. It was midnight, and he wasn't even sure he cared if he woke her, although he was sure he wouldn't. He had just left her.

"Hello?" She answered the phone sounding worried. No one ever called her at that hour. In fact, with rare exceptions for Monique, no one called her.

"I've just seen a ghost, and I'm terrified. It was ten feet tall and had horns and red eyes, and I think it was wearing my sheets. Do you want to come see it?" He sounded like a naughty child, and she couldn't stop laughing as she listened.

"You're awful. I meant that. People *do* see ghosts. I hear about it all the time at the historical society, and some of them can be identified. I've done research on it myself." She was trying to be serious with him, but she was still laughing at what he'd said when he called her.

"Good. Then come identify this one. I'm locked in the bathroom."

"You're hopeless," she said, smiling at her end.

"You're right. That's the problem. I'm going to write to Ann Landers in fact and sign the letter 'Hopeless.' I've met this woman and I want to be her friend . . . and I think maybe we're attracted to each other, but if I say anything about it to her, she'll hate me." There was a long silence as she listened to what he was saying, and he wondered if he had blown it with her forever. He hoped not.

"She won't hate you," she finally said in a soft voice, "she just can't do anything about it . . . she's too scared by what's already happened to her." She sounded very tender and he wished he could put his arms around her, but she probably wouldn't have let him, and he knew that.

271

"I'm not sure I believe that. I know you do," he said gently, "and I'm all banged up too. I'm not a pretty sight these days, and I don't know what the hell I'm doing. I haven't been out here in the world in ten years . . . more than that . . . eleven . . ." It had been ten months since Carole left him. "And I've been saying all the same things you are . . . but one minute I'm crying over Carole, and the next minute I'm . . . I'm talking to you, and feeling something I haven't felt in a long, long time . . . it's confusing. Maybe all we'll ever be is friends. Maybe that's all I have a right to. I just . . . I wanted you to know . . ." He felt like a kid again, and he was blushing, but so was she, at her end. "I just want you to know how much I like you," he said awkwardly. It was more than that. But he couldn't bring himself to say it.

"I like you too," she said honestly, "and I don't want to hurt you."

"You won't. It's already been done by experts. I'm sure you'd be an amateur in comparison."

She smiled as she answered. "So would you, Charlie. I really appreciate how nice you've been to us. You're a good person." And Pierre wasn't. Fantasy or no, she knew that. He had used her shamefully, and taken terrible advantage of all her decency and kindness and feelings for him. And no one else was ever going to do the same thing to her, not if she could help it. "Can't we just be friends?" she asked sadly, she didn't want to lose him.

"Sure we can," he said gently. And then he had another thought. "How about letting your friend take you and Monique to dinner on Monday? You already turned me down for tomorrow. You can't say no again, I won't let you. A quick dinner after work Monday night. We can have pizza in Shelburne Falls." There wasn't much she could object to, and he was accepting her terms on their friendship.

"Okay," she relented. He drove a hard bargain.

"I'll pick you up at six again. Okay?"

"Okay." She was smiling. They had survived the first skirmish. "I'll see you then."

"I'll call you if I see another ghost." He was glad he had called her. It had been worth it. And just before they hung up, he stopped her.

"Yes?" Francesca sounded a little breathless, and he loved it.

"Thank you . . ." he said softly. She knew what he meant, and she was still smiling when they hung up. They were just friends, she told herself. Nothing more. He understood perfectly . . . or did he?

And at his end, Charlie sat back in his chair with a smile. He really liked her. She wasn't easy. But she was definitely worth the effort. And he was so pleased with himself, and the fact that she'd agreed to see him again, that he picked up one of Sarah's journals to reward himself. He hadn't read them in days. And he had really missed her. And he wanted to know what had happened to her. But now, when he opened the small book, and saw her familiar handwriting, it felt like a celebration.

Chapter 17

TRUE TO HIS word, François de Pellerin came back through
Shelburne again in August, and when he did, he came to see
Sarah. She was working in her vegetable garden when he arrived, and she didn't see or hear him approach. He came on
silent feet, as he always did, and suddenly he stood beside her.
She turned with a start, and looked up at him, first with surprise,
and then obvious pleasure.

"I'm going to have to fasten a bell around your neck if you
continue to do that." And then she blushed slightly and wiped
her face with her apron as she remembered to thank him for the
bear claws.

"Have you been well?" she asked as he smiled down at her.
Her face was brown, and her raven-black hair was in a long braid
down her back which made her look almost like an Indian
squaw. And he noticed as they walked slowly back to her house,
that she had the same regal carriage as Crying Sparrow. "Where
have you been since we last met?" she asked him with interest as
they stopped at the well for some water.

"With my brothers," he said simply. "In Canada, trading with
the Huron." He did not tell her he had been to the capital, to

meet with Washington again, to discuss the continuing problems with the Miami Indians in Ohio. He was far more interested in her, and what she'd been up to. She seemed to be flourishing in Shelburne. "Have you been to the garrison to see Colonel Stockbridge?" he asked conversationally, as she poured a cup of cool water and handed it to him.

"I've been too busy to go to the garrison," she answered. "We've been planting for the past three weeks." They'd been planting tomatoes and squash and pumpkins in large quantities, and they hoped for a good-size crop before winter.

She had heard from Mrs. Stockbridge by then, begging her to leave Shelburne and return to civilization, and she'd had a letter from the Blakes as well, giving her all the news of Boston. But she was far happier here, and François could see it. "Where are you off to now?" she asked as they stepped into her sitting room, it was still somewhat cooler than it was outside, as that part of the house was shaded by elm trees. The men who had built her house for her had planned it well, and it suited her to perfection.

"I have a meeting with Colonel Stockbridge." The colonel was still concerned about the Kentucky volunteers who had sacked and burned several Shawnee villages the year before, and the fort that had been built at Fort Washington in violation of several treaties. The colonel was sure that there was going to be retaliation. Blue Jacket had already taken vengeance by crossing the Ohio River into Kentucky, and there had been numerous attacks on settlers there. But the colonel was afraid of more widespread warfare, as was François. He had said as much to Washington when he'd seen him. And Sarah listened with interest as François explained it.

"Is there anything you can do to stop it?" she asked calmly.

"Very little now. Blue Jacket still feels there has not been adequate retribution. He's a hard man to deal with. I've tried several times, but he doesn't like the Iroquois any better than the white man." He knew from firsthand experience in a meeting he reported to Stockbridge, when he first met Sarah. "All we can do is hope he gets tired of it, and feels he's had enough scalps to make up for the men he lost. I can't see how we'll stop him, unless it becomes a war involving several nations, and none of us wants that," he said calmly. He seemed to have a wise overview of things, and a sympathetic sense for both sides, although more often than not, his sympathies lay with the Indians, rather than the white man. The Indians had suffered more, and in François's view, were usually more honest.

"Is it not dangerous for you to be negotiating with Blue Jacket?" she asked, with obvious concern, as he smiled at her. "He must see you as white rather than Iroquois."

"I'm not sure it matters to him. I'm not Shawnee. That is enough to make him angry. He's a brave warrior filled with fire and anger," he told her, with obvious respect, and a certain amount of fear, which was not unfounded. Blue Jacket was not afraid to bring a whole new Indian war down on his people.

They talked about it for a long time, and when they went outside again, it was cooler, and as she always did, she asked him if he'd like to walk to the waterfall with her. It was a daily ritual she never missed. And they said very little to each other, as they walked the easy mile to where the cascade fell in all its beauty and glory. And when Sarah sat down on her favorite rock and looked at the water tumbling down so jubilantly, François looked down at her with pleasure. He wanted to tell her that he had been thinking about her a great deal, about the things she had said to him the last time, and what he had gleaned himself over dinner. He wanted to say that he had worried about her, and was anxious to see her again, but he didn't. He simply stood there, and watched her and said nothing.

They sat that way for an hour, lost in their own thoughts, communing silently, and then she turned and looked at him, and she smiled as their eyes met. It was good to see him. He looked brown and healthy after his time with the Iroquois, and it was difficult to believe he had not been born among them. And as they walked slowly back to her small farm again, she felt his bare arm brush against her.

"Will you be staying at the garrison this time?" she asked quietly as they reached her house.

"I will," he said, looking down at her, "I'm meeting some of my men there." And then she asked him to dinner, and he accepted. He knew he could spend the night in the woods, or in her barn, and go down to the garrison before dawn the next morning. He had no set appointment with the colonel.

He caught several rabbits for her, and she cooked them for him and the boys, and she made rabbit stew with vegetables from her garden. It was a delicious meal, and the boys thanked her enthusiastically before they left to do their evening chores, and she and François sat quietly in her comfortable kitchen. They spoke softly for a long time, and then they walked out into the moonlight. And within minutes they saw a comet.

"The Indians say that is a good sign," he said, looking at her carefully. "It's a good omen. You will be blessed here."

"I already have been," she said, looking around her. She wanted nothing more than this. This was everything she had ever dreamed of.

"This is only the beginning of your life here," he said wisely. "You must go on, do many things, bring wisdom to many." He sounded very much like the Iroquois as he spoke to her and she smiled at him, not sure of his meaning.

"I have no wisdom to give anyone, François. I lead a small life here." She had come here only for healing, not to teach others. But François seemed not to understand that.

"You crossed a great ocean to get here. You're a brave woman, Sarah. You must not hide yourself away here," he said firmly. But what did he expect of her? She could not negotiate with Indians, or go to see the president. She had nothing important to say to anyone. She couldn't imagine what he was thinking. And then he told her that he would like to introduce her to the Iroquois one day, which surprised her.

"Red Jacket is a great man. I think you would like to meet him." It frightened her a little bit, but she had to admit, it intrigued her too, and she knew that she would be safe there, as long as François was with her.

"I'd like that," she said thoughtfully.

"Their medicine is very wise," he said cryptically, "just as you are." He sounded very mystical, and she felt a strange, unspoken bond with him, as they stood in the moonlight, so much so that it made her nervous. It was as though, without a word, without a sound, without ever even touching her, he was drawing her slowly to him. And she knew she should resist, but she found she couldn't. She didn't even know where the pull she felt came from. It was almost like being ever so slowly drawn by mystical forces, as they tightened a rope around her.

And as they spoke, she walked him slowly to the barn, and when they reached it, he stopped and gently took her hand in his own and kissed it. It was entirely a gesture from another life, and something he would have done had they met in France in their other lifetimes. He was the oddest mixture of Iroquois and French, of warrior and man of peace, of mystic and human. She watched him walk silently into the barn, and then turned and walked back to her kitchen.

And in the morning, he was gone again, and when she went back to her kitchen, she found a narrow Indian bracelet made of brightly colored shells. It was pretty and she put it on, and as she looked at it, she realized that it was an odd feeling knowing that he'd been in her kitchen while she was sleeping. He was so silent and so strong, so handsome, with his shining dark hair, and she had grown accustomed to the buckskins and moccasins he wore. They looked completely natural on him. And she found as she went back to work in her cornfield that day that she missed him. She had no idea when he would come again, and she had no reason to wish him there. They were just friends after all. In fact, she reminded herself, she scarcely knew him. But he was so interesting to talk to, and his presence seemed so reassuring. They could walk along side by side for hours, without speaking. And at times, it seemed as though each knew what the other was thinking. He almost seemed to have mystical powers, he was so wise, and she was thinking about some of the more spiritual things he had said to her, as she walked back to the waterfall that afternoon. She hadn't been able to get him out of her mind all day, and her time at the waterfall was no different.

She was dangling her feet in the icy water, thinking about him, when something crossed the sun, and she looked up to see what had cast the shadow. She gave a little start when she saw it was François, standing not inches from her, blocking the sunlight.

"I suppose you will always surprise me," she said, smiling up at him, shading her eyes with her hand, unable to hide her pleasure to see him. "I thought you were at the garrison."

"I have met with the colonel," he said, and she sensed that there was more, but for a long moment he said nothing. He seemed to be struggling with something very powerful and very disturbing, and she sensed it.

"Is something wrong?" she asked gently, ready to listen to any problem, but he already knew that.

"Perhaps," he said, not sure whether or not to go on. He was not at all sure of her reaction. But he knew he had to say it. His own thoughts had tormented him all morning. "I cannot stop thinking about you, Sarah." She nodded and said nothing. "I suspect it is very dangerous for me to tell you." But she wasn't sure why he said that.

"Why dangerous?" she asked gently. He looked so troubled and so worried that it touched her. And she had been just as tormented as he was.

"Perhaps you will not let me come here again. I know how much pain you have had in the past . . . how much sorrow

. . . I know how much fear you have of being hurt again . . . but I promise you," he looked at her with anguished eyes, "I will not hurt you." She knew that too, but she also knew she would not let him. "I only want to be your friend." He wanted so much more than that too, but he also knew he could not tell her. Not yet anyway. And he needed to know how she felt first. But she didn't look nearly as frightened as he had feared she would. She seemed to be thinking.

"I have thought about you a great deal too," she confessed. "Even before you returned this time," she said, blushing, and then she looked up at him with the innocence of a child and smiled at him. "I have no one else to talk to."

"Is that the only reason why you've thought of me?" he asked, with a smile, as he looked into her eyes and sat down carefully beside her. But she could feel the warmth of his body next to hers, see his flesh and feel his buckskins. It was difficult not to be aware of the power of his attraction.

"I like speaking to you," she said quietly to him. "I like many things," she said shyly, and he took her hand in his own, and once again, for a long time they sat in silence. And then finally, they walked home. He poured a cup of water from the well for her this time, and then he asked her if she would like to take a ride through the valley on his horse, and she smiled at the prospect.

"I like to ride sometimes, when I need to clear my mind," he said as he led the paint mare out of the barn, wearing only its bridle. He rarely used a saddle. He preferred riding without one, and he handed her up behind him. She put her arms around his waist, and rode astride, with her wide cotton skirt all around them, as they rode down into the valley, and then across the valley floor for a while. Everything looked so rich and green, and he was right, it seemed to clear her head as they galloped along the river.

They were back by dinnertime, and she cooked dinner for all

of them, as she always did. And afterward, he said he was leaving. She did not ask him if he wished to stay. They both knew that he couldn't. Something had changed between them during his visit.

"When will you come back again?" she asked sadly, as he prepared to leave her.

"In a month, perhaps, if I can." And then he looked down at her sternly, and she was reminded of the night she met him in the forest and had been so frightened of him. But he didn't frighten her now, and she could only imagine how much she was going to miss him. And what troubled her most was that she didn't want to be drawn to him in the way she was, and he knew it. But neither of them seemed able to stop it. "Take good care of yourself," he said then. "Don't do anything foolish."

"What about all that wisdom you say I have?" she teased, and he laughed.

"You seem to use it for everyone but yourself. Take care of yourself, Sarah," he said more gently then, as he kissed her hand again as he had the night before, and then he mounted his horse, waved, and trotted out of the clearing. She stood looking after him, but he was gone in a matter of minutes.

And it was a month before he returned again, in the early part of September. He had business at the garrison, and he was there for a week, for meetings with Colonel Stockbridge and several other commanders who had come to see him. The meeting, as usual, was about the Shawnees and the Miamis. They seemed to be a constant concern to the army.

François didn't stay at Shelburne this time, but secretly came often to see Sarah, and when he asked the colonel politely how she was, it reminded the senior commandant of the garrison that it had been months since he'd seen her. And he immediately invited her to dinner.

She and François feigned surprise when they met, and pretended to have very little interest in each other. But Stockbridge thought he saw something in the Frenchman's eyes, and for only a moment he began to wonder. But he had far more pressing things on his mind, and by the end of the evening, he'd forgotten. They laughed about it afterward, when François came to her farm, to share dinner with her again. He stayed in the barn this time, and they had a very pleasant time, enjoying the last of the summer weather. They went to the waterfall, as they always did. And they rode together, on separate horses this time. She was an excellent rider, and balked at nothing, although unlike François she preferred riding with a saddle. She was afraid that in her wide skirt, she might slip off the horse if she didn't have one. And they both laughed at the mental picture she created as she described it to him. But no mishap occurred, and they spent several happy days together. Their friendship was becoming an ever stronger bond now, and François never dared to cross the line she carefully placed between them.

One day though, as they walked along, on their way back from the waterfall, he asked if she ever feared Edward might come to America to find her. It was a concern he had had for some time, ever since she had told François about him.

But she looked unconcerned as she answered. "I can't imagine him doing that. I don't think he ever liked me that much, to be honest. And it would mean his making a devilishly uncomfortable journey to get here." She knew that only too well from her two months on the *Concord*.

"But perhaps to reclaim his property, and a very valuable piece of property, I might add," François said with a small smile at her, "he might think it was worth it." He still looked worried, but she didn't.

"I doubt it. I think he knows that if I came this far, I would never return to England with him. He would have to bind and gag me, and beat me senseless to get me to leave here, and I think I'd be far too troublesome a prisoner. I'm sure he's doing very well without me." François thought it was hard to envision. He couldn't imagine any man letting her get away from him. It was obvious that her husband was extremely odd, as well as a brute. For one very brief, unfriendly moment, he would have liked to meet him. But whatever had happened before, he was glad she was free now.

And when he left her again, he felt troubled as he always did. It was getting to be harder and harder to leave her.

"Will I see you again?" she asked demurely as he prepared to leave, and she filled his flask with water. It was made of deerskin, and he had carried it for years. It was intricately beaded, Crying Sparrow had made it for him.

"No, never," he said in answer to her question. "I will never come back to see you," he said, sounding surprisingly firm about it and Sarah looked worried.

"Why not?" she asked, looking like a disappointed child, and he was pleased to see it. She wondered if he was moving to the Western region.

"Because it is too difficult to leave you. And after I've been here, I find everyone else intolerably boring." She laughed at his answer, and she suffered very much from the same problem.

"I'm very glad to hear that," she said, and then he turned with a serious expression to look at her. It made her tremble a little.

"Are you? It doesn't worry you?" he asked bluntly. He knew how afraid she was of ever getting involved with anyone again and he knew she couldn't marry. But in his mind, there was no reason for her to be alone forever. Her exile was self-imposed, her solitude unnecessary and stupid. But he still knew it was what she wanted. Or at least he thought so. "I don't want to frighten you," he said softly. "I never want to do that again." She nodded and said nothing. She had no answers for him. And he was troubled as he rode away. He had told her he would be back soon, but he didn't know when this time. He was traveling north again, and sometimes those trips took longer than he wanted.

But she was troubled this time too. She knew how close they were getting, and there seemed to be a kind of unspoken intimacy between them. They seemed to be able to tell each other anything, and they seemed to find all the same things either interesting or amusing. It was frightening, if she thought of the implications. And more than once she decided that she would tell him not to come again, when he next came to see her. But in the end, he was gone for so long that she was truly worried about him. She did not see him again until October. And when she did, the leaves had turned, and the entire valley looked as though it were on fire, it was all painted in red and yellow. She hadn't seen him in six weeks, and this time she saw him approaching the falls. He came on horseback, and she was standing in the clearing. He was wearing a buckskin shirt with bobcat sleeves, a deerskin mantle, and deerskin leggings with fringes. And he looked incredibly handsome as he galloped into the clearing. His hair was loose, but he wore a headband with eagle feathers hanging from it, and the moment he saw her, he was smiling. He reined in, and slid down gracefully to greet her.

"Where have you been?" she asked with a look of worry, and he was enormously pleased to see it. Something had told him for weeks that he had frightened her the last time they met, and he was deeply worried about it. He did not want her coming to the wrong conclusion. But he wasn't far wrong. She had tormented herself for the past month. And she had fully intended to tell him she didn't want to see him again, but the moment she saw him, she forgot all her good intentions.

"I've been sadly busy, I'm afraid," he said soberly, apologizing for his absence and then he told her the bad news, "I can't stay. I'm meeting my men at the garrison and we leave tonight, for Ohio." She looked deeply concerned as he said it.

"Blue Jacket again?" she asked, as though they were old friends and he smiled at her. He had missed her so much, and he was so happy to see her, even if only for a few minutes.

"They began fighting a week ago. Stockbridge has asked me to go out there with a platoon of his men, and a delegation of mine. I'm not sure what we can do, except support the army. We'll do the best we can," he said calmly, drinking her in with his eyes, but he didn't dare touch her.

"It's dangerous for you," she said, looking unhappy, wanting him to stay now, sorry she had ever thought of telling him not to come again. She wondered if he had sensed that, and that was why he hadn't come for such a long time. She was full of regret now, and terror that he would be wounded.

"Can you stay for dinner?" she asked anxiously, looking nervous and afraid he would tell her he had to leave before that, but he nodded.

"I can't stay long though, I need some time to meet with the colonel."

"I'll be quick," she said, hurrying toward the kitchen, and half an hour later, she had a very creditable dinner for him. There was some cold chicken left over from the day before, that she had left in the cool house over the river, and she had sent the boys running for it, and she'd cooked some trout they'd caught only that morning. There was fresh, plump squash from the garden, and pumpkins, and a mountain of corn bread. And this time, she asked the boys to eat outside, so she could be alone with François. And as he ate the delicious meal she'd prepared for him, he looked over at her with pleasure.

"I will not eat this well again for a long time," he said, and she smiled. Looking at him, no one would ever have doubted that she was entertaining an Indian. There was nothing about him to suggest he was actually a white man. But she didn't care what anyone said about her. Let them. "You must be very careful now," he warned her. "There could be war parties who venture this way from Ohio." It seemed unlikely, but anything was possible, or it might stir some unrest in the other tribes. He didn't want anything to happen to her while he was riding with the Army.

"We'll be fine." She had bought the guns, as she had promised. And she felt safe here.

"If you hear of anything from the settlers around here, I want you to go to the garrison, and stay there." He spoke to her as though she were his wife, and as though what he wanted her to do really mattered. But it did to her, and she listened to him calmly as he gave her orders. And as they exchanged thoughts and fears and concerns, and she tried to remember everything she'd forgotten while he'd been gone, the time passed much too quickly.

It was dark when he stood beside his horse again, and looked down at her, and without saying a word, he took her in his arms and held her. He just needed to feel her there, and not say anything to her, and she didn't say a word. She simply stood there and held him, wondering why she had been so foolish, why she had wanted to run away from him in the first place. What did it matter if her past life had been filled with pain? What difference did it make if she was still married to Edward? She would never see him again. He was as good as dead to her, and she was falling in love with this wild and beautiful man who looked like an Indian, and now he was going to fight with the Army. What if she never saw him again? How much they would have wasted. And there were tears in her eyes, as she pulled away from him to look up at him. Neither of them spoke, but their eyes said everything they needed.

"Be careful," she whispered, and he nodded, as he jumped onto his horse with the ease of any Indian brave, and she wanted to tell him that she loved him, but she didn't, and knew that if anything happened to him, she would always regret it.

He didn't look back this time as he rode away. He couldn't. He didn't want her to see that he was crying.

Chapter 18

*I*T WAS AN interminable time, waiting for him to return, and by Thanksgiving, Sarah had still heard nothing. She visited the garrison frequently now, hoping to hear news of him. It was a long ride for her, and the round trip took nearly all day, but it was worth it. There were snippets of news from time to time about the battles between the Indians and the armies. The Shawnees and the Miamis had done a great deal of damage, attacking homes and farms, killing families and seizing captives. They had even taken to attacking flatboats on the river. And the Chickasaws had joined them.

Brigadier General Josiah Harmer was in charge, but so far, it had been a disaster. His troops had been ambushed twice, and nearly two hundred men had been killed. But from everything Sarah could glean, by Thanksgiving at least, François was not among them. And by the time she sat down to dinner with Colonel Stockbridge and several of the Deerfield families he had invited to join him for Thanksgiving at the garrison, Sarah was deeply worried. But she could let on to no one. And she was very distracted as she attempted to make conversation with everyone, and inquire about their relatives and children.

And when she went back to the farm the next day, she was grateful not to have to talk to anyone. She had taken a Wampanoag guide with her. She didn't even have to deal with Lieutenant Parker anymore. Mercifully, he had been transferred.

She was lost in her own thoughts, as they finally reached Shelburne. She thanked the Indian who had traveled with her, and gave him a saddlebag full of food to take with him. And as she sent him on his way, she pulled her cloak tightly around her in the cold, and heard a rustling in the woods beyond the clearing. For a moment, she looked concerned, and walked as quickly as she could toward her kitchen, where she kept the musket François had left with her. But before she could reach the house, he came galloping into the clearing, in full war dress with his hair flying, a headband of eagle feathers flying out behind him. They were a badge of honor given to him by the Iroquois years before, and as she stared at him in astonishment, she realized it was François. He wore a victorious smile, and gave a tremendous whoop as he jumped from his horse, and ran to her, and this time there was no hesitation on her part, as he pulled her into his arms and kissed her.

"Oh God . . . how I missed you . . ." she said breathlessly when he finally let her go again. She could no longer remember a single reason for her reservations about him. "I was so worried . . . so many men were killed . . ."

"Too many," he said, still holding her tight, and then he looked at her sadly. "It is not over. The braves are rejoicing now, but the Army will come back again, stronger and more of them. Little Turtle and Blue Jacket will not win this war forever. They've been very foolish." He knew there would be more deaths, more murdered families, more slaves, more destruction, more anger, and the Indians would lose everything in the end. He hated watching it all happen, but he couldn't even think of it now as he held her. "You will never know how I missed you," he said, and kissed her again gently.

He swept her up easily in his arms then and carried her inside. It was cold in her kitchen. She had been gone for two days, and the fire had been out, for the boys had gone to a neighboring family for Thanksgiving. They had seven daughters and the boys had been very happy to pay them a visit.

And as soon as François set her down, he began making a fire for her, as she set her cloak down. She was wearing the blue velvet gown she had bought in Boston. She had worn it for Thanksgiving. And as he looked at her now he saw that it was the same color as her eyes, and he knew that he had never seen a more beautiful woman, not in Paris or Boston, or Deerfield or even among the Iroquois, not even Crying Sparrow, much as he had loved her. There was only one woman for him now, this slip of a girl who had always been so brave each time he saw her, the woman he had fallen so desperately in love with. He had never expected it to happen to him at his age. He had lived to see nearly forty summers, as the Indians said, and yet he loved her as though his life had just been beginning. He picked her up in his arms again then, and as he kissed her, he could feel her abandon herself to him. She had long since given her heart to him, and her soul along with it. And she had prayed every day for his safe return, and hated herself for not having given herself to him before he left, or at least told him how much she loved him. And she told him again and again now as he carried her to her bedroom. She had never loved any man but him, and as he lay her gently down on her bed and looked at her, she reached her arms up to him, and trembled as he held her. She had never known the gentle touch of any man, and no one had ever been as kind to her as he was. And he was infinitely gentle to her now, as he carefully took off the velvet gown, and placed her like a newborn child beneath the covers. Turning away from her, he let his buckskins fall quickly to the floor, and slipped into the bed beside her.

"I love you, Sarah," he whispered to her, and he no longer

289

looked like an Indian, but just a man to her, the man she loved, and there was nothing terrifying about him. He was all gentleness and kindness as he reached out slowly to her, and explored her body with the invisible magic of his fingers. And she lay in his arms moaning softly. And then at last, ever so gently he took her, and held her close to him, unable to control himself for long, he had wanted her so badly, almost ever since the day he met her, and he knew with total certainty that this was the life for which they had both been born, and as they lay together long into the night he felt as though his body and his soul had exploded in a shower of comets.

She lay silently in his arms afterward, lying close to him, feeling his heart beat next to her, and she smiled as she looked up at him in sated pleasure. "I never knew it could be anything like that," she whispered.

"It can't," he said just as softly. "It's a gift to us from the Gods of the Universe, it has never been like this for anyone before," he said, and smiled as he closed his eyes, pulling her even closer.

They slept in each other's arms that night, and when they woke in the morning, and she looked at him, she knew that they were one now, and always would be.

The next weeks were magical for them. He was free of his obligations to anyone, and he could stay with her for as long as they wanted. They walked to the waterfall each day, he taught her to walk with snowshoes on, he told her Indian legends she'd never heard before and they spent hours and hours in bed in each other's arms, making love and discovering each other. Neither of them had ever known a life like this one. And he told her that when the snows thawed, he wanted to take her to meet the Iroquois. As far as he was concerned, she was his wife now.

And two weeks after their life together had begun, he took her to the waterfall, and she noticed that he was looking very solemn. He was quiet as they walked, and she wondered what he was thinking of. Perhaps his son, she thought . . . or Crying Sparrow, but he looked as though he was worried about something, or deeply troubled. And when they reached the waterfall, he told her what he had been thinking.

The waterfall was outwardly frozen by then, but still spectacular to look at, and the world around them was blanketed with snow as he held her hand in his own and spoke very softly.

"We are married in our own eyes, little one . . . and the eyes of God . . . you can never have been married to that terrible man, in England . . . there is no God in any heaven who would want you to spend a lifetime of such torture. And in the eyes of God, you are free now. You have earned your freedom.

"I will not take you into bondage again," he said as he went on, still holding her hand, "but I will take your heart, and give you mine, if you will have me. I will be your husband from this day, until my death. I will promise you my life, and all my honor," he said, bowing to her, and then he quietly took a small gold ring from his pocket. He had traded for it months before, in Canada, during the summer. And he had wanted to give it to her, but he was afraid to. And now he knew it was the right moment. "If I could, Sarah, I would give you my title, and my land. I have no other heir, but all I can give you now is who I am, and what I have here. But all that I am and have is yours now," he said, slipping the ring on her finger. It fit her perfectly, and was a narrow band of gold studded with the tiniest of diamonds. It was truly a wedding band, and she only hoped as she looked at it that the woman who had worn it before had been happy. But she knew as she looked at François that he was all he said he was, and that in her heart, from this day forth, he would be her husband.

"I love you more than I can ever tell you," she whispered with tears glistening in her eyes, wishing that she had a ring to give him. But she had nothing, other than herself, her heart, her life, her trust, which was something she had given no one until François. And she trusted him completely.

They exchanged their vows at the waterfall, and then they walked slowly home, and made love again. And when she woke in his arms, she looked happily at the pretty ring on her finger.

"You make me so happy," she said, rolling over playfully on him again, and he could never resist her. And later, as they sat in bed, drinking tea and eating corn bread, he asked her if she cared what people would think now, if anyone discovered they were living together. "Not really," she admitted to him. "I suppose if I did, I would never have left England." But he still thought they should be careful. There was no need to bring the disgust of the entire parish down on them. If eventually they were found out, they would live with it. But there was no need to flaunt what had happened. Although neither of them thought they would be good at keeping a secret.

They got their first opportunity to try at Christmas dinner at the garrison, when they arrived separately and pretended to be surprised to see each other. But both of them feigned far too much innocence, and glanced at each other far too often. Had the canny Mrs. Stockbridge been there, she would have seen through them immediately, but fortunately for them, she wasn't. And they got away with it, this time, but Sarah knew that people would not be fooled forever. Someone would see them, or talk, and inevitably her reputation would be tarnished. But as she said to François, in the end, it didn't really matter, as long as they had each other.

As it turned out, their life went on quite peacefully through the New Year, and then one afternoon, while she was trying to break through the ice, and get water at the well, a man in city clothes rode into the clearing. He had a Nonotuck guide with him, a very old man, and the white man looked chilled to the bone, as he looked intently at Sarah. And she didn't know why, but she sensed something ominous about him, and she casually looked around her for help, and remembered that François had gone to one of the small forts on the river for fresh ammunition, and the boys had gone with him.

The man in city clothes rode straight up to her, and looked down at her with determination. "Are you the Countess of Balfour?" It was an odd question to ask her, and although there had been rumors about it for a long time, no one had ever dared to ask her quite this bluntly. At first she was inclined to deny it, and then decided it wasn't worth the trouble.

"I am. And you, sir? Who are you?"

"My name is Walker Johnston. I'm an attorney, from Boston," he said, as he dismounted. He looked stiff and tired, but she had no desire to invite him inside until she knew what he wanted. And the old Indian guide with him seemed to have no interest in the matter. "May we go inside?"

"What is your business, sir?" She didn't know why, but her hands were shaking.

"I have a letter for you, from your husband." For a moment, she thought he meant François and that something had happened to him, and then she made the connection. Her voice shook as she asked the next question.

"Is he in Boston?"

"Of course not. He's in England. I was hired by a firm in New York. They traced you to America quite some time ago. It took a little while to find you here though." He sounded as though he expected her to apologize to him for causing so much trouble.

"What does he want from me?" She suddenly wondered if this man and the old Indian were going to throw her over their horses and carry her back to Boston. But it seemed unlikely, knowing Edward. It was far more likely that the man had been hired to shoot her. But perhaps not, if he was a lawyer. She wondered. Perhaps he was only masquerading as an attorney. She was instinctively afraid of him, but she was equally determined not to be overcome by terror.

"I am to read you his lordship's letter." The man persisted. "May we go inside?" he asked with a look of frozen determination, and she could see that he was freezing.

"All right," she relented, and offered him a cup of hot tea, once he was in her kitchen and took his icy coat off. She gave the old Indian corn bread, but he was happy waiting outside. He was wearing warm pelts, and he wasn't bothered by the weather.

And with that, the attorney from Boston puffed up his feathers like an ugly little black bird and glared at her as he unfolded the letter from Edward. He was obviously prepared to read it to her, and she held out a hand with a look that would have told anyone her rank and title.

"May I read it myself, sir?" she asked, holding out a hand, and when he gave it to her, she prayed the trembling of her hand would not betray her.

She recognized Edward's hand at once, and the venom of his words no longer surprised her. He was clearly furious that she had left, and called her every imaginable name he could think of, most of them relating to her being a whore, and dirt beneath his feet, and no loss to anyone in the county. He spoke of her dismal failure to provide him with an heir, and at the end of the first page, he said he disowned her. But on the second page, he reminded her that she would receive no funds from him at all, would never reclaim anything that might have been hers, or had been left to her by her father, and that she would inherit nothing from him after his death, none of which surprised her. He said he was redoing his will now. He even threatened to bring charges against her for stealing her mother's jewelry, or better yet treason for stealing from a peer of the realm. But as the British no longer ruled in Massachusetts, she knew that there was nothing he could do to her now, except berate her. But he could bring charges against her in England, and he warned her never to set foot in England.

And then he reminded her quite cruelly that wherever she

went, whatever she did, she could not marry again, unless she wished to face charges of bigamy, and if she had children, if they lived, which seemed quite unlikely given her pathetic history, they would all be bastards. It was not a pleasant prospect, but one which she had considered long since. She knew full well that she could not marry again as long as Edward lived, and so did François, and they seemed able to live with it, so Edward's threats were empty.

But it was on the third page of his letter that Edward surprised her. He spoke of Haversham then, and said that he was startled she did not take him with her. He called his brother a spineless worm, and then referred rather mysteriously to his idiotic widow and four grieving daughters, which made no sense to Sarah until she read further. Apparently, Haversham had been killed in what Edward described as a "hunting accident" six months before, when the two brothers went shooting. But knowing how Edward detested him, and would have gone nowhere with his brother except under extreme duress, it was quite obvious to Sarah what had happened. Out of sheer boredom, or rage, or simple greed, Edward had killed him. And her heart sank as she read it.

He then assured her in the last paragraph that one of his bastards would inherit not only his entire fortune, but the title. And he wished her damned in hell for an eternity of agony and sorrow. And signed himself, Edward, Earl of Balfour, as though she didn't know him. But she knew him only too well, and the horrors he was capable of. She still hated him, and now particularly for what he had done to his brother.

"Your employer is a murderer, sir," Sarah said quietly as she handed the letter back to the lawyer.

"I've never met him," he snapped at her, annoyed to have been dragged all the way to Shelburne. And as soon as he'd put the letter away, he took out another. "I need you to sign this," he said, brandishing it at her, and she couldn't imagine what he was giving her now, but when she took it from him, she saw that it was a letter she was to sign, agreeing to renounce anything she could try to get from Edward, his lands, his title, any possible inheritance, whatever its source. He wanted her to agree to give everything up, and she didn't care at all for any of it, so it didn't matter to her. It also said that she would renounce the title of Countess from that day forward, which somehow amused her, as though she had been using it all over Deerfield.

"I see no problem with this," she said, and went to the desk in the next room as quickly as she could. She took out her quill, dipped it in the ink in the well on her desk, and signed it. And after dropping a few grains of sand on it, she walked swiftly back to the kitchen and handed it to Mr. Johnston. "I believe that concludes our business," she said, standing expectantly, waiting for him to leave, just as she saw a flash of movement and color fly by the window. She wasn't sure what it was, but it looked ominous somehow, and she grabbed quickly for her musket, as the lawyer jumped in terror.

"Now, there's no need to . . . not my fault, you know . . . you must have done something to make him so angry . . ." He was pale with fright and she silenced him with a single gesture and listened. But at the same moment, François burst into the kitchen and they both jumped. He looked absolutely terrifying in his winter Indian garb, with a bobcat head at each shoulder, and the skins down either arm. He wore a fur hat, and a bib of beads and bones that he'd been given in Ohio. He hadn't been wearing all that when he left, and she suddenly realized that he had put some of it on to terrify the stranger. The old Indian outside must have told him something of Johnston's mission, if he even knew it. Or perhaps François guessed it from what the Nonotuck told him. But in either case, he was playing the part to the hilt, and motioned Sarah against the wall as though he didn't know her. And the lawyer from Boston was shaking violently and holding his hands up.

"Shoot him," he said to Sarah violently, and she looked paralyzed. She was terrified she'd laugh suddenly and give the whole game up.

"I'm afraid to," she whispered.

"Out!" François grunted at him, pointing at the door, as though he were taking him somewhere. "Out!" He pointed so fiercely the man would not have argued. And grabbing his coat, he fled the room and ran out to his waiting guide and horses, but the old Nonotuck was grinning. He knew full well who François was, they all did, and like most of his tribe, he had a good sense of humor, and thought it was very funny. He had told François that he thought the man was up to no good. He had hardly given the Nonotuck any time for food or rest on their travels.

"Go!" François pointed at the horses, as the lawyer scrambled into the saddle. And with that, François reached for his bow, and an arrow.

"For God's sake, don't you have a musket, man?" Johnston said to the Nonotuck, but the old guide just looked helpless as he swung back onto his horse, and Sarah could see that he was laughing.

"Can't shoot. Indian Brother," the Nonotuck explained, as François got astride his own horse then, and made him dance as though he were going to chase them. But with that, the lawyer gave his rented hack a ferocious kick, and shot out of the clearing, with the old Nonotuck laughing uncontrollably as he rode behind him, with François pretending to pursue them. It was a full five minutes before François came back to her, and he was grinning broadly, but she scolded him when he dismounted.

"That was very foolish of you. What if he'd had a gun? He would have shot you!"

"I'd have killed him," François said bluntly. "His guide said he came to do something bad to you, but he didn't know exactly what. I hope he didn't have the chance." He looked concerned. "I'm sorry I didn't get home sooner."

297

"It's just as well you didn't," she said with a smile, still somewhat amused at his performance. It had been very convincing. "The poor fool is going to report a war party on the loose in Shelburne."

"Good. Then maybe he'll stay in Boston. What did he want?"

"To strip me of my title," she said with a broad grin. "I'm a commoner again, or reduced to my title before my marriage. It's only Lady Sarah now, you'll be sadly disappointed."

But François only frowned at her and said, "One day you'll be my Countess. Who was he?"

"A lawyer hired by Edward. He came with a letter from Edward threatening me and warning me there would be no inheritance, which I'd never have gotten anyway, so it really doesn't matter." The only thing that did matter was that he had killed his brother. And she told François all about it.

"What a bastard!" he said with feeling. "I don't like his knowing where you are now."

"He will never come here," she assured him. "He only wanted to humiliate me, and deprive me of something he thought I'd care about, but I never have . . . and I suppose," she said wistfully, "he thought I'd be heartbroken about Haversham. I'm sad for him, and poor foolish Alice and her children. But somehow it doesn't surprise me. I always feared Edward would do that. I think Haversham sensed it."

"You're lucky he didn't kill you," François said with feeling, and then smiled more gently as he looked at the woman he called his wife. "*I'm* lucky he didn't kill you." He took her in his arms then, and held her. He hated her having any contact with Edward, and was sorry he hadn't been there when the man arrived from Boston. But she didn't seem overly troubled by it, only by her brother-in-law's death. That saddened her, and she thought it unforgivable of Edward.

They spent the next month peacefully, with no incident, and in February, although there was still snow on the ground, he took her to visit the Iroquois, and she thought it a remarkable experience. They took a number of things to trade, and François took several gifts to Red Jacket, and Sarah enjoyed meeting the women. She could see easily how François had loved living with them. They had an honor and integrity that made a huge impression on her. They loved to laugh, and they told stories endlessly, and they were fascinated by her. And she loved their culture with their legends and their wisdom.

One of the wisewomen of the tribe spoke to her quietly one night, holding her hand in her own. François had been smoking the pipe with the men, and when he returned he knew that this woman was the sister of the powwaw, and she was a spiritual woman herself, but Sarah hadn't been able to understand her. And she asked François to translate, but when he listened to what she said, he seemed deeply concerned, and looked oddly at Sarah.

"What did she say?" It looked terrifying, from François's expression.

"She said you are very worried . . . very afraid . . ." he said quietly. "Is that true?" He wondered if she was afraid of Edward. But there was little he could to her now. And they both knew that Sarah would never return to England. "She says that you have come from far, and left many sorrows behind you." It was certainly true and gave Sarah a shiver as she listened. She was wearing a deerskin skirt and leggings that had been given her by the Iroquois, and she was warm and comfortable in the long house, which they used in winter. "Are you truly worried, my love?" he asked gently, and she smiled as she shook her head, but the woman was wiser than he knew, as Sarah watched her. They were sitting near the fire, with no one else near them, and there was no one to listen, as the woman continued.

"She says you will cross a river soon, a river you have always been afraid of . . . in past lives you have drowned in it many times. But you will not die this time. You will cross the river safely. She says that you will understand her vision when you think about it, that you know what she is seeing." And then she stopped, and François looked disturbed as they walked outside for some air, and he asked her what the woman meant. She was a wisewoman, a prophet in the tribe, and he knew her. Her visions were rarely mistaken. "What are you afraid of?" François asked her, as he pulled her close to him in her fur mantle. She looked like a beautiful Indian squaw, and they made a striking couple, but he sensed now that she had a secret from him, and he didn't like it.

"I'm not afraid of anything," Sarah said unconvincingly, as he watched her. He knew she was lying.

"You're hiding something from me," he said, standing closer to her, wanting to feel her warmth against him. And she did not answer. "What is it, Sarah? Are you unhappy here?" They were to go back in a few days. They had been there for weeks, and he had thought that she liked it. She seemed so happy.

"I love it . . . you know that . . ."

"Have I done something to upset you?" Their life was certainly unusual. Perhaps she was longing for the other worlds she had known . . . in England, or Boston. Though it didn't seem as though that was what she wanted, but it was something far greater that was worrying her, and had for a while now. And then he closed his arms tightly around her, locking her close to him as she smiled in pleasure. "I will not let you go until you tell me. I will not let you keep secrets from me, Sarah."

"I was going to tell you eventually," she began, as he waited, suddenly terrified that it would be something that would take them away from each other. He knew he couldn't bear that. What if she was leaving? But where would she go now? "Something has happened," she went on, with sorrow in her voice. The powwaw's sister had been right then.

"What is it, Sarah?" His voice was barely more than a whisper. He was filled with terror.

"I . . . I don't know what to say to you," she said, with tears spilling from her eyes, as he watched, feeling great distress for her sorrow. "I cannot . . . I cannot . . ." She could not go on, and he didn't know what to do for her as he held her, and then finally, in a whisper of grief, she told him. "I cannot bear you children, François . . . you have no sons . . . and you should have one . . . but I cannot give you what you deserve . . ." She was sobbing in his arms, and he was deeply moved by what she was saying.

"I don't care, my love . . . you know I don't care . . . it does not matter . . . please, my darling . . . no, you must not cry . . . oh, how I love you . . . my darling . . . no, you mustn't . . ." But no matter what he said, she could not stop crying. "It's not important."

"All my babies have died," she said as she clung to him, and he told her how sorry he was for the agony she'd been through, and then she stunned him completely, "and I know this one will too . . ." she whispered, and suddenly he understood, and pulled her away from him so he could look at her in disbelief and terror.

"Are you pregnant?" he asked, almost breathless at the thought of it, and then she nodded. "Oh my God . . . my poor Sarah . . . oh no . . . it will not happen this time. I will not let it." He held her closer to him as tears filled his eyes, realizing what she must have been fearing. And then he remembered the words of the wisewoman who had had the vision. "Do you remember what she said? That you will cross the river safely this time . . . it will not happen again, my love," he whispered.

"She said I would survive," Sarah reminded him, ". . . but the baby?" Why would this one live and no other? "I cannot believe that this time will be different."

"I will take care of you . . . we will give you herbs, and you will be round and happy, and you will have a beautiful baby," he said, smiling at her, as she nestled next to him. "Everything in your life is different now, Sarah. This is a new life for you . . . for both of us . . . and for our baby." And then he remembered to ask her, "When will it be?"

"I think at the end of summer," she said softly, "in September." She thought it must have happened the first time, because she had had the first signs of it by Christmas. It was almost three months now, but she hadn't had the courage to tell him. She had been carrying the worry for a long time. The woman with the vision had known that.

They walked slowly back into the long house then, with the others all around them, and he lay next to her, holding her, and when she slept, he looked down at her with his heart filled with love for her, and begged the gods to have mercy on her. And their baby.

Chapter 19

*I*T WAS LATE Monday afternoon, when Charlie put Sarah's journal down again. He needed to get dressed to take Francesca and Monique out for pizza. But he was filled with love and tenderness as he put the journal aside, and thought of the baby Sarah carried for François. As always, he wondered what had happened to it, but he didn't know yet. It was like a mystery in his life unfurling daily. It was so odd to think that it was so real to him, more real than the people he knew here. He was dying to tell Francesca about it.

And when he picked them up at six o'clock, he was still feeling pensive. Monique was in great spirits as usual. And Francesca seemed to be in a good mood too. She had said she had gotten a lot of work done on her thesis on Sunday.

It was an easy comfortable evening between the three of them, and Francesca invited him back to her place again after dinner, for ice cream and coffee, and he accepted with pleasure. And Monique was ecstatic to be with him. She seemed to crave a father-figure in her life, and being with her made Charlie think about children.

When she'd gone to bed, he and Francesca sat in the kitchen, drinking coffee and eating cookies. "She's a great kid," he said, and meant every word of it, and Francesca smiled appreciatively. She was crazy about her daughter. "Did you ever think of having more?" he asked, wondering about those feelings, and thinking of Sarah.

"I guess so, a long time ago. And then everything fell apart. Pierre wasn't exactly interested in me when his little cupcake was having twin babies. And now it's too late, so it doesn't make any difference." She sounded almost depressed as she said it, and it intrigued him.

"At thirty-one, that is crazy," he scolded her. "Stop saying it's too late for everything. Sarah Ferguson was twenty-four when she came to this country, at a time when that was middle-aged or worse, and she managed to have a whole new life with a man she loved, *and* get pregnant."

"I'm impressed," she said semi-sarcastically. "I think she's becoming an obsession." But listening to her, he made his mind up. He hoped he was right, but he trusted her, and she needed it more than he did.

"There's something I want to give you to read," he said thoughtfully, and she laughed.

"I know, I know. I did that too for the first year. I read all the psych books, all the how-to books, how to recover from your divorce, how to set the past free, how not to hate your ex-husband. But there are no recipes in there for learning to trust someone again, for finding someone who isn't going to do it to you all over again. There are no texts for finding courage."

"I think I have one," he said mysteriously, and then asked her if she'd come to his house for dinner on Wednesday. It was a school night, but he planned to feed them early. She looked hesitant at first, but he told her that he wanted to show her the house, and she said she wanted to see it. "Besides, Monique would love it." She hesitated, but he was so insistent that she finally accepted, and when he left her that night, he said very little but he could hardly wait to see them again.

And he spent two days dusting and cleaning and vacuuming, fluffing up his couch, buying wine and groceries, and baking cookies for Monique. He didn't even have time to read the journals, but he wanted it to be perfect.

And when he picked them up on Wednesday night and brought them there it was obvious that Francesca was impressed, not by his decor, which was nonexistent so far, but by the house itself, and the trouble he'd gone to. And like him, she was deeply moved by the mood she felt there. It was almost as though you could feel a loving presence in the house, even if you knew nothing about her.

"Whose house is this?" Monique asked, as if she felt it too, and she looked around with interest.

He explained to Monique that the house belonged to a really nice friend of his in Shelburne Falls, but it belonged to someone very special, a woman named Sarah, from England, a long time before that.

"Is she a ghost now?" Monique asked, undaunted, and Charlie laughed and denied it. He didn't want her to be frightened. He had bought some coloring books and some crayons for her, and he offered to put the TV on, if her mother didn't mind. And Francesca said she didn't. Then he and Francesca took a walk around the house, and he showed her everything he'd found himself, except for the journals. And just as he had, she stood at the window, looking out over the valley. She looked like a painting as she stood there.

"It's beautiful, isn't it," he said, pleased that she liked it.

"I can see why you fell in love with it," she said, admiringly, and grateful for all the little things he'd done for them, the coloring book for Monique, a cake he'd bought, the wine he knew she liked. And he was making Monique's favorite pasta. In spite of herself, she had to admit, he was terrific.

And they had a wonderful dinner in his kitchen that night, as he told them some of the things he knew about Sarah. But after a while, Monique lost interest. Francesca didn't.

"I'd love to see some of the books you've found about her," she said casually. "Actually, I think some of it interweaves with some of my Indian research a little bit. François de Pellerin was very instrumental in negotiating some of the treaties around here at the end of the eighteenth century. I'd love to know your sources," she said as he smiled. He couldn't wait to tell her.

He waited until Monique was engrossed in a television show, and then he went up to his study where he kept the journals. The trunk was still there, safely stored, and he took out the first one and held it lovingly for a moment. These books had become incredibly precious to him in the weeks since he'd been there. They had filled his days and his nights, and his life with wisdom. They had given him the courage to go on, and meet Francesca, and even face losing Carole, and he knew Francesca needed them as badly as he did. They were a gift not from him, but from Sarah.

He walked slowly downstairs, holding it, and she was standing in the empty formal living room that looked so much like a French drawing room. Looking at the parquet floor, the graceful ceilings and long windows, it was easy to believe she'd been a Countess. Francesca smiled at him as he crossed the room, and he could tell that she felt the magic of the house all around her. It was impossible not to. The love they'd shared must have been so strong that it had lasted two hundred years, and was still everywhere around them.

"I have a present for you," he said as they stood in the moonlight, "a loan actually, but it's something very special. No one else knows about it." She looked puzzled as he stood smiling at her. And if he would have dared, he would have taken her into his arms and kissed her. But it was not time yet. First, she had to read the journals.

"What is it?" She smiled at him expectantly. She felt warm and comfortable here with him, so much so that it surprised her. She hadn't expected to feel this way about his house, or about him, but it was difficult to deny the attraction.

He held out the small leather book to her and she took it from him, and looked at it. It had no name on the spine, and it was obviously very, very old. She handled it gingerly, and her love of old books shone in her eyes as she examined it, and then opened it and saw Sarah's name on the flyleaf. It was the first one. The one she had carried with her from England. Charlie had realized long since that she must have had others she left there. But this was the one she had started before her voyage on the *Concord*.

"What is this, Charlie?" Francesca looked puzzled, and then as she turned the first few pages, she realized what she was holding. "My God, it's her journal, isn't it?" She spoke in a whisper.

"It is," he nodded solemnly. And then he explained how he'd found it.

"How incredible." Francesca was as excited as he was, and he was thrilled to see it. "Have you read all of them?"

"Not yet," he confessed. "I'm working on it. There are a lot of them. And they cover her whole life from before she came to America until she died, I think. They're fascinating though. I thought I was falling in love with her for a while," he grinned, "but she's a little old for me, and she's so crazy about François, I don't think I would have had a chance." He was smiling, and Francesca still looked a little awestruck as they walked back to the kitchen. Monique was still happy with her coloring books and the TV show she'd been watching, and Francesca and Charlie sat and talked about Sarah. "I think what's impressed me most about her is how brave she was, how willing to try again. I think she felt just like we did at one point, that she'd been so badly burned she could never try again. And this guy even makes your husband look like a sweetheart. He beat her, he raped her, he forced her to have one baby right after another and they all died, or six at least, but she still started a new life, and gave François a chance. I know it sounds crazy about a woman I've never met, who's been dead for nearly two centuries, but she gave me hope . . . and she gave me courage . . . and that's what I wanted to share with you."

Francesca was so touched she didn't know what to say as she held the journal in her hand and looked at him, and then she couldn't help asking him another question. But this time, she thought she knew the answer.

"You've seen her, haven't you?" she asked in an undertone, so Monique wouldn't hear her. But she could sense something as she looked at Charlie. He returned her gaze for a long time, and then slowly, he nodded, and she almost squealed with excitement. "Oh God, I knew it! When?" Her eyes were a brilliant green as she asked him, and she looked so beautiful he could hardly stand it.

"When I first moved in. On Christmas Eve. I hardly knew anything about her then. I just came in from dinner with Mrs. Palmer, and there she was in my bedroom. I thought someone was playing a trick on me, and I was really annoyed. I checked the whole house, and the snow outside. I thought someone was having a laugh on me, I looked everywhere for her, and then I figured it out. I've been hoping to see her ever since, but I haven't. It was incredible . . . she was so beautiful and she looked so . . . so real . . . so human . . ." He felt a little crazy as he said it but Francesca was drinking it all in, and she could hardly wait to get home and read the journal. He hoped it would do for her what it had done for him. Sarah had done so much for him.

They went on talking about her for a while, and at ten o'clock he drove them home again. It had been a terrific evening. Monique said she'd had a great time, and Francesca's eyes were sparkling from what he'd told her, and what he'd given her. He hoped she felt for it what he did.

"Call me when you finish it," he said, and then teased her a little. "There's more where that one came from. You'd better be nice now," he warned, and she laughed.

"I have a suspicion this stuff is addictive," she said, her eyes alight with excitement. She was dying to start reading.

"Reading them is practically all I've done since I got here. I should be doing a thesis." He teased her.

"Maybe you should write a book about her," Francesca said seriously, but he shook his head.

"That's your field. Mine is houses." François had already built a monument to her, and Charlie was living in it.

"Somebody ought to write something about her, or maybe just publish her journals," Francesca said seriously.

"We'll see. Read them first. And when we're through, I have to give them to Mrs. Palmer. They're technically hers after all." Though he would have loved to have kept them, but he wouldn't. It was enough just to have read them. They had given him more joy than a thousand books he'd read in a lifetime. And now he was sharing them with Francesca.

"I'll call you," she said, and he knew she meant it. And as he left, she thanked him again for a lovely evening, but for the moment, she was no closer to letting him into the fortress where she was hidden.

And all he could think of as he drove home was how much he would have liked to have reached out to her . . . how much he would have loved to have had with anyone what François had with Sarah.

Chapter 20

BEFORE THEY LEFT the Iroquois, François had quietly spoken to some of the wisewomen of the tribe to ask what they suggested he do for Sarah. They had given them several herbs, particularly a very potent one, and some sweet teas, and they offered to be there with her when she had the baby. Sarah was very touched by their kindness to them, and she promised to take the herbs when they got back to Shelburne. And then she and François began the long journey home. They returned more slowly than they had come, and they slept under the stars at night, using the skins he carried for shelter. He wanted to be very careful with her, and be sure they had no mishap.

It was well into March when they got home, and at the end of April, she could feel the baby moving. It was a sweet, familiar feeling to her, but in spite of the herbs she took religiously, and François's constant reassurances, she was still terrified of the outcome.

By then people had begun to suspect they were living together. Several of the women from Shelburne had dropped by occasionally, and more often than not, they ran into François. There was talk at the Deerfield garrison by then and she had even had a letter from Mrs. Stockbridge begging her to deny the terrifying rumor that she was living with a savage. And with a look of amusement, she had quickly written to her and assured her she wasn't. But even Colonel Stockbridge knew the truth by then, and although she and François never said anything to anyone, people in the area knew that they were together. And by June, everyone knew she was having a baby. Some of the settlers were very kind about it, and a few of the women offered to help her when her time came, but many of them were outraged, and thought it was disgraceful. After all, they weren't married. But neither François nor Sarah cared a fig about what they were saying. What they cared about was each other, and their baby. They had never been happier, and she felt surprisingly well. For her, the problems usually came later. In fact, she'd been far healthier this time, and she wondered if that made a difference.

Even in summer, they still walked to the waterfall every day. The Iroquois women had told her that it was important that she walk a lot, they said it would make her son's legs stronger, and the baby would come more quickly. But in August, she could hardly make the distance anymore, and had to walk very slowly. It touched François's heart to see her lumbering along, and they stopped every few minutes so she could rest, but she seemed in good spirits, and insisted she wanted to do it. She would hold on to his arm, and they would talk all the way there. He told her whatever news he had heard when he went to the garrison, and she worried when she heard that things were still not peaceful in Ohio.

"They'll want you to go out there again one of these days," she said unhappily. She wanted him with her all the time now, and even when he visited the forts, or the garrison, she worried. He knew it was because of her confinement. But he had also thought about what would happen when he ventured from home again, because they both knew that sooner or later, that would happen. And he would have preferred leaving her in a house in a less remote area than her farm, and considerably more solid. He had had a dream for a long time about building a small château, a tiny gem, and now he talked a great deal about building it for her. But she insisted that the house they had was good enough, and she didn't need a "château." She had had one.

"Well, I shall build you one anyway," he said stubbornly, and they laughed about it, but one day when they were riding a good distance from the farm, with her in front of him on the paint mare, he stopped in a beautiful spot that overlooked the valley. You could see everything for miles around, and he looked at her with a smile as though he'd just come home, and she knew what he was thinking.

"It's lovely," she admitted.

"It will be beautiful," he said gently, and she didn't argue with him this time. She was too tired, and the baby was coming closer. She could feel it. She had been through this too often to think it would wait much longer, and every night now, she lay in bed, terrified, praying he wouldn't hear her cry in fear and sorrow. Sometimes, she got up and walked around outside just to get some air, and see the stars, and think of her babies. She couldn't imagine that this one wouldn't join them. But she could still feel life in it. In fact, it moved around a great deal more than the others. But then again, Edward wasn't beating her anymore, and she was endlessly happy with François. He took such good care of her, and sometimes he would talk to her, and rub oils on her the way the Iroquois women had shown him. He had all sorts of potions and magic for her, but she wasn't sure that even that would save this baby. Nothing they had ever done for them had saved the others. But she tried not to think of it as the time drew inevitably closer, and August melted into September. It was exactly two years since she had set sail on the *Concord*. Even she could not believe it. And neither of them could believe their good fortune. But she kept trying to brace herself for the sorrow she feared was coming, although she didn't admit her terror to the man she called her husband.

And at the end of a long day of picking corn for the winter, she asked him to go to the waterfall with her. She was tired, but she loved going there, and she wanted to see it.

"Don't you think it's too much for you now?" he asked gently. If her calculations had been right, and it had happened in the first few times they made love, the baby was due any minute. "Why don't we stay here, or just walk around the farm this afternoon?" he suggested sensibly, but she was stubborn.

"I'd miss the water." He agreed to go with her finally, because he was afraid she'd go without him if he didn't, and he walked with her very slowly until they reached it. She looked happy and strong, and he couldn't help smiling at her. Her belly was absolutely enormous. He had never seen anything like it, and he didn't want to ask her if it had always been like that. He didn't want to remind her of past horrors, though he could sense how frightened she was for their child, although she didn't say it.

They talked of other things now. He wouldn't speak to her of the unrest in the West, for fear of worrying her, and kept their conversations, as much as possible, to peaceful, gentle subjects. And on the way back from the waterfall that day, he picked her a bunch of flowers, and she carried them all the way back to her kitchen.

She was cooking dinner for him, which she still did every night, when he heard a soft moan, and hurried into the kitchen. And he knew immediately what had happened. It had started. And he was surprised by how strong it was so quickly. But she had had many children. This was her seventh, although she had nothing to show for her earlier efforts. But with Crying Sparrow, he still remembered, it had gone very slowly, and been very easy. Her mother and sisters had been with her, and she had only cried out once, as he waited outside to rejoice with her. But he could see now from the look on Sarah's face, as she leaned against a chair, that she could barely talk now.

"It's all right, my love . . . it's all right . . ." he said soothingly, as he picked her up easily in his arms and carried her into their bedroom. She had already taken the pot off the fire, and he knew that dinner would soon be forgotten. The boys would have to eat fruit and vegetables from the garden, but they wouldn't mind it. "Do you want me to call someone?" Several of the women had offered, but she had always said that she only wanted him with her. Neither of them had ever delivered a baby, she had always had a doctor. But the doctors had never been able to save her children, and she was very definite about being alone with François. There was also a doctor at the garrison, but he drank a great deal, and François knew she didn't want him.

"I just want you," she said again, but her face was contorted with pain, and she was clutching at him in agony and terror. They both knew the baby was very big, and it was easy to suspect this wouldn't be easy. Her other babies had been much smaller.

But she said very little as she lay there and writhed, trying not to make a sound, as he held her hands, and put cloths on her head drenched in cool water. It was a long night as she labored, and by midnight, she had begun pushing, but they couldn't see any progress. And in another two hours, she was exhausted, but she couldn't stop pushing. Each time she felt a pain, she couldn't stop the urge to push the baby out. But it wasn't coming, as François watched her. He looked almost as tired as she did, and he was wondering what to do for her as she began screaming with the pains now, and he didn't blame her.

"It's all right, little one . . . go ahead . . ." He was almost crying, and she couldn't even speak to him now. She seemed to be having trouble breathing. She was gasping as the pains came, and all he could do was hold her and close his eyes in prayer, trying to remember what the Indians had taught him, and then he remembered something Crying Sparrow had told him, and he tried to pull Sarah gently up to a sitting position, but she didn't understand what he wanted. "Try and stand up," he said, and she looked at him like he was crazy, but the Indian women said that a baby would come faster if you were squatting, and it made sense to him too. He would have tried anything at that point, and he didn't even care about the baby now. He didn't want to lose her.

He literally held her in his arms as he lifted her to the floor, and rested her legs against him, but he could see that it was easier now as she kept pushing. He kept her from falling with his strong arms, and she screamed each time she pushed, but she was saying something to him now as she did . . . it was coming . . . it was coming . . . she could feel it. . . . He wanted to look but he couldn't. He was still holding her in his powerful arms, and telling her to keep pushing, and then there was a long agonizing scream which was the same as the one he remembered Crying Sparrow make as the baby pushed through her, and then along with Sarah's cries, he heard the baby's, and he rolled an Indian blanket beneath her, and a moment later they looked down and the baby was looking up at them. It had big blue eyes like hers, and its face was very pale, but the baby looked huge to both of them, and they could see that it was a boy as Sarah cried in triumph. And then, just as they were watching him, the baby closed his eyes and stopped breathing. Sarah gave a scream of anguish, and reached down to him, and picked the baby up still attached to her by the cord, but François could see that it was dying. And with his powerful hands, he lifted her up and put her on the bed, and gently lifted the baby from her. He had no idea what to do, but he wasn't going to let this happen to her again . . . not now . . . not this time . . . after all that work . . . he held the baby gently upside down, and began patting his back, trying to will life into him, as Sarah sobbed, lying on the bed, distraught, watching.

"François . . ." She said his name over and over again, begging him to do something he couldn't. But she could see that the baby was dead, just like the others. And as François cried, he hit the baby hard on the back, and it coughed and a plug of mucus flew out as the baby gasped and began breathing.

"Oh my God . . ." was all she could whisper, and the baby cried loudly as his parents watched in amazement. He was beautiful, and François had never seen a lovelier sight as he put the infant to his mother's breast and she smiled at him in relief and gratitude. He was perfect. And then she looked up at François with all her love for him in her eyes. "You saved him . . . you brought him back. . . ."

"I think the spirits did that," he said, still deeply moved by the experience. They had come so close to losing him. But he looked fine now. François had never been so terrified in his life. He would have rather faced a thousand braves than lose their baby. And he couldn't take his eyes off Sarah and his son. They were truly miraculous as they lay there.

He helped her to clean up after he cut the cord with his hunting knife and tied it, and he went outside to bury the placenta. The Indians said it was holy. And as the sun came up, he thanked the gods for giving them this baby. And when he came back inside, he looked down at them with all the love and gratitude he felt, and Sarah lay in bed smiling at him and reaching her hands out to him, and when he went to her, she kissed him.

"I love you so much . . . thank you. . . ." She looked so happy and so young with their baby in her arms. Life had been good to her finally, after so much sorrow.

"The powwaw's sister told you, you would cross the river safely this time," he reminded her, but neither of them had been that certain of it, and it had come far too close for him to take anything for granted. "I thought I was going to drown in that river before you did," he teased her. It had been a long hard night, and it hadn't been easy for her and he knew it. But she didn't complain now. She was much too happy.

He brought her something to eat after a little while, and while she and the baby slept, he went out for a short time. He had to pick up papers in Deerfield. When she awoke, he was just returning, and he came into her bedroom smiling broadly.

"Where were you?" she asked, looking worried.

"I had some papers to pick up," he said, with a look of victory in his eyes.

"What kind?" she asked, trying to readjust the baby as he suckled. This was all very new to her, and she still felt a little awkward as François helped her. He was better at this than she was. And he put a pillow beneath her arm so she could hold the baby and she thanked him. He was as happy as she was. "What were you picking up?" she asked him again, and he smiled at her and handed her a roll of parchment tied with leather. She opened it carefully, and smiled at him when she saw it. He had bought it. "You bought the land then." She looked at him warmly.

"It's a gift for you, Sarah. We'll build a house there."

"I'm happy here," she said simply, but the land he had bought was in a splendid location.

"You deserve better." But they both knew that she didn't need another thing than she had at that moment. She had never been happier in her life, and was sure she never would be. This was heaven.

Chapter 21

THE BABY GREW visibly in the first two weeks after he was born, and Sarah was back on her feet by then, cooking for François and working in the garden. She hadn't walked all the way to the waterfall yet, but she was working up to it, but other than feeling a little tired from nursing so much, she seemed completely healthy.

"That was pretty easy," she said cavalierly one day to him, and he threw a handful of berries at her with a look of amazement.

"How can you say that? You worked for twelve hours, and it's the hardest thing I've ever seen anyone do. I've seen men pull carts up mountains that looked easier than that! What do you mean *easy*?" he teased her, but the memory of what she'd gone through had already dimmed, which was the way the Iroquois women said it should be. A woman was not supposed to remember the birth of her baby, or she would be afraid to have another. But François was just pleased they had this one. He was not inclined to be greedy, or push her to another possible disaster. He didn't want to do anything to spoil her joy now.

But at the end of September, he found he had to. Colonel Stockbridge rode out to see him himself, and an expedition was riding out to Ohio the following week, to see if they could finally subdue the tribes that were fighting the Army. It was always the same ones, the Shawnees, the Chickasaws, and the Miamis, led by Blue Jacket and Little Turtle. It had gone on for two years now. Everyone was afraid of a general Indian war if nothing was done to control them. And it was high time they were dealt with. François couldn't disagree with him, but he knew how upset Sarah was going to be when he left her. The baby was only three weeks old, and this had been just what she was afraid of. And the very fact that Colonel Stockbridge had come to see him told its own story. They needed him badly in Ohio.

As soon as he left, François went to find her. She was out in the garden with the little papoose firmly attached to her back while she picked beans. And the baby was sleeping soundly. He only seemed to wake at the exact moment when it was time for his dinner.

"You're going, aren't you?" she said with a look of anguish. She had known it the moment she saw Stockbridge. François didn't even have to tell her. But he had been at home for a long time, almost ten months now. It had been a year since the last attempt to subdue Blue Jacket, which had cost the lives of a hundred and eighty-three men and been completely unsuccessful. "I hate Blue Jacket," she said to François, like a pouting child, and he couldn't help smiling at her. She looked so sweet and so young and so happy, and he hated to leave her. But at least he had given her his baby. They had named him Alexandre André de Pellerin, after François's grandfather and father, and he would be the eighteenth Comte de Pellerin, François had told her. His Indian name was Running Pony. "How soon will you go?" she asked sadly.

"In five days. I need time to prepare first." He would need muskets and ammunition and warm clothes and supplies. He knew many of the men who were going, both Indian and soldiers. But to Sarah it sounded like a death sentence. All she had left was five days with François. She looked stricken.

And he looked agonized when he left her. He had lain in bed with her all night, they had both stayed awake, and she couldn't seem to let go of him. He had made love to her although he knew that Indian legend said he should wait till forty days after the baby, and it had been less than thirty, but he hated so much to leave her, and he couldn't stop himself, but she didn't seem to mind it. On the contrary, she was as hungry for him as he was saddened to leave her.

She stood outside the house and cried when he left, and she had a terrible feeling about what would happen. It was like a horrible premonition flying over her. It had to do with Blue Jacket and Little Turtle, and she was completely convinced that something terrible was going to happen. And it did. But not to him. The Shawnees and the Miamis overran Major General St. Clair's encampment three weeks later and left six hundred and thirty men dead and nearly three hundred wounded. It was the worst disaster the Army had suffered. And St. Clair was disgraced when everyone blamed him. It had been poor strategy and miserably handled. And for more than a month Sarah had no idea if François had survived it. She was frantic. And it was after Thanksgiving when she finally heard that he was alive and on his way home from Ohio. A party of men had arrived back at the Deerfield garrison before he did, but they assured her he wasn't wounded, and told her he would be home before Christmas.

She was wearing the papoose on her back the day he arrived and she looked like an Indian squaw, as she came out of the smokehouse. She heard hoofbeats, and before she could even turn around, he had dismounted and grabbed her in his arms. He looked tired and thinner, but he was safe, and he had terrible stories to tell her. He didn't know what could be done to control the unrest. And to complicate matters, the British had built a new post below Detroit on the Maumee River, in violation of the

Treaty of Paris. But he was so happy to see his bride that he no longer cared what Blue Jacket did in retaliation. He was home now, and she was thrilled to have him.

And on Christmas, she told him the news, but he had already suspected it. They were having another baby. It would be born in July, and he wanted to start building their new house long before that. He had spent hours at the camp fires drawing up plans and making little drawings, and he began hiring men in Shelburne almost as soon as he got home from Ohio. They would start the moment the snow melted, and hoped to be in before winter.

Little Alexandre was nearly four months old by then, and Sarah had never before looked so happy. François loved playing with him and wore the papoose himself sometimes, particularly when he took him riding with him. He was spending a lot of time in Shelburne, commissioning people to make things for their new home, and writing to cabinetmakers for furniture in Connecticut, Delaware, and Boston. He took the project very seriously, and by spring, he finally had Sarah excited about it.

They had just begun to break ground, when a man came to Shelburne, looking for her. He appeared at the farm unexpectedly as they rode home with the baby from the site of the new house. He was waiting outside the house and he didn't look pleasant. And he reminded Sarah vaguely of the lawyer who had come to see her from Boston, which was precisely what this man was. He was Walker Johnston's partner. But Johnston was still talking about the Indian attack that had occurred when he last came to see her. He said he had barely gotten out with his scalp, but never explained why he had fled, leaving her to fight the Indians herself, or how she had survived it. But this man was even more unpleasant. His name was Sebastian Mosley. And she wondered if his coming to see her had anything to do with the smallpox epidemic in Boston. It was a good place not to be now. But his visit had nothing to do with that, and he had no papers

321

for her to sign this time. He had simply come to tell her that her husband had died. And she looked up at François as he said it. She had no other husband. As far as she was concerned Edward no longer existed. But Sebastian Mosley had come to tell her that the Earl of Balfour had been killed in an unfortunate hunting accident, and although he had intended to recognize one of his . . . er . . . ah . . . illegitimate children, the attorney said uncomfortably, and the papers had been drawn up to do so, apparently his lordship had neglected to sign them, and his untimely death had been quite unexpected. It was apparently a complicated legal situation now, because she had waived all right to his inheritance, but by dying intestate, he brought that document into question, and there was no one else to leave either his land or his fortune to, since he had no legitimate children. The lawyer did not tell her that he had fourteen bastards. But what he wanted to know from her was whether she wished to contest the document she had signed a year and a half before. But for Sarah, it was extremely simple. She didn't have much, but she had everything she wanted.

"I suggest you give it all to his sister-in-law and his four nieces. They're his most direct heirs now." But she wanted nothing to do with it, not a penny, not a plume, not even a souvenir of Edward. And she said exactly that to the attorney.

"I see," he said, looking dismayed. He had been hoping for a little business if she decided to contest it. According to his counterpart in England, the Earl had had an enormous fortune. But Sarah didn't want it. And the lawyer from Boston left as soon as she said so, and thanked him.

They watched him ride away and Sarah stood there, thinking about Edward for a few minutes, but she felt nothing. It had been too long, too hard, and too awful. And she was far too happy now to have any regrets over Edward. It was finally over.

But as far as François was concerned, it was just beginning.

He had thought of it the moment he'd heard the lawyer. And he turned to Sarah as soon as they were alone again and asked her.

"Will you marry me, Sarah Ferguson?" There was not even an instant's hesitation. Just a tinkle of laughter, as she nodded.

They were married on April first, in the little log church in Shelburne in a simple ceremony, and no one was present except the two boys who worked for them, and Alexandre, who was seven months old. Their baby was due in only three months.

And the next time they went to the Deerfield garrison, François bowed formally to the colonel and presented Sarah to him. And he looked startled for a moment.

"May I present the Countess de Pellerin to you, Colonel . . . I believe you've never met her," he said, beaming.

"Does this mean what I think it does?" he asked kindly. He had always liked them both, and felt bad for their situation, although his wife thought it quite shocking. She had stopped writing to Sarah as soon as she'd heard about the first baby. And others had had the same reaction. But now suddenly everyone wanted to know them, and they were invited by some of the nicest people in Deerfield. They stayed at the garrison for a while and Sarah visited Rebecca. She had four children by then, and was expecting her fifth one, which was also due that summer.

But François was anxious to get home this time, he wanted to see how their new house was coming. And once they got back to Shelburne, he worked feverishly on it with the men he hired, and the Indians whom he taught to do the kind of work he had once seen in Paris. Everyone said it was going to be beautiful, and Sarah beamed when she went there. She loved watching them build it, and it was a passion with her too now. She was already planning her garden. They expected to have the outside of the house done by August, and be able to move into it in October, before the first snows came. And they could work on all the interior details all winter. Sarah was so excited she could hardly wait, and she worked there daily all through June, in spite of the encumbrance of the baby, but this time, even she was less worried. She was taking all the herbs she knew she was supposed to, and getting a lot of rest, and walking as the Indian women had told her to. Everything felt right, and she had little Alexandre to prove to her that miracles could happen.

But by July first, there was no sign of a new arrival, and Sarah was restless. She couldn't wait for the baby to come, so that she could see it and move around more freely. She felt as though she had been pregnant forever, and she said as much to François.

"Don't be so impatient," he chided her, "great works take time." And this time, he was more nervous than she was. It had been difficult the time before, as far as he was concerned, and he had been lucky to save the baby. He dreaded another terrifying experience like that one, although he was as excited as she was. But he just hoped it would go smoothly. He had even considered sending for the doctor in Shelburne, but Sarah insisted she wouldn't need him. And she seemed very lively in the first week of July, which convinced them both that the baby wasn't ready. Last time, she had slowed down visibly as her time came closer, and could sense herself that the baby was coming. But this time, as tired as she was of lugging a big belly around, she felt as though she could go on forever. She wasn't even tired. And he had to discourage her from riding over to the new house constantly, to attend to some detail.

"I don't want you riding over there alone anymore," he scolded her one afternoon as he saw her returning. "That's dangerous, you could have the baby by the side of the road," but she laughed at him. The last time she had plenty of warning, it had taken twelve hours, and the others far longer.

"I wouldn't do that," she said primly, every inch the countess.

"See that you don't!" He wagged a finger at her, and she went to make dinner. But they were both thrilled with the little gem of a house they were building. And everyone in the neighborhood was talking about it. They thought it was very fancy for Shelburne, to say the least, but no one seemed to mind it. If anything they liked it. They thought it added importance to the area, and was a real feather in the cap of Shelburne.

Sarah made dinner for him that night, and François went to pore over some more plans in their sitting room, while she cleaned the kitchen, and after she'd washed their dishes, it was still daylight, and she tried to convince him to go walking with her.

"We haven't been to the waterfall all week," she said, obviously in good spirits as she kissed him.

"I'm tired," he said honestly and then smiled at her, "I'm having a baby."

"No, you're not," she parried with him, "I am. And I want to take a walk. You heard what the Iroquois women said, it will give the baby strong legs." She was laughing at him and he groaned.

"And me weak ones. I'm an old man." He had just turned forty-one, but he didn't look it. And she was twenty-seven. But he followed her outside to humor her, and they had only walked for five minutes when she slowed noticeably, and stopped walking. He thought she had a rock in her shoe perhaps, and stood beside her as she clutched his arm, and then he realized what had happened. She was having the baby. But he was grateful they hadn't gone far from the house, and could turn back easily, but as he was about to suggest it to his wife, she fell to the ground beside him. She had never felt such pain in her life, and she could hardly catch her breath as he knelt beside her. "Sarah, what happened?" He wondered if it was a bad sign, as she lay on the grass by the roadside. "Are you all right?" He was terrified, and he wasn't even close enough to the house to call for the boys to get the doctor. He felt trapped there.

"François . . . I can't move . . ." she said with a look of terror as the pains ripped through her. But this was not the beginning, it was the middle and the ending, it was the worst pain she could remember, and then she suddenly knew the familiar feeling as he held her. "François . . . it's the baby . . . it's coming . . ." She looked panicked as she clutched him.

"No, it's not, my love." Would that it were that easy, he found himself thinking, but she knew better. She was suddenly gasping in agony and he could see that she was almost screaming. "Remember last time, how long it took," he said, trying to convince her. He wanted to pick her up and carry her back to the house, but she wouldn't let him move her.

"Don't!" She screamed out in pain, and then writhed in agony beside him, as he knelt helplessly beside her.

"Sarah," he said, feeling helpless, "you can't just lie there. You cannot have the baby so quickly. When did this start?" he asked, suddenly suspicious.

"I don't know." She started to cry. "I had a backache all day today when I went to the house, and my stomach hurt for a while, but I thought it was from carrying Alexandre." He was a healthy size now at ten months and still loved to be carried.

"Oh my God," François said with a look of panic. "It's probably been all day. How could you not know that?" She looked like a child suddenly and he felt sorry for her, but he wanted to get her back to the house now, no matter how much she said it hurt if he moved her. He would not leave her here, lying in the grass to have their baby. He tried to scoop her up again, and she screamed and fought against him, and then suddenly her entire face was clenched and she was pushing. He had never seen anything like it. She was delivering her baby and there was nothing he could do to stop her or help her, and then suddenly he realized how badly she needed him and he held her shoulders and tried to assist her. She was totally intent on her work, and making little sounds as she fought the pain, and then suddenly she began to scream as though a terrible force were tearing through her, but he remembered that sound, and he let her down gently on the grass, and lifted her skirts, and ripped off her pantaloons, and as he did, she screamed again, and he could see the baby coming into his hands, with its bright little face screaming at him in outrage. And within an instant, he was holding the baby. It was a little girl, and she was perfect and breathing, and screaming blue murder at her father.

"Sarah," he said, looking at his wife, lying on the grass in the twilight with a peaceful smile on her face, "you are going to kill me. Don't ever do that to me again! I'm too old for this!" But neither of them were. He leaned over and kissed her and she told him how much she loved him.

"That was much easier than last time," she said simply, and he sat down next to her and laughed as he put the baby on her chest. He had used his hunting knife again, and tied the cord neatly.

"How could you not know she was coming?" He was still overwhelmed by the experience, and it amazed him to see how peaceful she was after so much pain. She and the baby looked completely content, and he could still feel his knees shake.

"I was busy, I guess. I had so much to do at the new house," she said, smiling at him, as she opened her blouse and the baby found her breast easily and nursed there.

"I shall never trust you again. If we ever have another child, I will chain you to your bed for the last weeks, so I won't end up delivering a baby by the side of the road somewhere." But he kissed her again as he said it, and let her rest for a while as they lay beneath the stars that had just come out, but it was getting chilly. "Now, may I carry you home, Madame la Comtesse? Or would you like to sleep here?" He didn't want the baby catching a chill there, and neither did Sarah.

"You may carry me home, Monsieur le Comte," she said grandly, and he bundled her up carefully, and carried her the five minutes back to the house as she held the baby. It was not terribly comfortable for her, and she wanted to try to walk, but he wouldn't let her.

"This is the kind of thing the Indians talk about," he said in an undertone as they reached their farmhouse, "but I never believed really happened." But with that, the two boys had just seen them, and asked what had happened to Sarah. They thought she'd fallen or sprained her ankle, and hadn't realized she was carrying the baby. It was sleeping, exhausted by its hasty arrival. "We found the baby in the field," François explained with amusement. "It's amazing, she looks just like her," he was laughing and the boys looked stunned.

"Did she just have her like that, on the way to the waterfall?" one of them asked incredulously.

"Right on the way," he assured them. "Never missed a step, she's very good at this," he said with a wink at his wife as they admired the baby.

"Wait 'til I tell my mother," the younger of the two said, "she always takes forever, and by the time the baby comes, my dad's so drunk he falls asleep, and then she gets mad at him because he can't see the baby."

"Lucky devil," François said as he carried his wife and daughter inside. The boys had been baby-sitting for Alexandre but he had fallen asleep before he could see his sister.

"What'll we call her?" Sarah asked as François lay beside her on their bed. She was looking more tired than she admitted.

"I've always wanted a daughter called Eugénie, but it's not as pretty in English," he confessed.

"What about Françoise?" Sarah asked, grateful to be on her bed again, she was feeling a little woozy. With the speed of the delivery, there had been a fair amount of bleeding.

"It's not very original," he said, but he was touched, and finally agreed on it. They named her Françoise Eugénie Sarah de Pellerin. And she was christened in the little church in Shelburne along with her brother in August.

Their house was nearly ready by then, and Sarah had her

hands full with her children, but she went there as often as she could to observe their progress. And by October, they were in it.

The entry in her journal that day sounded jubilant, as she talked about every detail of the house. It made Charlie smile to read it. The house had scarcely changed since she and François had built it, from the sound of it, and as he set the journal down, he felt wistful thinking about their children. How lucky Sarah and François had been. What a full life they had had. He wished he had been as wise and as fortunate as they were.

He was feeling slightly sorry for himself, as the phone rang, and he almost didn't answer it. But he wondered if it was Francesca, reporting on her first reading of the journal. And with a small smile, he picked the receiver up, and spoke into it.

"Okay, Francesca, how is it?" But it was Carole, and Charlie was shocked when he heard her.

"Who's Francesca?" she wanted to know.

"A friend. Why? What's up?" He was completely confused to hear her. What could she possibly want from him? She had already called to tell him that she and Simon were getting married. Their divorce wasn't final till late May. So she wasn't waiting any longer than she had to. "Why are you calling?" he asked, still embarrassed at having called her Francesca. It made him feel very foolish, and even more so when he wondered if it would make Carole jealous. That was just plain stupid.

"There's something I want to tell you," she said sounding awkward, and he had a major case of déjà vu.

"Didn't we already have this conversation? We just went through this." He didn't sound overly pleased to hear from her, and she noticed it. But she still had this obsession about being decent to him, which Simon told her was crazy. He said she didn't owe Charlie anything anymore, but Carole knew better. "You already told me you're getting married," he reminded her. "Remember?"

"I know. But now there's something else I think I should tell you."

He couldn't imagine what it was, and he wasn't even sure he wanted to hear it. He didn't really want the intimate details of her life with Simon. "Are you sick?"

"Not exactly," she said, and he was suddenly worried. What if something terrible had happened to her? He was sure Simon wouldn't take care of her the way he would. "I'm pregnant," she continued, and knocked the wind right out of him. He was stunned into silence. "And I'm sick as a dog. But that's beside the point. And I thought you should know, Charlie. I didn't know how you'd feel about it. And it's going to show before the wedding." He wasn't sure if he hated her or loved her for telling him, a little bit of both, but he was really shocked, and it really hurt him.

"Why Simon?" he said, sounding unhappy. "Why not me during all those years? You never wanted kids, and suddenly zap, you get yourself a sixty-one-year-old boyfriend, and you're pregnant. Maybe I'm sterile," he said, and she laughed gently.

"Hardly," she said. She'd had one abortion before they were married. "I don't know, Charlie. I just turned forty, and I'm scared the opportunity will never come again. I don't know what to tell you, except this time I know I want it. Maybe if it had happened to us, I would have felt that way too. It just never did, that's all." But it was more than that and she knew it. In the last few years, Charlie hadn't been right for her. She wasn't happy with him. He was a relic from her youth, and Simon wasn't. He was the man she wanted to marry, and have children with. He was everything Charlie wasn't. "I didn't call you to hurt you, Charlie. I just thought you should know." Even if it was awkward to tell him.

"Thanks," he said, trying to absorb what she had said to him, and thinking about the future. "Maybe if it had happened to us, we'd still be married." It was impossible not to think that.

"Maybe," she said honestly, "or maybe not. Maybe this all happened for a reason. I just don't know."

"Are you happy about it?" he asked, suddenly thinking about Sarah, and her babies with François. Maybe there was a Sarah out there, waiting for him. It was a nice fairy tale, but he didn't really believe it.

"Yeah, I guess I am happy," Carole said, honest with him again. "I wish I didn't feel so sick. It's really rotten. But the idea of a baby is kind of exciting." Something about the way she said it moved him deeply. He could tell it was important to her, and for an instant, she sounded like a different person.

"Take care of yourself," he said, worried about her. "What does Simon think about all this? He must feel a little elderly to be folding diapers again, or does it make him feel youthful?" It was a mean thing to say, but Charlie couldn't resist. He was jealous of the guy. He had walked off with his wife, and now they were having a baby. It was a little hard to stomach.

" 'He's over the moon,' as he says," Carole said with a smile, and then winced at a wave of nausea. "I'd better get off, but I just wanted to let you know, in case you hear it via the grapevine." In some ways, London was a small town, and so was New York, but he was in neither of those places anymore. He'd been banished.

"The grapevine doesn't reach Shelburne Falls," he informed her. "I probably wouldn't have heard it till I got back to London."

"When is that going to be?"

"I don't know yet." He sounded vague, but he had nothing else to say to her. She had dropped her news on him and now he needed to digest it. "Take care of yourself, Carole. I'll call you one of these days." But he wasn't so sure he would now. There was nothing left to argue about, or to say. She was getting married, she was having a kid. And he had his own life to get on with. It was the first time he had really felt that, and when he hung up, he realized that it had a lot to do with Sarah. In an odd, subtle way, reading the journals had really changed him. And he was still thinking about that, when the phone rang again, and he figured it was Carole.

"Hi, Carole," he said. "What now? Twins?" He didn't sound overly thrilled as he answered, but the voice was not the one he expected.

"It's me. Francesca. Am I interrupting something?" She sounded puzzled and he groaned.

"I'm batting a thousand tonight. My ex-wife just called, and when I answered the phone I said 'Hi, Francesca.' Now you called, and I thought it was Carole calling back. Anyway, she just called me with another news flash." He sounded strangely unemotional about it, which surprised him. It wasn't at all like his reaction when she called to tell him she was getting married, and he had sat and talked to Francesca.

"Is she leaving her boyfriend?" Francesca asked him with interest.

"No, quite the contrary. They're having a baby. Apparently she'll be six months pregnant when they get married. Very modern."

"How do you feel about that?" she asked kindly, and he thought about it.

"I think it's hell finding a wedding dress in a case like that, and it's better if you do it a little sooner. Maybe even before you get knocked up, just to be old-fashioned." He was teasing her a little bit, and she wasn't sure if he was hysterical or indifferent to what Carole had told him. And he wasn't entirely sure either.

"I'm serious, Charlie. How are you?"

"How am I?" He thought about it for a long time and then sighed. "Kind of pissed off, kind of disappointed. I wish we'd had a kid, but we didn't. And if I were going to be honest about it, I'd admit we didn't want to. I *really* didn't want kids with her, and she *really* didn't want them with me. Maybe it was our own way of acknowledging that something was wrong even before she found Simon. I guess in a funny way, I feel free now. It's definitely over and I know it. She's not coming back. She's his now. I kind of hurt and I kind of don't. And after reading Sarah's journals, I really want a kid of my own now . . . or maybe Monique did that. But that's what I feel. And you know what else?" He sounded fairly chipper, and she liked what he was saying.

"What else?" she asked softly. It was late, and Monique was sleeping.

"I miss you. I was hoping it was you when Carole called. I was dying to know what you thought of Sarah's journals."

"That's why I called you. I've been sitting here crying my eyes out all night reading about what Edward did to her, and all those babies that died. How did the poor woman stand it?"

"I told you," he said proudly, "she was gutsy. So are you. So am I. We can make it. We've all been through a lot of stuff but this is only the beginning." After reading Sarah's journals, he really felt that. "Where are you now?" he asked, remembering each step of the way he had come. He envied her the fact that she was just starting. But he could imagine reading them all over again one day, a long time after he finished, and after he'd given them to Gladys Palmer.

"She's on the ship."

"It only gets better." It was like a secret club they shared, and she was so grateful to him for letting her read them. But he'd had another idea. He'd been thinking about it ever since he saw her. But he wasn't sure if she was ready. "How about a real date one of these days? A real dinner, just the two of us. I'll pay for the sitter."

"You don't have to do that." She smiled, and she felt she owed him something for letting her read Sarah's journals. "I'd love to."

"Saturday?" He sounded ecstatic and surprised. He didn't think she would accept it.

"Saturday," she said.

333

"I'll pick you up at eight. Happy reading." And they hung up then. It had been a long day, a long night. Sarah had had two babies. Carole was having another. And he had a date with Francesca. He wanted to kick his heels up and laugh when he thought about it.

Chapter 22

C HARLIE PICKED FRANCESCA up at eight on Saturday, and she looked beautiful. She was wearing a plain black dress with a string of pearls, and her hair hung straight and sleek to her shoulders. It was a great look for her, and Charlie's heart gave a little leap when Monique gave him a woeful look, sitting in her bedroom with the sitter. She wasn't happy not to be included. But her mother had explained very nicely to her that sometimes grown-ups just need to be together. Monique said she thought it was a stupid rule, and she hoped they never did it again. Besides, the baby-sitter was ugly. But she seemed to be managing, playing Monopoly and watching TV when her mother and Charlie left for dinner.

He took her to Andiamo in Bernardston, and after dinner they went dancing. It was definitely a real date, and for the first time since he had known Francesca she didn't act as though she were going to run out the door every five minutes when they were alone. And he couldn't help wondering what had happened.

"I don't know. I'm growing up, I guess," she said when he commented on it. "Sometimes I even get a little tired of my war wounds. Wearing scars around like jewelry gets a little boring," she said, and he was impressed. He wondered if the journals had done it, or simply time. Maybe she was healing. And then she surprised him by saying she was going to Paris that week. Her lawyer had called, and she and Pierre were selling their last piece of property and she had to sign all the papers.

"Can't they send them to you?" Charlie said, looking surprised. "It seems like a long way to go just to sign some papers."

"They want me to do it in person. Pierre doesn't want me to be able to claim that he forced me, or there was fraud involved, or I didn't understand, not that I would. I guess he figures that if we do it face-to-face there won't be any misunderstanding."

"I hope he's paying for the trip," Charlie said bluntly, but she smiled.

"It'll come out of my profits. I'm not so worried about that. I'm more worried about seeing him, and the little mother. It used to make me sick just seeing them, now I'm not so sure. Maybe it'll be a good test. Maybe I don't care as much as I used to think I did. Sometimes I wonder." She looked pensive as she looked at him. Just in the short time they had known each other, he could tell that she was changing.

"Are you scared going to Paris this time?" he asked honestly as he reached out and took her hand. It was hard to go back sometimes. In a way, as much as he wanted to return, he was dreading London.

"I'm a little bit scared," she confessed sheepishly. "But I won't be gone long. I'm leaving Monday, and I'll be back on Friday. As long as I'm going, I want to see a few friends, do a little shopping."

"Are you taking Monique with you?" he asked, concerned about both of them. He could see that the trip was going to be a challenge.

"She has school, and it's better if she isn't there for this. I don't want her to feel pulled between us. She's staying with a friend from school."

He nodded. "I'll call her."

"She'd like that," she said, and then they danced for a little bit, and neither of them said anything. He loved holding her in his arms, but didn't dare do more than that, though he would have liked to. But he could still sense she wasn't ready. And he wasn't so sure he was either. A lot of things had gone through his mind in the last few days, a lot of changes, a lot of new ideas, like wanting children, and not being quite as angry at Carole. He wasn't sure he was angry at all anymore. He wished her well. He just wished he had as much in his life as she did. Like Sarah and François.

They talked about the journals on the way home, and the house, and he wished he could find the plans that François had worked on. For him, that would have been really exciting. But the journals were even better. And when they got to Francesca's door, he walked her inside and she paid the sitter. Monique was sound asleep by then, and it was nice being alone with her in the silence.

"I'm going to miss you when you're away," he said, and meant it. "I like talking to you." He hadn't had a friend in a long time, and lately, she had been one. He didn't know yet what more she would be, but even having someone to talk to was rare and precious.

"I'll miss you too," she said softly. "I'll call you from Paris." He hoped she would, and she told him where she was staying. It was a small hotel on the Left Bank, and it conjured up dreams for him. And he wished he could go there with her. It would have been so romantic, and he could have supported her when she saw her ex-husband. Like François protecting Sarah from Edward. He said as much to her, and they both laughed at the image. "You'd make a good knight in shining armor," she said gently, standing very near him.

"I think I'm a little rusty," he said, aching to kiss her. But he took her hand and kissed her fingers instead, remembering

François's gesture. "Take care of yourself," he said. He knew it was time to go, before he did something foolish. And as he drove away, she watched him from the window.

He read a little bit of the journals again that night but most of it was about the house, and everything they'd done to it that winter. And he fell asleep dreaming of Francesca.

The next day, he thought of dropping by to see Francesca and Monique, but in the end, he didn't. He took Mrs. Palmer to lunch instead, and had to fight himself not to tell her about the journals. But he wanted to let Francesca finish them before he turned them over. And Gladys Palmer was happy for the attention, and there was plenty to talk about. He wanted to tell her about Carole, and Francesca.

But as the day wore on, all Charlie could think about was Francesca. He called to see if she and Monique could have dinner with him, but they were out all afternoon, they had gone ice-skating, and when he finally reached them they had already eaten. But Francesca sounded touched that he had called her. She was sounding wistful these days, and he suspected she was worried about her trip to Paris in the morning. She was leaving after she dropped Monique off at school, and he offered to take her to the airport but she had already made other arrangements.

"I'll call you from Paris," she promised again, and he hoped she meant it. He felt like a kid being abandoned.

"Good luck," he said before they hung up, and she thanked him and told him to say hi to Sarah. He wished he could, and that night, as always, he listened but heard nothing.

The week crawled by interminably, and Charlie felt distracted. He tried to do some work, started a painting, read a little more in Sarah's journal, and looked at all the architectural magazines he could lay his hands on. He called Monique a couple of times, but heard nothing from Francesca, until Thursday. And then, finally, she called him.

"How did it go?"

"Great. He's still a jerk, but I made a lot of money." She laughed into the phone, and she sounded terrific. "And the little Olympic champion is getting fatter by the minute. Pierre hates fat women."

"It serves him right. I hope she weighs three hundred pounds by the next Olympics." She laughed again, but there was something else in her voice, and he couldn't tell what it was. It was morning for him, and afternoon for her. And she was catching the plane to Boston in a few hours. She hadn't been in a rush to call him. "Can I pick you up tomorrow, at the airport?" he offered, and she hesitated, and then accepted.

"That's a long drive for you, isn't it?"

"I think I can make it. I'll get the coach out and hire a couple of Indian guides. I'll be there on Sunday."

"Okay, okay," she said, and then seemed to be in a hurry. "I have to pack. I'll see you tomorrow." She was due in at noon, local time, on Friday.

"I'll be there," he assured her. And he felt like a kid the next day, as he drove to Boston. What if she never wanted more than to be friends with him? What if she stayed scared forever? . . . what if Sarah had never gotten over Edward? . . . he was beginning to feel as though he should have been meeting her in buckskins and eagle feathers, and the thought of that amused him.

She went through customs before he could get to her, and it was one o'clock before she came through the gate and saw him. She looked better than ever. She was wearing a bright red coat she'd bought at Dior, and she'd had her hair cut. She looked very French and very striking.

"It's great to see you," he said, and walked swiftly beside her and carried her bags to the garage, and as soon as they found his car, they set off toward Deerfield. It was odd to think of how long it had taken Sarah two hundred years before. Four days, as opposed to an hour and ten minutes. And another ten to Shelburne Falls. They chatted easily on the trip, and she said she'd finished the first journal. They talked about it for a while, and she asked him if he'd read any more that week, but he looked at her sheepishly and shook his head. "I was too nervous," he admitted.

"Why?" She seemed surprised, and as he drove, he was honest with her.

"I kept thinking about you. I didn't want him to hurt you."

"I'm not sure he can anymore," she said as she looked out the window. "That's the funny thing. I haven't seen him for a long time, but somehow I kept endowing him with these magic powers to ruin my life. He almost did. But I don't know what happened since the last time I saw him. Something changed that. He's just this very self-centered, not quite so good-looking French guy I used to be in love with. And yes, he hurt me a lot, but I think I'm past it. It really surprised me."

"You're free now," he said gently. "I think that's what's happened to me with Carole. I haven't seen her, but how involved can you be with a woman who's marrying someone else and having his kid . . . and never wanted mine . . . it's kind of a losing proposition." That was the difference. They were losers. Pierre and Carol had screwed things up, or maybe they'd just gotten what they wanted and didn't have. But Francesca and Charlie wanted to be winners.

Sarah had won the prize in the end. She had found it all with François, once she had the courage to leave Edward. And Francesca nodded in agreement and they both fell silent as he drove her to her house, and helped her with her bags. He looked down at her in the doorway with a question.

"When am I going to see you?" he asked pointedly and she looked him straight in the eye with a small smile, but said nothing. "How about dinner with your daughter tomorrow night?" he suggested, not wanting to pounce on her too quickly, although he would have liked to.

"She's going to a sleep-over birthday party," Francesca said, feeling slightly nervous.

"Can I make you dinner at my house?" he asked, and she nodded. It was a little scary. For both of them. But Sarah would be there, at least in spirit. And Charlie kissed her on the cheek then. She was a very different woman now than the one he had first met. She was cautious, hurt, still frightened sometimes, but she was no longer bitter, angry, or destroyed by what had happened. And neither was Charlie. "I'll pick you up at seven," he said, and turned to leave and she thanked him for the ride from Boston.

And then he went back to his house, and out of sheer nervousness, he picked up the last of the journals. He had left them comfortably settled in their new house, and François had not ridden out with the army in a long time, but Sarah continued to report on the situation in the West between the Shawnees and the Miamis and the encroaching white settlers. It did nothing but worsen.

And in the summer of 1793, a year after Françoise was born, they had another baby. Another little girl this time, and she came almost as quickly as the last one. And as Charlie read the journals, he realized she had been born right in the bedroom he slept in. They had named her Marie-Ange because Sarah said she looked like an angel.

Sarah was ecstatic with her little family, and with the fact that François wasn't riding with the Army, and hadn't in ages. He kept improving on the house, and she recorded all the architectural details in her journals. It made Charlie want to pore over the house again and find every nook and cranny she spoke of. He suspected that most of the details she described would still be there.

She also wrote that Colonel Stockbridge died that same year,

341

and was mourned by all who knew him. And the new commandant was far more ambitious. He was a friend of General Wayne's, who was the new commander of the Western Army, and had already been spending a year drilling troops to go after Little Turtle. But so far, nothing had happened since General St. Clair had retired in disgrace after his crushing defeat the last time.

It was a time for her family, and Sarah sounded peaceful but busy and she wrote less and less often in her journals. It seemed as though she had her hands full with three young children, the farm, and her husband.

But in the fall of 1793, Sarah mentioned with concern that one of the Iroquois, Big Tree, a friend of François's had attempted peace talks with the Shawnees again, and been rejected. The problem was that the Shawnees had previously allied themselves with the British, so that when the British were defeated, the American Army felt that the Shawnees in the Ohio territory should disappear with them, relinquishing their land to the settlers. But the Shawnees did not wish to go down in flames with the British, and were now refusing to give up their land, and demanding a fifty-thousand-dollar repayment for it and a ten-thousand-dollar annual annuity, which was out of the question. It was unheard of. And General Wayne was not listening. Not even for a minute.

He continued to train his troops at Fort Washington, and Forts Recovery and Greenville in Ohio, through that winter. Nothing was going to sway him, and everyone agreed by then. Blue Jacket and Little Turtle, their two proudest warriors, had to be defeated. But so far no one had succeeded.

There was talk of a campaign organized by General Wayne in May of 1794, but it never got under way, and Sarah was enormously relieved. She was looking forward to a peaceful summer, and had begun to tease François about being a settler, no more the warrior or the Indian brave. He was "an old man" now, a "farmer." And she loved it. At forty-three, she wrote that he was as handsome as ever, and she was glad he was no longer risking his life constantly to ride with the Army. In fact, they were thinking of visiting the Iroquois that summer, with all three children, since for once, she did not appear to be pregnant. It was the first respite she'd had since she and François were married, and even before that. And it was obvious from what she wrote how much she loved her children. But it was equally clear that she adored her husband. François was truly the love of her life, and she wanted more than anything to grow old with him, and enjoy their family together. She worried about his being restless at times, but for a man like him, that seemed normal and for the most part he was content living with his family.

But as Charlie read her entry in early July of that year, he could see clearly that her hand was shaking. There had been an attack on a pack train and its escort of a hundred and forty men in Ohio on the thirtieth of June, led by Blue Jacket and Tecumseh, followed by an attack on Fort Recovery by the Ottawas, and within days, the new commandant of the Deerfield garrison had sent a message to François. Within a month nearly four thousand men, from the regular Army and militia men from Kentucky were to go to Fort Recovery to attempt to regulate the problem It was an enormous number of men, and even François had never heard of anything like it. And predictably, General Wayne wanted François to go with them. His vast knowledge of Indian tribes, his ability to deal with all but the most hostile braves, was invaluable to them. But Sarah did everything she could to fight it, including beg him not to go, for the sake of their children, and insult him by telling him he was too old to survive it. But all he did was try to reassure her.

"With so many men, how can anything happen to me? They will not even find me," he told her gently, keenly aware of his sense of obligation.

"That's nonsense, and you know it," she argued. "There could be thousands of men killed, and there will be. No one can defeat Blue Jacket, and now he has been joined by Tecumseh." Thanks to all that François had explained to her, she had become knowledgeable about these things, and Tecumseh was known as the greatest warrior of all. Sarah did not want François anywhere near them.

But by late July, Sarah had been defeated. François promised her he would never go again, if that was what she wished, but he could not let General Wayne down now, after he had specifically asked for him. And he knew that in truth, he could be useful.

"It would be wrong of me to abandon my friends now, my love." He was, above all, a man of honor. And although she argued with him about it constantly, she knew he could not be stopped now. But she cried piteously all night, the night before he left her. All he could do was hold her close to him as she sobbed, and kiss her. And just before the dawn, he made love to her, and Sarah found herself praying that she would become pregnant. She had the most terrible premonitions about him leaving her this time, but François kissed her gently and reminded her that she had those same feelings whenever he went to Deerfield. "You want me tied to your apron strings, like your children," he said, grinning. It was true, in part, but she also knew that if anything happened to François she would not be able to bear it. And even as she saw him astride his horse in the dawn, she knew who he was, and whom she loved. He looked like the same warrior who had terrorized her four and a half years before when she met him in the forest. He was a proud eagle high in the skies, and even she knew she could not force him to earth quite so swiftly.

"Keep safe," she whispered as he kissed her for the last time, "come back to me soon . . . I shall miss you."

"I love you, brave little squaw," he smiled down at her from his paint mare that had been a gift from the Iroquois long ago in another life. "I will be home before the next baby," he laughed, and then rode off into the valley at a gallop as she watched him. She stood for a long time, and could still hear the hooves of his horse on her heart, as she went back inside to her children.

She lay in bed for hours that day, thinking of him, and wishing she could have stopped him. But no matter what she told herself, she knew he would have gone anyway. He had to.

And in August she heard at the garrison that they had reached Fort Recovery safely, and built two new forts, Fort Defiance and Fort Adams, and their spies had told them that Little Turtle was ready to negotiate peace, but neither Tecumseh nor Blue Jacket were willing to hear it. They were determined to defeat the Army. But the fact that at least one of the great warriors was willing to yield seemed a good sign, and the men at the garrison felt sure that with four thousand men at his command, Wayne would defeat both Tecumseh and Blue Jacket quickly. But through the entire month, Sarah could not feel easy. August droned around her head like a swarm of bees, stinging her constantly with her own terrors. And at the end of the month, she felt still more worried. There had been no news. And then finally, the entire garrison was alive with what they considered a rout. General Wayne had made a brilliant attack on Blue Jacket on the twentieth of August at Fallen Timbers. Forty Indians had been killed or severely wounded, and very few of the Army. They had used great strategy and defeated the Indians mercilessly, and within three days, Blue Jacket retreated. And General Wayne was moving victoriously toward home through Ohio. There was cause for celebration, and yet Sarah felt almost ill as she listened. She knew she would not find peace again until François returned to her safely.

She waited for him to return or for news of him from the few men returning to the area. Many men had stayed in the West to continue the battle. Blue Jacket had been beaten, but had not yet conceded total defeat, nor had Tecumseh. Perhaps François had also chosen to stay in the West, to follow the battle through to its ultimate conclusion. But that seemed unlikely. That could be years or at the very least months, and she didn't think François would stay to do that.

But by mid-September when she heard no word she was frantic, and she appealed to Colonel Hinkley, the commandant of the Deerfield garrison, to get what news he could from the men returning from Fallen Timbers. For nearly two months now she had heard nothing. And he promised to see what he could do to alleviate her anguish.

She rode home that afternoon, with only one of her hired boys to accompany her, and when she got there, she found the children laughing and playing, and as she sat looking at them in their games, she thought she saw a man watching them from the treeline. He was wearing Indian dress, but she could see that he was not an Indian. He was a white man, but before she could question him, or send someone else to, he had vanished. And she stood for a long time that night, watching the sunset. She had an uneasy feeling.

And two days later, she saw the man again. But this time, he seemed to be watching her and then disappeared even more quickly. And the week after her visit to the garrison, the commandant came out to see her himself. He had just had the news from a scout returned from Ohio. And Sarah knew even before he said it. François had been killed at Fallen Timbers.

Only thirty-three men died, and he had been among them. And yet she had known it. She had always known that Blue Jacket would kill him. She had felt it. And then she knew who the man in the woods had been. The man she had seen watching her, and who had seemed to vanish in thin air . . . had been François, come to bid her farewell. She had seen him.

She sat very still when Colonel Hinkley told her the news that shattered her world, and he left her very quickly. And she stood looking out over the valley he had loved, the place where they'd met, and felt in her heart that he would never leave her. And at dawn the next day, she rode quietly to the waterfall they had loved, and where he had first kissed her. There were so many memories . . . so many things still to say to him . . . and she already knew there would be no more babies . . . Marie-Ange had been the last one.

François had been a great warrior, a great man, the only man she had ever loved . . . White Bear . . . François de Pellerin . . . she knew she had to go to the Iroquois to tell them. And as she stood at the waterfall, she smiled through her tears, remembering all he had been, all she had loved . . . and knew she would never lose him.

And as Charlie read the page, huge tears rolled down his cheeks. How could it have happened? They had only had four years together. How was that possible? How could one woman give so much, and get so little back, only four years with the man she loved, and yet Sarah didn't feel that. She felt grateful for every day, every moment, and for their three children.

The entries were fewer and shorter over the next years, and yet he could see that she had a good life. She seemed peaceful. She had lived to be eighty, in the house he'd built for her. And she had never loved another man, or forgotten François. He had lived on through his children as she did. She never saw the man in the clearing again. It had been François come to say good-bye to her, and she knew it.

And the last entry in the last journal was in a different hand. It was written by her daughter. It said that her mother had had a good life, and lived to a great age, and although she had never known her father, she had known what a fine man he was. She said that their love, and their courage, and the bond they shared was an example to all who knew them. She had written it on the day Sarah died, when she found the journals in the trunk in her bedroom. And she had signed her entry on the last page, François de Pellerin Carver. And she had written after it, God Bless Them. The date was 1845. And the handwriting was almost the same as her mother's. There were no further entries after that. No way of knowing what had happened to her children.

"Good-bye," Charlie whispered, as tears continued to roll down his cheeks. For a moment, he couldn't imagine what he would do without them. What a gift Sarah had been in his life, what an extraordinary woman . . . and François, how much he had given her in such a short time. It was hard to imagine. Charlie was deeply moved by everything he had read, and knew about them. And as he went to his room that night, thinking of her, he heard the sound of a silk skirt moving swiftly across the floor and he glanced up, almost without thinking. He saw a shape moving swiftly across the floor in a blue gown, and then it was gone, and he was no longer sure if it was real or his imagination. Or was it like the man she had seen at the edge of the clearing. Had she come to say good-bye to him? Could she even know that he had found her journals? It seemed impossible to believe that. And seeing her again was like the final gift from her, as he stood feeling bereft in the silence.

Charlie wanted to tell someone that she had died, to call Francesca and talk to her about Sarah and François. But it wouldn't be fair. And it would spoil the rest of the journals for her. He couldn't do it, and besides, it was three o'clock in the morning. Instead, he lay down on his bed, still seeing her as he had, still thinking of everything he'd read, and mourning François's death at Fallen Timbers, and hers so many years later. There was no sound in the house and in a little while, he was sleeping deeply.

Chapter 23

C HARLIE AWOKE WITH the sun streaming into his room the next day, and the feeling of a weight on his chest as though something terrible had happened. He had woken that way for months after Carole left, and he wondered if it was her again, but he knew it wasn't. It was something else, but he couldn't remember . . . and then he knew what it was. It was Sarah. François had died. And so had she, nearly fifty years later. It was such a long time to live without him.

And the worst thing for Charlie was that there was nothing to read now. She had left him. And she had taught him yet another lesson, that life was so short and the moments so precious. What if she had never opened the doors of her heart to François? They only had four brief years, and yet it was the best part of her life, and she had borne him three children.

It had made everything that had happened to her before seem so unimportant. And as he stood in the shower that morning, thinking about her again, his mind wandered back to Francesca. She had changed since her trip to Paris. He had seen it in her eyes when he picked her up at the airport, and it was even more significant that she had let him. And all of a sudden, as he dressed, he could hardly wait to see her. He realized that an entire new life could be waiting for both of them. The day was going to seem endless until seven, when he was supposed to pick her up. And as he thought of it he heard the knocker on the front door downstairs. He wondered who it was, probably Gladys Palmer. No one else in town knew him, other than Francesca, and he wasn't seeing her until that night for dinner. He couldn't imagine now why he hadn't asked to spend the day with her. It seemed so stupid. But as he hurried down the stairs, and looked out the window, he saw her. She was standing there, waiting for him, and she looked worried. It was Francesca.

"I'm sorry," she said nervously, she was frowning, but she still looked beautiful as he asked her in, and she stood in the front hall. He was smiling. "I just thought . . . I dropped Monique off at her friend's, I wasn't far from here and . . . I wondered . . ." There were tears in her eyes, she was so nervous, and she thought she shouldn't have come, but she had done it. "I finished the journal last night. She's in Boston, and she's about to come to Deerfield."

"You're only just beginning," he said thoughtfully, looking down at her. "Maybe we all are. I finished the last of them last night . . . I was feeling as though someone died," and someone had, but a long, long time ago. But he still mourned her. "I'm glad you came by. I couldn't imagine who was knocking at my door, it had to be either the police or the landlady . . . I'm awfully glad it was you." He looked gently down at her, and suddenly had an idea. Maybe it would bring them luck, or have special meaning to them later. "Do you want to take a drive with me?"

"Sure," she said, looking relieved. It had taken so much courage for her to come to visit him, she was still a little bit shaken. "Where are we going?" she asked nervously.

"You'll see," he said mysteriously. He grabbed a coat, and went back outside with her, and drove her the short distance that

Sarah had walked so often, even when she was pregnant. And then Francesca recognized it. She had been there with Monique once. They'd loved it. They'd brought a picnic. But only Charlie knew it was the waterfall that Sarah had written about so often in her journals. "It's beautiful, isn't it?" he said as he stood next to her, the falls were iced over, but they still looked so enormous and so majestic. "It was a special place for them." He remembered why, though Francesca didn't know yet. And without another word he pulled Francesca slowly close to him and kissed her. They had said enough to each other since they met, about the past and the present and the future, what they wouldn't do, and couldn't stand, the people who had betrayed them, and the scars they would keep forever. Maybe it was time to stop talking, and follow Sarah and François's example.

She could feel his heart beating hard against her chest, and she smiled at him when he finally pulled away from her, and she put a finger on his lips ever so gently.

"I'm glad you did that." She spoke in a whisper.

"So am I," he said breathlessly. "I didn't think I could stay away from you for much longer . . ."

"I'm glad you didn't. . . . I've been so stupid," Francesca said as they sat down on a rock that had a familiar curve to it, and Charlie couldn't help wondering if it was the same place where François had kissed Sarah. He hoped so. "When I read about her, I realize that all that stuff that happened to me was so unimportant." Francesca looked so much more free now.

"It's not unimportant," he corrected her, and then kissed her again. "It's just behind you . . . that's different. You've resolved it." And she knew that Sarah had helped her too.

She nodded, and then they walked for a while, and he put his arm around her. "I'm so glad you came over this morning," he said, and meant it.

"So am I," she smiled at him, she looked years younger than when he had met her. He was forty-two and she was thirty-one

351

and they had a whole life ahead of them. They were roughly the same ages François and Sarah had been at the end of the life they shared, and theirs was just beginning. It was a remarkable feeling, particularly after they'd both been so convinced that their lives were over. And now there was so much to think about, so much to dream, and hope for.

They drove back to his house eventually, and he asked if he could still cook her dinner that night and she laughed at the seriousness of the question. "I was afraid you'd be tired of me by then," he explained, "since you came over so early."

"If that were true, that could be a serious problem. But actually . . . I don't think it is . . ." she said as he kissed her in the car, and then again when she got out of it, and all of a sudden she couldn't take her hands off him, and all the loneliness and the pain seemed to melt away from them, and the anger, and there was nothing left but warmth and relief and happiness, and love for each other. They stood outside, in the garden for a long time, as they talked and they kissed, and he told her he was going to talk to Gladys Palmer about buying the house from her, and for the past few days he'd begun to think about opening an office in Shelburne, with the intention of restoring old houses. And Francesca smiled as she listened. They were so busy talking to each other, they never saw the woman smiling at them from an upstairs window. She was watching them with a look of satisfaction, and then she disappeared slowly behind a curtain, as Charlie unlocked the front door and walked into the house with Francesca. He was saying something to her about the house, and Francesca was nodding. And then they walked upstairs, hand in hand, each trembling a little bit, and neither of them made a sound as they walked into Sarah's bedroom. There was no one there. But they hadn't come to find her. She was gone now. They had come to find each other. For them, it was just beginning.